A BUZZARD *to* LUNCH

by

GORDON CHANNER

Valley of Dreams series

CORNISH BOOKS
5 Tregembo Hill
Penzance, Cornwall, TR20 9EP

*To Caravanners and Campers everywhere,
and to all those who would do something
different!*

Bound and printed in UK
Cornish Books
First Published 2000
Copyright © Gordon Channer 2000
IBSN 0-9537009-3-3

Contents

The Family at Relubbus

Gordon	Father
Jan	Mother
	(Age at start of book)
Chris	Fourteen years two months.
Sharon	Twelve years six months.
Stephen	Nine years five months
Jim	Grandfather (Jan's father)
Audrey	Grandmother (Jan's mother)
Max	The big yellow excavator.

Period.   Feb 1975 – Apr 1978

Sketches and notes – see end of book.

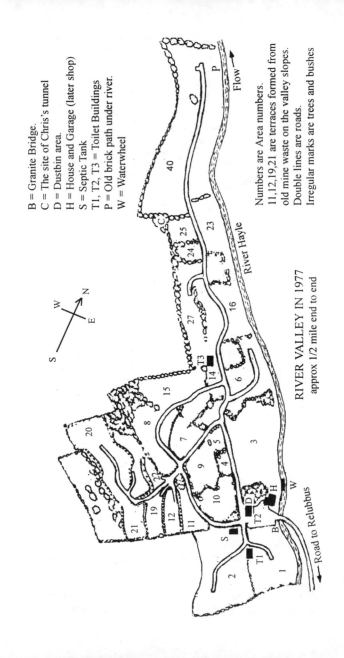

B = Granite Bridge.
C = The site of Chris's tunnel
D = Dustbin area.
H = House and Garage (later shop)
S = Septic Tank
T1, T2, T3 = Toilet Buildings
P = Old brick path under river.
W = Waterwheel

Numbers are Area numbers.
11,12,19,21 are terraces formed from
old mine waste on the valley slopes.
Double lines are roads.
Irregular marks are trees and bushes

River Hayle

Flow

RIVER VALLEY IN 1977
approx 1/2 mile end to end

Road to Relubbus

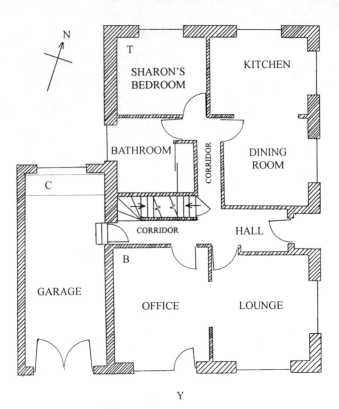

The House in which much of the novel takes place. Knowing the layout may make the action more real - which in fact it is, for this is a true story. The ground floor is shown, there is a basement below in which the rooms are almost identical, the stairs leading down to it from the hall are made of concrete. There are two bedrooms in the roof, another flight of stairs wind up to them from the garage end of the corridor. These too are concrete, except for the top two treads which are wooden.

Y indicated the tarmac yard where arriving caravans draw up.

B is the tree with the bird carvings.

T shows the trap door in Sharon's room, her escape route in a
    previous book.

C indicates the pit where coal was stored.

Single lines show the windows. Those in the kitchen, dining room, lounge and office face partly towards the river and bridge.

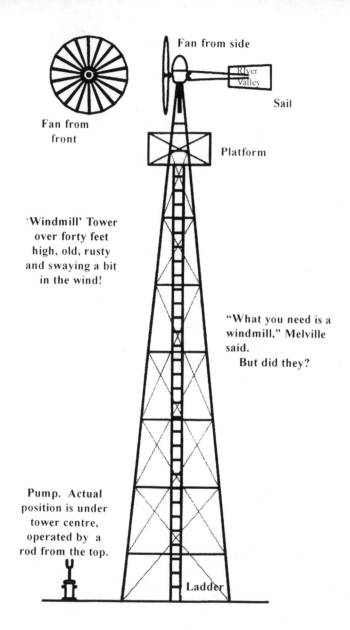

Fan from side

River Valley

Sail

Fan from front

Platform

'Windmill' Tower over forty feet high, old, rusty and swaying a bit in the wind!

"What you need is a windmill," Melville said.
    But did they?

Pump. Actual position is under tower centre, operated by a rod from the top.

Ladder

Reviews

Village by the Ford (1st Book in series)

A seemingly crazy and impossible venture... but the story itself is a compelling one. THE CARAVAN CLUB MAGAZINE

Told with good humour in a collection of anecdotes of crises and triumphs. CHOICE MAGAZINE

an engaging and... amusing account... vividly evokes the family's adventures WESTERN MORNING NEWS

If you liked Nevil Shute's A Town like Alice, you will appreciate Village by the Ford. I couldn't put it down. TOURER MAGAZINE

This charming story...makes a good read. WEST BRITON

It is by turns funny and touching... recommended reading for all. MMM

A fascinating, readable, well-told tale THE CORNISHMAN

A gentle tale... Looking forward to the sequel RADIO CORNWALL

...and all the adventures that came their way PRACTICAL CARAVAN

Turned to reality his dream... the absolute limits of endurance CARAVAN MAGAZINE

...story of a young family's struggle CAMPING & CARAVANNING

Reviews

House by the Stream (2nd Book in the series)

Is this everyone's secret dream? RADIO CORNWALL

Woven through with a rich vein of romance...will appeal
to readers of all ages... Nature plays an integral role...
happily devoid of crime & violence. THE CORNISHMAN

Written as fiction... the experiences are real...
an eye-opener. CARAVAN CLUB MAGAZINE

A heartwarming story of... improvisation... but most of
all, endurance... packed with interest WEST BRITON

A gentle story of an idyllic life.
THREE PAGE ARTICLE – CARAVAN MAGAZINE

...pulls very few punches... told simply and effectively...
I'd recommend Gordon Channer's books to anybody...
how a real family made their dream come true. MMM

To anyone who enjoys a good easy family read this is the
book for you... full to overflowing with their adventures
...a book worth reading. CAMPING & CARAVANNING

Cornish dream became reality...a gentle book, packed with
incidents and a real unique feel for the Cornish landscape.
PAGE HEADLINE. WESTERN MORNING NEWS

Full of human colour... the reader is there willing them to
succeed. BH&HPA JOURNAL

It's a very good book with a great deal of humour about
real people and real situations. Once I have picked it up I
don't want to put it down. CARAVAN LIFE

VERY YOUNG GROWING UP

See note on final page.

BUZZARD NOW FREE

BUZZ AWAITS LUNCH

BILLY AND BESSIE BIRD TREE

*The author thanks readers for their letters
on previous books in the series
and may be contacted through the publisher's address
or Email   Gordjan@AOL.com*

BUZZARD LANDS

- AND SETTLES.

The Valley of Dreams Series.
by Gordon Channer

This is a novel, not a work on Buzzards –
but it is based on a true story, and who
could resist taking the photos?
There is an experimental web page with more photos
entitled:- www.Cornishbooks.com

The series is available through your local bookshop or can
be ordered direct from, Cornish Books,
5 Tregembo Hill, Penzance, Cornwall, TR20 9EP
Email   Dreams@Cornishbooks.com

CHAPTER 1

Patience

The young girl lay shaking in the darkness. As she turned, hiding her head deeper under the bedclothes a tear rolled down one wet cheek to the corner of her mouth; the tip of her tongue reached out nervously – it was salty. Sharon swallowed, wanting to call out, call to her mother asleep in a room upstairs, but dare not. There would be questions; she should not have been eavesdropping the night before, crouching hidden behind the door as her parents discussed the devastation created by those big machines that had churned up their beautiful wild valley. The secretly overheard words, the serious tones in her parents' voices and the doubts they expressed to each other about the future, those were the things that had kept her long awake; unhappy hours, falling at last into fitful slumber and the nightmare from which she had just woken.

The big excavator that chased her in the dream was resting not far away, parked for the night a short distance up the track that ran beside the small stream. Now immobile, engine dead, bucket with extended metal teeth resting limply down, it would sit, a silent sentinel biding its time – waiting. She must pass close by in a few hours; near enough to touch! No way to avoid it! The valley had no other exit, no other road. Her way to the village, to school, to the wider world beyond, lay past that machine. Daylight would see it in action again, creating more havoc, tearing at the surface, spreading huge mounds of sticky

1

soil across her path; clambering around and over those heaps of wet mud was unavoidable. When she did pass, would that gaping bucket reach out to grab at her once more as it had in her restless sleep?

With a shudder, one small hand reached up to pull the bedclothes more tightly round. She wished someone else were awake, someone to talk to, and for the first time felt envy for her brothers, Stephen nine and Chris fourteen, sharing the room directly above. She was proud of having her own room but company would be so welcome now, just to have someone near even if that person had been asleep – but there was no one. Softly, through the curtains, a gentle swish pulsed; the waterwheel turning in the clear little stream not far from her window. For a long time she lay, listening for any sound, awake and frightened in the darkness; time in which her mind wandered back.

Only five years had passed since their first arrival. Why did her parents sell the big house and buy this lonely valley? The first small caravan, ten feet long and six feet wide, smaller than a normal bathroom, had been very cramped for the five of them. That first year had been fun but a real struggle to be ready for holiday visitors; campers and caravanners who must come to provide money for the following winter's food. Life had been hard with no mains water or electric, but they had managed, working together to build the necessary facilities. And the visitors had come; not too many but conditions had gradually improved, particularly after they built themselves this house, then the waterwheel to provide power. "I never have as many new clothes as my friends," the little resentful thought crept in, "and I still get in trouble for leaving lights on; or rather I did," she corrected herself. It was true enough, for under normal circumstances the house battery soon ran flat; but not at the moment! That big machine had cut the cable; now there were only candles. They had been in the house for nearly three years and life was much more comfortable – or it had been until that horrid sewer reached their

2

valley. A shudder passed through her young body in the darkness, a muscle spasm triggered by thoughts of that excavator ripping up soil and tree roots for the sewer that must be laid. Eventually, tension in the small clenched fists relaxed as sleep came and silent hours flew by.

The parents rose early, Jan cooking breakfast for two, Gordon anxious to push forward repairs to that trail of destruction where the big pipes had already been buried. The damage was extensive! It crossed the entire site; almost a mile including the entrance road. Now, in February it would be light by seven. They ate together by candlelight before he hurried away.

Jan filled a large jug with corn, then picked up an empty bucket for water from the river; one should be enough, Chris would fetch more before he left for school. It was better collected in the early morning – the sewer men used it sometimes as a latrine. Once, when the gang had been nearer the house, she had watched from the shadows as a man had stepped to the river's edge and sent his own stream arching out across the water. It seemed less funny now the gang was working upstream; made the clear river water seem so much less palatable but there was little alternative. The road was impassable by car and lugging large water carriers on foot from Jim's bungalow half a mile away was so difficult. Leaving the house she headed down the bank to the water's edge, slipping and catching her balance on the dewy grass, then filled the bucket and returned to leave it on the step. Opening the shed door released a wave of ducks; she watched that first dash for the river, waiting until they satisfied their need to drink, swim and dive under, before feeding them on the bank. Sundry other outside chores demanding attention took another fifteen minutes.

Returning to the house and surprised to find Sharon not yet awake, she opened the bedroom door quietly. Light now filtered strongly in; leaning across the bed to draw back the thin curtains, Jan saw one tear stained cheek surrounded by a mass of dark hair on the pillow. Pausing, then drawing the curtains closed again, she left without speaking, wondering what had caused the distress. It contrasted strongly with her own mood. A few minutes earlier while returning to the house she had glanced to the clear sky, squinting slightly at half a sun peeping over hills to the east then swung to where its beams fell. Up the valley's gently sloping sides the trees while still bare, somehow promised the coming of spring, tiny specks of white appearing on bushy willows and nearer at hand buds everywhere were swelling. Birds would be nesting soon and flowers bursting into colour, another season was about to start – everything should have been great! What had upset her daughter? Drawing back the lounge curtains, she looked upstream to where the entrance road lay devastated with mud. Was it that? The water, telephone and electricity were still cut off and the access obstructed; even on foot one must of necessity, climb mounds of squelchy spoil alongside deep trenches that cut through the stone surface. With a shrug, Jan turned from the window. Who knew the cause; twelve was a difficult age for a girl – could Sharon's tears be for some boy at school? She was growing up. What about the facts of life? Perhaps Gordon should have a talk with her about birds and bees? A smile replaced the frown at the idea of Dad trying to explain. Yes, she would ask him one evening when the family gathered.

About mid-morning the news came through. Where the sewer passed near the house, one large manhole stuck high above the surrounding soil and might require the big excavator's return. Fear of this had delayed restoration of the household electrical supply. The sewer authorities had now decided the excess height need not be adjusted. It was fine they insisted; no one would stumble, even in the dark. That seemed overly optimistic but with the matter resolved it was at last safe to reconnect!

Gordon set to work replacing the severed cable that

4

carried current from waterwheel to house. To make the system safer, the battery now rested inside the building and a larger replacement cable would run deep underground inside a protective pipe, no longer in its old vulnerable position a few inches below the turf.

Jan offered help and had fetched the necessary pipes, but digging trenches was too physically demanding. Now she watched through the window, glancing out intermittently, seeing muscles beneath the shirt flex backwards and forwards as the pick rose and fell. It would be good to have lights again. For weeks they had used only candles, the pressurised oil lamp long since ceasing to function and new parts no longer available. At first it had been a novelty, nostalgic almost, but reading in the dim light strained the eyes. Candles had not been too helpful either with the children's homework and all three would be so pleased to have television restored. The small power supply limited viewing each evening to about an hour usually, the time varying as river levels rose and fell according to season and rainfall. The TV took more current than the waterwheel produced, leaving the house battery to supply the rest – until it ran flat. Now at least that pleasure would again be available, though viewing reduced drastically if someone was forgetful and left extra lights on. Jan looked out again, saw the job was nearly finished and returned to her own tasks.

The children arrived from school a good hour before sunset and finding Dad already at the house, tea was eaten together earlier than usual. As they chatted, neither parent thought to mention the reconnection and the youngsters dashed off soon after. When the light began to fade they gathered again indoors, making for easy chairs in the lounge. Chris sat, reached for a book then rose again, picking up matches and moving towards a candle. Jan opened her mouth to stop him but Stephen's sudden jump from his chair distracted her momentarily. Although the lad said nothing, an intense expression on his face

5

prevented her speaking. In seconds he reached a cord hanging by the door; the ceiling switch clicked and light flooded the room. Flooded, might be an exaggeration but the intensity did seem bright when compared with the candlelight they had become used to. Sharon looked up startled; Chris stared towards the ceiling, a match now in one hand, box in the other. "Who..." he turned to his mother, the match still held as if to strike.

"Dad, of course, who did you think? They told us this morning the digger won't come back because that high manhole cover is not being moved, so he remade the connection. It's the only service not coming down the track from the village; the only one they can't now cut us off from."

Sharon moved towards the window. With the light switched on it seemed much darker outside. She could no longer see the big excavator in the distance but had passed it on the way home and knew it was still there. "It's a little farther away now," she thought. It moved on a few metres each day. Unconsciously she strained harder to see but could not. Another thought occurred; the stronger glow at their window would show from outside. "Is it watching us? Is it greatly disappointed at seeing the lights restored?" A small smile touched her lips, "Good. Serves it right." Realising she had spoken the last words aloud, Sharon stepped away from the window, seeking some distraction. "Who told Stephen?"

"Not me," Gordon glanced towards Jan who shook her head. It was obvious Chris had not known or he would never have reached for the matches. All eyes settled on Stephen. With a ghost of a grin, the lad looked away.

"Stephen!"

At his sister's explosive, commanding call, the lad turned slowly towards her but said nothing.

"Tell me!"

If ever an expression alone could say 'No, shan't', young Stephen's said it then, lips tightening, chin forward,

6

taunting his sister to try and make him tell.

"Perhaps," Dad interrupted, "he's just more observant?"

Chris frowned, gazed again at the bulbs on the ceiling, then suddenly rose, crossing to the window – it was gloomy outside but not really dark. Returning he nodded to Stephen in happy understanding, plonked himself down in a chair and faced his sister with amusement.

Jan looked at Dad, seeing a contented smile, then at the children.

Lost and unsure of herself, Sharon faced the two boys with a sulky expression, then tossed her head in the air and trying to appear casual, crossed to the window to gaze out. Nothing appeared to have changed. She turned back to her mother.

Jan met the unhappy eyes, then asked of the boys, "Well?"

Stephen leant against the wall pretending not to be aware. Chris glanced at him, then at his father as if asking permission.

"You'd better. Women are so slow," Dad shrugged at the boys who nodded back grinning, both watching as Sharon's hands came up to rest on her hips, her face a mask of annoyance. "I..." she stopped abruptly as Jan put a warning finger to her lips and winked, spoiling what would have been the boys' delight at their sister's outburst.

"Well," Chris started, hesitating in an attempt to rile Sharon further, but caught his mother's eye and continued. "It's the waterwheel speed. We should have known when we crossed the bridge. It's much slower tonight, producing electric, not running free any more."

Jan nodded, casting a glance in Stephen's direction. He would be ten next autumn; his hair had grown darker as time passed, no longer so fair as in earlier years but he was still apt to find trouble. Raising her eyebrows in a way that asked confirmation, she received a small dip of the head but no words. How different her children were.

7

Glancing back to Sharon, Jan silently thought, "Yes, and if you had seen it my girl, you could never in a thousand years have sat through tea and nearly an hour afterwards until darkness started to arrive without giving the slightest indication that you knew." Another glance at young Stephen brought a shy smile, quickly masked. She smiled back, speaking directly to him, "Dad dug a trench by hand for the cable; less mess than using Max." Everyone knew Max was their own excavator, a friendly machine not half the size of the one laying the sewer. "You can hardly see where the turf went back and the battery is in the basement now, not outside."

"I hope it's near a vent," Sharon spoke archly, recovering some of her poise.

"Why?" Dad asked.

Sharon looked at her brothers, waiting for an answer, but none was offered. "Hm! Batteries give off hydrogen gas while charging. It could explode! Don't men know anything?"

"Not a lot, otherwise we should have one of those lights you can switch on and off from upstairs or downstairs." Jan smiled at Gordon, awaiting his excuse.

"That's not so easy, not like a normal house. With twelve-volt electric the length of cable needs to be short; that's why all our switches are ceiling switches, it shortens the cable runs."

"Pity, never mind. Someone more clever might..." Jan gestured to Sharon, the two girls grinning. Chris and Stephen turned away, not in the least bothered by walking up the dark staircase to reach the switch and certainly not prepared to support their sister's contention about males.

Seeing the girls' smiles, Gordon sought an answer and not finding one, changed the subject. "It's the first day of March tomorrow. Even though no one can reach us, we'll be open – officially that is."

Mid-morning the following day, a back-packing

8

couple, their shoulders loaded with haversacks and a roll that must have been a folded tent, emerged from the wood across the stream, a direction from which very few people approached. The season's first would-be customers, but it was not to happen. On hearing of the absence of water and showers, they asked only for somewhere to rest a while and cook a small meal on their portable stove before moving on? Jan pointed to the rear field, noticing the girl seemed tired and wondering how much farther the pair must now walk to locate an alternative site. Within an hour they had re-shouldered their loads and marched off, leaving the valley empty again. Gordon was working farther downstream, still repairing areas damaged by the sewer as he had been all winter. Jan alone in the office waved to the departing couple as they crossed the bridge, shouting a warning about the mud that lay ahead, then returned to the house, busying herself in an attempt to push the problems from her mind.

At coffee break, she explained the visit, waving a hand towards the area where the couple had rested. "They've gone," her voice flat, without sparkle. She watched Gordon rise, cross to the window and look out. Under normal circumstances it would have offered an opportunity to bate him, accuse him of not believing her, but the situation was beyond fun. She spoke again as he returned to the chair.

"Couldn't we make the Council do something? How long can we survive with the entrance closed?"

"All summer if necessary; provided you don't want to eat in the following winter. I've already contacted everyone I can think of, but there's not much they can do."

"Sue them?"

"Better not. Remember the camping. If we raise legal matters, someone may start checking our planning consent and see tents were somehow omitted. We need two more years before they find out – that will give us rights. It shouldn't matter then."

"I suppose." Jan put a hand to her mouth as if to bite a fingernail, took it away again and reached for a nail file. "It's being cooped up in the house that gets to me. I want to thump someone. I can't really help much with the heavy work and now the telephone is cut there's not even the occasional caller to chat with. It's all right for you, talking to birds – don't think I've forgotten that robin. Sane people can't do that!" She threw both hands forward, almost shouting the last words, the frustration showing.

Gordon moved back a pace in mock alarm. He didn't want to discuss Robin; that had not been madness, just a device to pass lonely hours. He sought to calm her, to bring comfort. "You should be able to get the car out soon; they're nearly past the worst part." He glanced at the desk. "The telephone will be reconnected by then, so you'll have to go at weekends when the children are home to take the bookings. Jim could do it if you fetch him in the car, he'll never make it on foot with his bad leg and the road in its present state. Be patient."

"Isn't there a job we could do together near the office, something to get me out of this house?" Jan's voice had an urgent quality; she paused then hurried on. "We could give the toilets a thorough spring clean. Even if they do reconnect suddenly, I can reach the phone if it rings."

"Okay. A change of job wouldn't do me any harm either, but I doubt they'll reconnect this week. If they do, I'll do the running when it rings. Men are faster, more agile and athletic." He watched her hands tighten on the arms of the chair and was only just fast enough as she sprang up and lunged for him, a smile taking the sombre expression from her lips. It was what he had aimed at; for a moment they stood watching each other, both ready for action – and then they were together.

After a while she lay a head on his shoulder and whispered, "Let's do it now."

They both leaned back, she with a small mischievous grin, he nodding, understanding it was the toilet building

10

she really referred to. It would be good to do something different, even if no paying holidaymakers could get through to see the results. They hurried outside, fetching more buckets of water from the river and carrying them into the nearer toilet building.

"If I clean under the sinks and round the urinal, will you do the tops of all the partitions?" Jan left no time for a reply, assuming he would agree. "When you fetch the stepladder bring a bottle of bleach, this one is empty."

Bleach proved particularly effective on urinals, since it dissolved the limescale. He slipped out to the service passage that ran between Ladies and Gents toilets, separating the two. This narrow space contained much of the pipework and since the public had no access, it formed a convenient place for a workbench and for storage. Hoisting the steps nearer to the door, he bent to collect more bleach from its usual place but there was none. A brief search confirmed supplies had run out. Picking up the steps he returned with the news.

"No bleach, use your disinfectant for now and we'll give a thorough scrub later. You must slip to cash-and-carry once the car can pass and..."

"*We'll* give a scrub?" Jan interrupted. "*I* will you mean! Don't pretend you'll tear yourself away from those turf repairs to help up here for another hour? I might not stand the shock."

"Don't be facetious. Make a list first, there must be other things we want."

"Dozens. Speak to the sewer gang, ask them if they can clear a way wide enough to get past before they leave this coming weekend."

In the event, a narrow way was cleared mid-afternoon on Friday, and in addition the water had been reconnected. Jan drove off with a wave and a huge smile. Gordon watched the car disappear, pleased to see her so happy. Knowing the road was now open, he was torn between staying near the office in case someone arrived, or

11

continuing work on the damaged grass. Remembering the small dispute about the stairway light, he retreated inside. A tiny 12-volt bulb like those used in very old buses, was fixed at the top of the staircase. Beside it hung a cord from a pull switch on the ceiling. There was no other switch, no way to turn it on or off from below. He ran up the stairs, reached for the cord and gave a tug. The light glowed dimly; it hardly showed in daylight but was effective enough after dark. This system had two disadvantages. Firstly, anyone retiring to bed must climb the stairs in darkness before the light could be switched on. Secondly, a person coming downstairs before dawn on a winter morning must switch the light off and descend in darkness, for they could not turn it off once they reached the bottom. Switching off was essential; no unnecessary lights could be left burning since it reduced the supply available for other purposes. Only three small bulbs could be supplied from the waterwheel without drawing extra current from the battery. A cluster of three was used in the dining room alone and at the moment they were still needed for breakfast. Of course, morning darkness would not be a problem much longer; very soon it would already be light when they rose at six, but the single switch arrangement was substandard and in the evenings that stairway light was still needed. He pulled again switching it off and looked at the possibilities. The boys might not care but Jan and Sharon would refer to it forever if they were losing an argument. Never mind, he had an idea. There was perhaps, a way?

The staircase was concrete except for the top two steps, which were wooden. It was through one of these timber steps that he drilled a slender hole close to the wall. Removing the cord hanging from the ceiling switch, a longer piece was substituted and fed through the new hole so it hung down into the hallway below. This cord could now be reached either from upstairs or downstairs. Descending again, a quick pull then a few steps back along the short corridor to gaze upward, confirmed that it worked. Another pull turned it off. With the cord cut to the correct level and a bead tied at the end for easy pulling, everything was ready. He climbed the stairs again, taking the cord and drawing it upward until the bead pressed solidly against the ceiling below. Good. The surplus was coiled and pushed under the carpet edge out of sight. The cord rising to the ceiling switch was still visible, but everyone was used to it hanging there; with luck no one would notice the increased length.

This proved to be the case, for on returning with the bleach Jan quickly mounted the stairs to reappear in older clothes before donning rubber gloves and hurrying off to the urinals. She failed to notice the switch cord had been altered, as did both boys when on arriving from school they dashed upstairs to change.

That evening, in a rare display of unity, all three children were keen to watch the latest Bond film, but it was long and even with a full battery, the power might fade too soon. Without prompting, Chris took a hooked steel rod from the hall and with it, cleaned every scrap of debris from a grid in front of the waterwheel, returning for the grease gun to lubricate all the bearings. Gordon, who had withdrawn after tea to finish reseeding an area of torn grass, returned as darkness was falling, surprised to see the lounge lit with candles again, then realised the cause. The TV program's start lay half an hour ahead but someone was making sure the batteries were fully topped up. This system was not new; abandoning lights and using candles had been done before when a special program was due.

Entering the room, Gordon crossed quickly to draw the curtains. Jan watched him reach awkwardly from one side as if hiding his body, then step rapidly across the opening, reaching out to draw the other end at arm's length. She smiled silently, at the animal caution. It was so stupid, idiotic, but somehow... why did she love him so? A glance at the children revealed faces watching the cards of

13

a game they were playing; they had not noticed. Good. It was something private, a difference between the parents, something that added, well... she could not quite define what it added, but while shaking her head, felt pleasure at the little act.

As program time arrived the set was switched on then quickly off again; the film had not yet started and time was so critical it could not be squandered. The delay, however, proved acceptably short, all eyes soon glued to the screen. An hour passed, Sharon defending herself once when the girl in the film did something stupid, but those few words that flew back and forth between the children in the flickering light were automatic, their attention still fully on the drama. They watched intently until twenty minutes before the end, then Stephen pointed. He said nothing but there was little need; they had all been expecting it. The power supply was failing, a black border round the picture growing steadily wider. Five minutes later the screen went blank. Switching off the set they moved to the dining room. Stephen started another candle, Dad reached up to light the gas lamp in the adjoining kitchen and Sharon filled the kettle, lighting a gas ring – disappointment in all their faces.

"Someone at school is bound to have watched, you'll have to ask them on Monday." Jan suggested.

"Not me!" Sharon shook her head. "I'm not telling my friends we have a television that doesn't work properly. I'll pretend I wasn't watching. Let the boys ask, I'm not going to!"

Mum turned to her sons, "Well?"

"No." Without expression or elaboration, Stephen declined.

"I'll find out," Chris offered, a little movement of the hand indicating it was no trouble, that he could handle the situation with ease.

"You'll look silly," Sharon warned. "Hope none of my friends get to hear of it."

Gordon and Jan glanced at each other then back to the children, particularly Chris. He had a funny smile, more a grin, aware they awaited his reply.

"No I won't. You might, but you only look stupid if you don't know how to do it." He spoke not defensively, but quietly, as if addressing someone of lower intellect, or a child to whom everything must be explained, another small gesture of the hand saying how simple it was for a more mature person.

Sharon, knowing immediately she was being talked down to, put one hand on her hip, drawing in a deep breath and hunting for but not finding a suitable response. Turning away, she looked towards the door, not sure whether to stamp off but somehow realising that that would mean defeat. Swinging back with pointed finger, "You..." She just couldn't conjure the words. Seeing Chris's smile, her cheeks reddened, aware that her parents were standing to one side silently watching was no help either. Finally she managed to force out the words, "All right then, if you can ask and pretend our television was still working – go ahead, tell us how!"

"No problem. For instance I could say that my sister cooked tea, so naturally I was ill at the vital moment and..."

He got no further, Sharon was on him; though at twelve she was two years younger, it took all Chris's strength to keep his sister at arm's length while not retaliating and trying to pretend it was so easy. The sound of Dad clearing his throat brought them both up short, but their father said nothing. Chris glanced over to see his parents were still leaning against the far wall holding hands. For a moment there was silence, until Mum spoke.

"The kettle has almost boiled, let's have that coffee and discuss this round the table." She looked across in Stephen's direction, then to Sharon. Knowing what was required the girl pivoted on her heel with a "Hm," and strode over, reaching for the cups as Stephen lifted the

15

candle saucer from the worktop and carried it to the table.

Five minutes later found them all seated, coffee far too hot to drink steaming beside each one.

"Right?" Jan started, "Chris, I believe you said *one way* of solving the problem was Sharon's cooking. What other method did you have in mind?"

"There's nothing wrong with my cooking! He doesn't have another way Mum, that was..." A raised hand cut Sharon off.

"Give him a chance and we might find out." Dad signalled Chris to continue.

"Well, there are plenty of reasons. I could say we had a visitor at that time and had to switch the set off, but something more impressive would be better. You remember uncle Clive? His girl friend went to Adelaide and he once said he might go too. When my friends ask why I didn't see the end, I could say that Clive rang me from Australia, wanted some advice about fishing and he always rings at that time because he's just had breakfast when it's eight in the evening here. They wouldn't laugh then, they'd be impressed. I might pretend he rang me about caravan parks rather than fishing because some of the boys at school, their fathers own fishing boats and they know more about fishing than I do. What I..."

"That would be telling lies!"

"Let him finish." Jan stopped Sharon's interruption, allowing Chris to resume.

"What I'll really tell them is the truth; that our waterwheel couldn't produce enough for the whole program. You think they'll laugh – girls might do but men are interested in mechanical things. Most of my friends already know about our wheel, think it's great, wish they had one. They understand it produces less as summer approaches and the river is lower." Chris yawned and stood up, making as if to go upstairs but stopped in the doorway to speak again. "Of course, all my friends know that most of our electrical problems come because my sister keeps leaving lights on!" And he was gone as Sharon bumped her knee with a loud "Ouch," trying to rise from the table in a hurry to give chase. A few seconds later Chris's head reappeared at the doorway, realising he hadn't drunk the coffee.

The little discussion that followed as they sat together again was surprisingly good-humoured. Sharon, having suddenly understood that lads were interested in water-wheels, was keen to investigate this possibility further without appearing to do so; not yet from any physical attraction, just a young girl's natural wish to make a good impression. Shortly, the drinks finished, Jan rose, pointed to Stephen then towards the ceiling indicating time for bed, but another voice interrupted.

"Tonight, we'll all go upstairs together. I've something to show you."

Attention around the table swung towards Dad, questions were asked but received no reply. "Women and children first as they say at sea. Mum, you lead the way, I don't want anyone racing ahead." Ushering them out into the corridor and following on behind, Gordon waited until they turned the corner towards the stairs then jumped to reach the bead on the ceiling and pulled down the extended light cord, taking up the slack. As they reached the bottom step, another pull switched the ceiling light on. It was still faint, for the battery condition had not yet much recovered, but in the dark stairway no one could mistake it.

Over the weekend the road remained passable with care, but the presence of the excavator parked alongside still gave an impression of excessive narrowness and it was hardly expected that anyone would take the risk. When a medium size motorcaravan appeared, Jan hurried to the door, waiting as it crossed the small bridge and drew to a halt beside the house.

A window wound down, "Can I top up my freshwater

tank?" the driver asked.

"Certainly," Jan called back, then seeing the face at the window look round the entrance yard and sensing his intention to take water and go, she quickly added, "It comes free with the night's fee."

The head disappeared. There were obviously discussions going on. Jan waited. She thought they might leave but one thing was certain; if money was too tight to replace the clothes that Sharon was rapidly growing out of, then no motorcaravan was using the facilities free!

"How much is one night, just two of us?"

Jan called out a figure, hurriedly adding, "That includes hot showers and as much water as you like."

A man descended from the cab, entered the office and paid. Jan led across to the front of the nearest toilet building, picked up the hose, turned on the tap and let the full force of water wash down a nearby drain behind the Cornish wall. "I'll let it run for a minute, you're the first to arrive this year. Why do we always get more motor-caravans at the start of the season?" They stood discussing the valley and the area, Jan's advice of a hardstanding pitch bringing a pleased response. Judging that any old water in the hose had now been properly flushed, she twisted the tap-head easing the flow and reached out, caught a handful, drank it and murmured, "Um, good," passing the hose with a smile. Showmanship was after all, part of running a caravan park. Gordon had suggested the move a year before. "If you take a swig yourself, they can't eat something bad, get ill, then blame our water and sue us."

"Don't be ridiculous," she had said at the time. Now, watching the man struggle to remove the tank cap she smiled at the thought. Her hand remained on the tap, increasing the flow once the pipe was in the tank, then turning it off as water started to overflow. "I'll show you to a pitch."

"Where can I empty the waste tank?"

18

Silently Jan gave a little curse under her breath. All motorcaravans seemed to be getting them; they were awkward, most needed to get very close to a drain, certainly the one behind the wall was no good. Gordon usually lifted the lid of an inspection chamber in the road near the chemical point, but it was hard on the fingers and she couldn't manage it herself. "I'll show you," she walked off without waiting, one hand held out, indicating the way. Stopping at the manhole Jan pointed down at the galvanised lid. "It's a bit stiff, I find it difficult but I expect you..." she left it unfinished but let her eyes wander down his body and up again to the shoulders, smiling with a little nod as if to confirm her opinion of his strength.

Immediately he knelt, pushing two fingers inside both the small lifting points, and pulled upwards. When it failed to rise, the man jerked harder, aware he was still being watched. The lid resisted a moment then came away with such speed he almost overbalanced.

"Let me show you the pitch first," Jan escorted him to a small sheltered area of hardstandings behind the toilet building, then returned to the office.

At tea that evening, Chris, having spotted part of the roof above the surrounding bushes, asked, "The motor-caravan, how long?"

"Only a day. It really didn't want to stay at all, just to top up its water tank free." Jan heard a splutter and out of the corner of one eye saw Gordon spill some liquid on the table, rapidly put the cup down and try to clear his throat of coffee that had gone down the wrong way. "Relax," she grinned at the children. "What did you think – that I gave him a free night? I'll tell you something though; you need an easier place for these motorcaravans to empty their waste tanks. That lid is too stiff."

The vehicle disappeared by mid-morning the following day and on Monday the road was impassable again. Jan had planned to fetch Jim, her father in the car, leave him to tend the office in case of any visitors, then drive off to

19

Truro. That was pointless now, Jim's presence no longer necessary for no visitors could arrive, but neither could her own car get out.

That evening when darkness fell she sat reading, but her mind wandered. How much longer would the obstruction continue? Early holiday-makers ought already to be here. Work to repair damaged grass was proceeding non-stop but they still had no telephone in spite of several promises that its restoration was 'imminent'. At least the water was back and the lighting restored. Jan glanced upward then back at her book, seeing the print so much more clearly now the candles had gone, but not able to clear her mind to read. Thank goodness for coal and Calor gas, at least the heating and cooking facilities had remained working throughout, though it had been necessary to add the occasional bucket of river water to the central heating system to maintain liquid levels at the boiler and avoid the risk of explosion. The boys were making something at the workbench in the basement and had taken a candle, there was not enough power for lights in several places at once. Sharon lay in her room, reading on the bed under her gas light. It was very quiet in the house. Unable to settle, Jan let the book rest gently on her lap and looked across to Gordon as he read. After a few moments his head lifted as if sensing her gaze, "Yes?"

"How did you... I never asked anything?" She spoke defensively.

"Something is bothering you though?"

"No. What makes you think... You don't charge for looking do you?"

"How rich would I get if I did? Don't tell me, I can guess. Not very?" He saw her nod but it had somehow a sombre touch. Without appearing to watch he had seen the book in her hands tilt several times at an angle impossible to read, and knew she was restive, something on her mind.

For a time they sat silent, he waiting, she not knowing quite how to start.

"Do you... This sewer business, how badly will it affect us?"

"Impossible to say," he shrugged. "Depends how long they take. Seems bad at the moment but they must be clear soon – I hope."

"What about the mess? What about money? Must I still hold off buying Sharon's new outfit? She really needs one."

"I think we must wait. Don't spend anything that's not vital." He saw her about to interrupt and hurried on. "Yes, I know she thinks it's vital, and that her friends all have new clothes and she wants to keep up, but having something to eat is more important, next winter that is. You ask about the mess; it *is* improving, not as fast as I'd like of course, but even when the entrance does reopen I'll still have some weeks before people come in any volume. The grass should be presentable by then; that's all I can say for sure, but it won't be very thick. Pray for dry weather at peak season."

"That money from our cashed life policy, must you spend it all on tarmac?"

"I think so. The roads where the big lorries ran are totally destroyed. I've done my best but the surface is unacceptable. It must affect trade badly unless we get that main section tarmaced. Even so we can't afford enough. Just have to see how far it will stretch, then hope the season comes good."

"When will we know the worst?"

"Things should be back to normal by May – as normal as they're going to get this year. If trade is really bad, next winter could be difficult."

"Sharon must have clothes before then," Jan warned. "Stephen will need some too."

"We'll see. Chris and I can cut logs for the boiler to save buying coal, but with luck it won't come to that. Some people when they first arrive, look at the entrance and at reception then decide how long to stay from what they see. Could we make the office more welcoming?"

21

"You could sell the snooker table and buy more chairs?" Jan had tried several times to lose the big table, believing it spoiled the room. Used only by the family, mainly in winter, it stood to one side of the office; it had to, nowhere else had sufficient space. True the mahogany covers looked good and provided a place to display pamphlets, but it made the room smaller. Seeing his reluctant expression, she gave way. "Never mind, I know you and the children like it in the dark evenings. I'll change things round and try to improve the appearance. All your bird carvings on that chest behind the desk, people like to see them but couldn't we show them better?" Jan stopped as the basement door opened and Stephen emerged with a candle, blowing it out as Chris followed. On hearing the voices, Sharon quickly appeared. With the children now present, further discussion was postponed.

The following day did see the telephone restored as promised and eventually the road was cleared sufficiently to drive along, allowing visitors to arrive. Numbers however, were down, caravans no doubt reluctant to squeeze by where the big machine still worked. Downstream along the riverbank the tedious and seemingly unending task of repair and re-seeding continued. The battle of appearance was being won, but time was running out.

As April approached, the valley, while by no means restored to its former glory, had attained as presentable a state as was possible in the time available. Many of the site roads retained their uneven stone surface but those worst affected had been tarmaced by a Cornish firm; two coat work nearly four inches thick, machine laid, followed by a heavy roller to give a good finish. It looked magnificent. The entrance road on the other hand, remained a mess. However, arrangements had already been made that this too, be resurfaced once the sewer gang departed. Gradually things were coming together but Sharon in particular, viewed the low number of visitors with dismay.

CHAPTER 2

Leaks

"Hey!" Gordon jumped from the doorway across the intervening steps waving vigorously to a motorcaravan, then changing his mind he ran urgently towards the bridge, sprinting across and signalling the driver to follow. Racing clear of the tarmac to where the old stone road still showed, he waited until the vehicle caught up, then called to the open window, urgently addressing the driver. "You're leaking. Hope that's not diesel oil falling on my new tarmac!"

The man climbed down, stooped to peer underneath, then straightened. "No. It's my waste water tank. Sorry, must not have turned the drain tap off tight." He strode to the rear, knelt to reach underneath, moved something and the liquid stopped. "Tap is a bit touchy," the driver said. Gordon nodded, happy that no harm had been done and started back.

Chris, already home from school and surprised at his father's sudden burst of speed, had watched from the office step.

"Waste water tap not turned off," Gordon muttered as he re-entered house.

The motorcaravan drove slowly away to be almost hidden by trees, the top visible here and there above the willows. Lounging against the wall, Chris continued to observe its progress until a little further on the roof stopped again for perhaps thirty seconds. Having a natural

23

curiosity, particularly concerning people from the site, he strolled off in that direction, covering the ground quickly but in an apparently leisurely fashion, a laid back image, a touch of the John Wayne's that he had started to adopt as many fourteen-year-old young men were apt to do. This stretch of road had not been touched by the sewer excavation. At the moment, no rain having fallen recently, the stone surface was quite dry if a little the worse for wear from the many heavy lorries that had used it over last winter. At roughly the point where the vehicle had stopped, he searched the ground, moved on a few paces and shortly found what was half expected; a darker moist patch on the dry surface and a narrow trail leading off towards the village. Pleased, he turned back and on reaching the office, quietly entered, eased the door closed and crossed to the desk. The signing-in book that held everyone's address contained other information: the vehicle registration, the area where it was pitched, the number of people and whether caravan, motorcaravan or tent. Chris knew the vehicle's number, had memorised it crossing the bridge; his finger slid up the outer column. Ah! There it was. The finger moved horizontally. Yes, a motorcaravan with two people pitched on Area 9, that was a hardstanding. The daybook revealed more; it had arrived only that morning and paid for three nights. He ambled off to examine the immediate area and the roads leading from it, but any signs of liquid had evaporated. "Hm? Not much point in watching for the return, it's probably out for the evening." Tomorrow he would be at school. Pity. Still, if it went out at this time one evening, might that not be habit?

The following day Stephen arrived from school first as usual. Returning home with Sharon, Chris entered the house and chatted briefly, looking for a way to leave without arousing curiosity. Taking a piece of bread he sauntered out, leaving the office and heading towards the river. Feeding the ducks aroused no suspicions, something they often did at teatime. Most visitors were still out for the day and the ducks had grown hungry. A few pieces torn off and thrown, rapidly drew a small flock. Chris flicked the remaining slice into the water to a flutter of feathers as they fought for a share. Glancing round with apparent nonchalance he decided no one was watching and made off down the riverbank, cutting quickly across to find the motorcaravan still parked with no one apparently about. Ah well; he returned for tea.

As they ate, an engine noise caused the lad to turn. Through the window, a large vehicle moved slowly to the left; his target was crossing the bridge. Hurriedly he finished the meal, excused himself and with disguised haste left the office. On the far side of the yard, a trail of liquid led both ways. Glancing towards the bridge, Chris followed the wavering line with his eyes, then quickly strode off in the other direction, tracing it back to source, anxious to collect the final evidence of what he already suspected. Sure enough, the dark stain continued right back to where the motorcaravan had been parked. The trail terminated in a tiny puddle, a discovery that had taken only a few minutes.

"What are you looking so self-satisfied about?" Jan asked, as he wandered back into the dining room where the family still sat talking round the table.

Chris resumed his seat. "I... er, know something that Dad doesn't."

Eyes that had rested idly in his direction awaiting the answer, now showed growing interest. For a while he sat, smiling and pleased with himself, but volunteered no further information. The parents waited, glancing at each other then back at Chris, but it was Sharon who asked, "Well?"

Pleased with his minor coup, Chris regarded the ring of waiting faces. "I know Dad wasted his time chasing a motorcaravan yesterday."

"It hasn't come loose again, has it?" Gordon frowned.

"No, I don't think it has."

25

"Mum!" Sharon shook her mother's arm where it rested on the table. "What are they talking about?" Jan heard the agitation in her daughter's voice and made a shrug with her shoulders indicating she had no idea, then turned back as Chris spoke again.

"It went out just now, leaking again."

"A hole in the tank?" Dad asked then corrected himself. "No, can't be. It stopped when he shut the tap off yesterday; I watched him. It must be loose."

"No. He sets it like that deliberately when he starts off."

"To save emptying, you mean?"

"Would you men mind telling the rest of us what you're discussing?" Jan asked, "or don't you want any breakfast tomorrow?" She winked at Stephen.

Gordon held a hand towards Chris, indicating he should explain.

"There's a motorcaravan, the one that drove across the bridge while we were eating; it goes out leaving a trail of water from the waste tank... You know, where dirty water from its sink and wash basin is stored. Well, instead of emptying his tank down the drain, this chap leaves the tap slightly open and spreads it along the road while he drives." Chris beamed, still pleased at having detected what others, particularly his father, had missed.

"Ugh. Not very hygienic," Sharon wrinkled her nose. "He'll make his pitch smell."

"No, you're wrong. He only turns it on just before they drive away." Chris made a small gesture with the hand as if all should now be clear.

Sharon frowned. She had disliked not knowing what they were talking about and been pleased when the chance came to make her own contribution. Her suggestion was not going to be made light of so easily. "How do you know? You were in here when it drove out."

"I know because I checked and found a wet patch where he parked, but too small to have been leaking for

26

long. Besides, if he left it open all the time there would be none left to leave a trail; that's pretty obvious. Yesterday when Dad made him shut off the tap, I watched it drive away. He stopped again nearer the village, so I went up to investigate. Another little wet patch and a wet line leading towards the village showed where he'd opened it again." Chris leaned back smiling.

"Hmph," Sharon got up, collected a handful of plates and made for the sink. "Wish I had time to stand around watching motorcaravans."

Easter came with the sewer not quite finished, the big excavator drawn well to one side near the entrance. Fortunately some people did risk squeezing past but the numbers were poor; couples mainly, with few children and only three tents. The boost to finances was welcome but depressing small. After the holiday, workmen returned to lay the last of the sewer pipes, then a large low vehicle arrived, collected the big machine and trundled off. This accomplished, work to repair and tarmac the half mile entrance road from site to village swung into action. Much of the preparatory work had already been done and the tarmac itself took only one day but as another week passed, the finished surface failed to bring any influx of visitors. What more could they do?

Re-seeding grassy areas was well underway if not exactly finished, but the growth remained sparse, nowhere near its pre-sewer standard. Improvement elsewhere was even less encouraging! Heathers along the riverbank showed little signs of regeneration, and cars bounced going onto or off those roads already tarmaced where the new black surface rose several inches above the adjoining grass. It was only to be expected; there was a limit to what two people could do. Not everything could be fixed in one season.

Audrey and Jim, Jan's Mum and Dad, had been trying to help, working on the garden of their bungalow half a mile away in the village; it was the first thing caravanners saw as they left the main road. Jim, had come down to the site a lot in previous years but the bad surface had prevented that over the past winter, his stiff leg unable to cope with the slippery conditions. Now suddenly, he appeared riding a tricycle, the new tarmac providing a suitably smooth surface. What gave him the idea, no one knew; a suggestion probably, by some visitor who called on him for a chat and perhaps a nip of whisky that Jim was so apt to offer, using the excuse to drink one himself. His first appearance on this new machine made the family laugh – and there had not been too much to laugh at recently! Jim, in spite of his age, was a big, very muscular man; in his own time few were tougher. Seeing him now, rolling along on the spindly wheels was a sight with a hint of comedy or so the family thought – until they tried it themselves and found riding that tricycle not quite so easy. On corners it refused to lean over like a bicycle, with a definite tendency to overturn. Jim rested against the house wall, his chance to laugh heartily at the ungainly efforts. Only Stephen, standing on the pedals, unable to reach the seat, mastered it quickly. With his usual eloquence he said just one word, "Easy!" and tore round the yard in wide circles.

With the entrance road smoothly tarmaced, Jim could now travel the half mile from his bungalow to the site with relative ease and promised to do so whenever help was needed. That offer brought a smile to Jan's face, for the telephone had kept her in the house; it could not be left unattended – certainly not this year when every possible booking was so direly needed!

For Gordon too, life was changing. Through the winter he had toiled every daylight hour. Long evenings when darkness prevented further work saw the carving of more birds, a hobby to some extent combating depression at the extensive damage. As early May arrived, it was not darkness but stamina, or rather the lack of it after more than ten hours of heavy work, that sent him indoors in the evening, those longer days and the dryer, sunnier weather bringing a handful of extra customers, though not nearly as many as previous years. The last few days had been easier, that same good weather now prevented further work on the grass; any lifted turf tended to shrink and curl and seeds would no longer germinate. It forced a change to other jobs, but ones not involving noise; visitors were precious and they came for the quietness. A long dry-stone wall above the first terrace on the valley's western side was currently receiving attention. Towards one end a hazel bush growing through the outermost fringe of old mine waste had fallen over, probably due to a poor depth of soil. Only drastic cutting could save the root. One part was a mass of stout limbs in all directions. Sawing off this large complicated section of branches, Gordon heaved it across to the front of the terrace, laid it on the ground, then clambered down the stone wall to the level below. Reaching up, he pulled down the trunk, balanced it on a shoulder, picked up the bow-saw and took a shortcut back to the house.

At the office, a sign sellotaped to the glass said, 'Back in 5 minutes'. Where had Jan gone? Cutting off bits of branch here and there gradually reduced the size until it passed through the doorway. Entry achieved, he stood in the office wondering where and how to mount it, one hand steadying the tree, fresh spring leaves sprouting on all sides, some brushing a light that hung from the ceiling.

While he stood thinking, the door opened. Jan entered and pulled up short.

"Wha... I was out searching for you. That drain is blocked again." She pointed to the nearest toilet building then walked round the tree, inspecting from all sides. "I know I'll regret asking, but just what is that for?"

"Hm. I thought it would go quite well on the chest of draws in the corner; what do you think? Do you like it?"

Her nose wrinkled, an expression similar to one seen the previous day when she accidentally stepped in something a duck had dropped. "Oh yes, wonderful! Do tell me, why do we need a tree in the office?"

"It's unusual, you don't see many about."

She took a threatening step forwards and he quickly offered an explanation.

"You wanted the bird carvings better displayed so visitors can see them. Remember? To improve the office and increase trade, you said. Or try too! Well, if the leaves and small branches are trimmed and the size reduced a bit, I can mount all the birds on this and..." He hesitated, watching for a reaction before hurrying on. "I did promise never to let your life become dull, so can you help me get it up there."

"All right," she nodded, laughing now. "Don't mind if I take my coat off first do you? Go fix your drain."

Easy as that! Perhaps after twenty years a wife got used to her husband's... er, he was thinking hair-brained schemes, but mental revised it to 'occasional touches of genius' – it made him feel better.

The drain was quickly cleared and an hour later, after much trimming and sawing, offering into place several times and taking down for adjustment, the tree was finally manoeuvred into a suitable position on the chest of draws behind the office desk and they stood back together, taking in the effect. When the birds were later mounted it would be fine, well probably, at least he thought so. It was just a matter of convincing Jan. Turning towards her he spoke, the enthusiasm perhaps a little exaggerated.

"It should look great with all the birds on. You'll like it when it's finished."

"Not a lot," she rolled her eyes to heaven.

At least it wasn't total rejection. Press on before her mind changes!

"I'll get my drill; needs screwing to the wall at the top. At the moment it's only balanced; if someone opens the door in a gale it might fall!"

"Do you think it could?" she asked thoughtfully, stopping him as he made to leave, then pushed him round behind the desk.

"Sit there, I want to see how it will appear to a visitor." She moved towards the door, ostensibly viewing the scene as a customer would.

Being a chap, he was not vain of course, but anyway sat upright, threw the shoulders back, lifted the chin and put on his best smile, modestly thinking, "Between us, me and my tree together – pretty irresistible! This should bring a twinkle to her eyes." He moved his face slightly to the right to catch the light better.

Nodding approval she walked slowly backwards, surreptitiously reaching for the doorknob with a hand hidden behind her back. Suddenly it swung wide open, and when the tree didn't fall, slammed again with a great bang!

Dashed from grandiose thoughts, belatedly realising her intent, he ducked, lifting one arm in the air to fend off the tree, half-swivelling round to stare upward in alarm. It teetered unsteadily; he leapt from the chair but the tree stayed upright.

"Pity." Jan said sweetly, walking off to the kitchen.

A lady with two children mounted the short square steps and entered the office. Finding the room empty, she peered through the large opening into the adjoining lounge and seeing no one, stood for a while looking at the door which communicated with the rest of the house. This room, although it had a desk, was unlike the reception area on most caravan parks in that it formed part of the house and was obviously lived in, with ornaments, books and even a large covered billiard table. One hand reached down to hold the younger child, restraining it from touching, and her feet shuffled restlessly, uneasy at being alone in someone else's home. Shortly the woman led her children outside again, and in closing the door saw the sign, "Please Ring."

Lifting a finger towards the bell push, she hesitated, embarrassed to have already stood inside unannounced, and instead moved away, starting across the yard.

Jan, hurriedly preparing a midday meal in the kitchen, thought she heard the outer door. Interruptions were a regular feature of any day, especially now numbers were beginning to increase; it took only a moment to turn down the gas, pop through to the office, grasp the handle and poke her head outside. "Did you want something?"

Halfway across the now tarmaced yard, the lady stopped, reaching out to guide her children round and back to the door. Inside she held up a small snippet with one five-petalled pink flower and dark, well-divided leaves on a reddish stem. "Sorry, we thought there was nobody in. Do you know the name; not campion, is it?"

"Gordon usually does the identification, he's seeing two caravans to a pitch at the moment but I think that's Herb Robert, one of the Geranium family. Just a minute. Here." Jan reached for the Collins Guide, carefully scanning the pages. "Oh... look, the shape is right but the leaves show too green." She held out the open book, pointing, waiting a few moments before flicking to the back. "Where is that index? Ah, page 51. Hold on... Yes, it says *'often reddish, especially on the stems'*. I think that's the one, it grows quite a bit in the valley."

After a brief conversation, the woman left. Visitors often brought plants to the office or described birds they had seen; it was to be expected from people who came in search of quietness and the country. A little collection of books, bought over the years to assist in answering these questions, stood on a nearby shelf and word had got round that 'the office would know'.

Fixing the tree, apart from making the office more attractive, had also been intended to help people identify birds they had seen. However, when the first models were mounted on the various branches, although people

32

admired them, they proved of little assistance since colour formed the main means of identification for all but the most expert ornithologists.

"That one?" Sharon followed the outstretched finger of her friend. "I think it might be a chaffinch." She spoke doubtfully to a girl of her own age as they stood in the office at the weekend. Later, over lunch she asked, "Why can't they be coloured? I looked a fool not knowing which was which."

Never having painted before, Gordon tried one evening with watercolours from Stephen's paint set. Colour fastness was an idea completely foreign to him, it came as a surprise a week later to find the paint on a bird inadvertently left in full sun on the window sill was fading.

"I could try oil paints," he tentatively suggested, "but they'll cost and you know how tight money is. What do you think?"

Jan looked at the tree. "How expensive are oils? We certainly need to attract more customers; if people want colour, let's provide it."

"I calculate eleven extra caravan-nights would cover the cost. Surely a good display will achieve more than that – provided I can paint well enough!"

While visiting the bank with a handful of cheques, the purchase was made from a shop in Penzance; a few brushes and a selection of tubes, the colours chosen sparingly. The way oils blended during painting without any tendency to run, added an unexpected and appealing facility to the new medium. When finished a few days later, the display did add something to the office. The oils had another advantage too as they found out later. Dust could now be removed with a damp cloth, whereas those still in watercolour required more careful treatment, traces of paint dissolving when touched with even the slightest trace of moisture. Timber too, affected the appearance; teak in particular absorbed paint at certain grain angles giving an occasional striped effect, but most types of wood seemed

33

to take oils well.

When all was finished the display looked good but had little influence on customer numbers. Trade, though increasing marginally was still terrible compared to previous years. What else could they do. With the final carvings re-mounted, ambition took a hand, soaring beyond painting robins and chaffinches. Think Big! The tree was fine, but it needed a background. Why not paint the whole wall behind? A vivid seascape perhaps, something to set the birds off. Jan wouldn't mind, would she? Instinctively he felt that assumption to be a mistake. How to overcome it? Make painting a wall seem nothing unusual, the sort of thing everyone does!

Removing the screws he called, "Would you give me a hand with the birds please, I'm going to paint the wall behind."

She appeared in the doorway. "Good, it's getting grubby," and helped lift the tree down then returned to the kitchen.

Gordon watched her retreating back with a faint smile before concentrating on the wall. Work downwards, that seemed the best way to begin. Start with a deep blue then while working lower, add white to give distance someone had advised at school in the dim and distant past. He checked outside; it was true, deeper blue overhead. Splotch in some rocks, mark out the cliffs, add a bit of green bank as foreground. Within fifteen minutes a general outline streaked the wall. Now to fill in the detail. As he stood on a stool reaching for the highest parts, Jan came through from the kitchen.

"What!!!" She paused, astounded.

He savoured the dramatic effect; she was not often stuck for words. Smiling down, raised eyebrows questioningly asked her approval, his very expression suggesting she should be delighted.

"Oh fine! If the children did that you'd blow up." Having recovered, Jan snorted the reply with derision.

True. True. He nodded silent agreement. That was indeed a good description of his probable reaction, though he tended to stay calm if things were critical. Too busy thinking what to do in serious situations, no time to be annoyed then – but small things? Hm, yes, sometimes he did speak first and think after. What could he say? Surely it wasn't necessary to let Jan have the last word. He had heard the heavy sarcasm in her voice, she obviously didn't appreciate artistic flare.

"Well, there have to be some advantages to being head of the household." He nearly said Master of the household, but thought better of it. "And anyway, it's going to be a masterpiece."

"Really?"

Such a put-down in one word.

"And why shouldn't it be?"

"Of course, if you say so dear." She blew him a little kiss, and smiled. That smile announced she never truly believed a word of it, but her eyes were full of love, as were his for her.

"All right, if it turns out badly I'll wallpaper the lot just to keep you happy," he grinned, sweeping one hand in a gesture across the wall. After all, she could truthfully have pointed out that this would be the first full picture he ever painted. These verbal skirmishes were fun, part of the zest of life, lightening the sombre mood which present circumstances all too often caused. They gazed at each other for some moments before she spoke again.

"I should stop you, but if it's what you really want, go ahead and damn the consequences."

Her words played in his ears; had she spoken of the wall, or read his thoughts? He shook himself back to reality. Stepping off the stool left them standing very close; she didn't back away. Softly their lips met, not in passion, but friendship and affection – finding in each other relief from mounting worries.

A few days later the painting was finished and the tree

remounted. Chris wandered into the office, glanced at his parents in the lounge, then eased himself quietly into a seat behind the desk and reached for a sheaf of booking forms hanging on the wall.

Jan turned, catching his eye but neither spoke. She guessed his purpose; it was Friday night, just after seven o'clock on a fine evening in mid-May, but the splendid weather had still failed to attract many holiday-makers. In spite of fresh tarmac the entrance road still looked poor; previously attractive green verges on each side had disappeared during the sewer's progress under a coating of drably brown mud, now baked hard in the sun. Tomorrow, Saturday, should be the week's busiest day. Jan knew Chris was checking if any boys his own age would be arriving; the booking forms showed such information, including very often, the Christian names. Would he find a Henry or a George, she mused then wondered if it might not be a Maureen or a Susan that he really sought?

After a while Chris put the forms aside, wandered over to the lounge and stood gazing out through the window. Stephen was crouched at the water's edge with another young lad dangling a line in the river. Sharon too was absent, gone off with two recently acquired friends somewhat younger than herself. Chris scanned the few caravans sprinkled across the field, "We aren't doing very well, are we." It was a statement, not a question.

Gordon straightened from the graph spread out on a board on his knee, putting aside a scrap of paper and the pencil he had been scribbling with, and looked at Jan. The parents had known for some time they were in trouble but had not thought the children would notice. Turning back, Gordon hesitated; at fourteen Chris was entitled to know.

"No, we're not. You're right, numbers are down; considerably. I'll tell you." He reached for the scrap of paper, scanning it, then ran a finger down the graph. "Every year since we started has shown a big increase; that's normal with a new business, but this year we've dropped for the first time. By May 10 last season we'd been paid for 591 caravan-nights, but that figure is now down to 469, a fall of twenty-one percent!"

"What will it mean to us? No school camp?" Chris sounded casual enough, not particularly bothered.

Aware of her son's recently acquired habit of not showing too much feeling, Jan wondered if he really was so unconcerned. Did this 'play it cool' tendency come from the many cowboy films watched on their small TV or from friends at school? Gordon should not have been so open; the younger pair might now find out. Sharon was already worried; best play the matter down.

"We'll see. The situation is not that bad. Dad says the two of you can cut logs to use this winter instead of coal, okay?"

Chris nodded agreement, "Shame the goats are gone."

About to speak again, Gordon caught a sharp warning expression on Jan's face and changed what he intended to say. "Any ideas how we could do better?"

Chris shook his head, then remembered, "One of my friends said his father hated wet shaving, wanted somewhere his electric razor would work. They might have stayed longer if..." a motion of the hand finished the suggestion.

"Difficult. Like the hairdryers people ask for. I've thought about it a lot but without mains electric there's no safe method that's really practical. Razors don't use nearly so much current, but they still need 240-volts."

"What about the gadget you fixed for my Vacuum and food mixer?" Jan asked.

"Yes, that does convert 12-volt to 240-volt and it's fine in the house. You use it for maybe ten minutes a day, but think how long it would be switched on for visitors. The waterwheel could never handle it."

The office door opened and Sharon burst in, two young friends in her wake. "I'm invited out, to Mullion tomorrow morning. Alright Mum?"

37

"Yes. Who with, and what time should I expect you be back?"

Three heads leaned together to whisper before the reply came. "Mrs Robinson. I'm invited to lunch, we may be out until late afternoon?" There was a question asking approval in Sharon's voice. Receiving a nod from Jan, the three girls made for the door, Sharon stopping on the threshold to call back, "Steven and his friend have caught a trout; they have it in a bucket." And the girls were gone leaving the door open, giggling voices drifting back inside as they faded away. Chris stepped casually to the office, slipping outside, closing the door behind him and strolling along the riverbank, no doubt interested in the fish.

"What was that fierce expression for?" Gordon asked when they were alone.

"I don't want the children worried; well not unnecessarily so. They realise this is no great year but you needn't let on just how bad things really are; to Sharon especially, she's quite upset already about the clothes situation. No need to make her more depressed. Twenty-one percent is not so bad, I can manage on that sort of reduction."

"It's worse than you think. That was what I was about to point out when you stopped me. Half our money, well perhaps not half but a fair bit, goes on fixed charges, the insurances, rates, and standing charges; the sort of thing that doesn't go down if less people come. Costs have gone up too, even toilet rolls. Another thing you've forgotten; this is our first year registered for VAT and we didn't raise prices to cover it. Another eight percent we lose. It really is quite serious; never mind clothes, think about eating next winter!"

They sat for a while, considering the situation, it was not new but the full realisation had somehow crept up on them. Was it only the sewer? What about the site? Doubts crept insidiously in. They began to wonder, confidence always a fragile façade of human nature. What about themselves? Should they change to Lifeboy soap?

Certainly the toilet facilities gleamed and sparkled as always and ducks gathered in their usual numbers. What else? Could anything further be done; some improvement, some way to increase people's pleasure? They had discussed it before but it seemed more urgent now.

"More advertising?" Jan asked.

"Sure. It would certainly help, but what with? The tarmac took all our reserves. Anyway we're in all the caravanning magazines already, and both Club magazines too, they were given top priority, booked and paid for earlier in the year while we still had money! Bigger adverts could help next year if we can afford it, but what we really need is something great to put in them, something that will make people feel River Valley is *the* place to come."

"What sort of thing – by appointment to HRH?"

"Yes! If only! Not really feasible though, unless... you wouldn't like to stand outside the palace in a very short skirt and try your luck with one of the Princes? No? I thought not. Something more modest then. More articles like that one on the waterwheel in last January's edition of Peninsular West, or we could set about winning a competition like the Magazines run sometimes. We need one that's keen on the simpler things, quietness and quality rather than lots of activity."

"You mean be *Best Site in the Southwest*?" Jan emphasised the title, "Think we could? What would we need?"

"Hm. Everything that makes a site better; cleanliness, facilities and appearance I suppose. What else? Finish moving the old mine waste from that top terrace, build the dry-stone walls, get more topsoil," Gordon stopped, trying to remember, but there were so many things. "Probably take several more years to fix everything. Some places at the downstream end are still a jungle but that might not matter."

"Cleanliness should be okay. How many owners clean

their toilets at six every morning? But the motorcaravans still need somewhere easy to empty their waste water; even the younger men have trouble lifting that manhole lid."

"Been watching them have you?" Gordon raised a questioning eyebrow.

"I, er, there was one yesterday, lovely tan, tight little shorts and lots of muscles..." Jan paused with a far away look; two could play games. "Wondered if I should go over, ask him if he needed anything. Bet he would fix me an emptying point in no time."

Gordon nodded, well aware that she teased, but pleased to see the fun come back into her face. He had concentrated so much on getting those roads ready for tarmac and the grass repaired that there had been no time for the emptying point earlier in the year. Once the season started they had avoided building work in deference to visitors, few though they were. "Too late to start now, with people here. It needs excavation, a new manhole a run of pipework, not a one day job. I'll do it next winter – provided we survive! The recreation field is still terrible; all cut up where vehicles parked and manoeuvred, I could work down there without upsetting anyone."

Halfway to the village was a field, marshy in places and partly overgrown; it had recreational permission. Older boys playing football or cricket had been sent there in previous seasons, it saved complaints from visitors about balls hitting their caravans.

"Yes. I noticed yesterday. What will you do eventually; build a pavilion? Oh! We slipped up there, or rather *you* slipped up! When the sewer went past you should have made them put a connection in. Trust a man not to think of it!" She gave him a shove.

"Actually, I did mention it once. What would you have done?"

"Insisted! Made them run a sewer pipe across the road and into the field."

"Would you really? Suppose they want to make a yearly charge?"

"Rubbish. Now if you want one, we'll have to rip up the new tarmac... what are you smiling abou... *you devil!* That pipe is already in! I know that stupid little grin. I'll murder you!" She shoved him against the wall, pummelling with small fists, resisting as he drew her closer, then felt her feet swept away and tried to hang on, first to the doorpost, then the handrail as he carried her up the stairs. "Stop it, someone will come," but her heart was not in the words and her grip on the bedroom doorway at the top of the stair was no more than a token effort before her body landed on the bed.

CHAPTER 3

The Best?

Being in bed was foolish in the daytime; foolish and different, that little extra element of risk, of excitement. Unique too, it had never been done before, at least, not while the site was open! By some marvellous chance no one interrupted, neither the phone nor the doorbell rang, but a little later as they lay recovering side by side, the office door opened and Sharon, surprised at finding the office unmanned, called "Mum!"

Quickly both parents slid from the bed, snatching clothes, Gordon hesitating a moment to watch long legs step into a pair of lacy panties before struggling on with his own gear as the voice called again and footsteps sounded below. When Sharon's head appeared round the door Jan was still buttoning her blouse, Dad turning away to pull up a zip. On the point of saying something, the twelve-year-old girl stopped suddenly, her body freezing, eyes opening to saucer size with understanding; her mouth dropping open.

"Go and put the kettle on," Jan urged, breathlessly.

"Mum!" Sharon stayed unmoving, then at a flick of the fingers from her mother, turned and raced off.

Downstairs the three sat over coffee, Sharon with a grin as broad as a cat that got the cream, looking from one to another; the parents tongue-tied and uncomfortable, sneaking small sidelong glances at each other and trying to pretend everything was normal. With remarkable speed

Sharon drank her coffee and was off.

Jan slipped out to the office to make sure she had really gone, and seeing her race across the yard, returned to the kitchen to stand gazing out over the river. "She's off like a rabbit before the fox. You know where, don't you?"

"To tell her friends?" Gordon rose from the table to stand nearby. "They may be too young to understand. I thought perhaps Sharon still was?"

"Not from where I stood. Did you see that look on her face when it dawned on her what had happened? I never told you before, but a few months ago I thought about asking you to explain the facts of life to her." Jan saw his expression change to alarm then amusement.

"Am I let off now? Not really necessary do you think?"

"She'd giggle the whole way through. We should have been more careful though."

"It served one useful purpose – got you laughing again," He reached out, taking her hand. "Me too; we've both been a bit sombre lately."

About to move closer, Jan recalled the earlier argument and stepped abruptly back, "Oh yes! We were discussing that sewer pipe. How *did* you get it laid?"

"Well, like I said, I mentioned it to the bloke who seemed in charge, told him we might need one at some future time. He muttered an acknowledgement, obviously with no intention whatever of doing it, so I left. As you know, I had formed the habit of walking up regularly to keep an eye on progress and the latest damage; well that same afternoon the road was almost blocked. I enquired casually if the Fire Engine could get through in an emergency or should a Bailey bridge be erected; that's those temporary steel bridges you see sometimes – very expensive. Anyway, he said it wasn't necessary, that they would be clear soon. I just said 'Okay' and before he could walk away, asked, 'by the way, that pipe into the field?' I got no further, he cut in straight away, 'we plan to

43

do that first thing tomorrow morning.' We nattered on a bit and he assured me it would cost nothing and there would never be any fee unless it was actually used. I waved and walked away."

"You pig, not telling me! But I'm not angry with you; not now. I was though, before we went upstairs. I could have..." she lifted a small fist, then lowered it. "Anyway, this Best Site competition; if appearance is so important, do something about the house, it's too square. Come on, the children are not back yet, let's stand on the bridge and pretend we're visitors coming in for the first time. You said yourself that what they see can affect how long they stay!"

Knowing it was true, he was about to agree when she grabbed his shirt sleeve and pulled towards the door. Naturally he displayed a proper reluctance, protesting there was bookwork to do, and anyway he couldn't possibly go outdoors in his slippers!

Jan stopped pulling and stood facing him with a warning smile. "Do you really want to clean the toilets on your own for the next week?"

"I... I can't think about that now. Must go and check from the bridge, see what can be done. You don't realise how important it is!" He jumped sideways through the doorway, she chasing until they stood together, arms round each others waist on the far side of the river, looking across. The toilet building directly ahead was already surrounded by a Cornish wall, two layers of stone with soil between. From this soil grew various conifers and other shrubs intermixed with low growing annuals now full of colour.

"The house front, it's very square. That gap between house and toilets is scrappy and untidy too." Jan frowned.

"Not much I could do with the house, not at this time of year, but the gap," he hesitated, absentmindedly rubbing fingers against a slightly rough chin, lost in thought. "The Cornish wall could be extended, the new part wider with

44

more planting room; something special to greet arriving visitors?" An arm swept sideways indicating the tangle of half-dead bushes and the dustbin area beyond, "A new wall would hide all that."

How much effect such a display would have no one knew; but lacking a brighter idea, anything was preferable to sitting watching business decline. A stockpile of large stones already lay in a partly hidden corner, each carefully collected while shifting the big heaps of mine waste. Some had crystals, others reflected the golden glint of pyrites, or green malachite, a transient copper decomposition product likely to wash away gradually in the rain. The most attractive pieces, particularly those with white quartz surfaces, would form the front wall. They could start tomorrow!

On a sunny Saturday morning the children were pleased enough to help, at least until some new friend appeared. Stephen's young companion had left, travelling overnight to miss the traffic as some caravans did. The young girls Sharon played with would not be back until evening; they were off to the Scilly Isles with their parents and had left early. Only five caravans arrived in what should have been the morning rush; even so, work was not started until after ten-thirty.

"Most people are off to the beach now," Gordon rose from his chair. "I'll tow the trailer over; if you all help we can load it quietly by hand."

Running 'Max' the digger was rare in May, deliberately so, in keeping with River Valley's reputation for quietness. This time of year saw mainly retired people, not many young families; always a slack time and even more so this season. Half an hour later the stone lay ready in a pile, the trailer hidden again behind some trees and Max had trundled off to collect topsoil.

In this irregular shaped piece of stonework, the two separate walls varied from three to five feet apart. By lunch it stood eighteen inches high and the family took time for a brief snack; only another foot to go. When work

45

resumed with the sun continuing to shine brightly, the valley was empty baring three couples laying out on loungers and in chairs. Each of these caravans was visited with an apology, the need for a few loads of topsoil explained and a promise given to finish by three o'clock. Hardly anyone else would return before then.

Worked stopped at one point, interrupted by two arrivals, both most welcome, one a caravan the other a tent. They were soon pitched and Max rolled off again, returning shortly, front bucket brimming with topsoil from a stockpile far downstream. The machine rolled to a standstill, tipping its load on the partly completed wall. Nearby, the children waited ready to level and tread down the soil. As Max reversed, turning for the next load, Stephen led the dash forwards, placing one hand on a stone, preparing to leap up.

Suddenly he jumped back! The others drew up quickly, curious but wary, peering past him. Swinging off the tractor, Gordon joined them. Four hands with outstretched fingers pointed to a small snake like object wriggling slowly through the soil.

"An adder?" Sharon asked.

Without offering a reply, her father moved cautiously forward, bending closer in careful study, then to gasps from Jan and the children, reached out, taking the squirming reptile and laying it across one hand. As it coiled round his fingers, he held the hand out towards the watchers. Sharon jumped backward with a shriek while Chris, the nearest, stood his ground but made no move to take it. Only Stephen stepped forward, half lifting his arm in that direction but hesitating, undecided.

Dad smiled at their reluctance. "It's not a snake. This is a slow-worm, a sort of lizard without legs. Quite harmless, not poisonous and doesn't bite."

Stephen lifted his arm higher, taking it gingerly. After a few seconds Chris also moved forward but Stephen, having mastered any doubts, stepped aside, not yet inclined

46

to pass over the little reptile coiling smoothly round his hand.

No detectable injury had been inflicted; perhaps it was stunned in some way because in moderately hot weather slow-worms are normally anything but slow. Like all cold-blooded creatures they move fastest when warm, slowing down as the temperature drops. Sharon peered closely at the slender body now gliding from Stephen onto Chris.

"I don't like the forked tongue that keeps flicking out. Are you sure it can't bite."

"Yes." Gordon confirmed, but seeing Sharon's half-extended hand swiftly withdrawn as she took a pace backward, he tried to be more clear. "I mean, yes, I am sure it can't bite. It doesn't have fangs; the notched tongue just gives that impression. Be careful, the texture is quite hard but that tail is brittle and can easily break off."

Stepping forward, Jan reached a little reluctantly, then expressed surprise. "It does; it feels like porcelain, not a bit slimy. Where do they like to live?"

"Anywhere with places to hide. On this wall or just behind would be good if it will stay; they eat little slugs; gardeners love them. I read somewhere they can live for fifty years or more. If that's true it could still be here when you children are sixty. There might be more by then, they have six to a dozen live young each year."

The family stood in a close circle as Sharon took the little reptile, accustoming herself to the unexpectedly solid feel.

Watching her daughter, Jan said in a whisper, "Poor thing. Never mind our wall, it might have a mate waiting."

So the small reptile was taken back downstream and slipped into bushes behind the topsoil heap from where it first came. By mid-afternoon while most people were still out, the construction was finished. Planting required more time, money again a problem, but Jim and Audrey having seen the new wall insisted on helping and by Monday evening the trees were all set. Larger, more mature specimens would have been preferred, but of necessity, smaller, younger trees were chosen – because of cost! The final effect however, was fine, another step towards that important first impression on arriving visitors. The extended wall matched the previous one in its balance of conifers and other shrubs, and should improve over the years with the trees growing nearer their mature height. Several new species now complemented those previously set, including Chameacyparis Lawsoniana Stuwartii, and Elwoodii, a taller, darker version of the Elwoodii Gold used before, together with Pisifera Boulevard, another Juniperus Squamata Blue Star and a Blue Carpet, the same colour but lower growing. A few other shrubs including three camellias and a fuchsia would set off a host of smaller, more colourful annuals. While in the gardening mood Jan planted a Clematis Montana beside the telephone box. A duck ate it the same day.

Having finished this project and with the season still very quiet, they considered the rest of the site; not for more walls, but for anything amiss that could be fixed without noise? There must be a reason to account for this lack of people. Walking round together as so many times before, they looked critically, trying to see as a visitor would. The valley was marvellous, trees in every direction clothed in a hundred shades of green, short and bushy close at hand, taller more majestic ones in isolated patches up the valley slopes. Short grass, browning a little perhaps but still predominantly green, and everywhere verges blooming with wild flowers, a myriad varieties of colour and shape. None of these verges were cut before autumn, allowing seeds to mature and scatter. Campion grew abundantly, here and there yellow flags, the pinky mauve of mallows and patches of clover, more yellow from hawkweed, toadflax, with the first yellow bartsia beginning to show. They strolled on, a bank to the left alive with tufted vetch, richly violet against the green, a single red poppy, and knapweed too. These flowers, plentiful and

48

easy to find, dotted all the unmown parts, a handful of rarities also present in isolated clumps. The unknown fern carefully worked round more than a year earlier was still thriving, overshadowed by a large oak. A royal fern the textbook said, the only one found; it showed no inclination to spread and they had decided against disturbing the roots. Another plant rare in the wild grew nearby, red hot pokers or more properly, kniphofia, confined to one solitary patch, only the leaves showing now but autumn would see its full spectacle. As they walked past Jan pointed.

"How many times did we spread the seeds?"

Every attempt had been unsuccessful. Each plant it seemed, had a mind of its own concerning habitat. It had been decided several seasons before to leave little rough areas where any wild flower could thrive, letting each stay where it wished, rather than trying to impose a pattern on nature. On the right a pile of recently disturbed topsoil showed the marks of Max's bucket.

"Where did you put the slow-worm?" Jan asked

Gordon climbed the heap, careful in placing his feet, and pointed down between soil and the bush behind. "In there. Nice of you to think of its mate, pity in a way we couldn't catch them both and feed them on the new wall."

"Better not," Jan shook her head. "Remember the frog? If young Stephen put one of these in the ladies toilets, they'd have hysterics!"

Ahead lay the jungle of bramble and gorse that had as yet not been tackled. They veered towards the river, crossing the track of the not yet fully recovered sewer and turned upstream to head homeward. At one point where the river changed direction in a dog-leg shape, the sewer had run slightly inland and this section of bank suffered less damage, recovering quicker. The grass was shorter here, the soil poorer.

"Look." Jan pointed. A dozen or more southern marsh orchids grew on the sloping bank. Below, the water flowed past, clear as crystal; two butterflies in some sort of aerial combat fluttered by. She sighed. "Why aren't they coming? How *can* anything be wrong with this valley? It marvellous – perfect!"

Still holding hands they walked slowly back to the house.

That night in bed they discussed again the outlook; it was depressingly difficult to put the thoughts aside; outside the weather was changing, a roof tile moving in the rising wind but eventually sleep came. Later Gordon found himself half awake but was unsure why. Coming sleepily to the feeling of something wrong yet unable to grasp the cause of this unease, his ear gradually isolated the offending sound, a clank, quite regular, about every five seconds. His mind toyed with the percussive note, trying to place it. Suddenly it clicked.

"Jan!" he shook her vigorously "Get dressed!" As the light flashed on she raised a hand, shielding her eyes to look drowsily at the clock.

"It's gone midnight, what's the matter?"

"Paddle loose in the waterwheel; must fix it – could cause damage! Need someone to hold the torch." He was already pulling on trousers and polo-necked sweater.

"Someone? Not me by any chance?"

"Anyone will do, but yes, you're elected. Everyone else is asleep."

"Why did I ask? Who else is stupid enough to wake at midnight for a waterwheel?" Jan's reply held resignation and a faint suggestion of amusement.

The sarcastic inference was missed, his mind totally on the damage that might occur, calling back as he made for the door, "I'll get the tools, see you downstairs."

Minutes later they were outside, winding down the sluice to divert the water's flow. The wind howled a minor gale, carrying away words but few were necessary. Rotating the now stationary wheel by hand located a loose paddle that hung by one screw on each side, flapping backwards and forwards like a saloon door in a Western. Probably some branch had floated downstream, gone under the wheel and this paddle had smashed against it, wrenching out the fixings. Extra screws were quickly driven in. A cursory check of the remaining paddles then opening the sluice started the wheel turning – electricity flowed again, the whole operation taking less than fifteen minutes.

Stepping back inside the house, cut the wind like a switch. That disturbing change from untroubled slumber to hurried activity left them feeling drained now the emergency had passed, drained but restless. Sleep would not come when they returned to bed. After a while as both moved uneasily, Gordon whispered softly.

"Told you I'd never let you get bored with life."

"Gee Thanks!" A moment later a pillow swung with considerable force, smashing down on him out of the darkness.

***

The phone rang; a hand reached out to rest on the receiver but waited, making no attempt to answer. It rang again then stopped; Audrey's signal from the bungalow in the village. The road was empty. Sharon rose and crossed to the window, watching, expecting something to appear. She was temporarily in charge, her mother having rushed off with an urgent telephone message about someone taken ill. It had not been a familiar name but a quick search through the signing-in book revealed both the area where the caravan was pitched and the car number. Jan had taken a stick-on message label and a pen in case they were out. Gordon was also absent dealing with a dripping standpipe, replacing the faulty tap with one that had already been serviced. The spring-loaded taps that automatically turned themselves off were complicated. He would bring the dripping one back to the work bench and deal with it later, inserting new washers and other parts from a large stock of spares, then use it again when the next tap started leaking – another of those tricks to ensure

51

nothing was ever out of order for more than a few minutes.

A motorcaravan appeared, slowly approaching down the road and halted astride the bridge; new arrivals often stopped, drawn to stream below. The head of a girl leaned out behind the driver to gaze down at the water. Sharon watched from the window, it pleased her; there were no girls her own age on site at the moment. She opened the office door and stood waiting, hoping it would hurry before her parents returned. As if in answer to the silent plea, another car appeared round the toilet building heading outward, forcing the motorcaravan to drive clear of the bridge, stopping near the office. A family descended, stretched themselves and moved forward, acknowledging and responding to the smiling face welcoming them in. Sharon turned, leading the way, pleased that people accepted her more now than in earlier years – not nearly so surprised to be met by a lass of nearly thirteen as they had been when she was only eight.

"Do you want Christian names?" the woman asked as she sat in the chair, writing her address in the book.

Christian names were optional; Jan would have said 'If you like.'

"Please," Sharon nodded confirmation, wanting to know the other girl's name and saw the upside-down word 'Carol', then looked up as the outer door opened again.

Jan entered, smiling at the new arrivals, pausing briefly to say 'Hello' and to pass a few pleasantries, then intending to head for the kitchen. However, Sharon rose from behind the desk, a little movement of the hand indicating she wanted her mother to take over. That was unusual; once either Chris or Sharon had started to book anyone in, they were normally allowed to finish – unless there was something amiss. Sliding into the chair to check the books, Jan's eyes ran guardedly over the three strangers, wondering what the difficulty might be, but saw no problem. Sharon had hurried off down the hall; perhaps she needed the toilet.

Having learned the girl's name, Sharon had headed off for an entirely different reason. Entering not the toilet but the kitchen, she lifted the bread bin lid, opened the plastic bag and took out a slice of bread then not sure if one would be enough, took another, concealing them inside her blouse. She would like to have left by the window; under similar circumstances Chris would have done so but the drop was a good five feet. Deciding against, she walked out through the office, avoiding her mother's questioning glance then hurried towards the river, retrieving one of the slices and showing it to the ducks, walking backwards throwing tiny pieces until they gathered round not far from the office door. Shortly it opened and the visitors emerged, pausing by the little flock. Carol watched with a touch of envy in her face, an obvious desire for contact with those friendly feathers – Sharon had the other slice ready and held it out.

Casting one restrained look at her parents Carol moved forward taking the bread, stepping closer and kneeling, to be quickly surrounded by hungry beaks.

Standing on the threshold, the key in her hand ready to lock the office door, Jan saw and immediately understood her daughter's earlier intention. Replacing the key in its normal place she left the door open, calling to Sharon, "Answer the phone if it rings. We'll be on Area 10, will you show your friend there afterwards." Striding on Jan signalled the visitors, "Follow me, I'll take you to a pitch."

Later that afternoon when the boys arrived home and they sat together at tea, another vehicle approached. Gordon was spreading his bread when Chris, hearing an engine, saw it cross the bridge and warned, "Caravan coming."

His father carried on spreading the slice.

Jan, signalling with her eyes, quickly enlisted the children's support. When Dad looked up expecting someone to go to the office and see the newcomers in, all the children and Mum were silently waiting, each with hands

53

under chin, elbows on the table, staring fixedly in his direction.

"Hm. Does anyone think it's my turn by any chance?" He rose, going through to the office and closing the connecting door behind himself.

The family smiled broadly at each other with success, congratulating themselves.

"Do you know what your father did this morning?" Jan asked, and getting no reply, continued. "He had insisted I set the alarm half an hour earlier, at 5.30. After it rang he told me under no circumstances to pull the chain or use any water, then he dashed off somewhere. When I'd dressed and gone downstairs, he was sitting across the bridge gazing down at the water meter like it was gold-dust, and checking the watch on his wrist. Five minutes he sat there before coming back to the office."

"Why?" Sharon asked.

"Testing for leaks," Chris pointed with his knife. "At that time in the morning the meter should show no movement; that means nothing is leaking."

"Yes he is a big-head," Jan agreed in answer to Sharon's whispered comment about her brother, "but he *is* right. Dad thought the amount of water used was too much for the number of holiday-makers but the meter never moved; there were no leaks. People use more than in previous years, that's all." Jan had addressed her final remarks to Chris, but now turned back to Sharon. "Well, how was your new friend Carol?"

"How did you know her name?"

"I read it in the signing-in book. You're not the only one who can do that. Yes, I know; I've seen you check the entries whenever another girl arrives, and that good-looking boy the other day too!"

Chris and Stephen's heads rose sharply. Sharon stared down at the table, colouring slightly, giving herself time to think. "It was his hair cut. I thought it might be a girl."

Jan leant over towards Stephen and whispered loudly

enough for all to hear, "Do you know what she did to meet Carol and get talking to her?"

Stephen shook his head and looked at Sharon, Chris showing obvious interest. Recounting the escape to the kitchen, the bread and the ducks, Jan turned to Sharon.

"Hope you appreciated the help I gave." Seeing her daughter's puzzled face, she explained. "Did you notice before taking them to a pitch, I asked you to show Carol where it was later? Before I spoke, the mother was about to call her to go with them."

"Sharon would never be bright enough to think of that," Chris apparently spoke to Stephen, but both boys, while pretending to look at each other were watching their sister expecting a reaction.

However Sharon sat back, smiling. "Girls are brighter than boys, they're brighter even than some men – than Carol's dad for instance."

The boys were disappointed but intrigued. Something unusual must have happened. Chris was eager to know, but realising Sharon wanted to be asked, he said nothing and waited. Stephen took his cue from Chris and across the table both sides sat, no one willing to give way.

"Sharon may be right," Jan deliberately broke the stalemate, "but I think she had better explain." The suggestion suited everyone, particularly Sharon.

"Right. Carol's father wanted to empty his waste tank but the proper drain hasn't been fixed yet. He tried to lift that lid over by the chemical point..."

"I showed it to him when we chose a pitch." Jan interrupted, waving a hand for her daughter to continue.

"Well, he couldn't move it, the thing was jammed or his fingers lacked the necessary strength. He left the motorcaravan right there and popped into the toilets. I took Carol to one side and told her we could do it. She didn't believe me but we ran to the service passage and borrowed some things Dad has been making. You slip them under the lifting lugs and they have a kind of handle

55

that gives a really good grip. We used both tools on one end and pulled together, forcing it up, then the other end until that too was clear. When we rested the lid carefully back in place, you couldn't easily tell it had been moved. I took the tools back and hid, watching from behind the building. As her Dad reappeared from the toilets, Carol knelt over the lid. She said *'Let me try Dad,'* and pretended to struggle then lifted the cover clear. He could hardly believe it; didn't know what to say. She slipped away afterwards and we walked together downstream; it was great! Don't you tell them Mum! They think Carol is amazing."

Later in the evening, when Jan slipped out to make coffee, Sharon followed, and entering the kitchen, closed the door soundlessly behind her. Jan saw the action, wondering why but said nothing and filled the kettle.

"Mum... did you ask Dad about my new clothes?"

"We did discuss it but things are still difficult. Why do you ask now, did Carol have a big wardrobe?"

"Bigger than mine and that's only what she brings in the caravan. But it's not really that."

"What then? Anyway, what do you need most, tops or bottoms? Are they too tight?"

"Tight is not so important. Some girls at school wear them that way, particularly the senior ones, but mine are old and worn. They all have new things, it gives them an advantage when we meet..." Sharon hesitated uncertainly, "When we meet... together."

"Nothing to do with boys then?" Jan asked the words quietly, with understanding.

"No! Well perhaps... not really in my year. Some of the older girls talk with Chris and his friends. We like to look nice though, make an impression; you know?" Sharon gave a shy smile, "Mum, what made you choose Dad? How did you catch him?"

"Catch him? You think I should have thrown him back?"

56

"Yes, and found someone richer. No, I didn't mean it – that's just how our group talk."

They smiled at each other, Jan leaning back against the sink. "When we first met I was barely two years older than you are now. It was in Pitman's College in Southampton Row, London. I walked into one of the classrooms and there he was, sitting at the desk. My friend Vicky was with me, she was really classy, all the boys went for her. '*Oh*,' she said, '*Wonder who he is?*' But it was me, not Vicky who found out!"

"How?"

"Walking past his desk, I slipped, kind of accidentally on purpose, and knocked his books on the floor. Helping pick them up I read his name on one of the covers."

"Mum!"

"Don't worry, I'll convince your father you need something; not expensive mind, we really are in trouble."

"I'd like to cut my hair too, should I ask Dad first? About here." Sharon indicated a level slightly above the shoulder, some twelve inches shorter than at present.

"No. Go ahead, do it and tell him afterwards. Say it was costing too much in shampoo so we cut it ourselves to save money. Come on, they'll be in here for the coffee if we're not careful."

***

"I say!"

Sorting through the line of dustbins, replacing full ones with empties, Gordon heard a voice. A tall man in a white open neck shirt waved some sort of paper, walking forward across the yard, a man he recognised as having been before.

"Look at this!" A magazine was held out. "You remember I asked earlier in the year about using my electric shaver?"

Gordon nodded, he did remember, vaguely. It was difficult to be sure, a good many people had asked. The man's finger pointed to a drawing or maybe a photo, some

57

type of small electric box with a socket for a two pin plug. 'Transhave' said the caption underneath.

"I was thinking of buying one for my caravan," the man said, "have you seen them before? Are they any good?"

"No idea. Didn't know there was such a thing." Gordon looked more closely. "Can I borrow the magazine? I'll try to find out. I'll bring it back!"

"Go ahead. You know where I am?"

"Sure, your car number is CKX, right."

"Right!" The exclamation showed surprise. "How can you possibly remember with all the cars staying at the moment?" The man shook his head, waving a hand as he left.

Gordon watched him go. "Good memory? Hm! Just as well I wasn't asked his name!" Trade had improved but there were not *that* many cars on site yet. The letters were easy enough, Buckinghamshire registration seen every time the vehicle passed the office; more people were known by car registration than by name. It was always the letters that were remembered – unless of course, somebody should show up with an 007. No one had yet, but a visitor from Essex might contrive it by altering the spacing.

Stuffing the magazine inside his shirt, he quickly tidied the line of bins and returned to the office, sitting down at the desk with a magnifying glass to study the tiny print. After a while he picked up the phone and dialled.

A female voice confirmed that they did offer 12-volt shaver sockets, and no, three couldn't be ordered by phone because they must have the cheque first. A suggestion that they send the sockets with an invoice met with a cool response. "No. Cheque first, goods afterwards; that is the company system!"

Gordon blew a little snort into the handset; he did not want to wait. The season was getting busier, the last week bringing a long overdue surge in trade.

"How would you like your sockets displayed in one of the leading southwest touring parks?"

58

The line went silent, he waited, hearing faint conversation; someone had laid the phone down and was talking, the words indistinct.

"Sorry to keep you, how big is this park?" a male voice asked.

"Licensed for 250 caravans." Gordon resisted any temptation to explain that not even half this number had ever been achieved.

"Three complimentary units? Where would you like them sent?"

Five minutes later Jan entered the office to be whisked off her feet and swung round, legs flying as they gyrated together between billiard table and bookcase. As the movement slowed to a stop, her body slid down against his until the tips of both toes touched the carpet. "Grrr!" He bent forward, lips crushing against her own.

After a while she staggered back, "What was that fo... Never mind, forget I asked. Whatever it was, keep taking the tablets!"

"That's power, raw power!" He flexed an arm muscle, clenching the fist and bending the wrist inwards. "I just got three Transhave units free! Free because *we* are a leading southwest tourist park!"

"Oh good. I always wanted one, doesn't the fur keep falling out?"

"Can't stand clever women. It's a little device that works ordinary electric shavers from a 12-volt battery. I shall install one in each Gents."

"Chauvinist! Ladies use shavers too, for their legs."

"They can creep in the Gents at midnight, I'm not putting sockets in the Ladies, they'll plug in their hair curlers and burn the units out."

"We've only two toilet buildings, why have you ordered three? Wait! The third one is..." she held up a hand with one finger extended, bringing it down as a signal and they spoke the final words together. "A spare!"

With clenched fists she pummelled gently at his chest,

59

then murmured, "Well done. When he gets home, Chris will be pleased to hear you've found a way to act on his suggestion. That may cause a few to stay longer; we can do with them. Still down aren't we?"

"Yes, but not nearly so much." They looked together at the front field now liberally dotted with caravans, and then more westerly to a good collection of colourful canvas.

"Those tents," Jan whispered, "Will they have to go if the Council discover we don't have proper permission? Will they find out?"

No one knew the answer.

CHAPTER 4

Arthur

Three days later the Transhave units arrived and were fitted the same morning, one in each building. Two car batteries purchased for the purpose would provide power. Compliments flowed as several regulars called in at the office to comment, and especially when the magazine was returned to CKX and the man told he could try them out himself now and see how they worked.

After the first few people had said how much they appreciated this new facility, Jan cornered Gordon as he entered the office after pitching another caravan. "These shaver points, they really like them, even a lady came in to say how good they are."

"How did she find out?"

"Said she didn't mind kissing her husband now! I told her I wouldn't know – forgotten what it's like." Jan swung casually away, leaving one cheek obviously exposed. He moved forward to oblige but a man appeared in the doorway.

When the visitor left carrying a full gas bottle, Jan asked, "What is this secret weapon for lifting manhole lids that Sharon speaks of?"

"Oh yes, I meant to show you. Hold on." He disappeared to the service passage which ran between the Ladies and Gents toilets, returning with a kind of claw, a piece of steel bar bent sharply round at one end, a stout handle at the other. "There are two, they hang on the wall by the gas heaters. Lend them to anyone who wants to empty their waste tank."

"I thought you were making a better arrangement."

"I intended doing it this coming winter, but will it be worthwhile? I could only connect to the septic tank and we won't be allowed to use that soon. We need one that goes to our new drains but they lead nowhere until the sewer is working. This," he waved the hook in the air, "must see us through until next year."

Seeing him reach for the door handle, Jan touched his arm with a restraining hand, stopping him. "I was spring cleaning my cupboards this morning. Those jars of bramble jelly, the ones you over-cooked when I had to go out; they're still on the shelf. Couldn't we... well, get rid of some. And that old coffee jar, there's something inside wrapped up in a plastic bag; what is it?"

"The bramble jelly? Let's not throw it away. You never know, one day we may need..." Gordon stopped, seeing a smile spread across her face, then tried to justify himself. "It can't be more than four years old and there's no mould." Quickly he changed the subject. "The coffee jar; that's Sharon's hair, the length she cut off. I liked it better long but if short is more economical you can't really argue."

"Where will you be if I need you?"

"Trimming back long brambles round the pitches. Didn't get chance in the winter." And he left.

Trade was still fairly slack, a few caravans and two tents came before midday, and towards teatime something else arrived. Arthur was a pigeon; he entered the office on a man's shoulder just as Stephen came home from school. Another couple were booking extra nights at the time but everything stopped for the introduction.

"Why Arthur?" the lady writing a cheque asked, pen still poised in her hand.

The man lifted a finger to the bird, ruffling the breast feathers. "I'm a miner from Nottinghamshire. None of us had much to do while the strike was on, so a group of us took to this pigeon. It won't fly you see; not injured or anything, just refuses to fly, thinks he's a person. It's such a stupid bird that we called it Arthur. Afterwards, when the strike was over, I got stuck with it – been trying to lose it ever since." He pushed his finger upwards until Arthur stepped on, then offered it to the lady. Laying the pen down, she tentatively held out a limp hand and the bird hopped happily across.

"You can keep it." the miner offered hopefully.

She reached out, quickly passing the bird to young Stephen who stood watching nearby. The lad took it in silence, with great care, eyes shining. The miner opened his mouth to repeat the offer, but caught Jan's forbidding glance and the firmly shaken head. Not wanting to cause offence, he took the bird back.

Stephen too, had seen his mother's silent warning. Being a boy of few word, he was perhaps more aware of body language than either Sharon or Chris might have been. Standing quietly in the background, he waited until attention turned back to the desk, then slipped out through the door and off to a hidden observation point, settling down to watch. The first couple emerged and walked away; Stephen saw them go but remained hidden. Arthur's man left the office next, waiting while Jan locked the door, then with the bird still on his shoulder, climbed into the towing vehicle and was led away. Following secretly until the caravan pulled onto a pitch, Stephen hid quickly behind some bushes knowing his mother must pass close by when returning to the office. Shortly after, judging it safe, he emerged from the leafy cover, quickly rounded a corner then dawdled past the newly arrived caravan. The man winding down the steadies looked up, recognised him and called a greeting; Arthur strutted around on the ground nearby. Stephen stayed for a while stroking the bird, and over the next few evenings visited Arthur regularly, taking with him sometimes a young friend staying in a tent. So it was that late one afternoon, finding the caravan hitched up and ready to pull off, Stephen ran up to handle the bird one last time. He was standing with Arthur on his shoulder when the man climbed in his car, wound down the window and asked, "Would you like to keep him?"

For a long time Stephen stood, first watching the caravan disappear, then gazing at the empty roadway. He had nodded at the man's suggestion, only a single slight tilt of the head, knowing it to be wrong, knowing that his mother had already said 'No,' but somehow unable to resist. It was not the first time he had disobeyed. Would she let him keep it? Usually he worried more about his father, about those extra jobs that might be given in return for misbehaviour, but this he sensed, would be Mum's decision. Aware suddenly that he stood exposed to view from other caravans, Stephen moved, disappearing quickly behind trees to make his way downstream where a wild mixture of willow, bramble and gorse still made some parts practically unapproachable. Having reached relative safety, the problems remained; where to keep Arthur and how to feed him? Duck food perhaps? But that was in the shed and one of his parents, or sometimes Chris or Sharon, opened the door each morning freeing the ducks. They closed it at night too, shutting them in; discovery there was inevitable.

Thinking that wild pigeons found their own food, the lad reached up, let the bird step onto his hand and lowered it to the ground, bending a seed laden stem of grass towards the beak. Arthur ignored it and stood on his shoe, anxious to be picked up again. Absently, Stephen complied, placing the bird in the crook of his arm and gently stroking the feathers as it snuggled down with closed eyes. There were two other choices; the basement or the bedroom he shared with Chris. The basement would do temporarily but it was dangerous. Dad or Chris often went down without using lights, feeling a way through to the underground workroom and only pulling a switch

64

when they got there. They might tread on Arthur in the dark. Sharon would be safe enough, she switched lights on everywhere, left them on sometimes and ruined the evening television, but if she saw the bird she might tell – unless she too was in on the secret. Slowly he headed back towards the house. It was difficult now to move without being seen by visitors but they were so used to Arthur on someone's shoulder that few would notice anything different. Reaching one side of the nearest toilet building, he eased a way round the mass of dustbins, casting a glance at Max the big excavator now standing unused at the rear of the area, then pushed through a thin screen of escalonia and quickly into the duck shed. Arthur did not want to stay but Stephen placed him carefully on a shelf, knowing he would not fly down. Shutting the door was chancy, it was never normally closed in the daytime and someone might notice, but it seemed preferable to risking the bird's sudden appearance in front of the office, for it just might muster courage enough to jump from that shelf.

Entering the house he found both parents in the lounge, it was a quiet time, visitors settling for the evening. The bell would probably ring for a gas bottle at some stage or a motorcaravan could come, they often arrived a few hours before darkness, but it was unlikely that anything would happen to remove both parents. Arthur must be smuggled in somehow, and in the next hour! Dad always shut the duck shed door at night; he would investigate why it was already closed. Stephen peered along the hallway and saw Sharon's legs, horizontal where she lay reading on the bed; they were visible from the lounge with both doors open. He must speak to her but if he tried to enter that room a loud protest ordering him out would almost certainly draw Mum's attention and put her on the alert. With apparent aimlessness, he strolled off into the kitchen and sought some way of attracting Sharon, something that would not also bring Mum. Looking round, he knelt next to the cooker, opening the nearest cupboard door. Inside

65

were an array of saucepans, frying pans, cake tins, large flat roasting tins and other containers, all lain against and on top of each other. His hand reached out to rattle a small cake tin. He waited. No one came. Giving a bigger utensil a good shake produced a louder more effective noise, and another wait. Again nothing. Reaching for a handle, a sharp jerk intended to raise the sound level a touch higher caused a saucepan lid from above to slide down with a clatter. Desperately he made a grab, trying to catch it, knocking more pans in the process and in that second of panic the whole unstable mass slid – lids, tins, pots and pans clattering against each other and onto the floor below!

At the explosion of sound Sharon shot from her bed, dashing for the door. Stephen, his hands still steadying a large saucepan, looked over one shoulder at his sister's eager expression, then saw another more anxious face appear behind.

Relieved to see him unhurt, Jan asked, "What were you searching for?"

Stephen pushed the big saucepan farther onto the shelf, then reached for another, balancing it on top and picked up a tin, but said nothing. Sharon moved forward to help and the lad rose, collecting a lid that had rolled across the room.

Jan watched, catching his eye once but he swung evasively away. She sensed then that there would be no answer, no excuse such as Chris might have invented. The lad's very expression warned that mischief was afoot but there was something about this quiet resistance that made her want to reach out and hold him. It was too late of course... much too late. Five years ago she could have hugged him, cuddled him to her, but not now; he would resent it, be embarrassed. Did Sharon sense it too? Jan watched her continue to help, stacking things quietly away, taking the lid from her brother without question, as if protecting him. What had he been up to?

With the cupboard repacked and closed, Stephen

66

made for the door, headed along the corridor, through the office and outside. He offered no reason, just walked away towards the river then followed its flow, not seeing the solitary face still watching from a window.

The footpath would have led eventually to St Erth but that was not the intention. One caravan had pushed itself right to the river's edge, blocking the path; he dodged round it and continued downstream for a hundred yards then cut inward to the cover of some trees and retraced his steps to settle finally in the tangle of trees directly behind the house. From here it was possible to watch without being seen, but time was running out. Somehow Arthur must be carried inside the house, smuggled up the stairs and made comfortable in the bedroom – but how? He had no plan. Mum was far too suspicious for him to approach Sharon again. Chris was not available, he had recently joined a judo club at Goldsithney and had cycled off there immediately after tea; Stephen wished he knew when his brother was due back; Mum would know but questions would be asked.

The noise of an engine drew his attention; through the trees a vehicle approached, a car towing a caravan. For once he hoped it would not have children. At this time of year visitors with youngsters were rare and were invariably placed on the field directly in front of the house; it helped them find friends more easily and kept the other areas quieter for the retired people. If this new arrival was pitched so near, then his father would always be in sight of the office door, whereas couples without children invariably went to the downstream pitches; that might take ten minutes, maybe more by the time they finished chatting.

Stephen waited. The caravan stopped and two people walked to the door. He knew now that his father would leave the office, it was part of the service taking everyone to a pitch, offering a choice and helping shove the caravan into position. But what about his mother? How could *she* be persuaded to leave? Patiently he continued to wait, crouching behind an ivy covered trunk, peering through rather than over the glossy green leaves. The office door opened and the visitors emerged, walking towards their car; his father followed, pausing suddenly halfway across the yard to look at the closed duck shed door, taking a step towards it then changing his mind and hurrying ahead to lead the caravan away.

That had torn it; now something must be done! Hurrying from cover Stephen entered the service passage wondering what would bring Mum out. It had to be fast! The roar of a gas burner overhead drew his attention. There were two, one for wash basins, one for showers. Leaning over the bench, neck bent upwards he sought the flame; which one? Ah, the one farthest from the door; somebody was having a shower. It might be more than one person; four showers worked from the single heater, two in the Ladies, two in the Gents. They were instant heaters, firing up and giving hot water whenever required, better than storage heaters Dad said, because they never ran out – never that is, unless the flame died! Quickly Stephen fetched a stepladder stored against the far wall, spread its legs near the heater and climbed up. Without hesitation he reached for the control and cut the gas! The main burner died and in a second the pilot light also extinguished – but it could not be left like that! His father would know someone had switched it off. Stephen had started counting immediately; one, two, three... on the count of six a shrill scream sounded through the wall from the Ladies, followed by raised voices. With the gas cut, the water had suddenly run cold! Someone was bound to dash to the office and Mum would come. He counted on, ten, eleven, twelve... must reach twenty-five before turning on again. The safety device that stopped gas leaking if the flame went out might malfunction if the probe remained hot he had once been warned. Nineteen, twenty... there were footsteps running across the yard towards the office...

twenty-four, twenty five – he twisted the knob, held a spill of paper to the other heater's pilot jet, transferring the flame, carefully but quickly relighting the gas in the shower heater before taking three downward steps and jumping to the ground. Collapsing the ladder and putting it, almost throwing it, back in its proper place, he raced off closing the passage door, ran to the duck shed, snatched that door open, found Arthur still on the shelf and lifted him fast but with care. Remembered to close the shed door again since his father had noticed it shut, Stephen saw a woman back out of the office still talking to someone inside. He vaulted the low wall and dived horizontally behind it, protecting Arthur with both hands, arms outstretched before him.

Voices crossed the yard, voices and hurried footsteps. He risked a quick look, only one eye raised above the wall, glimpsing his mother and another women, then dropped down again in a flash. Five seconds later he was on his feet and running for the house, up the steps, bursting into the office... and stopped dead! Sharon, equally shocked, was standing in the hall doorway. She saw Arthur and drew in a breath! For a moment they stood, held by the unexpected impasse. Stephen, fearing the greater danger behind, moved, closing the door, signalling with a finger to lips and made for the hall. Sharon blocked his way.

"Does Mum know..." she broke off. Stupid question, the answer written clear in her young brother's face. The scattered saucepans came to mind but she could see no connection, then another idea, "The hot water!" It was an accusation that needed no elaboration. "How did you get it? The man has gone."

"Gave it to me."

"Mum will be mad. She'll make you take it..." Sharon broke off again. How could Mum make him take it back? The caravan had left.

"Only if she knows," Stephen spoke in a low voice. "Get some corn, bring it upstairs."

Sharon was hit by indecision. She hesitated, torn between shouting this news from the housetop or being part of the secret. Snatching the advantage, Stephen slipped by and was up the stairs, then rapidly constructing a barricade under the bed with books, pillows, anything to hand. Long before Jan returned Arthur had been fed, matters had been sorted and a strategy agreed. Sharon would keep the secret and have Arthur sometimes when both Mum and Dad were out. She would also be the one who took Chris aside and told him the story; that had been the clinching point in their pact.

Jan meanwhile, stood in the Ladies toilets, surrounded by a gaggle of women. A lady before her was holding forth, more amused than upset, pleased perhaps to find herself the centre of attention. She was full dressed now, hair in a turban-like towel, having dried off and donned her clothes in haste. "It was lovely, they always are; so much force, not a poor little spray like some sites. Anyway, I have it hot, that's another thing I like, you can adjust the temperature. Well, I tend to keep inching the hot tap open a little wider as I get used to the heat until it almost burns on the skin." she paused giving a little shudder of pleasure. "Anyway, I'd just reached the maximum I could stand and was washing off my hair when, Wham!" she threw her arms wide. "It hit me! Suddenly from nowhere, icy cold water streamed down like... like... I can't tell you, it was shattering. I think I screamed."

"You certainly did!" A laughing voice to the left interrupted, a hand pointing, "Good job I was already sitting in that little cubicle. Scream? You surely know how! I jumped so much five feet of toilet roll unwound and dangled on the floor."

Discussions broke out between several of the women. Apologising, Jan hurried off to relight the gas heater but found the pilot jet already burning and returned to check by operating the actual shower. It quickly ran hot – a mystery? Heading back to the house, she entered to find Sharon at the desk, something supercharged about the girl, an aliveness, an excitement that Jan could not place. Chris arrived home shortly afterwards and she watched wondering as Sharon dragged him off outside, talking animatedly, moving her arms, Chris obviously listening.

When the children had gone to bed, the parents sat in growing darkness, Gordon listening to the strange happenings of the evening.

"They're up to something, all of them but particularly Stephen," Jan warned.

He was not sure if she imagined it but hearing of the shower failure, insisted on taking a torch to check again that the pilot light still burned. It was fine, nothing amiss that might have caused the problem. They retired together for the night and were weary enough to sleep soundly until the alarm rang a few minutes before six next morning.

Sharon had risen early too, and heard water running in the bathroom. She was already dressed but lay in bed pretending to still be asleep in case Mum should enter with instructions about breakfast. Muffled voices reached her, then the sound of the office door closing. Had both parents left? They usually went cleaning together; if not never mind, she had felt restless and woken early, that would be her excuse. It was not so unusual, there didn't have to be a reason. Throwing bedclothes aside, she eased the door open and crept carefully to the office window, seeing Dad across the bridge bending down to read the water meter as he did every morning, pen and notebook in hand. The house was empty! A quick trip to the top of the stairs and a small tap on the bedroom door received no acknowledgement from the boys. Stealthily she entered, moved to the far end of the room and knelt, feeling under the bed. The thin orange curtains were still drawn but the light filtering in was adequate. Something pecked her finger; she reached farther in, gathering up Arthur, hugging him gently and started to rise when a hand grabbed her.

"What you doing!" Stephen's challenge was low but fiercely urgent.

"Sh!" Sharon moved closer, casting a warning glance at the sleeping Chris and whispering, "Mum and Dad have left. We've thirty minutes at least. Arthur needs a walk. Get dressed, catch me down the riverbank." She wrenched the arm away and was gone.

Stephen started to dress, then moved to the other bed. Would Chris still help if he was left out? A small hand reached across to shake the sleeping shoulder.

When Jan returned at sometime after six-thirty, she found breakfast already cooking on the stove and more surprisingly both boys dressed and sitting at the table.

"I made them make their beds properly this morning, Mum. You won't even need to go up and check. Is Dad coming in?" Sharon reached for another egg.

"You did? Yes he's coming; just letting the ducks out. Why is everyone up so early?" Jan looked at the boys; their faces showed such angelic innocence that she knew for certain something was afoot. As she swung round, Sharon quickly turned away. Breakfast was eaten in what could only be described as rebellious silence; glances passing between the youngsters changed to bland looks when intercepted by their parents, and questions were evaded by pretending not to understand. At one point the centenary celebration at the little chapel in the village was raised, it had opened for worship in 1875, but that conversation too, petered out. Quickly finishing eating, the boys returned upstairs, *'to prepare our books'* they said. Jan suspected some other motive, to avoid further questions perhaps, but made no progress in confirming her suspicions. She watched later as the three walked up the road together – they were far too pleased with themselves.

There was an hour at least before the shops in town would be open. Gordon was out catching up with trimming some hedges that last winter's intense repair work had prevented. He used secateurs and chose vacant pitches so not to wake any visitors. She had wanted him to clean the high windows on the toilet buildings but in spite of trade being slack, he refused outright to enter the Ladies at this busy period in the morning.

"Frightened you might get assaulted?" she had asked, knowing he could be a little unsure when dealing with other women.

"Well yes. Told you before, a young chap like me can't be too careful!" He had promised however, to be back by nine. Leaving the office door open and the outside phone bell switched on, Jan took a bucket and some scissors to start dead-heading the annuals in the nearby Cornish wall. When Gordon returned she had not yet finished but hurried off anyway, leaving the part full bucket in the service passage, popping indoors to change and grab cheques for the bank, then drove quickly off.

Two people changed gas bottles, but no early caravans arrived. Gordon settled down at the desk with daybook, totting up figures and marking extra dots on the graph. A group of customers walked by, heading towards the bridge with bread in their hands; he looked up, following the movement, then back down at the paper. Every point plotted lay below that of the previous year, hardly a surprise. The line was almost finished when a noise caught his attention, it seemed to come from upstairs. Sitting quite still and listening, no further sound came. Imagination probably; another column of figures was totted but before the final dot could be made on the graph, the sound came again, a series of small taps. Surely that was from above? Rising, he stepped softly to the door, into the corridor and along to the first stair tread, looking up to the landing above and listening. There it was again. Who? Jan had taken all the cheques and what little cash there was but a burglar was not to know that. It paid to be careful! Slipping quickly outside, he grabbed a long handled mainly straight blade with a hooked end, a tool used on

73

matted vegetation, a cross between a machete and a sickle. A trial swing, then another to bolster courage, and he was off! Soft but determine steps returned to the stairs, mounting two at a time; there was no possibility they would creak and give warning for each tread was cast in concrete.

Carefully stepping over the last two, the only ones made of timber, he stood on the small landing breathing deeply. A hand wiped unconsciously down against trousers, then reached to grasp the door handle and slowly turned. Standing there in that momentary hesitation before action the irrelevant thought came that this was a job for a left handed man – the hinges were on the right. Crouching slightly, one leg backwards for more drive, Gordon thrust on the door, muscles bunched, long knife at the ready!

Thump! It swung wide, hitting the wall and sending a gust of air across the room. On the floor near the foot of Stephen's bed, Arthur gave a jump and a backward step, two bright pigeon eyes pointing up at the tense figure crouched in the doorway!

"Arthur?" With a sigh, Gordon eased his grip on the handle, laying it aside in one corner, flexing the hand that had grasped the shaft with such force. "How did *you* get here?" He fell on one knee and the bird ran forward, trying to climb the thigh, happy when a pair of hands reached out to pick it up. The question had not really been to the bird. He never talked to Arthur the way he had, and still did, to Robin and Blackbird in the winter months. The enigma remained however, the bird was here in the house and it certainly never flew through a window for none were open. Not that it made any difference; if every window in the house had been thrown wide there was no way this stupid bird could fly in! Perhaps it was cross bred with a flightless species and grounded in consequence. Was that what would happen when some idiot scientist started fooling with bird genes? Typical! For a hundred and fifty million years birds happily survived against every catastrophe, then man comes along and having lived a tiny fraction of that time, thinks he knows better!

"A long time, a hundred and fifty million. What do I know about the Jurassic period? Much of Britain was covered by a shallow sea laying down clays and limestone; today's cement comes partly from there. Someone drilled a borehole at Portsmouth back in the 1930's, to encounter over 4000 feet of Jurassic rock..." Gordon broke off, stirred from his reverie of bygone college days by an impatient movement on his shoulder; he reached one hand absently to a feathered wing. Someone must have carried the bird here. Was that in some way connected with the strange happenings of the previous day. An idea occurred. Still balancing the new lodger he hurried downstairs, opened the daybook and dabbed a finger on one entry. That miner from Notts left yesterday. Had the children taken Arthur without his knowledge? No, none of them would; too fond of animals to separate one from someone that cared for it. Well then, what? Left behind accidentally perhaps, or was it deliberate? That hardly seemed right. Jan did say the man had tried to give Arthur away. Hm. Maybe, but for anyone with a caravan, a non-flying bird could have been abandoned anywhere long ago. No, he must have known it would be cared for; must have succeeded in giving it to someone before leaving. The thought raised another question. If he left yesterday, where had Arthur been overnight? Mounting the stairs quickly Gordon enter the boys' bedroom again. The wardrobe showed no signs of droppings or food, nor any of the drawers though he doubted they would ever put it in such a confined space. The under-bed pen could not stay hidden long, there were so few possibilities. A cloth laid over the carpet, a little scattered pile of corn and a plastic container of water told the story.

"So! Well what do we do with you then Arthur?" He reached up to the bird again and ruffled its feathers with a finger. "Mum is going to be delighted!" There was irony in the thought. "She said the man nearly offered it to Stephen and she only just stopped him in time. Stephen? Hm, probably. Come on, let's decide on a temporary home for you."

The loft of the farther toilet building provided a suitable place, Arthur would never try to fly down and it was only until late afternoon. A handful of corn and another plastic dish of water should ensure his comfort.

When Jan came home she bustled into the office, "Wait here. Don't you go away! Let me get this shopping in then I've a bone to pick with you." She hurried through into the kitchen and on returning looked surprised to find him still seated at the desk. "Typical male! Are you just going to sit there being useless? Aren't you helping unload?"

"I was told to wait. I always do as I'm told."

"Do you hel... some people could make a saint swear. I've had enough trouble this morning because of you!"

"Me?"

"You took Mr Robinson's money! Next time see that he signs his cheque. The bank girl spotted it and asked me to check the column of figures again – without a calculator! Get out and help empty that car. Now!" She stood by the desk, arm outstretched pointing, deliberately not moving back so he would have to brush against her to get past. Gordon rose, made to push by but leaned over as if to steal a kiss. Jan stepped sharply away, still pretending anger, but his move had been a feint. As she swayed back he jumped clear, racing for the open door then across the yard, to be caught of course at the car. There they stood close to each other, pleased with the little theatricals, a more satisfactory conclusion deferred by a small group of visitors standing on the bridge.

When teatime approached, Dad returned to the house early, he gave no reason other than to say briefly, "No time to start another job." He did not explain his intention to be present when the children arrived, nor why on this particular night he should want to witness their homecoming.

Stephen, not yet at the senior school, came first. He was early, not having stopped to see Jim and Audrey at their bungalow as was usual, but instead giving a wave and running on. The satchel that he normally dumped somewhere on the floor was taken immediately to his bedroom. Shortly after he descended again and wandered through to the kitchen. Jan preparing a salad, looked up and smiled. Stephen smiled dubiously back, expecting trouble; then glanced towards his father sitting at the far side of the table. Gordon, apparently reading a book, appeared not to notice. The lad slipped out and returned upstairs, hunting more thoroughly then left the office and started up the road to meet Chris and Sharon. It was three subdued children that eventually entered the house, Chris immediately running upstairs, returning to join the others with the briefest shake of the head.

Tea was quieter than usual, Jan asking once if anything was wrong. Chris shrugged. Sharon asked "Wrong?" as if it were a mystery and Stephen looked down at his plate. An inevitable interruption occurred part way through the meal; Sharon rose to go, but Dad stopped her. "I'll get it, you sit still and eat."

Someone wanted a gas bottle; that was by far the most frequent cause. He slipped a key into one pocket, took the money, carried the empty to the service passage and passed over a full bottle. Instead of returning to the house, a sprint to the far toilet building, a quickly turned key, up the ladder and Arthur was retrieved. Locking up and crossing back to the house, he entered, still with the bird on his shoulder and made for the kitchen.

"Look what I've found wandering about the yard."

"Arthur! Oh, he did leave you! I had hoped... never mind," Jan walked across, stroking the bird. "Everybody likes you don't they? What are we going to do with him?"

"I thought perhaps the children could take charge, let

77

him run anywhere in the daytime, put him in the duck shed at night?"

Three faces nodded, turning to Mum for approval. She looked back at them, "Okay, it's not your fault but try to keep him out of the house."

"You can do something else too," Dad suggested, addressing the boys, "Give your room a spring-clean before Mum has to go up and see to it."

"That's not necessary. Their room is clean enough," Jan smiled at the idea.

"Perhaps, but they should check. Might be dust or something under the beds?"

"We'll do it Mum," Chris offered urgently; two other heads nodded agreement and they turned towards Dad, smiling at him a little more broadly than was customary, then back at Jan with a touch of concern, then at each other. Sharon gave a little giggle.

Now Arthur's presence was known to all the family, he roamed freely and his character became more obvious. Arthur was stubborn, difficult, and totally out of touch with reality – and it wasn't just his refusal to fly! He showed no fear and had no respect for anyone, insisting on entering the house, thwarting constant efforts by every member of the family to chase him back to the shed put at his disposal. He would enter tents and invade caravans, anyone's caravan provided he could jump up the steps without the need to fly. In no way did Arthur behave as a normal pigeon should.

At first they suspected a wing defect but careful examination revealed none. In an attempt to teach him, Arthur was carefully tossed in the air with the family each holding the corner of a blanket, stretching it out to catch him. Arthur handled the exercise with no problem. Moving the blanket farther away eventually induced flights of over thirty feet but he insisted on walking back, like a dog fetching a stick, as if saying 'throw me again'. Stephen climbed a tree and left him on an exposed branch with a clear way to fly down. Two hours later he clambered back up to effect a rescue. It wasn't that he couldn't fly down; he was going to have his own way and just wouldn't. Arthur definitely held the opinion that other birds were wrong and he was right. Efforts to instil normal behaviour came to nil but it didn't upset Arthur, he still came to be picked up, still barged into any accessible caravan, and still absolutely refused to fly. The silly bird was quite prepared to ride the carrier of Jan's bicycle, but would he fly back? No! One sunny weekend afternoon when the children were home and Arthur had jumped up the step into the office for the umpteenth time, she addressed him with a mixture of affection and irritation.

"You stupid bird! I'll teach you to fly!" She picked him up, collected her bicycle, let him cling to the handlebar basket and rode off downstream. Many people were laying out on loungers or various types of ground sheet as she passed but few saw her stop, turn the bicycle, throw Arthur high in the air and pedal off looking over one shoulder. The bird fluttered easily to earth, landing lightly, then ran along the roadway at top speed trying to catch up. Even when the cycle disappeared round a corner he still refused to fly. Jan hid behind a bush and in a few minutes Arthur came pelting by, little feet going ten to the dozen, suddenly stopping as he saw her. Slowly she pushed the cycle back, the bird happily keeping pace.

It was typical of Arthur that he took things to the absolute extreme. When a visitor walked by with his dog, Arthur was among the ducks, pecking now and then at corn strewn on the ground. As the spaniel charged forward to be stopped abruptly by its lead, the ducks scattered in every direction in one great flurry of feathers. Even Francis who could not fly properly, scampered for the river, his unbalanced wings flapping so hard that those big webbed feet hardly touched the ground – but not Arthur! He stood there unconcerned, facing the snarling dog, driving it mad with rage.

Jan at first worried about Henry, the old ginger Tom who often prowled the site. Henry came more to get fed by caravanners than in hope of catching anything. He was so old that there was very little slow moving enough to remain within his capability. Jan feared however that Henry just might be fast enough to kill Arthur because the stupid bird would not fly away. It wouldn't even have surprised anyone if Arthur stopped to tell Henry that it was totally against his principles to have cats running around killing top class pigeons like himself! The risks therefore were clear. However, short of shutting Arthur up, which might be difficult and probably unkind, there was nothing they could do. Against all sensible predictions, the pigeon survived. To some extent the increasing numbers of caravanners protected him, for most delighted in Arthur's boldness and cheek; it was beyond their normal experience of birds, something new and therefore memorable. Many photos were taken and they referred to him often in conversation. 'That stupid bird' became a term of affection for many, or exasperation for those who tried without success to bar him from their caravans, for in the hot weather most people preferred to leave their doors open.

CHAPTER 5

The Awning

A car came too fast across the bridge. Hearing the engine, Jan caught a glimpse as it passed but her hands were covered in flour. Gordon would probably flag it down on his way back to the office and have a word regarding speed. It was one of the few things about running a caravan park that neither of them liked – ticking people off; embarrassing but necessary occasionally and if they were clever, done without giving offence. She always found that difficult. Gordon was better, less self-conscious but depressed when he made a mess of it. How would he handle this one, 'Hi, Sterling! Did you forget you're on holiday?' A man could get away with things like that, she'd heard him before – seen it go wrong sometimes too. The doorbell rang.

"Damn. It must have stopped." She must speak to it herself after all. A check on the time showed just after 9a.m. Business had continued to improve with the school holidays nearly arrived. Wiping hands and hurrying through to the office she opened the door but there was no car, only a lady with an unhappy face.

"Where can I get milk, please?"

"Did you try the man from the village?" Jan pointed to a van on the far side of the field with the back doors open and several people standing in line.

"He's run out again, says he's none up at the shop either. All the decent newspapers are gone too – had to buy *The Sun* this morning. I hate the way my husband drools over page three!"

"Goldsithney is the next nearest. Turn right at the main road and it's two miles. Sorry about this, we don't have any control..." Jan raised a hand palm upward towards the distant van. The woman understood but was still less than happy. Understandable of course, people wanted fresh milk for breakfast, expected it to be available; it always had been when Sampson Polglase ran the village shop. More might have been said but someone else came to the door wanting to stay longer and a caravan drew up in the yard. Having taken for the extra nights then booked the caravan in, Jan chatted, asking about the journey, glancing now and then through the window and wondering why Gordon was taking so long. "He'll be back soon – taken a tent to a pitch, must have got a difficult one."

They talked some more; the woman pointed at the tree and on learning the bird's were wood carvings, went to the door and signalled her husband to come in. Turning back she continued to talk, pointing, "That woodpecker, is it the greater sp... Oh!" she broke off, giving a little jump of surprise when a pigeon coming from behind, passed close to her foot.

"Arthur! Get out!" Jan made a shoo motion with both hands but the bird took not the slightest notice, walking right up to her and waiting to be picked up. Kneeling she lifted it as the man entered, and seeing the expressions on the two faces, made the introductions, warning that Arthur might well try to enter their caravan given half a chance. As they talked a car skidded round the toilet building, shot across the yard, over the bridge and sped away.

"Good job you were not out there then," Jan lifted Arthur level with her face and addressed him, "that one wouldn't have stopped for you like all the others do. Wonder who they were? Definitely not one of ours!"

It may have seemed idle conversation but in those few words apparently directed at a bird, the newcomers were warned to watch out for Arthur on the road, and had also been reassured that the behaviour just witnessed was not normal on the site. At that moment, Gordon appeared round the corner and strode to the office.

"What happened?" Jan asked.

"Oh, nothing. Three young men who got themselves lost. No problem." He led the caravan off, taking a little more care and giving extra time and trouble in the choice of pitches offered; an attempt to compensate for any bad first impressions. On his return to the office, no one was waiting; it was tempting to say "Good," but they needed the trade.

"Well?" Jan asked as the door closed, but he shrugged and turned away. Sensing evasion she caught his arm, "Come on. Tell me what really happened. I could see by your face there was trouble. What did they want?"

"The three young lad's? I didn't see them arrive; that last tent I took round was, how shall I say... choosy! He wanted to see everything, landed up with a pitch on the very last area downstream. Walking back I came across three chaps putting up a tent – made them take it down again. They were a bit surly, thought for a while I might get clobbered but I stood there until they pulled off. Did you see the clothes they were wearing?"

Jan shook her head. "Not at the speed they came past. Talking of clothes, what about Sharon's. I should buy them soon, time will be short next week. Are we okay for money now?"

"Yes, within moderation. Can you meet her tonight from school, we're too busy at weekends."

"Tonight is her judo night, she doesn't want to miss any, the tournament is due soon. We'll do it tomorrow."

Sharon had followed Chris's lead in taking up the sport, one of her friend's parents bringing her home on those evenings.

***

Two eyes peeped downwards, staring through a narrow

83

gap, a hand at each side holding the bedroom curtains apart. "That's another pulling in; there are..." the eyes roamed round the yard counting, "five more, perhaps six already. I think one has two cars but it may be a separate tent. Come on, it's started again." Jan drew the curtains closed, knelt back on the bed reaching for the light switch, pulled it and looked at the clock. A quarter to six. She pushed the alarm button down, switching it off; no longer needed. That last arriving car had woken them early. Just as well, this first Saturday of the school holidays was always hectic.

Gordon rolled from the bed, he had been awake already, lazily lying still, happy in the closeness of her warm body. "You start the cleaning, I'll move that last arrival to a temporary pitch; anyone else who's awake too, the entrance will block otherwise."

"Right," Jan pulled on a jumper, "Tell them to come to the office at... I'll get Sharon to make breakfast... say 7.30, okay?"

When the first couple knocked on the door it still wanted ten minutes to the specified time but the toilets had been cleaned, breakfast eaten, and everything was more or less ready. By 8.15 the early arrivals were all comfortably pitched, the site gradually coming to life. A woman came in asking for milk but the shop man had not yet appeared. Changing gas bottles, taking money from people booking extra nights and a steady stream of arrivals carried them non-stop towards lunch; even the post lay unopened on the desk. Stephen stayed mostly in and around the house, watching for new friends, running small errands but with no specific task, free to come and go as he pleased. Chris and Sharon had no such choice, the one morning of the year when both stayed on duty, helping with whatever came up. Chris dashed off to change some dustbins that a man had reported were full, Sharon hurrying with a dustpan and brush to the Ladies toilets when news came of a bottle smashed on the floor. Neither objected; their presence in and around the office offering a certain status and an early opportunity to meet the many arriving young people. Sharon cooked lunch, first for herself and Chris before the younger pair took over the office while their parents ate.

"If anyone comes in the next twenty minutes, tell them to wait," Gordon advised.

"Ask them to wait, don't you mean, Dad?" Sharon suggested as she left the kitchen.

"That told you," Jan laughed quietly when they were alone. "She's quite fair at handling people now, not as good as Chris but..." Jan saw a smile on Gordon's face and whispered urgently, "Don't you dare tell her I said that." They ate for a while in silence, then back to clear the queue, which had accumulated even in that short time.

By Monday the influx moderated, the children no longer needed full time. By arrangement they would take turns, one staying to help while the others followed their own pursuits, but today being the first opportunity to make new friends, all three were released. Numbers had nearly doubled in three days and more were still arriving, though no longer in an endless stream but rather at intervals or in small groups. A couple approached the office about mid-morning, the wife stopping short of the steps and urging her husband on. He entered the office.

"My wife is... she's not very happy."

"Oh. Something wrong with the facilities?" Gordon asked.

"No, just dogs. Ours is a small spaniel, we keep her on a lead like the rules say but it's not very nice when bigger animals come sniffing round. We're parked near the river, someone walked along with his dog running free. Is it a footpath?"

"Yes. I'm sorry. Not many strangers pass by and most keep their animals on a lead. You'll probably find it won't happen again but I can offer a position away from the river if you like, near the oak trees straight across from where you are now? Chat to your wife about it, let me know if you want to move and I'll come and help push."

As the man left, Jan came through from the kitchen. "Coffee in the other room, go and drink it, I'll mind the office." Taking turns for coffee had become habit on busy mornings; it was difficult drinking in the office. Many caravanners were old friends, it was tempting to offer a cup but that caused resentment if someone else was not invited.

Jan looked along the road, checking no caravans were coming. No, only a car, probably someone already on site. How many were still due to arrive? She reached across for the booking forms but stopped as the car swung into a parking space opposite the house. There was only one person inside, a man on his own. Unusual, what did he want? A figure emerged, opened the rear door, leaned in and his hand came out grasping a large notebook. He wore a dark suit, definitely not holiday attire! An inspector? Jan, knowing she could not easily be seen at the back of the room, took a tentative step towards the door, wondering whether to call Gordon, but the man flipped over a few pages, then strode confidently towards the rear field. Most families in that area had tents. Tents! A possibility struck her. "Gordon!"

Hearing the urgency, he was by her side before the man disappeared from view, his eye immediately drawn to the dark clothing. "Who is he?"

"No idea. He parked and marched off, hardly glanced in this direction. Did you notice the notebook? You see where he's gone!"

"An inspector on some sort. Yes, towards Area 2, tents mainly. You think the Council have..." Gordon broke off as a smaller hand slip into his own. Both knew they were vulnerable, had half expected the Council to discover the planning discrepancy long ago. By some oversight that they had not even noticed themselves at first, the site's main planning consent made no reference to tents. Loosing them would be devastating – tents represented perhaps a third of the peak season income.

"They can't stop us at the moment, not while we're on the temporary permission, but that expires once the sewer is working and then..." he stopped, there was really no need to explain, they had probed all angles of what might happen and the consequences so often before. The coffee would be getting cold but somehow it seemed not to matter. They watched and waited.

The arrival of another car towing a small camping trailer was a diversion, a relief. This tent was booked in then escorted off to a pitch. It was tempting to offer one of the downstream areas, somewhere hidden, some little niche surrounded by bushes that Mr Dark Suit would not discover. However, partly from bravado and partly from an intense desire to see what was going on, the tent was led straight to where the inspector, if that's what he was, had disappeared. Offering a selection of pitches enabled a thorough search of the area, the newly arrived campers believing this attention to be solely for their benefit. Indeed, seeing the young couple so spoiled for choice and so delighted was therapeutic, temporarily pushing more sinister matters into the background.

Walking back to the office, offered no further glimpse of the enemy and they waited together inside, unable to concentrate on the many tasks still requiring attention. When the man did return, his approach went unnoticed for they sat together in chairs in the lounge, no longer talking but watching the river flow under the bridge and ducks on the water – wondering silently how badly their lives would be affected. The office bell shot them both upright. Gordon hurried through the opening into the adjoining room to see a soberly dressed man standing at the door. A sudden vision of the child-catcher from Chitty Chitty Bang Bang flashed to mind as he reached to ease the handle, swinging the door open.

"Good morning. I'm from the Council. We're inspecting all touring sites, is it convenient to have a word?"

"Er... yes, come in."

"Now, oh... madam," seeing Jan step into the room Dark Suit acknowledged her, then continued, "Generally, your standards are very good. Those little handles fixed at low level to the toilet buildings, are they for tying dogs?" Receiving nods of confirmation he lifted the book and scribbled a short note. "Good, I've not seen that before, and the spacing between units is excellent – except two small tents that are quite close to caravans on one of the areas." He paused trying to work out in which direction they lay, pointing towards the west, "Somewhere over there, a grassy section with a wood behind..."

"Area eight," Gordon offered.

"Yes, well I'll have more to say about tents in a moment, but those two; can I take it they are both family units with the caravans they are close to. Let me explain. If a tent belongs to the same family it can ignore the proper six-metre fire regulation gap, provided there is only one cooking source! Some park owners don't appreciate that. Your tarmac roads are unusual on caravan parks, you may find sleeping policeman helpful but it's not a regulation. What do you do about fast drivers?"

"We speak to them, remind them they're on holiday, but the ducks slow everyone down." Jan spoke quickly, with an unintentional sharpness, nervously awaiting what they guessed was coming.

"Yes. They probably do," The man gazed towards the river, then at a handful of ducks in the yard. "Yes, good. Now, about the tents. This is perhaps the most difficult matter. We don't think those tent should be..." he paused, looking towards the rear field, then plunged on, "There are several caravans on that area too, and we feel, well this is really a personal feeling, that they shouldn't be there." He made an awkward gesture, and stood waiting.

Jan and Gordon leaned closer, her hand reaching again instinctively for his, but neither could bring themselves to reply.

Taking the silence to show reluctance, Dark Suit tried

again. "I don't mean you should change anything right away, but when the opportunity arises as people come and go, could you get rid of the caravans from that area. It's far better to keep caravans and tents in separate places."

Jan looked up in surprise, a glance at Gordon's rigid face warning her to keep control, to disguise the elation within, but it was too late! That first bolt of understanding had shone from her features like a beacon. The inspector smiled back, probably believing the sudden radiance to have resulted from not having to make any immediate adjustments. Only when he walked to his car and drove away did the pair in the office give rein to their full feelings, hugging each other, laughing, punching the air, celebrations quickly cut short by the arrival of more visitors as was only to be expected in late July.

At mid-afternoon, Audrey rang from the bungalow, "Can you send Gordon down when he has a minute? It's ice pack trouble. Oh, and ask if he ever managed to check whether this place really was a pub at one time like some people say."

"I'll tell him," Jan promised. "The pub question; he spent an afternoon on it way back, early this spring I think – one day when it poured with rain – went to the Cornish Studies Library, the one that opened last year over in Redruth. Can't tell you about it now, there's a queue in the office. I'll send him down later."

Jan rang off, not asking for details; her mother's voice had carried no tones of urgency. It was a safe guess anyway that the freezing system would be in trouble, they had half expected a problem. With no mains electric on site, all visitors had their ice-packs frozen in a big chest freezer at Audrey and Jim's bungalow half a mile away up the entrance road.

"Sorry about that," Jan reached across the desk, taking the cheque a woman had written out, entering the amount and the number of extra days in the book. Two more visitors waited, one moving forward to sit by the desk; Jan turned towards the hallway and called. Chris, now helping again, appeared in the doorway, saw the gas bottle and automatically picked it up, hurrying off for a full one. Leaving the office he saw his father busy moving dustbins, and another caravan rolling in across the bridge.

It was nearly seven o'clock that evening before the opportunity occurred to drive up to Jim's bungalow. As Gordon drew in the gateway, the sun-room door opened and Audrey stepped out, Jim with his stick following behind. Leading into the garage, she lifted the chest freezer lid, reached in and passed over a paperback sized translucent plastic container filled with some blue substance. Gordon took it and squeezed; the pack was still soft.

"Twenty four hours that one's been in; there are so many! It's only the last few days, we were fine before that."

"Are they grumbling?"

"Better not!" Jim spoke from behind.

Audrey smiled, shaking her head. "Some are not too pleased but they don't really grumble. I've said we'll get another fridge, can you arrange it?"

"Yes, I suppose we'll have to. Good job the money is coming in again. Where will it go?

"Right against the wall next to the other one." Jim waved his stick, "That leaves me room by the work bench. Come in for a drink."

"You put the kettle on, Jim." Audrey stayed by the chest. "I'll tidy the packs and close the lid."

Jim moved off and Gordon prepared to follow but a hand on his arm stopped him. "Get a really big one, there's plenty of room since we sold the car," Audrey urged quietly. "Don't worry about cost, we'll be paying. Gives us a lot of pleasure, all the people calling in. Anyway, I've been saving up; ten pence for each pack frozen and any soft ones are free – that's really why people don't grumble." Audrey led the way indoors and they sat down together.

"Did you learn any more on the history of this plot," Jim asked.

"Yes. The rumours are true, it was a pub once."
Gordon produced a bundle of papers, a mixture of photo
copies and scribbled notes. "I wrote down the names of
all the landlords, let's see... there was a deed dated 25
March 1808 from Francis Gregor to Richard Milldrum, a
carpenter, leasing two thirds of a dwelling house now a
public house known by the name The Lord Nelson Inn.
That's when it first became a pub. Several more landlords
followed, finishing with a Mrs Anne Opie in 1873, then
Joseph Tyack in 1879; he appears to be the last. A sheep
shearing match took place here in early July that year.
There was other information too, a note dated 1849 said
Relubbus Fair at the end of August was normally held at
the Lord Nelson. Should we revive it? It still shows as a
pub on the 1880 map but reverted to five cottages after
that."

"There was another pub in the village so they say, the
Hawkins Arms." Jim lifted a bottle from the sideboard.
"Have a whisky with that coffee?"

"No thanks, this is fine. The Hawkins Arms was
definitely a pub, er, here we are, 1856 to 1897 it says; the
landlord in 1869 was John Verdant. Must have been
plenty of drinking done in those days, the records show
there were six pubs in Relubbus. Well, two pubs, the other
four were kiddlywinks."

"Kiddlywinks?" Jim had poured himself a good
measure and took a drink.

Gordon ruffled through the papers again for details.
"Kiddlywinks were beer houses after the 1820 Beer act,
often a single room in a cottage, a sideline to bring in extra
cash. The payment of £2 a year to customs and excise
allowed a householder to put his name over the door but
he could only sell beer, not spirits. However, on the fire or
in the fireplace was usually a type of kettle known as
a kiddly, supposed to be full of soup. Traditionally it
contained something much stronger! A customer wanting
spirits had only to wink at the kiddly to get what he

needed. The proper pubs, The Hawkins Arms and our Lord Nelson didn't need to use a kiddly, they were legally entitled to sell liquor and their licences were dearer, £10 a year I think. There's a book on old Cornish Inns by a Mr H.J. Douch if you want more information. Relubbus had a blacksmith and a farrier too, and..." he rustled through the papers, "Ah yes, you know Trewhella Lane at the top of the hill? A Matthew Trewhella farmed there in 1856; must be where the name came from."

They chatted on for a bit, but even at this time, gone 7.30 in the evening, a caravan drove by and Gordon hurried off, following on behind to find it a pitch.

In the mid-week days, arrivals were less numerous, leaving the children free more often to join their many friends and meet new ones. Sharon called back at the house as another caravan drew up in the yard. From the back seat of the car a girl of her own age emerged, a girl she recognised from last year – but what was her name? Sharon waved, straining to decipher the numberplate and memorising the first three letters, pleased to see it was still a P registration, not a new car; that meant it should be in last year's records. Quickly, before they entered the office, she opened a drawer, snatched a book and disappeared to her bedroom. It took a few moments only to trace the equivalent week in the previous season, then follow the car numbers until a match was found. In one margin a pencilled note in her own handwriting read 'Sadie'. Back in the office the recent arrivals were gathered at the desk, the lady writing in the signing-in book. Sharon, having grabbed a piece of bread from the kitchen, stood slightly to one side and read the upside-down name Roberts. Fine! That confirmed it. She moved towards the door.

"Hello Sadie, come and meet the ducks again."

With a glance to her parents for a nod of approval, Sadie followed. Near the river they stooped to feed hungry beaks and stoke feathered backs; behind them the office door opened and shortly after, the caravan drew off.

"They know I'll find them." Sadie held out another morsel to a nearby beak. "Anyway I'd rather wait a while. We have a new awning... takes ages. We've only put it up once but they'll never remember how it fits together with so many pieces."

"Should we go and help?" Sharon asked.

"Not unless you've a magic wand. Let's keep out of the way. Are any of the other girls here?"

"Mary is, she came Saturday. I'm not sure if she's in; let's check."

They headed together downstream looking for Mary's big frame tent but it was zipped up with no one about. The two girls wandered slowly back along the riverbank to find Sadie's parents were still struggling with the awning so Sharon left for lunch, agreeing to meet again later. At the meal it became apparent that Chris too, had met a friend. Contrary to his usual appearance he wore a tie, causing Jan to assume his new companion was not male. Sharon noticed the smarter attire and tried to unearth who this girl might be but without success. When she spoke of her own friends and of Sadie's awning problem, Chris, far from passing derogatory comments on the ability of girls as he might have in earlier years, showed instead a keen interest, saying casually, "You must introduce me sometime."

"Then I won't see her for the rest of the holiday I suppose. No, you keep away. Find your own introductions!"

But there was no animosity in the banter, both happy, Sharon secretly pleased with her big brother's interest in her friends but not disposed to show it. They were eating a salad that included tomatoes, lettuce, cheese, grated carrot, some nice little spring onions, and ham; something that could be consumed at any time without getting cold. Dad for instance had not yet returned to eat. The meal finished, Chris carefully removed his tie, laid it on the sideboard and made to leave.

"If you're not wearing the tie, you should undo the top button," Jan suggested

"I'm putting it back on in a minute, just want to clean my teeth."

"Why take the tie off in the first place then?" Sharon demanded.

"I get toothpaste all down it otherwise. When I lean forward it dangles in the basin. You don't know much about men do you."

"No, I'm still hoping to meet one some day!" Sharon turned with a broader smile, making her way out to seek her friend again.

Later that afternoon she was sitting outside the caravan with Sadie; her parents having succeeded in erecting the awning had walked off down the riverbank. Chris strolled casually across asking Sharon if she had any preference for the evenings viewing, offering several options that he had memorised a few minutes previously. Since both had been busy with friends in recent evenings, the subject of viewing hardly seemed relevant. Sharon's immediate instinct was to expose the contrived question, but something in Sadie's expression made her hesitate. This season, with friends a year older, she had begun to notice a certain interest in her big brother that did her own standing no harm. Pretending the hesitation was in choosing the program, she gave her selection then made the proper introductions, inviting Chris to stay and explain how the waterwheel worked.

They sat together on the ground talking, Chris hoping the awning question would somehow arise, but not wanting to broach it himself. As the chatter ranged through various subjects, two caravans rolled down the road and across the bridge.

"Will you be needed at the office?" Sharon asked

"No. Mum knows where I am if she wants..." Chris stopped, realising they would now understand his approach had been planned. As the girls looked at each other and giggled, he waved an arm self-consciously, then seeking to divert attention enquired directly of Sadie, "Sharon said you had trouble with the awning?"

"Er, my parents do. It's not like our old one. So complicated, too many bits."

"Would you like to make it easy... for next time?" Chris had their attention again, his deception forgotten, or perhaps just forgiven.

"Sure, if you know a way. Go ahead, show us." Sadie rose, bending to unzip the awing front and signalling Sharon.

Following the girls inside, Chris produced a roll of sellotape, a pair of scissors and a neat handful of small paper squares each with a single capital letter marked clearly in black ink. Sharon picked a few up, inspecting them; there seemed to be two of each letter. Immediately she understood.

Within a very few minutes, small letters started to appear, attached with a circle of selltape to the hollow metal tubes that made up the framework. At each side of each joint the letters matched. After the first few, Chris asked Sadie to hold the letters in place while he applied the sellotape. Several times he reached carefully to take her hand on the pretext of adjusting the position.

Arthur, the stupid pigeon, strutted on into that early August rush, slowing cars, convinced they would never dare run him over, invading anyone's caravan and enjoying the increasing numbers of visitors. People, he regarded as his subjects, harmless and slightly inferior but at his beck and call as suppliers of food. The bird showed a slight preference for Stephen, but anyone, child or adult who would make a fuss and give him attention was quickly accepted. The weather continued mostly fine; Chris, encouraged by the record catch of a one-pound ten-ounce herring featured in *The Cornishman,* cycled off with his rod the three miles to Perranuthnoe when his help was not required. He had many holiday friends, mostly young men with fishing interests but a few girls too, including a rather pretty one who had won a junior beauty queen contest. Sharon had no trouble attracting companions either, though they were all female. She talked sometimes to various boys, but invariably from the safety of a group of girls, not yet ready to stroll off down the riverbank with a single lad. All three children still took turns in helping in the mornings, sometimes in the evenings, and particularly on busy Saturdays. Several times at breakfast Gordon complained that the water meter readings were high and people must be wasting it, but on the whole, things were going well. The larger chest freezer had arrived and been installed in Jim's garage, solving completely the ice-pack problems. With both old and new chests sharing the load, packs were now solidly frozen overnight. Caravanners batteries arrived at the house in increasing numbers, several sets of short jump leads connecting up a whole series as more were carried in for charging, the waterwheel working at maximum day and night to cope. To get them charged quickly, the grid that collected debris in front of the wheel was cleaned twice a day and household electrical use curtailed, the vacuum avoided and candles used in the basement. Few other lights were needed in the long days and although television in the evenings was still allowed, often the children were not home to watch and the parents too busy, leaving the set unused.

Through all this activity Arthur strutted on, making an amusing nuisance of himself – then suddenly he was gone, disappeared without trace, his fate unknown. Jan did think when she next saw Henry, that the old cat wore a self-satisfied smile; that slightly holy one-upmanship grin of a politician who had just convinced the public he was honest, overworked, underpaid, and his long summer break had not been a vacation, but an in-depth investigation of the continental wine trade.

CHAPTER 6

Henry

The hot August days passed and September arrived, traditionally a month when pressures eased and the family could draw a deep satisfied sigh, pausing to contemplate the gentle close of another season. This year it brought instead, trouble, deep trouble; a threat of arrest! The Law descended in haste one dark evening.

Jan and Gordon knew nothing until a police car drew up outside the house sometime after eight o'clock. An officer came purposefully to the door, extracted a notebook from his pocket and asked about foreign families staying on site. How many? How long had they been resident? Had anyone actually seen inside their caravans? The questions were searching but no mention was made of any particular nationality.

The officer offered no reasons, not even a small hint as the interrogation continued. They were left to speculate what crime had been perpetrated, but the officer's manner, his terse urgency, suggested the worse! In addition, every car that passed the window caused him to break off and stare into the deepening gloom outside. Seeing their puzzled expressions the policeman spoke again without a flicker of a smile.

"Expecting backup."

Phew! This was getting serious. Backup? What backup; an armed squad? Jan drew in her breath sharply.

Catching the sound, the officer eyed her suspiciously.

97

"Do you have any Germans?" the demanded was sharp, probing, more accusation than question, his tone daring her to deny it!

What now? Did they perhaps have a murderer, maybe Herr Great Train Robber or his equivalent?

"Yes," Jan admitted, feeling a stab of guilt. "There are Germans staying, two very nice..." she stopped suddenly, mouth open, realisation dawning. A few seconds ticked by, seconds in which the policeman never once took his eyes off her face, not even to blink. She swallowed protesting defensively, "Well, they seemed nice! One family speaks really excellent English, the others know only a few words."

This was unusual, most Germans were fluent English speakers. Of the main continental travellers, Dutch were the best linguists, closely followed by Germans, while Italians and certainly French were normally pretty poor, almost as bad as the British themselves at learning other peoples languages.

The policeman knew where to find the caravan he wanted, and described its position. Murphy's Law dictated, naturally, that this was the family that spoke little English. Another car pulled up outside. The single occupant, a man in a suit, strode quickly to the office door and entered without knocking. He drew the policeman aside and spoke in low tones, glancing down at his watch during the brief conversation. Shortly they both stepped forward, the plain-clothes man introducing himself.

"I am a Customs officer." He flashed some sort of card, slipping it quickly back into a pocket.

"Customs?" Jan paled, swallowing. The man extended an arm but there was no greeting in the motion, no warmth in these new eyes that coldly regarded her. Briefly shaking the hand, her thoughts raced. "Opium smuggling?"

"We could be more helpful if someone would say what is going on?" Gordon suggested. They two officers seemed doubtful.

98

Jan, apprehension making her edgy, was becoming annoyed. "You suspect us of something?" When the two officials remained silent, obviously uncertain what to say, she turned to Gordon, "Shall I ring Jim?"

"Who is Jim?" The customs man spoke sharply.

Seeing aggressiveness rising on Jan's face Gordon stepped in quickly to forestall trouble. "Jim is my wife's father. He recently retired from the force. You might feel easier talking to him."

The two officials looked at each other, nodded and the policeman began.

"Hmm. That won't be necessary. Well sir, madam," he paused, remembering to address both, "it has been reported that this German family is hiding a cat in their caravan on your park!" He regarded them accusingly, pausing to let the words sink in before continuing sternly, "There is an alert on. It appears likely quarantine regulations have been breached."

The customs man added his weight with a warning, "You do realise this animal might carry rabies?"

A long silence followed. Neither official apparently had anything further to say but again their eyes never flickered as they watched for reactions.

Finally Gordon asked, "You have a description of this cat?"

"Yes. Very scruffy, light ginger colour and appears either old, *or ill*." His last words carried heavy emphasis.

"That's Henry." Jan's reply was automatic, triggered by surprise before she could stop herself.

"Henry?" The policeman pounced, actually leaned forward, body stiffening, his whole stance tightening, hands not moving but one index finger rising unconsciously to point. An admission of guilt? A knowledge of this animal's existence?

Feeling the accusation, the censure in that single word, she almost took a backward step. "Henry or Heinrick?" The thought was silent, read in those challenging eyes. With an

99

effort she drew her shoulders back, breathing in, the anger returning. "Yes! You only had to ask! It belongs to the cottage up the hill. Spends long periods on site, gets quite attached to some visitors."

She stood ready to say more but he turned away towards his colleague. As relief then irritation crossed the men's faces, she felt her own anger evaporate.

"I hope it is a false alarm, even if it has wasted a lot of people's time. You can't be too careful with rabies." The policeman spoke, justifying their previous actions. His colleague, more businesslike, looked to the details.

"We must see your visitors; have to check. If it is this particular cat, what d'you call it... Henry; then we need to take it home for the owner's confirmation."

"Ah!" Gordon nodded with satisfaction. So no heinous crime had been committed after all! Of course. Thoughts of sinister foreigners miraculously evaporated. Hardly their fault they were unfortunate enough not to be British! Always said they were nice people. Yes, but these Germans who spoke little English, might they be alarmed by a policeman at their caravan door after dark? He hesitated a moment, still thinking, anxious to protect both his visitors and the park's reputation.

"Would it be a good idea if I persuaded the fluent German couple to come round? You could explain the situation, they might be willing to act as interpreters." Seeing resistance in the officers' expressions, and wondering what argument would most impress the official mind, he tried again.

"An international incident could be embarrassing?"

"Hm." The customs man shifted his weight to the other foot, looking uneasily toward his colleague "Well, yes. Certainly... good idea!" A small gesture of the hand sent Gordon on his way.

The German couple were a little concerned at first but most co-operative once they grasped the full facts and that their help was needed. The man came to meet the policeman, flattered to be asked to make the translations. While the rest of the little group trooped off to locate Henry, Jan busied herself putting the kettle on and preparing glasses ready for the return.

As circumstances panned out, the interpreter's presence smoothed a tricky situation. The visitors with the cat were out for the evening, except for the teenage daughter who opened a zip in the awning at some word of greeting in German. Seeing the group, she stepped back in surprise and alarm, allowing them to enter. There lay mangy old Henry, sprawled on the carpet fast asleep, a bowl of milk and another bowl of something resembling chicken nearby, living the high life of total contentment. No wonder he wanted to stay. All that special attention, not that he couldn't get just as good at home, but that's cats, faithful when it suits them.

The young lady's first alarm soon eased as the other German spoke to her. She understood some words of English so could follow part of the conversation even without an interpreter, but he supplied translations for the missing words and a general explanation, bringing smiles and amusement where so easily might have been concern and apprehension. The two officers popped off to see the owner, "To make absolutely sure," the customs man said, donning heavy gloves and gingerly lifting the reluctant Henry, taking the cat with them.

"Go on back to the house, we'll meet you there shortly to do any paperwork," the policeman suggested, excusing himself with a hand raised to the young lady.

It was a happy band that eventually sat round the lounge. The German girl had come along, leaving a note for her family; perhaps not wishing to stay alone now that Henry had gone. The other German had collected his wife and the officials returned, pleased to confirm the cat had been identified by an amused owner. Coffee or something stronger was on offer; the interpreter went without hesitation for whisky, the other men being still on duty, regretfully opted for coffee. While drinking, the policeman made calls on his radio to give the all clear, and shortly after left, accompanied by the customs officer. The three Germans remained, the women talking together with frequent cross chatter in a mixture of language, aided by regular interpretations, all becoming friends. The talk was still flowing when the children arrived home, having spent the evening with Jim and Audrey to watch an extra long TV film. The youngsters, still excited by the action on screen, had raced down the road in the dark to tell their parents. The presence of three strangers held them back at first, but after an introduction, Chris, with many interruptions from Sharon, explained the plot, pausing at intervals for the words to be translated. Stephen contented himself with occasional short comments.

A few words in each language were exchanged with the children learning to count to five, but what caught the visitors interest most was the strange electrical arrangements and the fact that long films could not be watched at home. They gazed upward when their attention was directed to the three little bulbs on the ceiling, not having realised before that this was different from normal English standards of house lighting.

Gordon almost said, "We keep them dim in case the bombers come over tonight," but suppressed the urge, not being quite sure of their new friends' sense of humour.

The German interpreter, when leaving, thanked them and commented on the politeness of English policemen as if this was not necessarily normal practice back home.

Towards the season's end a customer arrived, one super fastidious about levelling his caravan. Having taken a long time choosing his place, which was fine with trade no longer busy, he produced a thin line with a heavy weight on the end. This he proceeded to hang from a hook on the ceiling just inside the door; it had to line up with a spot on the floor. While Gordon chatted to the wife, an interesting woman with a good knowledge of flora, her husband went round the caravan tightening first one leg then another until the weighted line indicated that it stood exactly level.

Strange! Most visitors used a little two way bubble mounted on the tow bar, or the front shelf, or somewhere convenient to get the caravan roughly level and that was generally good enough. Some people even put a little water in a pan on the stove, a level cooker being more important than the level of anything else. One caravan had been deliberately sloped to the side, "Water won't run from our sink otherwise," a lady had said. Another visitor simply placed a tin of beans on the table adjusting the steadies until the tin no longer rolled. What was so special that this outfit needed such precautions? Finally satisfied with the adjustments, the man walked across to express satisfaction with the pitch, and explained the reason.

"Fridge trouble. We didn't have one in the previous caravan. A great improvement this, but only when the level is perfect; it doesn't work otherwise. There's another thing, the flue outlet," he pointed to a grid in the caravan wall near the door. "That needs to be downwind – that's why I chose this pitch."

Gordon left quickly before the wind changed direction again.

**

"Nonsense, there's no such thing as a negative number," Jim dismissed the idea.

He and Audrey had come to tea, a rare occurrence even though they lived so near. Audrey loved her own bungalow at the entrance and spent hours in the garden, seldom going out, always happy and contented. The couple were visited by many old friends among the caravanners, welcoming company but not needing it, equally as happy in winter when visitors were few, always finding sufficient interest around the home or just outside. Every visitor who used ice packs came to know Audrey well, calling regularly to drop off or pick them up from the deep freeze chests that now lined one wall in her garage.

Today however, ice packs were not available, a note left on the door advising people to call later. It was September 3, the family had gathered not exactly for a party but a special celebration tea – Jim and Audrey's 43rd wedding anniversary and Stephen's tenth Birthday both falling on the same day. Sharon's thirteenth birthday, which being in August had been largely ignored, was also included. She looked very smart, wearing yet another swingy tartan skirt received that morning, dark hair now a full twelve inches shorter, touching her shoulder. At her best in company she chattered happily, expressively outgoing, the one member of the family least able to withstand being shipwrecked alone on an island, but also the one who made friends most easily. Stephen too was happy though without the demonstrative relish of his sister. He had done better that anyone, receiving a bicycle, disproportionately expensive compared to Sharon's presents, but by buying it jointly with the grandparents the cost had been bearable, in spite of a relatively poor season. The older pair already had bicycles of their own and he needed to catch up.

Jim's denouncement of negative numbers was directed at Chris. Discussions had turned to homework. Jim, who would be seventy in a month's time, could still add a column of figures in his head quicker than Chris could do it on paper. This prowess originated in a Grocer's shop in Birmingham around 1912 and had never included negative numbers.

"If you have two apples," Jim said, "and you give one to Sharon, that leaves one. If you give that to Stephen, that leaves none, so you can't give one to anyone else because you don't have any more. Zero is the least you can have, you can't get less. Negative numbers are nonsense!"

Chris thought for a while, not inclined to accept Jim's statement.

"What about if I borrow an apple from a friend, and give it to someone else? Then I owe an apple – that's less than zero. If I had zero then when I get another I could eat it, but now it must be given back to the person it's owed to, so I can't eat it. That must be minus one apples."

Jim, unable to handle the argument, smiled changing the subject, and directed a question at all his grandchildren. "All right then, tell me this. How many beans make five?"

They looked back at him puzzled. What did he mean?

"Five," they muttered among themselves, unsure if they had grasped the question right. He shook his head, repeating the question and supplying the answer, speaking almost too fast for them to follow.

"How many beans make five? I'll tell you. Listen carefully then repeat it as fast as you can. A bean, a bean, a bean and a half, half a bean and a bean!"

With most aspects of the site, visitors had been happy; it would not be an over-exaggeration to say delighted, but their needs were changing. That had been obvious not only in extra ice-packs frozen and increased numbers of batteries carried in for charging, but most of all in discontent over milk and newspapers. Deliveries that season had not been well received; people's expectations had risen; they wanted other things, bread or rolls or baps for instance, and not only in the mornings. The tents in particular needed fresh milk at teatime in the hot weather and were surprised to find it not available. Often the shop in the village had run out too. Some other arrangement must be made, but every scheme considered had drawbacks.

"If we have crates of milk delivered early each morning, visitors can collect them whenever they like. That's fine, but what about the pints that don't sell; will they keep fresh until evening or the following day? You know how hot it gets in summer." Jan's concern had been expressed before and no solution found.

"We could have a mobile shop; park it over there."

Gordon pointed through the office window. "Some have fridges that plug in overnight with enough cooling elements to last most of the day. A second-hand one shouldn't be too expensive."

Jan considered the idea; it had possibilities. "You mean leave it plugged in up at Jim's bungalow, then drive it down here for the caravanners each morning? It might work. Normally, we finish cleaning the toilets before seven, Sharon can get breakfast if necessary but I should have time. You'd need to collect the shop by eight. Sounds good; where do we find one?"

"*The Cornishman* or *The West Britain* might have one but not many operate in this area. Try *The Western morning News* as well. Look for those with deep freeze cabinets; we could sell other things then. Your Mum will still need to cope with visitor's ice-packs; no mobile freezer will handle those. Pity they don't make bigger Calor gas fridges."

Searching the relevant columns revealed several likely vehicles; second-hand as agreed, new ones were far too expensive. Most were for sale in the London area. One unit in particular caught the eye but someone with a heavy goods vehicle licence would need to drive it home. Tommy Thomas who had often welded Max, the excavator, held such a licence and agreed to help. The three set off shortly after two o'clock one morning. Three hours later and still in darkness, breakfast was taken in a transport cafe, a fresh experience for Jan but the food tasted good – hunger perhaps, not having eaten before starting out. Pushing on, London was busy as they arrived around eight o'clock. One delay, until the sales area opened was followed by another for the commercial salesman to arrive. He led them miles across London in his Range Rover, eventually drawing up in some type of goods yard, parking near a large enclosed wagon with an auxiliary engine on the roof. A right con man he was, with tales of missing keys when asked to start the engine and various other tactics.

"No engine, no sale," Gordon said, and a set of keys miraculously appeared. It started eventually, but not the auxiliary engine for the fridges.

"Got a bit damp standing here, that's all," the salesman glibly passed it off with a wave of the hand.

Taking all into consideration, £900 was too much. An offer of £600 was rejected. The salesman knew they had travelled up from Penzance that morning and probably figured no one would make such a trip and leave empty handed. With a shrug, Gordon murmured "We're not meant to have it," That had generally seemed right in the past, and in this case not only right but a lucky escape from what could have been an unwise decision. They returned westward away from the swirling city traffic, a 600-mile round trip for nothing, but splitting the driving, with Tommy taking the final leg, they were home again before teatime.

While eating, the children pressed avidly for information. Jan gave them the details with a wry smile. The trip had been a tiring waste of time and petrol to a grimy, busy place where almost everyone would have envied this green Cornish Valley. To the eager faces before her however, it was a glamorous opportunity missed – a voyage to a glittering city of people, tall building and bridges over the Thames.

"We were talking at school," Sharon said, "A group of my friends were really jealous. London for the day! Only one had ever been."

The parents smiled at each other. Some thrill!

A month later a small mobile shop appeared in the local paper; it was not far away, they jumped in the car and viewed it together. A man from Goldsithney had found that selling groceries mainly to outlying houses was costing almost as much in petrol as the profit it made. He had given up delivering, sold his stock and was left with the vehicle – so it was cheap! The bodywork had seen better days and Jan advised against the purchase, but

Gordon insisted it would look reasonable when repainted. As nothing better seemed likely to come on offer, Jan gave way with good grace, aware she could probably not change his mind anyway. It cost £250, much more economical and without need of a heavy goods vehicle licence.

***

"Keep it still!" the shout echoed across the empty valley. Hearing the call, Jan stepped closer, holding the staff more tightly where it rested on top of the channel supporting the waterwheel. "Okay!" the voice came again. A distant figure bent over, one eye to the instrument, scribbled something in a notebook then straightened and stretched before lifting the tripod and signalling that they were finished.

Back in the office with the equipment put away, she sat on the edge of the desk.

"Well, what did you learn? Was it worth the effort."

"It may be one day. This is for the future, to look back on and check how much the wheel settles from the constant rotation. It's forty-four feet seven inches above mean sea level. The difference between upstream and downstream surfaces is one foot nine and a half inches. There, didn't you always want to know that?" Gordon asked.

"Oh sure! I'd rather know what *this* contains." Jan tapped one finger on a letter that had arrived as they carried the equipment out. It lay still unopened on the desk, a message from the bank for sure, a return address in small print revealing the origin. Had the year been successful? What chance now for dreams of becoming Best Site in the Southwest? Gordon ripped the envelope open, unfolded the statement and they gazed together at the balance.

"I can do the housekeeping on that," Jan pointed to a figure, "but how much will you want to spend on the site? We've no house to build, nothing really expensive this year, is there?"

"Not a great amount. I've still some sewer damage to

108

remedy but that's physical rather than expensive. Another 200 gallons of diesel, and rates and insurances, but not much else. The children have had their new clothes and Stephen his bicycle; bit rash perhaps, but we're still okay – should survive the coming year."

Jan glanced at the mobile shop standing in the yard. "Lucky we didn't buy the bigger one; gives us more to play with."

She must be right. They had suffered a financial setback but with luck, things should improve. How much River Valley's reputation had been injured by the aftermath of sewer laying could only be guessed, but the roads were better – at least, those that had been tarmaced were. There ought to be enough cash until visitors came again given reasonable care. Before the sewer started they had thought their days of being careful were past; never mind, a full winter's work should improve the valley's appearance. Max could do with another coat of paint sometime. Pity there was no place to store the machine out of reach of visiting children.

"Now Gurlyn is sold, will it make any difference to us?" Jan walked to the window, gazing out across the river to the farm opposite. There was little to see, some fields at a higher level were half hidden by a wide belt of willow, hazel and oak that stretched from the river part way up the valley slope. No farmhouse was visible from where they stood.

"I wouldn't think so. I met the chap, Melville I think he said, seems nice enough – didn't have chance to say much, he was in a hurry. Wonder if we'll get any statics this winter."

Six static caravans of various sizes were now available, some privately owned, others offered for holiday renting, and all connected to mains water. They were a sideline, touring visitors remained the chief interest, the preferred type of trade. Keeping the permission for larger units however offered flexibility for the future, in case a caravan tax, high petrol prices or some other catastrophe should kill the touring trade. The other benefit could not be ignored either, this regular small source of extra income being most welcome.

***

A sycamore leaf fluttered down, one of the last, the site closed and the valley deserted again. Plenty of land remained to be cleared but days were easier now. From a numbers viewpoint the season had not been good and existing pitches had coped adequately. With luck more could be needed next year if trade picked up again. No one knew if it would of course, they must press on anyway, it had become second nature. Some work remained repairing sewer damage but the main task would again be shifting spoil from the old Wheal Virgin mine. With any luck the last would go this winter, though that might prove optimistic for several thousand tons still remained. In any case it would not entirely solve the appearance question; those terraces already formed from the waste heaps still drew the eye, a noticeable but diminishing scar on the valley's beauty. More dry stone walls and planting along the front edge of each tier would soften them further. That too was planned for the coming winter.

Customers were absent now, even walkers rarely seen; the days pleasant but lonely, coffee breaks lengthening, sometimes to half an hour as the two sat together, reluctant to separate and looking forward to the children's arrival home.

"What will it be like in the future, when the children are gone?" Jan asked.

They were growing fast. Apart from the peak season, their help was needed less now than in earlier years, the older two in particular developing their own friends and interests. Chris had commenced his fourth senior school year and was out much more in the evenings; twice a week to the judo sessions at Goldsithney or cycling to meet friends in various places for football or fishing or perhaps

110

some more secret activity, for not all his friends were boys. Neither parent probed too deeply when he seemed reticent, thankful perhaps that he travelled mostly under his own muscle power rather than needing to be taken and collected in the car. Chris had always been sensible, but sharp words sometimes passed between father and son when he returned extra late. Sharon too was well established at senior school and had joined the Guides. Running her to and from meetings could be a major problem next summer. She still went to the judo club but getting home from there was easier, her friend's parents normally dropped her off at Jim's bungalow. In the recent judo tournament she had met with mixed success. Having been paired against a very aggressive girl, Sharon lost her bout, but fortunately the home side won and all the girls in the team, win or lose, received a gold medal! She had also begun bringing home dishes from her cookery classes, but disliked the use of that name.

"It's Domestic Science, Dad! The family is supposed to give an opinion, make constructive suggestions and say how good they are." Sharon waited, hoping for compliments.

Some chance! Chris and Stephen would combine, sometimes aided by their father to criticise and find fault; Sharon could still be fun when aroused. The boys made a point of protesting strongly whenever her efforts appeared on their plates.

"Why can't we have proper food?" Stephen asked, egged on by Chris.

Actually her preparations were good, some really excellent, but only Jan was prepared to tell her so. For the rest, admitting it would spoil half the fun. Among her best work were some rather tasty small cakes. The plate was about to be offered round for a second time when Sharon objected.

"No! Don't give any more Mum, they don't appreciate it. They can go without!"

111

Jan turned to the boys, awaiting some favourable comment. No one spoke. She shrugged at Sharon, then addressed the three males of the family with heavy emphasis.

"You do like them, don't you!"

"Oh yes," Gordon rolled his eyes, nodding to the boys, "they're wonderful." He spoke in exaggerated tones; Chris and Stephen nodded back solemnly, adopting similar expressions.

Jan smiled wryly at her sons, "Sarcasm is not very nice," and turning slightly, regarded Dad with pursed lips, "Wonderful? Like Brutus is an honourable man? Don't know why your daughter cooks for you at all." She offered another anyway.

After taking a bite, Gordon insisted, "They really are superb!" and pulled an 'Ugh' face towards Stephen and Chris, making sure that Sharon could see.

"I won't bring any more of my cooking home! Ever!"

Chris muttered "Yippee," under his breath. Everyone knew they were intended to hear. Even Sharon laughed, so they relented, telling her the cakes were, "Quite good really; for a girl," still not ready to confess to anything more but adding as an afterthought, "We wouldn't mind if you made a bigger batch next time."

That was as near a compliment as Sharon was ever likely to get.

Seeing her daughter's pleasure and knowing she deserved more, Jan suggested, "Ask them to put it in writing!"

Visitors during the year had shown a tendency to choose pitches away from the stream. That was unusual, almost certainly due to some bare, uneven surfaces still evident after sewer laying. Most existing pitches had now been repaired and once turf, heather and shrubs recovered to their former state, old preferences for a riverside position should again prevail. It seemed sensible therefore to concentrate on clearing further areas beside the river, making better use of this favourable feature. Walking downstream hand in hand as so often before, they reached the remaining untouched region and stood surveying a tangle of unruly growth ahead and to the left. Along the riverbank on their right the contrast was marked; all vegetation had disappeared, leaving a flattened swathe of largely bare soil that still marked the passage almost a year previously of machines laying the sewer, a place where every living thing had been stripped away. There had not yet been time for much renovation here. Closer inspection revealed tiny green shoots widely spaced, some natural some from seed that had been sparingly scattered, but how long would it take?

"When you've finished this," Jan pointed to an area near at hand that was currently being levelled with mine waste, "what will you do about access?"

Gordon lifted an arm, tracing the route. "The land is quite narrow here. A more or less central road curving round those trees and bushes will leave broad strips of grass on either side; at least they will be grass if we ever get enough topsoil. I'll give preference to preparing the riverside strip but the road must come first." The pointing finger dropped; they could see no more from here and wandered across to the river's edge then onward downstream again, following the current. "Roads are so important! Don't laugh. You may not realise, but they are! The main part of the site that's already laid out is much wider. Many people think the circular road, the big oval that serves all those pitches, is just chance but it's not. Do you ever wonder why our grass survives so well in wet weather?"

"Not really. The ground I suppose. Cars do arrive from other places with their wheels all muddy. I hadn't really thought about it much – no chance of escaping the explanation now is there?" Playfully she shoved him towards the river but felt herself spun round over the sloping bank edge, to land looking steeply upward into his eyes.

"I might not tell you now," he threatened, pulling her back to stand, toe to toe, arms around each other, lips meeting in that deserted valley. After a while they moved on again.

"Might not tell me? Pink elephants might fly!" Jan broke the silence. It was more than a gentle tease, she knew one of them must give way, must speak first – they understood each other's moods, even thoughts sometimes. With clever sensitivity, she broke the impasse with a jibe that had them both smiling.

"Can't stand intelligent women! Okay, I *am* going to tell you, and no, you can't escape. Why do good roads stop muddy patches? Think of all our pitches; can you point to any instance where more than one car crosses the grass in the same place? Every pitch is near a road without being close enough to be uncomfortable. Not all are tarmaced yet, I admit that, but they serve the purpose just the same. Each pitch is reached by branching off at a slightly different place. We have no restricted openings where several cars must cross the same grass – that's where the mud starts. One road down the centre of this narrower section will do the same. Okay?"

"I'm glad you can't build straight, they're much better curving round the trees, but that's luck, not skill!" She threw the challenge down as they stopped facing westward over an area of gorse and willow. "Maybe not even luck, probably drunk at the time," Jan prodded again, trying to get a reaction.

"I can do stupid enough things without alcohol. I once spent seven shillings and six pence on a silly gir..." He stopped abruptly, pretending injury as she punched him lightly in the ribs. Together they strolled back, retracing steps, crossing to the stone road and on to where the surface had already been tarmaced.

Gordon pointed to the edge. "Before starting more pitches I'd better complete this job." A drop of perhaps four inches showed between the new black surface and the existing grass, another hangover from the sewer, due partly to an extra layer of stone necessary before applying the tarmac. On most areas the problem was already dealt with, three widths of turf had been lifted and more soil spread beneath, raising the grass in a gentle curve to meet the new road edge. Unfortunately there had not been time to finish all the repairs.

He returned later with turfing iron, shovel and wheelbarrow to make a start. Two things could definitely be said about lifting and replacing turf; it was hard on the muscles and tedious! Though necessary for visitor's comfort, the finished work showed little change in appearance; no sense of achievement. An hour passed, and another; he pushed on determined to finish one section before changing back to moving mine waste. When Robin flew in to settle on the ground not far away, Gordon was pleased and searched a recently lifted turf for a worm. Extracting one, he threw it to the waiting beak, welcoming the chance to talk again with his feathered friend and wondering if Blackbird would also appear.

While lifting more turfs, he chatted away having a little grumble, telling how monotonous the work was, then realised it was easier now with a companion. The bird seemed to listen but as the afternoon wore on and work moved farther up the road, the nature of the ground began to change, the underlying soil poorer and few worms appeared as the turfs were lifted. Knowing Robin so well, it was easy to see when the bird prepared to leave. Resting on the turfing iron, Gordon apologised. "I'm sorry. Not my fault." The little feathered head cocked on one side tilting up at him. As so often before, he sensed the thoughts, or perhaps heard them, the difference lost in those solitary hours. *"If you had sensible cars with wings instead of wheels you wouldn't need all this,"* and it flew off.

CHAPTER 7

Courage

It was good later in the afternoon to find human company to talk with. When the family sat down for tea, school work came under discussion as it often did while they were eating.

"We had two questions in algebra. First, if a car travels at sixty miles an hour for ten miles, how long will it take?" Chris turned to Sharon, waiting for an answer but none came. Mum shook her head too. Dad nodded but continued eating.

"He'll crash if he don't slow down on corners," Stephen muttered.

"There are no corners, it's a motorway," Chris smiled, pleased no answer had come. "There are sixty minutes in each hour, so he travels a mile every minute. Ten miles takes ten minutes. Easy. Now try this. If he travels at half speed for the first five miles, how fast must he travel the second five miles to take the same overall time?"

"Um, 120 miles an hour," Sharon pointed a finger. Mum agreed and Stephen nodded. Dad put another forkful in his mouth, there might have been a tiny shake of the head, but again he said nothing.

"No." Chris positively glowed with triumph. "If he goes half as fast it will take him twice as long, so the first five miles will now takes the full ten minutes! There's no time left; it doesn't matter how fast he travels the other five miles – he can't do it!"

116

"He could take a shortcut," Sharon suggested

"You can't do that if you're travelling in a straight line, stupid."

"Why not!"

"Because a straight line is the fastest way between two points, any idiot knows..."

"Dad doesn't believe it," Jan's interruption, broke the argument. "He's starting to extend the road downstream, says it's only curved to go round the trees, not because he can't build straight. What do you think?"

The family as usual, sided with Mum at Dad's expense. He listened for a while before commenting.

"It looks better and stops cars going so fast. We were trying to uncover ways of improving the site. Any ideas?"

"Sell ice cream. My friends say most camps have it." Stephen looked up from under unruly hair, confident neither his brother nor sister would disagree.

"Will I serve in the new shop?" Sharon asked.

"Probably have to in the school holidays; you too," Jan looked to Chris, "I know you'll want to be doing other things but we'll need some help."

Chris shrugged in resignation. "What about Sunday trading? One of my friends has a relative who owns a shop and Penwith Council are to prosecute people who open on Sunday. Does that mean we get Sundays off?"

"I saw that in the local paper," Jan remembered, "And no, you don't get a free day, we'll be open as normal; people will want milk and papers. I think the law is, that you can sell anything perishable. Do you know what that means?"

"Bananas, tomatoes," Sharon suggested, "and er, tins have sell-by dates on now, does that make them perishable too?"

"Probably." Jan nodded. "I think we're allowed to sell any foodstuff, but perhaps not camping spares. A customer can buy a luxury like strawberries and cream but not a gas bottle. It's stupid. You know something else we couldn't sell on a Sunday? A bible! That's not perishable."

"If some inspector catches us selling a gas bottle, couldn't we say it has a slight leak?" Chris suggested.

"Why?" Sharon asked. "What difference would that make?"

"Not a bad idea," Dad smiled. "If it *is* leaking it must be perishable!"

"Don't encourage them," Jan frowned, "If anyone arrives without something vital, like their water carrier, we can lend them a new one and tell them to pay on Monday, but I think the restrictions may not apply to shops on caravan parks. Oh, by the way, for Christmas we'll be in Buckinghamshire, travelling up the morning before and staying a few days. I'm telling you early so don't go making any arrangements with friends for that time." Questions about the trip were cut short by the phone ringing. Jan rose and left the room.

"Have you bought Mum's present yet," Sharon spoke quietly, almost a whisper, directing the question at her father.

"Er, no. Not sure exactly what..." He paused, making a gesture; it had been on his mind for some time. "You think another saucepan would be... a bad idea?"

They nodded, eager faces making it obvious that from their point of view, no present could be better. "Mum will slaughter you," Sharon warned with relish, for once with full support from her brothers.

The approach of Christmas in no way affected work. Extending the road downstream required more stone from the upper terraces, a job temporarily suspended while those final turfs were lifted and levelled. When Max trundled off one morning to restart the loading work, a pair of strange robin-like birds appeared, staying near until the midday break. The plumage lay somewhere between a robin and a bullfinch. At lunchtime, after they had eaten, Jan fetched the *Pocket Guide to British Birds*.

"Describe them. Should be here if they're not erratics."

118

The valley lay on a migratory passage. From time to time strange birds would pass through which were not naturally British. When news of such an event circulated, people with binoculars would sneak up, skulking in the shadows and appearing unexpectedly from behind various gorse bushes. Shortly after first purchasing Muscovy ducks, a rather dark stumpy bittern had walked up the bank in front of the house. A very keen bird watching friend, Bertie King, phoned later with a request to watch out for an American bittern known to be in the area. Gordon, slightly gloating, described the bird and told of its slow deliberate steps, almost as if testing the ground before transferring its weight, along the riverbank towards Relubbus. Without knowing its rarity they had watched the unhurried progress for perhaps five minutes. Even Jan could hear the shriek from the phone earpiece.

"What! Lucky devil, I'll be there in 15 minutes, keep looking!" He had arrived shortly after, parking his car in front of the house. They saw him at intervals for the rest of the day prowling up and down the river, half a dozen others had joined him, all clutching binoculars and all entirely without success.

Due to this bittern and other migrants, Jan was aware the species she now searched for would not necessarily show in any British bird book. As Gordon began reciting the main features she flipped the pages.

"More than anything they were like robins, about that size, maybe a touch smaller but the head of the male is black. He's braver than the female, she hung back but he actually perched on the bucket when I stopped the machine. He had a white half collar, she too, but not so pronounced. I deliberately tried to remember every detail in case we don't see them again. Both had a white flash on the wing coverts, both had red chests, his brighter... not quite like a robin, more pinkish, halfway to chaffinch colour, fading to almost white lower down."

Jan turned more pages, backwards and forwards a few

119

times comparing, then reaching a decision, held the book towards him. "Only a stonechat has all those features. There; the whinchat doesn't have a black head, the redstart doesn't have a white collar and you know the linnet and bullfinch. Better be careful your Robin doesn't catch you talking to them."

It was a point of contention; Jan had never been intended to know that working alone over long winter months he talked to the birds, but she had overheard on several occasions those chats with the robin. It was useless to make a denial, instead he moved to the window pointing, "Look, Francis is at it again. Not much use this time of year."

Jan glanced out, then back at him, both smiling and well aware of the attempted diversion.

Chris was quiet at tea, glancing once or twice at his father. Jan noticed and wondered if, unbeknown to herself, there had been an argument. Her son was growing, testing his independence, his fifteenth birthday in a few days. Seeing nothing to be gained by raising the subject now, she carried on talking to Sharon then rose to clear the table as Gordon left.

"Where has Dad gone?" Sharon helped carry some plates.

"Servicing the digger before it gets dark." Returning to the table and seeing Chris still sitting lost in thought, Jan eased herself into the chair. "Some problem?"

"No."

"You were very quiet, I saw you look at Dad. An argument?"

"Just wondering how things had gone today." Chris looked evasively away.

"Why, what did you want?"

"I... could we get our goat back soon? The grass areas are recovering now." Chris paused, anxious not to cause an outright refusal. "Well, we did say perhaps Judy could come back if the man will sell her – when spring comes I mean, and people start arriving again?"

Sharon and Stephen who had been talking over by the sink slipped into the adjoining chairs, waiting for the reply.

Jan looked at the three children, it was not something she alone could decide. "Dad would have to agree. What stopped you asking him? Anyway, I heard the property she went to has changed hands. Wherever Judy is, she may be harder to handle now she's been running wild for two years. We could enquire. Do you all want her back?"

"As long as she doesn't escape again," Sharon grinned, recoiling as Stephen leaned across, lashing out with a small clenched first.

"Steady," Jan held up her hands. "Why all the argument; she never escaped before, did she?"

"Only once Mum," Sharon smiled at Stephen's angry face, then turned to Chris, awaiting his nodded agreement before continuing. "Well, just after the house was first built we were home from school one evening and something happened. Dad had injured himself, I think. You both dashed away; you were driving Mum, it was still light and as the car left Dad shouted to us through the window to put Judy away and get ourselves something to eat then go down to Jim's. We watched the car disappear; it was December and darkness was approaching. The three of us had never been left alone before – except Chris and I were, that time Stephen hurt his back." Sharon paused for agreement.

"That's right," Chris remembered. "Me and Stephen went to find where the goat was tethered and Sharon started cooking. I searched downstream but Stephen found Judy over by Bluebell Wood and led her back to the shed."

"He came to the house afterwards and tea was nearly ready," Sharon cut in. "I sent him back to look for you." She made a small movement of the hand passing the tale to Chris.

121

"As we ate, the light started to fade. When the meal was finished I went to check Judy was comfortable but the goat had gone, the door wide..."

"Wasn't my fault." a low voice checked Chris temporarily, but he continued.

"The catch was difficult sometimes, Stephen was only six then. Anyway, I had a quick look at the nearby places but it was nearly dark and Judy was mainly black, so I went back for help."

"We were frightened she would be lost," Sharon took up the commentary. "There was only one torch, I took it and the two boys went off without one, racing down the footpath together, dashing downstream to cut her off, then worked their way back up while I searched nearer the house. We found her in the end but Judy decided not to be caught, something must have frightened her. Following a black goat after dark is not easy! We chased around hoping you wouldn't come back too soon. Even with the torch I didn't like those shadows."

"We got her in the end," Chris smiled. "Cornered her near some brambles, the three of us together. I grabbed a horn and Stephen hung on her hindquarters. Once we got a grip and stroked her for a while, she calmed down and Sharon went for a rope to lead her back. She'd just left when some car lights started down the road, you can see them a long way off, so we didn't wait, but ran holding the collar. Judy ran with us, we didn't need to pull, she came willingly, didn't want to be left behind. We pushed her into the shed and fixed the door properly as the car swung into the yard." Chris paused, allowing Sharon to finish the account.

"I'd found the rope and was with them again by then. Thinking it was you and Dad, we crouched out of sight, plotting what excuse to make, but the car swung right round and drove off. This was before the waterwheel existed. We sprinted for the house, it was in complete darkness; the candles had been put out for safety before

122

we found Judy. I wanted us to run down to Jim's but Chris took the torch and led the way inside. We lit candles, drew the curtains and pretended to play cards when you came home." Sharon finished with a flourish of the hand.

"When exactly was this, and why did you never tell us?" Jan shook her head in wonder.

"Thought we'd get told off," Stephen murmured.

"About three years ago, Mum." Chris calculated.

"Well! I must write it down. Sharon will never in her life keep another secret that long! I'll speak to your father, persuade him to find where Judy is and buy her back. You're right about waiting for Spring! I'll ask him when we start getting visitors again; he'll be more receptive with money coming in."

Christmas was approaching. The previous year they had stayed home, not daring to leave, desperately struggling with repairs and concerned what else the big sewer machines might do if they were absence. Last December, just before the festive season, there had been much discussion on the radio about the undesirable dietary effect of aluminium. As a Christmas present Gordon had bought Jan a very expensive stainless steel saucepan. In spite of several smaller presents, it went down badly!

"It should be something personal, something special that a girl gets for Christmas," she had said resentfully.

"But a saucepan is useful. Presents don't come much more useful than this. It will help you every day."

"A girl doesn't need useful presents. She wants something unnecessary, foolishly extravagant, something romantic to show how much you love her, to woo her a little!"

No doubt about it, he was in trouble. What could he say? What excuse could he offer? Attack! According to the old saying, that was the best form of defence!

"Yes, I see that. But you're not a girl; you're a wife. Why should I want to woo you? We're already married."

Well aware he was teasing, she entered into the proper

123

spirit with a vengeance, swinging the saucepan in a big arc, only just giving him time to duck. He had caught her arm as it swung by, pulled her towards him then kissed her gently and whispered, "Sorry, thought you'd like it. I promise to buy something very personal next year."

That had been twelve months ago. For this Christmas the 'something personal' had become more than just a problem; with the family going to Buckinghamshire, to his mother's, it was an essential! The present must be wrapped, put in the car and taken along. Only a few days remained; all attempts to locate that 'special gift' had failed. Deep trouble loomed ahead; a solution must be found! Using the builders' merchants as an excuse, he climbed into the car and headed for Truro with a pocketful of money, well half-full... or to be exact, twenty pounds; money was still tight. Considering perfumes, which he cordially detested, dresses and other such things in various windows, eventually landed him in the lingerie department of Marks. Here, on one of the plastic models was the very thing; a diaphanous underwired half-bra, at least it seemed like only half a bra. Ideal! But what size? Ask an assistant. He looked guardedly round, hoping for an elderly sales person but the only one free was a rather attractive young lady who came sweeping forward with a smile.

"Can I help you Sir?"

"Ye... Humph..." His voice seemed to have gone somewhere. He struggled to recover. "Yes please, I want to purchase one of those bras, like on the model," the words were quiet, almost a whisper, forcing her to lean closer. "I... er, that one," he shuffled awkwardly, nodding his head to indicate which one, not wanting to be seen pointing. It was a slight movement, followed by a quick glance round in case anyone had noticed, a finger rising to ease his collar, an unconscious reaction hoping perhaps to give the impression that some irritation had caused the nod. Hesitating again he looked at the floor, "I don't know what size."

The girl stood waiting, expecting more. It was embarrassing, she hardly seemed old enough to consult on such a matter.

"Do you think it would suit you sir?" He gave a start, but those nervous words came from within; the young assistant silently waiting. Swallowing hard, he tried again. "Surprise present for my wife."

A smile spread, sympathy perhaps and she asked, "How big is your wife?"

Was it imagination or did the 'your wife' bit have that emphasis which said, 'I believe you but thousands wouldn't'. Cupping his hands he started to say "About like this," but chickened out and instead, fluttering a downward glance at the nearby breast, suggested, "About your size, I think."

She whisked over to a shelf, her skirt swaying nicely from the hip. Always having liked skirts that swayed, he watched, admiring the movement but looked quickly away pretending to gaze in another direction as she turned, coming back with the small box. He didn't want to take it, hated the thought of standing holding it in the queue at the till – would have much preferred that she took it to the counter and wrapped it quickly. A young hand reached out towards him offering the dubious prize; he accepted it – could hardly refuse without drawing attention.

"When you pay, keep the bill so your wife can change it for a different size if necessary."

He thanked her, took the box and turned it over hoping to conceal the contents, only to find another acetate window on the reverse side. Holding it against his body, half concealed by a hand, he walked across to the cash desk to pay. The queue dispersed quickly but another woman had joined behind; he slid the purchase across the counter, withdrawing the arm as if it were hot.

Taking the money the till-girl asked, "Would you like a carrier sir?"

"Yes please, that would be fine." What a question! Did this young cashier think he would walk through the street carrying the box, its small plastic windows displaying the contents to all and sundry? No chance! He left the store both relieved and pleased, with a touch of elation, a growing feeling of achievement, invincibility perhaps, like shooting Niagara Falls and surviving! A see-through bra! You can't get more personal than that. There should be a prize just for the effort of will required to make the purchase.

Next question – how to wrap it? Christmas paper seemed so tame. Suddenly, passing a shop an idea struck! The very thing. Wrap it in a saucepan! Nipping in to make the purchase, he hunted for one that would take the little bra box snugly inside; stainless steel of course, but smaller and necessarily cheaper than the year before. Why are assistants always young girls? This one was looking at him strangely. Never mind, his courage was up, he could do anything now! She had seen the frilly bra through the acetate lid as he tried the box in various saucepans. Locating the right size he turned towards her. She took a step backwards, the expression on her face a mixture of apprehension and pity, her thoughts not hard to read.

"A manic. What sort of man buys a saucepan to boil an unused bra without even unpacking it?"

He glanced down again at the pan and the little box in his hand. Mad? Never! Men must do this all the time! Head rising, he prepared to explain, but seeing the assistant's sharp intake of breath, decided against it. She thought he was mad, Okay! He hunched his shoulders slightly, rolled his eyes, peered furtively in each direction – then took a step closer.

For a moment it appeared she would scream. He straightened up, smiling.

"I'd like this saucepan, could you find a box to pack it in so my wife can't see what I've bought her."

The girl stood for a second, rooted, unmoving.

"I thought..." She reached for the saucepan with an unsteady hand, and took it away. Not only did she produce a cardboard box but packed it with newspaper to prevent rattling, sealed it up neatly then beckoned him over to the till.

Extracting notes from a wallet he became aware that other young assistants were watching him, making faces and signals to each other, one sniggering as she moved away to serve another customer. The confidence so recently built up began to crumble; he stood, knowing his colour had risen but not sure what to do. An odd idea began to form. He recalled that old urge to climb on the house roof at midnight and send Tarzan calls echoing across the valley then sit watching all the caravan lights come on. If one possessed the courage, would such a call now send all these cheeky girls fleeing for the nearest exit? No way! Instead he straightened up to look at one; she gazed back for a few seconds then turned away; a short stare put the next to flight, hurrying off to move boxes on a shelf. The rest was easy. He picked up the parcel and walked out. In another shop Christmas paper and sellotape together with a little card attached to a ribbon rosette were purchased to finish the job.

Back at home Jan watched as he lifted the box from the car, carried the brightly coloured package inside and deposited it on a pile of other presents. Kneeling she inspected the card and seeing her name, smiled suspiciously. There was no way to tell the contents but she issued a warning. "I'm opening this it front of all the family, it had better live up to your promise... very *personal,* remember?" The word *personal* was emphasised strongly.

On arriving home, Sharon saw the extra parcel, stooped quickly to pick it up, felt the weight then put an ear to the paper and shook it. She had done the same with all the other presents as they appeared. The boys too were now showing curiosity. On an instruction from her mother Sharon carefully replaced the box. "What is it?"

"Ask your father. He was out for a long time today. I hope..." Jan left the sentence unfinished, not sure how to

127

express that hope and aware that the children's attention had already switched.

Gordon smiled back at the waiting faces but gave nothing away.

"Don't worry, we'll find out soon enough – then watch out!" Jan thumped a fist on the table. "By the way, this came in the post." She waved a green form and passed it to Stephen.

Chris leaned over and read the large print at the top. "Certificate of Registration." Lower down the page was a handwritten note, 'Storage and Sale of Ice Cream'. Mum's finger pointed, "This gives us permission. We're allowed to sell ices next season like Stephen suggested. There's something else too; Sharon, get that copy of Cornish Life I was showing you?"

Sharon jumped up, hurried off to her room and reappeared holding a magazine. "Volume 2, Number 9," she read from the cover, not passing it to her mother but leafing through, searching for a particular page and placing it on the table near Chris and Stephen. "There! The library van in the village. You can see Jim with his stick by the door and Charles Clouter sitting on the bridge."

"Mr Clouter to you, show some respect," Jan corrected.

"Audrey always calls him Charles. I can too. My friends call lots of older people by their Christian names – we're not still children, Mum!"

With a snort of derision, Chris pulled the magazine forwards for closer scrutiny. "Part of our sign and the Private notice shows. Not recent though, taken last summer; look at the trees."

"I see the new Scillonian is going ahead," Jan changed the subject. "The government has lent a million pounds towards it. The contract was signed in the dining room of the Union Hotel... that's where the death of Nelson and news of the victory at Trafalgar were first announced it says here in *The Cornishman*. Do you think they'd lend us a million?"

In the days that followed the children were out often with friends attending those special events that crowd the pre-Christmas calendar, the presents largely forgotten until the time came to pack the car and drive off to Buckinghamshire. Frank and Ivy, the grandparents, greeted their arrival; it was colder than in Cornwall, Jan popped a coat on as the presents were unloaded and the cases carried in. Later after a meal, when questions were asked about the site, Chris spoke of problems caused by the sewer and explained how one evening the boys had climbed into the trench after the men left. "We crouched down, eased ourselves into the last pipe and crawled along to the next inspection chamber. It was still open at the top, so we climbed up and out."

"You could have got stuck." Sharon warned.

"I don't think they could, not really," Gordon shook his head. "The engineers inspected the pipes that way on one length. After all, it is two feet diameter. I saw a bigger one years ago when working in Slough; thirty six inches diameter, it was. Did I ever tell you how we went down an inspection chamber one day and not far away in the sewer was a full size child's pram. No one ever found out how it got there."

"Fifty years ago in my school days," Ivy said, "we'd never heard of sewers, not in the country anyway. We were a big family. My Gran, Sara Evans, had two cottages – she needed them with twelve children but there were no drains or flush loos, it all went on the garden. She was married to Job, like in the bible, people called him Joeby that's your great-great-grandfather. He used to like a drink..."

"I'm not surprised with twelve children!" Jan pointed at Sharon, "Twelve like that would make me drink too. How many were girls?"

"Let's see," Ivy took up the story again. "There was Nora, Maggie, Alice, Bertha – that was my mother, and Vie... well, she was meant to be Violet Elizabeth but when

129

the registrar came to write her name down, Joeby had been drinking and forgot, so he said *'Dob her down as Sal'*. We never did call her Sally, she was always known as Vie. When Bertha had me, I lived there too. I remember a band of travelling players visited the village each year and acted a different play every night. Local people used to put them up and feed them."

"How did your Gran cook for so many people?" Sharon asked.

"Her own children were grown up when I went there but she still cooked for most of them. The men were the important ones, the ones that everything had to be exactly right for. It was a man's world in those days," Ivy looked across at Frank but he only smiled and turned back to his book. "Dumplings were the mainstay, five parts of flour mixed with two parts of suet – old fashioned suet cut straight off the meat, chopped up fine with a knife then mixed together with water and rolled out. All the men had their own favourite fillings, steak and kidney or liver and bacon, some with sage others with mint, each one done separately then folded over, rolled up in a cloth and dropped into the big cauldron to boil for three hours or more; sometimes for half a day. Gran always knew which one belonged to each man, though how she could tell them apart I was never sure."

"Who were the men?" Chris asked.

"Alf, Will, Bert, Ted, Stan, Frank... I must have forgotten one. Three more youngsters arrived while I was there. Alf's wife got ill and had to go away. Sara, my Gran, didn't want the children taken to the workhouse in Old Amersham so fetched them to live with us. I remember Ted was killed in the war. Joeby, my grandfather, the one who liked a drink – he and two other chaps put Hyde Heath Village Hall together in er, 1924. An important local man had built the post office and the church before I was born... in 1911 I think it was. Rumour had it that he wanted to do the hall in the same style but he died. The

130

hall still got built though, from a big army hut. We had lots of dances there in the Second war. Even young boys and girls danced in those days – your Dad for instance, he danced with young Audrey, and with other girls too. Those were the days of Victor Sylvestor and his dance band."

Eyes swung to Gordon, then to Jan to see if she was annoyed, but they were smiling at each other.

"What did you do about water?" Sharon asked.

"Drinking water you mean? Mostly it was fetched from a communal village pump. Non-drinking water came from wells filled by water running off roofs. Everyone had their own well. My father, George, died before I was born but later when my mother, Bertha, remarried to Jack, they bought a house. The well in their garden was lined with copper and had a pump over the kitchen sink. That was quite something then. At the bottom of the garden was a shed where very often a dead pig hung from the roof and in one corner was an open lavatory, just a bucket with a seat. I suppose it kept the flies away from the meat. It was emptied on the garden with everything else. People were hardier in those days. In the house, water inside the bedroom would freeze on cold nights." Ivy folded her arms round, making a little shudder towards the children.

"Did you have pocket money?" Sharon asked, glancing at her father.

"I had half a penny a week which I mainly spent on acid drops for grandfather, I liked him best, he'd let me do anything – took me with him sometimes, especially on a Sunday when he went to the pub in Chesham. I stayed outside in the horse and trap. Usually someone helped him back out at closing time, for very often he couldn't walk. Then they gave the horse a slap and it found its own way home while Gramp slept in the cart, at least I think he was asleep; maybe just unconscious. I wasn't worried, he always recovered and the horse knew where to go. I just sat up on the seat watching the hedges fly past. Another cart came round regularly, a butcher with meat all laid out in the bottom, not very hygienic but no one seemed to get ill. The village had its own baker, Frank Craft; at this time of year he used to cook turkeys in his big bread oven for anyone whose own oven was too small. They were good days." Ivy sighed.

Later, the big television was switched on, providing entertainment late into the evening but ideas that this might make the children sleep later on Christmas morning, were doomed to failure. They waited with impatience for breakfast to finish before presents haphazardly placed under the tree were given out. To Sharon's delight, the privilege of handing them round fell to younger members of the family. Jan eventually received her box and began to open it. Seeing Gordon hurriedly move out of range, she warned, "This had better not be another saucepan!"

Her exclamation drew attention; as she reached into the box the family waited expectantly, howls of laughter greeting the saucepan's emergence. Jan looked thunderous, shaping as if to throw it.

"Personal?" she asked glaring and lifting the handle.

"Look inside!" Gordon urged hastily, holding up a hand before his face to fend off the heavy missile.

Lifting the lid, she took out the box, gazed through the acetate window, then extracted the bra. Not her usual style, quite a bit more daring, a present for a lover not a wife – but then she was both really. She smiled, obviously pleased, not even minding the "Oh la la" and similar comments from the family. Inspecting the box her smile broadened. "You got the right size, how did you manage it?"

"Experience." Seeing her happy laugh and raised fist he relented, "I got the assistant to help me."

"Oh yes? Tell me more."

"Well, she was a nice little girl, I said you were about her size."

Leaning over ostensibly to kiss her cheek, he whispered, "Thought you might wear it tonight?"

So it ended okay. A grand few days with the family

then back to Cornwall and Relubbus.

One Saturday early in January the phone rang. Sharon, alone in the office, took the call from a Redruth motor agent they had approached last autumn about a mobile shop. The man explained he had purchased one in an auction, emphasising the vehicle's advantages and how good the condition was. Sharon listened, then wrote down the telephone number on a pad.

"A bit late. Pity Dad didn't wait." Jan frowned as Sharon repeated the gist of the message. It must, she thought, be better than the tatty van purchased against her advice but they had been watching the local papers for several weeks when it appeared and were not sure if another would come along. She had guessed at the time that all objections would be swept aside but regretted now, not trying harder to stop it.

"Couldn't you persuade Dad to swap?" Sharon asked.

It seemed unlikely; this new offer was bound to be dearer. The existing vehicle had been driven to Camborne a month earlier for a few repairs in preparation for the following season.

"Doubt it," Jan shook her head, "Still, I might convince him. He mentioned yesterday that we should call sometime to inspect progress on the old one; we would pass that garage on the way to Redruth. Did the man say anything about price?"

"Five hundred and something pounds I think, he spoke quickly, probably thought it would sound less. How much did Dad pay for the other one?"

"Never you mind, and don't go mentioning the cost! If he thinks it's that much I'll never persuade him even to look. It'll have to be Monday now, they'll close midday for the weekend."

Monday dawned fine and clear with a chill in the air; there were even faint traces of snow on the ground in Camborne, only ten miles away. The previous evening's news had been full of great drifts, roads closed and farms isolated 'upcountry', a Cornish expression for any place north of the river Tamar, but none had been expected in the far southwest. No depth had fallen and the local roads were completely clear. It lay only in isolated patches in the lea of walls and hedges, blown there by the wind. There had been none at Relubbus but that was a mere fifty feet above sea level whereas Camborne sat 300 feet higher; even so the difference was surprising. Reaching the garage, the old mobile shop stood in one corner; not a thing had been touched. Gordon asked the mechanic just to make sure.

"Nothing," he said. "We'll be starting it directly."

'Directly' – another word much used in Cornwall and varying somewhat from the definition shown in standard dictionaries, having acquired a meaning akin to 'eventually' or in many cases not as strong as that, more 'maybe it will be done sometime'. Feeling assured that no work would start in the immediate future, Gordon thanked the mechanic and must have forgotten to look displeased. When they returned later, their mobile shop had moved to centre floor with headlamps hanging out and tools strewn all round, as good a job of window dressing as you could ever wish to see. It just showed the deviousness of human nature. If the mechanic had thought they wanted it done, waiting would have been the order of the day. Because they could be loosing interest – worse, might prefer the job not done at all, then it must be started immediately.

However they were not to discover that for another hour and went off happily to see the newer mobile shop, which apart from having one side ripped out, was a splendid vehicle. Jan walked quietly off when the man mentioned a figure of £520, this to include replacement and re-spraying of the damaged side. Gordon had warned her on the journey not to appear pleased whatever price was offered but she had moved away for a different reason; to avoid giving any indication that this sum was known to her in advance.

"That much?" Gordon frowned, eyeing it doubtfully. "What about the one already bought; it would have to be part exchange."

The salesman paused, gazing blankly towards a wall, his face showing little enthusiasm for the idea, then said offhandedly, "Depends on the price."

"We paid £300 for it." Gordon exaggerated, having added on the cost of parts for the various repairs he had carried out himself. After some bargaining they settled for £275, unseen. Not bad, not exactly a profit, but not too much of a loss either. The salesman, while trying not to show it, seemed well pleased. Obviously he had picked the damaged one up for a song. Accompanying them back to the garage where the original model now showed every sign of being worked on, he walked over to the mechanic and pointed to the hanging headlights.

"Screw those back in place, I'll pick it up this afternoon." And that was that.

A week later, with the damaged side repaired and resprayed, and trade plates hanging fore and aft, he drove the vehicle across the bridge to stop near the door.

Gordon spent that afternoon painting the site name on the front, and 'Mobile Shop' on one side. Evening approached while finishing the last letters and they didn't seem to be drying. At Chris's suggestion the gas blowtorch was hunted out. Without letting the flame actually touch the paint work, the aluminium was gradually warmed, working backwards and forwards over a wide area. It did the trick. Fifteen minutes later a careful finger found the paint no longer tacky. Once working, this mobile shop should provide a better service. Customers could rise early, or if they preferred, lie in bed for most of the morning – it didn't matter now, the milk for breakfast or whatever else they wanted, would still be readily available. Was it another step towards that Best Site label they so wanted?

Through January the heavy work of moving mine waste

continued but an unprecedented spell of frost interrupted progress. Water frozen solid in a bucket gave warning. Immediately Gordon hurried round to kick Max's big rear tyres. Ouch! – like iron. The water inside, designed to add weight and give better loading power, had frozen! Using the machine in this condition might cut the tyres to ribbons. Never mind, alternative jobs were plentiful and the cold spell passed in three days. As if sorry for the trouble caused, the weather reversed itself, becoming warm for the time of year; excuse enough Jan suggested, to take a break before the season opened. It was however, several weeks before she succeeded.

One fine weekend in February the family did take a day off, driving together to St Ives and picnicking on those superb silver sands. The winter sun shone surprisingly warm from a clear sky, the lightest of breezes wafting in off a blue sea.

"They hung a man here last week," Chris claimed, gaining for himself a moment of undivided attention amid the family chatter. Sharon, recovering quickly, expressed her disbelief, proclaiming it untrue, forcing Chris to justify his comment.

"They did, on a rope from the church tower; a man one of my school friends knows. That's the truth and nothing but the truth as they say."

"Did you forget something Chris?" Jan asked. "Remember I'm a policeman's daughter. What about the middle bit; the *whole* truth?"

"Ah, if you want that... well, the hands on the church clock stuck and they hung him down twenty feet from above so he could reach to free them."

Chapter 8

Pay Up

"Mum will thump you," Stephen offered the opinion as he walked in the door, his friend waiting outside.

The site was open again, moving the final mine waste postponed for the season, hopes of finishing it proving over-optimistic. Max now rested at the rear of the dustbin yard, abandoned in favour of quieter jobs that preserved the park's reputation. With Jan out shopping in town, Stephen was nominally helping in the office but it was April, help only needed when a caravan arrived. His father was drawing with a pencil on the office wall, taking rough measurements from a map of West Cornwall and enlarging them to show the area for fifteen or so miles in every direction. Stephen beckoned the other lad in and they stood watching, whispered remarks passing between them as to what Jan might do on her return. After a while they slipped outside again but Stephen, suddenly remembering why he had entered in the first place, returned and hurried through to the kitchen. Grabbing a slab of Cornish heavy cake from the tin, he waved it at Dad as he passed and ran off again to the river.

Gordon stepped to the window, watching them settle downstream from the waterwheel with a fishing line, and guessed Stephen would try part of the cake on the hook, even though such bait was frowned on for trout. Returning he selected a tube of blue paint and commenced to outline the sea. A caravan drawing in brought the two boys haring

137

back, anxious not to miss any arriving youngsters. Seeing only and elderly couple, they waited outside, taking over the office when the new visitors were ushered away. As he left Gordon issued a warning, "The paint is wet, keep away." He doubted they would obey but it might make them careful to leave no traces.

The afternoon was quiet for a Saturday but at this time of year that was scarcely surprising. Interruptions were few, the phone rang occasionally and a car returning from sightseeing stopped briefly for the mobile shop. This slack period had given the vehicle its first test, an easy introduction to refine the arrangements, which in general had worked tolerably well. The necessity to drive to the site entrance each evening and plug into Jim's electric to keep the fridges cold proved inconvenient but not too great a drawback. Whether the system would stop ice cream from melting in midsummer remained to be seen. The customer left, and work on the painting resumed. An hour later the wall map was almost complete; roads had been painted in, place names added, a crossed arrow indicated compass points and a series of circles marked contours at 5, 10, and 15 mile distance from Relubbus.

As Jan returned, driving across the granite bridge, she slowed to gaze over low parapets at the water and ducks below; many people did that.

Seeing the car, Stephen ran to open the garage doors, then hurried through into the house. "Mum's coming!" He leaned against the billiard table waiting with a demon grin, watching his father still adding the final touches of paint.

Catching a glimpse of them while passing through the hallway, Jan deposited her shopping bags in the kitchen then bustled back, suspicions aroused by her young son's behaviour. For a moment she stood watching, then asked "What gave you that idea?"

"Stephen did." Dad pointed towards the lad, whose eyes grew suddenly round with alarm.

Before he could gasp a denial, Jan swung towards him.

"Well done. I like it."

Over the next few weeks the map did prove useful with visitors and not as they had supposed, just for showing where places were. It did more; demonstrating how very central the site was, giving easy access to everywhere. Several families, having looked at it, booked more nights than they originally planned.

April was coming to an end but grass growth had hardly slowed. Chris did much of the mowing on evenings when he had no homework or at weekends if no friends were about. Many areas were still empty, which made mowing easier; he still tended to sing sometimes while driving round but on warm days complained about bumble bees.

"There are thousands on the clover; I can't help mowing over some." It had always been a problem, not that the bees ever retaliated but it seemed such a shame to destroy the small creatures. They had attempted once to make a bee-bar, a horizontal stick with plastic strips dangling, the whole thing arranged to project some distance in front of the mower. The purpose was to frighten bees away before the blades damaged them but those first efforts had proved unstable and not very effective in moving bees. They intended to produce something better but had never actually got round to it again, other work always needing attention. The general rule seemed to be, the bigger the bee the more friendly, but not everyone believed it. An arrival was being shown to a pitch and as they passed a large tent, the occupants suddenly rushed out.

"What's the matter?"

"A great bee, buzzing everyone inside."

"May I?" Gordon stepped into the area at the front of the tent; it was really like a closed awning, an addition to the main living and sleeping areas behind. Near one wall a large furry black bumble buzzed, constantly bumping against the canvas as if trying to break through to the

139

sunlight filtering in. A few steps, two cupped hands and it was trapped, taken outside and released. They watched it fly away. Bumbles very seldom stung if treated carefully. The new arrivals chatted to the already pitched visitors for a short while and decided to camp nearby. Still concerned they asked did bees fly in often and what about wasps?

"Wasps? No, too early, later a few will appear, in June perhaps. Plenty of bees already around but they come for the clover, only enter a tent if they lose their way. Guide them out with a hand or if you prefer, an empty jam jar and a piece of paper will do the trick. If you're lucky enough to get another, call me and I'll show you an easier way?" Gordon waved and returned to the office.

"Our shop is getting much more use," Jan, having disposed of the early morning queue, entered the house, crossing to fall into an armchair. "What shall we do in peak season?"

Time had moved on and visitor numbers increased. Discouragingly, they were again slightly down on the previous year – a hangover still from the sewer probably. The mobile shop did cause extra work but had proved popular. After cleaning the toilets at 6am then eating breakfast, there was still time for other chores before nipping down to Jim's to unplug the overnight electric lead and drive the vehicle back for its normal opening time of 8am. Nevertheless, it was one more thing for the morning list of changing dustbins, checking for stray rubbish, replacing gas bottles, preparing the office and if time permitted, a certain amount of housework which was seldom possible later in the day. There were ducks to feed too, more of them now; some Campbell and Aylesbury ducklings recently purchased, the fluffy white Aylesburys quickly becoming favourites with the caravanners but it all added to the work. Even with the site less than a quarter full, the shop caused some difficulty. Invariably a continuous string of people needed serving in the first

140

hour, all anxious for an early start. If Gordon was pitching a caravan, it left no one in the office to answer the phone. At weekends the children could handle such calls, otherwise Jan pushed her way down the vehicle steps, past any queue that had formed, raced across the yard, up the house steps, wrenching open the door and into the office, grabbing the receiver!

What would happen in the peak season and how to cope when numbers trebled – the matter had been mulled over often enough but never really solved. Life would be a scramble, that much was clear enough. Perhaps Jim would help more, though mounting the shop steps was not easy with his bad leg. As they talked Jan rose, grabbed the daily newspaper, folded it twice then reached over to swot a bluebottle delicately against the window using minimum force so not smear the glass. When it fell stunned, the paper smashed down again, a great angry thump, an impact squelching the fly to pulp on the sill.

"Are you sure it's dead? Couldn't you hit the poor thing a little harder?" Gordon asked smiling.

"Not really – I already pretended it was you!" she swished the paper again in his direction. "Why can't we hang a Vapona in the room?"

"I like to breathe fresh air not some chemical concoction. All the windows are open, it would soon have flown out again."

The postman arrived, passing in a handful of mail at the door and took two letters for posting.

"Three bookings I think... handwritten addresses." Gordon extracted the likely letters, passing the others over. "One from Exeter on the top looks like a bill; what have you been spending?" He grinned down at some papers on the desk.

"In Exeter, at this time of year? Hm, must be that mink stole I sent for!" Jan watched his head shoot up, and smiled. Tossing away an unwanted catalogue on children's swings and slides, she reached for the paper knife, opening

141

the top letter. Scanning it through caused a frown; she re-read the words more carefully, looking out into the yard and checking the number.

"You'll love this!"

"What is it?" He carried on making notes on a pad.

"A summons."

The pen stopped abruptly. "For what? From the police?"

"No. Exeter City Council. They're prosecuting you for parking in one of their car parks without paying."

"I haven't been to Exeter. Neither of us has... nor has the car."

"It's not the car. They say the mobile shop was parked there. They've got the number right too, I've checked. Come on, admit it; you crept out at midnight for a secret assignation on the Council's property. Pay up."

"I will not!" He spoke with feeling, glaring at Jan, unable to see what was so funny as she collapsed into a chair doubled over with laughter, pointing at him and trying to speak.

"You and the boys all laugh at Sharon when she gets indignant; I should have a tape recorder to play back your words – *I will not!*"

Certainly the number on the form tallied with that of the mobile shop, which as a couple of hundred people could witness had stood by the river every single day. No way could it possibly have appeared over a hundred miles away. The reply, dispatched by return, denied the vehicle had been at Exeter and offered to supply witnesses to prove it, in considerable numbers if necessary, explaining the circumstance that made it easy to produce such evidence. No more was heard, no apology or explanation offered.

Local authorities should insist a vehicle's make and colour be checked, to help avoid mistakes. How many ordinary motorists have been prosecuted in other places for such an offence? How many can prove the exact whereabouts of their vehicle several weeks afterwards and anyway, would they be believed when protesting their innocence? Not very likely!

***

Choosing an evening when three caravans arrived together, each booking for ten days, Chris again raised the goat question. His father led the new visitors to a small sheltered area that suited them very well, and returned to the house in ebullient mood – happy not only from the inflow of funds but at the compliments and general good feeling expressed about the valley and the pitches.

It was then that Chris put the question, adding a tentative reminder, "You promised we would buy one when the sewer was finished."

"Yes, you did." Sharon offered support as Stephen nodded agreement.

There was no denying that the promise had been made. Attempts to repurchase Judy failed, so Jan combed the local paper hunting for a likely advert. A Saanen goat was found, white all over, friendly and with a pedigree though not a terribly impressive one, certainly not from a line of champions. Even so she was fairly expensive but not stubborn as Judy had been, following to heel and jumping in the back of the car without the slightest protest.

Stephen saw the car arriving home across the granite bridge and turned to shout. Chris and Sharon quickly appeared.

"What is she called?" Chris asked, taking the goat's lead.

Jan shook her head, "The man says she has no name, choose one between you."

Sarah, they eventually agreed. No one could call Sarah a majestic goat, coat dirty white even when clean and she had no horns but Chris, the family's keenest goat fan, liked her. At first milking Jan smiled with surprise. "This is so easy; she just stands there, you don't need to hold her at all."

Chris, who had attempted to milk Judy once or twice but never really acquired the knack, suggested that

143

perhaps he might now try again.

"Get a footstool then," Jan directed, then noticing how tall he was growing, changed her mind. "No, perhaps you better kneel, here opposite me; remember what we tried before. Watch and copy what I do."

After a few attempts he looked up disappointed. "Nothing comes out."

"Loosen your fingers on the up movement, the milk goes back again if you keep them tight all the while."

A few more pulls and Chris, with an exclamation of triumph, directed a stream into the pail, then trying to sit back as if it were easy, squirted the next over his trousers. One hand automatically reached down to brush the wetness away but he withdrew it quickly, continuing the task, pretending nothing had happened, bending closer and concentrating to direct the stream more accurately. Stephen, however, had seen the error, a little grin spreading across his face.

Persevering, Chris improved, settling to a more rhythmic movement, still occasionally missing the pail. Each such error elicited another snigger from Stephen as he continued to watch closely. After one such guffaw of delight, Chris stopped.

"All right, you try then. Bet you couldn't do it!"

"'Corse I could!" Stephen moved forward.

"No. That would be unfair." Jan held up a hand. "Sarah is very obliging, not like Judy used to be. Let's not upset her. One learner a night is enough, you can try another day."

Disappointment faced them at breakfast. The milk was tainted! The really strong unpleasant flavour made it unusable, the cereals dumped and omelettes cooked instead. Judy's milk had always been good except occasionally after eating too much ivy, but no one could drink this. Varying the diet, more or less oats, more grass less roughage and vice versa over the following week was all to no avail. They asked advice from a more experienced

144

goat keeper.

"Some goats are like that; nothin' you can do about it. Best sell her to someone who doesn't want the milk."

It seemed unlikely anyone would want Sarah on these terms but a notice was stuck in the office window anyway. The following morning with Jan serving in the shop, Chris sat alone at the office desk when a caravanner entered.

"The goat that's for sale, is it the white Saanen I saw you with early this morning?"

"Yes," Chris agreed reluctantly. "But her milk is bad, you can't drink it."

"I don't want milk, only a goat. How much is she."

"You're not going to eat her?"

"No lad, I'm not. I want her to run with the cattle. I've a small farm, hardly a farm, more a smallholding, a hobby rather than a business. We retired and kept a dozen or so acres... run a few cows and hens. In the old days, many farms kept a goat. There's a disease that affects certain grasses sometimes, and can turn the tops black. It's called ergot, bad for cattle but is said not to affect goats; they like to browse the top shoots best. Having a goat is supposed to keep the cows more healthy in a natural way. That's part of the reason, but mostly we'd just like to have a goat around the place." The man smiled at Chris, "Well, how much?"

"You know they take the bark off young trees if they run free." Chris asked hopefully.

"I know. Our fences are good, we had sheep for a while. Don't you want to sell?"

"Well I..." Chris looked away, moving his weight uneasily to the other foot, not wanting to see the goat go but knowing Mum or Dad would sell her soon anyway. Making a decision, he straightened up.

"All right, you can have her. Sarah's a nice goat except for the milk. Mum says get what we can. How much would you offer."

"What changed your mind, would you take ten pounds?"

145

"Yes, okay. I did hope no one would ask so we'd keep her, but, well... she'll have to go eventually and I suddenly realised the next offer might not be somewhere so nice. Your place; you did say she can run free?"

"Completely, and other animals to keep her company. Perhaps I could have bought her for only five?" The man held out a ten pound note and seeing Chris's embarrassment, he knew that was right. "Don't worry, tell your mother you made a bargain. We leave next Wednesday, can you keep Sarah for me until then? We live quite near, a couple of hours away. I'll sit in the back with the goat while my wife drives home."

The man left, pausing in front of the office to bend down and stroke a gaggle of ducks that barred his way, apologising to them for not having any bread. The Aylesbury and Campbell ducklings bought early in spring had long since lost their fluffy down and were nearing full size but for a variety of reasons no Muscovys had yet hatched. Some had found their own nesting places, hiding under bushes and among tangles of ivy but they were somewhat clumsy birds and all these nests had been raided. The two that wisely chose the shed had started late and were delayed further by thieving magpies until that problem was eventually solved by young Stephen lying in wait with an extra large fishing net on a broom handle.

Happily, all were now sitting again; goodness knows how many there would be by September – the extended flock could be expensive come winter! At the moment they hardly needed feeding; the visitors, particularly the children, loved them. As with previous seasons, the occasional bird was lost, but mainly drakes at night while the sitting ducks slept safely in the shed. As a precaution, the young Aylesburys and Campbells, but not the wild Mallard, were also put in before darkness fell, and not without difficulty. Previous years had shown that once the tourists departed, all would be simple. Stop offering food in the afternoon, then put corn in the shed at night and

146

stand clear – the hungry ducks would enter eagerly! Often Chris had gone out on a winter evening with a bucket and called, "Come on! Come on!" They followed in a line, jostling to be first when he threw corn on the shed floor.

Now however, with many children stuffing bread into them most of the day, the attraction of corn was an insufficient inducement to go in, especially with the light evenings. Like naughty children the ducks would dash to the river, swimming to the far bank as Gordon ran up and down with a big stick splashing the surface, trying to frighten them off the water. River Valley ducks did not scare so easily – too well treated, that was their trouble! They would sit treading water, paddling gently without concern as if to say, "Whatever is that ridiculous man playing at?" The crowd of campers that regularly gathered on the bridge, probably agreed, adding words of encouragement until either the ducks were successfully persuaded to go in, or the attempt was abandoned leaving them to sleep on the river. Failure occasionally resulted in losing one during the night, after which they would be meekly compliant for a few days. Sometimes the children donned swimming costumes and waded in, a technique invariably successful and thoroughly approved of by the watching visitors. Privately however, the family considered this measure a defeat. Surely it should be possible to persuade a few ducks off the river without actually entering the water!

Drakes were excluded. In the shed, they would only fight and cause trouble, so nobody tried to catch them; they took their chances outside.

"Males are expendable!" Jan claimed with relish. With ducks that was indeed true; there were always far too many drakes. Little chance of infertile eggs, every duck was mated many times a day whenever she wandered far from the dominant drake.

Each morning one of the children, they took turns, undid the shed door while their parents cleaned the toilet facilities. Many ducks hurried to the river, anxious for that first drink, but those intent on hatching eggs generally stayed, not leaving until later in the day. When they did leave, it was as much to dispose of the waste matter held within their bodies as for food and water. Normally, a bird's digestion varies from fast to almost instantaneous, an essential evolutionary trait; those that fly can afford no unnecessary weight! However, a sitting duck will hold these droppings within her body for twelve hours or more, another stronger dictate of that same evolution. A nest that has no smell increases survival chances, for most predators have keen noses. Once well clear of the nest however, a duck anxious to relieve herself would let the waste come away with explosive energy. Stand well clear! Few things smell stronger or more obnoxious. Some ducks were obliging enough to reach the river first but many a load was dropped halfway, not far from the office door! It was a priority job for whoever detected such a mess, to douse it quickly with several buckets of water; even customers had to wait while this was done in the greater interest of the site as a whole.

Sharon, on opening the shed one morning, stood back to watch that first rush for the river, some flying, others running, jostling each other for position. Walking towards the bridge with the intention of watching as they dived under, wetting and preening feathers in a morning wash, she came across such a dropping. Some sitting duck had decided on an early swim, that was obvious. Where was the bucket? Ah yes. Throwing the first pail dispersed the thick dark mass; two more drawn from the river completed the job. Now why had that duck left her eggs so early? Sharon returned to the shed, peering in, approaching slowly, chatting to the other ducks for reassurance as all the family did, so not the disturb them. She heard tweets before seeing anything, then discovered the ducklings, newly hatched, some bright yellow, others almost black with yellow on chests and lower face. Squatting with great joy she reached out to touch, and when they cowered away, spread her hands over them allowing the palms to lightly touch the little fluffy heads much as the mother ducks feathers would do. Shortly the chicks, far from trying to escape, crowded under, pushing against each other for there was insufficient hand-space to cover them all. After a while Sharon moved, taking one hand away and stroking individuals, smiling as little beaks pecked experimentally against her skin. How many were there? Four, five, eight, gently they were moved to one side, individually or in groups by careful fingers as each was counted... ten, twelve, lucky little thirteen, pure yellow without a mark anywhere. Oh yes, and one more hiding in the corner. "Come on, join your brothers and sisters." The tally complete, all were guided back to the centre; the nest a flat square of straw and feathers inside a big cardboard box on the broad timber shelf. A single unhatched egg remained, Sharon lifted it to an ear and listened... a faint cheep sounded from the chick inside. Her fingers searched the surface; a tiny blip, a pimple of raised shell indicated where the egg tooth had tried to break out. Not much hope for this one, late chicks seldom survived but perhaps it would still hatch.

Returning the egg and spreading her hands again, the little brood gathered beneath. They were at an impressionable age, only a few hours old, happy now to accept the substitute Mum, offering as it did the protection of something warm above their little backs. Sharon chatted to them happily, glancing occasionally through the open door and hoping no one would come. At breakfast only she would know; an inner happiness glowed at that thought and at the soft movements beneath her down-turned palms.

After a while the mother duck returned, jumping onto the bench, not disturbed by the girl's presence; happy perhaps to have the brood protected from opportunist magpies during the brief absence? When Sharon re-entered the house there was something serene, some transparent happiness about her manner. Her mother, having returned from cleaning and now busy cooking breakfast, noticed a dreamy, disconnected glaze in her daughter's eyes and almost spoke, but decided against and instead watched guardedly, wondering about the cause. Dad and the boys, sitting discussing gas bottles were less observant.

"Chris, if you make sure there are two ten pound gas cylinders in the mobile shop each morning," Dad was saying, "Then Mum won't need to go to the shed when people want one!"

"Should I put a Gaz cylinder too, for the tents? Couldn't Sharon take a turn on her morning to let the ducks out?"

That was reasonable enough, Gordon indicated his agreement. Chris grinned with success, anticipating a protest, but Sharon smiled benignly back in a way that made him feel somehow thwarted, robbed of victory. Defensively he hit out.

"'Bout time she did something."

Stephen nodded positively and the boys waited, relishing their chance to gloat, fully expecting a resentful outburst, sure from long experience that their sister could never accept the chore without complaint.

Sharon, now also sitting at table, received the jibe with equanimity, shoulders straight, head back and looking slightly down her nose at her brothers. "Okay, but I may have other things to do!" The happy expression, the sublime indifference – no retort she could possible have made would have annoyed the boys more! Jan watched, eyeing her daughter carefully. What went on here?

"What other things could *you* do?" Chris's demand was belligerent, suggesting her incapable.

"That's for me to know, and you to find out!" The triumph, the joy of supremacy, shone like a beacon from her manner, waving like a red rag to a bull; it even moved Stephen to a few muttered words.

150

"She's a pistachio shell."

Eyes turned, wondering. A frown on the young face faded, replace by that little satanic grin with pursed lips, head tilted downwards, looking obliquely up under that lock of brown hair on a lightly tanned forehead. For some moments he said nothing, silently regarding each person round the table; then uttered two low, almost inaudible words, "Nut case."

It restored the boys' pride. Jan laughed lightly, pleased to see everyone in such good spirits but still unsure what it was that lit Sharon from within; obviously some discovery had been made, something must have affected her daughter deeply to keep it secret so long – but what?

"Don't you think you better tell us?"

Sharon beamed at her mother's words, aware she was now centre stage, had everyone's full attention. "Well, I found..." She paused. "They're mine, all of them! I saw them first... so fluffy under my hands."

"How many?" Dad asked.

She turned eagerly to the voice, "Fourteen!" Then swinging back, anxious not to lose the limelight, "ducklings, five completely yellow, the rest normal. They love me holding them. One egg is still not hatched but the chick is live inside. I heard a cheep. The shell is pipped, but only very slightly. Will it live Dad?"

"Probably not. If it does hatch there may be something wrong; often is with the late ones. Have a look before you leave for school. You may see the duck standing over her chicks now, not sitting. If that's the case, bring the egg inside and I'll fix it under the desk light. Can you locate that thermometer, Jan?"

After breakfast the egg was carried indoors and rested on a bed of corn that had been pre-warmed inside a shoebox. A thin covering of feathers borrowed from the nest spread the desk lamp's heat more evenly, its height adjusted until the thermometer alongside read thirty-nine degrees. With great care, slithers of shell were lifted where

151

the beak had tried to break out; this hole would be enlarged by small amounts as the day progressed if the chick failed to manage by itself.

The children, having dressed quickly for school, hurried back to watch these preparations.

"If it does hatch, at least there won't be so many flies here to pester it," Sharon suggested. "The duck store is full of them. It's awful!"

"Hm, duck sheds do tend to draw flies." Gordon shot a sideways glance at Mum and the boys then beckoned Sharon closer, pretending to whisper but doing it loudly. "Why not use the Vapona your mother smuggled in yesterday and is hiding under the sideboard?"

"How did you..." Jan stopped abruptly. "So the ducks are more important than we are!"

"Just stop arguing and put it in the shed. We don't have a problem in the house, except for the occasional one. Anyway, knowing you're fanatical about flies, I made a small purchase, something far more suitable for indoors." With a smile, he slipped through the doorway into hall and from an anorak pocket produced four small cylinders in a plastic bag. Climbing on billiard table with one of them and hanging it from the lampshade, he pulled the looped end. A spiral of glistening brown paper descended to hang down about a foot long.

"Flypapers! They're disgusting!"

"Why? They don't smell, don't give off chemicals – what is wrong with them?" He held out a hand, palm upward.

"They look horrible."

"Oh never mind that, who cares what they look like."

"Typical of a man! I care! And where do you intend to put the others?"

"I thought one in the dining room and one in the lounge."

"And the last... Oh no! Don't tell me. It's a spare?"

When he nodded, she picked up a newspaper, folded it

152

carefully twice, slowly and with precision, broadcasting her intention as they smiled into each other's eyes. Taking a deep breath, Jan swung the paper baton with force, striking an arm flung defensively above his head. Still smiling broadly, she displayed the now buckled swatter. "The only real pest around here is your father; time he stopped messing around and fetched the mobile. Look, someone's already waiting. Now get off to school before you miss the bus!"

A caravanner coming in to book extra nights saw the artificial nest, and later several more visitors enquired after the egg's well being but news travelled slowly in June for the site had mainly retired couples. When the school holidays came, word would spread faster; children have fewer inhibitions about talking to strangers. By evening, Number Fifteen as it had become known, was free of the shell but not too perky, moving weakly, still absorbing the yoke. Over the following day its appearance improved, more fluffed up and healthy but not too steady on its feet. The other ducklings were already enjoying a shallow tray of water and pecking up food sprinkled on the shed floor; a robust brood but for a day or two they would be safer inside unless someone stood watching over them. No question yet however, of Number Fifteen joining its siblings.

"It ought to have a proper name. What shall we call it?" Chris asked before departing again for school. Automatically the family assumed that Sharon would choose; she flushed with pleasure at being afforded the privilege.

"Do we know if it's male or female, Dad?"

"I never check, not worth upsetting the chick. Ducks are preferred, but it makes no difference to their treatment, we look after them all equally, male or female."

Sharon thought for a moment, reaching out to take it in her hand. "What shall I call you. You're not very strong, a funny wobbly little thing, probably not very bright – Fred! Let's call it Fred."

Both parents immediately turned to Christopher, but his face was blank, unaware, thinking Sharon's smile was only from pleasure at choosing the name.

More people called to see the improving duckling as the news continued to spread. Several caravans arrived, their owners also showing great interest. Jan had put little Fred into one lady's hands while her husband entered details in the visitor's book. When he asked for two days, the woman nudged him, "Why not book for the week right away?"

Later a large motorcaravan with German number-plates drew up, a man entered, saw the box and swung round to call something from the office door. The words were unintelligible but the 'come here' beckoning signals with one arm were plain enough. Two boys descended from the vehicle, running to the office, a woman following. Fred was now in a bigger box on the floor – the lamp alongside continuing to supply warmth. Trade was only moderate, as was usual mid-afternoon in June, so there was no rush to get people pitched. Perhaps that was just as well, for the duckling caused considerable delay. Eventually the man paid for a single night before explaining.

"We would like three days, but I have no more English money. I must find a bank. You can change German Marks perhaps?"

"Sorry."

"I could leave fifty Marks until we have more pounds – in case you get full. It would be in order?"

"Not necessary," Jan insisted, speaking more clearly and precisely than she normal did but not slowing down as had been necessary with the laughing Italian family who came in yesterday. Taking the proffered note, she examined it with interest then passed it back. "We will not be full but I shall put you down for three days. Bring the money in after you find a bank."

By late afternoon when the children came home, Fred was pecking up food happily enough and some discussion took place on his future. The other fourteen were taking a first swim on the river at the moment, watched over by Stephen and two visiting children together with a group of older people. It was decided to wait until the brood returned to the shed and later when darkness came, to tuck Fred under the mother duck's feathers, hoping the proper smell might make it more acceptable by morning.

Taking advantage of a lull in activity, Gordon took the duckling cupped in his hands to see Mini Jenkins, the old lady who lived halfway down the track, right next to the recreation field. Arriving at the cottage a voice called 'Come in' before he could knock at the door. She was seated at the table stringing runner beans.

"I promised to show you when the chicks hatched. This is the runt of the litter, hatched a day late. Sharon named it Fred. Here, see if he'll come to you."

Released onto the table top, the little webbed feet took a few indecisive steps and with no other hands in sight, headed for Mini. Hands had come to mean warmth and safety to this temporarily orphaned duckling. Fred took a few more steps forward, pecked experimentally at one finger, then climbed onto the old lady's open palm and sat comfortably as the two people talked.

"We hatched it under a light bulb, this is Fred's first journey outside the house. I tried him just now among the grass on top of the wall," Gordon pointed through the window to a long Cornish hedge leading off toward the village.

Stroking the fluffy down with one finger, Mini looked up, her expression serious.

"You be careful of that wall. Snakes. You remember Emma, my sister."

"Sure, I carried her along the trench when we dug the water main, back in our first year."

"She liked that, talked about it for weeks. One summer, oh, quite some time ago when we were much younger, Emma was out by that wall picking wild mint. We grew proper mint in the garden but she preferred the wild, used it a lot, not just on lamb..." Mini broke off, absent-mindedly stroking the duckling with a finger and gazing vacantly into space, then sighed, looked down at Fred, and continued. "I can see her now, leaning over to pluck another stem, and that was how it happened. Must have been coiled up sleeping there in the sun like they do; an adder – it bit her! The doctor said there was nothing to be done, keep her quiet and hope for the best. Well, she got very bad, but I cured her; never mind what the doctor said, I knew what to do!" As Mini talked she held the duckling close, chuckling it under the chin with a finger. "I poured half a pint of neat gin into her. She was right as rain next morning."

They laughed together sitting for a while in the cool of the thick walled stone cottage with its small windows. Half a pint was probably an exaggeration, and whether Emma recovered because of the gin or in spite of it no one might ever know, but it was time to go. Smiling down again at the fluffy little bundle, its eyes trustingly closed, fast asleep, Mini sighed, "They should never grow up."

Chapter 9

Hooked

The latter end of June was a splendid time, the valley sheltered, weather fine, ducklings now sporting full feathers and testing their wings, dabbling in the clear waters then sleeping for hours on the bank – a lazy carefree existence. Life for the family was pleasant too, not yet the mad rush it would be in a few weeks, still time to relax between visitors. During this most pleasant of months, Gordon, taking advantage of a quiet period, decided to put into effect an idea dreamed up after an unexpected discovery behind the house.

"Some people," he told Jan, "may not have a bottle mine. What will they do when the world runs out of bottles?"

"Some people?" she echoed his words. "I've got news for you! Nobody has. More than that, no sane person would want one."

"Of course they would! Anyway, I want one. I'll start it tomorrow."

She didn't argue, only smiled gently, rolling her eyes towards the heavens. One thing was certain, there would never be any shortage of bottles here! Great piles of glass containers continually appeared in the rubbish, every type except milk bottles which were put in crates by the office door for the milkman to collect. Jettisoned in the bins were squash bottles, pop bottles, sauce bottles, jam jars, pickle jars, cider flagons, and wine bottles of many colours! Tall and slender or short and fat, round, oval, square; cross-sections of every shape – glass everywhere. It seemed to multiply each year, accounting for a good percentage of dustbin space.

"Break them up!" he had thought the previous year, hoping many more would fit in one bin, for a bottle is mostly space; could hardly serve its purpose otherwise. However the practice proved too noisy and little flying shards made it dangerous, so the idea was abandoned, but surely there must be some use for all that glass?

"Ask the dustmen," Jan suggested. "They know about rubbish."

The following week while helping as usual to empty bins onto the cart, he asked one of the chaps, "What can I do with all these bottles?"

Returning towards the house as the dustcart left, Jan stopped him. "Well?"

He looked at her blankly, then shrugged.

Frowning with annoyance, she sighed. "You forgot again, didn't you? Forgot to ask about the bottles."

"Oh that. No I did remember." He resumed walking towards the house but on entering the office an arm from behind grasped his shoulder, swinging him round.

"I'm waiting?" She stood, feet apart, hands on hips.

"Waiting?"

"What did they say?" She took on a threatening air, reaching to the bookcase for a heavy volume.

"You don't want to know. Anyway it's physically impossible!"

Having tried all sources locally, they wrote to the Department of the Environment asking what could be done with bottles. Compared to the dustman's suggestion, the reply was polite, extremely so, by some chap who had swallowed a dictionary – but equally unhelpful.

"Listen to this," Jan waved the letter. "Persons or organisations desirous of effecting the environmentally bene-ficial disposal of any superfluity of discarded receptacles of a vitreous or primarily quartz origin... Here, read it yourself, it goes on quite a bit. This chap will probably make Prime Minister!"

Apparently, cullet, the proper name for recovered glass, was recycled by glass manufacturers at the rate of nearly fifteen percent. Impressive! Fifteen percent of what it failed to say. So much for the good news. The bad news was, down here at the tip of Cornwall, nobody wanted it.

This useless information had been discovered earlier in the season. Never mind, the new idea, the bottle mine, resulted from a more recent find; a large almost square hole in the ground situated under a group of trees behind the house, a thicket as yet unexplored, a place given no attention since it was never intended to pitch caravans there. Max's bucket could not reach under the low branches without causing damage, but something must be done to make it safe. The first thought had been to pack the hole gradually over the years with ashes, a big pile of which had steadily accumulated behind the house, some dating back to their first winter in the valley and that second-hand caravan with a boiler. Well instead, this hole could be packed with bottles! Not only would that fill it quicker but should also solve the glass problem; not permanently, but for one season at least, and thereby postpone any need to buy more dustbins. Brilliant!

Enthusiastically he started right away, filling a spare dustbin, hauling it over to the hole in the ground, then climbing down to fit each bottle flat on the bottom like a jigsaw. The nearby pile of ash proved useful too, filling in the gaps and forming a thin covering between layers. They might become bottle millionaires. If a glass crisis ever arose they could be rich!

In the slack of the afternoon, work continued; it was close enough to the office to be called if needed. Had Robin or Blackbird appeared, Gordon would have chatted to them about his plan, but being alone it was only natural that thoughts freely came and went. "How will we find it again in years to come? Perhaps I should mark the burial place. What sort of label? A stake with a name board, obviously; but what name? What suitable epitaph?

"An empty bottle layeth here,
Cast aside when out of beer.

"Be sensible! Something grand and imposing. Letters carved in wood... or stone? Hm, stone would be stronger... last a long time, like that Roman stone at St Hilary church. Bit presumptuous perhaps, hard to carve? Better be fairly short, not too many letters. How about 'Relubbus Interment Project'? I could just use the initials."

The idea had promise. It was nice to imagine some chap in the twenty-second century, digging down to plant a tree, coming unexpectedly across a layer of bottles, then another and another. Would an archaeological dig be called to examine this strange phenomenon? Perhaps some professor of history would appear on TV, offering the nation his learned opinion on a society where bottles were precious enough to be hidden underground. Little men with shovels would stake claims all over River Valley.

Gordon paused, realising where his thoughts had run. Mad? No, no! Imaginative maybe, but perfectly normal.

The bottle mine filled more quickly than expected; wine bottles the most numerous. Holiday-makers must be enjoying themselves? Before the month ended, the hole was filled to the brim and turfed over. No other holes were found so more dustbins had to be bought in the end. Never mind, though no sign was ever erected, the evidence lay there waiting – someday someone would certainly find it.

Early July saw more motorcaravans than usual, due partly to an increase in Continentals. These European visitors normally stayed only a night or two, restlessly anxious to cover the country, see the next town, the next city. This year they were staying longer – longer than in previous years and longer than the owners themselves had expected. Many were booking extra nights, finding both this valley and the Cornish countryside very much to their taste – so thoroughly enjoying the quiet atmosphere that they spent odd days of relaxation without leaving the park. Naturally another day was needed to see those missed landmarks but that was the beauty of camping and caravanning, the ability to stay or move on at will. Largely these were last minute decisions, taken on the very day visitors were due to leave and as a consequence several ran low on funds and asked to change foreign money. The family were beginning seriously to wonder if such a service should be provided. Extra days were gratifying, flattering even, something they wanted to encourage. On a whim while visiting cash-and-carry, a *Financial Times* was bought to provide exchange rate information. The idea was scrapped when a phone call revealed the bank charged £15 for each currency transaction.

"My Dutch friend has a motorcaravan," Sharon pointed obliquely through the office window. "Her parents were one of those asking about currency. She persuaded them to stay longer, can I invite her round?"

"Does she look respectable?" Gordon asked.

"Very! You should see her wardrobe. Speaks good English too, but very proper, each word so distinct." A little upper crust tone crept into Sharon's voice for those last words but it faded, replaced by enthusiasm as she continued. "They've a super 'van, its own shower and toilet, central heating, real plushy upholstery and insect screens at all the windows! They're posh!" She pointed to the lounge with the flypaper hanging down, fixed by a piece of string to the little bulb socket high on the ceiling. "Not like our house with those things everywhere!"

Dad rose, picking up the newspaper they had used for checking the exchange rates, folded it and stepped over to strike twice against the glass. "Posh is not having a big wardrobe and screens at the windows," he collected the two bodies dropping them in a waste bin. "Posh is swatting your flies with a pink paper!"

161

***

Since motorcaravans were normally absent during the day, it was becoming difficult remembering which pitches were taken. Some, probably the more experienced, placed a sign 'Reserved for XYZ 123' to reserve their space, others were asked to leave something on the pitch. A plastic waste-water bucket was most frequently chosen, cheap enough to be easily replaced if lost and dirty enough that no one would want to steal it in the first place. Not that anything ever was taken, but new visitors were not to know that. Occasionally a driver forgot, or for some reason decided not to leave a marker, only to learn on returning that someone else had taken the pitch.

The advantages and disadvantages of these vehicles had always been a matter for debate in touring circles; sometimes criticised by those with towing caravans as clumsy, petrol guzzling, ostentatious, and other less kind remarks, but fiercely defended by their own supporters for being more convenient and comfortable. Mostly such arguments were friendly and good-humoured, but a sharper edge could easily creep in. One proud owner of a moderately large motorcaravan, on finding himself the butt of jokes about the weight of his vehicle by a group of towing caravanners, was overheard to say, "Yes, they're not for the unskilled driver or for those whose mouths are bigger than their wallets!"

These pros and cons were quite different for a site operator. On the downside, very level pitches were required since they did not have the same ability to 'level up' as a towed caravan. Being generally heavier, damage to grass if the ground was soft could be substantial. That was particularly true of motorcaravans with awnings that were left permanently on the pitch, for in order to connect one to the other, their wheels must pass along exactly the same tracks both when going out and returning, often creating deep ruts. River Valley had these two features well covered, having extensive, carefully levelled hardstanding, a surface ideally suitable even in wet weather, where motorcaravans could neither sink nor get stuck. Not all parks were so lucky.

What about the upside, the advantages? Well, a point of which even the drivers are not normally aware is that these vehicles tend to be both Local Authority proof, and revenue concealing! Tax inspectors hate motorcaravans! This special quality was highly favoured by some site operators. The local Council, being of a distrusting nature (probably with some justification) had recently arranged for a light aircraft to fly over all the caravan parks in their area and take photos. From this evidence some diligent clerk could if required, carefully count the numbers, checking the licensed quantity had not been exceeded.

"We are not spying," a council official once claimed. "West Cornwall is a prime holiday area. We need to know that there are enough pitches to satisfy the demand. These aerial shots allow us to check that."

He may well have been right, but most park owners were to say the least a little cynical! On that first occasion, few people were aware of the little spy plane's purpose but news, as bad news will, leaked out! Fortunately it had not appeared until mid-morning and when this tardiness became known, it delighted those parks that overran their permitted numbers. The reason was simple. By ten o'clock each morning, ninety percent of motorcaravans had already left for the day! Site owners had their own organisation, soon to be renamed The British Holiday and Home Parks Association. Regular meetings were held at which the finer points of life were discussed, like how to remove a grapefruit some moronic idiot had stuffed round the U-bend in a loo – worse still if they were sadistic enough to use the appliance afterwards! Some chap volunteered the suggestion that a few piranhas in the pan might deter mischievous hands; he thought however, these might not be appropriate in the Gents! The spy flight, when it was discovered, also formed a topic of conversation at such meetings.

"Did you hear the KGB flew over last month? Good thing they leave it so late in the day; never heard of early birds I suppose."

"I doubt the clerk in charge knows one end of a motorcaravan from the other, just don't realise time makes any difference."

General opinion proposed that while site operators were thoroughly good fellows rising early to tend their visitors needs, spy pilots and senior council officers were something else! Such creatures might consider themselves a cut above ordinary people but nothing short of a mortar bomb, or perhaps a British Rail sandwich, would shift them from their beds of a morning. It is just possible that these opinions might have been a teeny bit biased.

Seeing a light plane circle overhead one afternoon, Jan shook her head. "They're wasting their time with us, we don't need to exceed our licence! If we ever do get those 250 units allowed, we'll be rich anyway!"

While River Valley had no need of the special daytime invisibility quality of motorcaravans, these vehicles were most welcome and did find the valley attractive, particularly the hardstanding pitches. Another point appreciated and commented favourably upon by folk who carry everything with them wherever they go, was the absence of any tarmac bumps, those sleeping policemen that tend to shatter crockery as well as rear springs. The ducks made a splendid alternative having definitely decided that all cars were harmless and would stop for them. They waddled around regardless of oncoming vehicles, to sit occasionally blocking the way entirely, refusing to move until someone jumped from a car to shoo them away. The funny thing was, far from being annoyed, the tourists loved these obstructions, beaming with happiness as if chasing over-tame Muscovys was the highlight of their day.

Indeed the ducks were right, they were kings of the road, everyone did slow down, especially after the ducklings hatched. Nobody wanted to hurt one, and so far no one had, but there were hazards other than cars! One Mallard drake unwisely swallowed a fishing hook. The little lad who caught him was upset. Shocked to see a drake where a small trout had been expected, he let go the hand line and stood unsure what to do. The drake, in an effort to dislodge this new irritation, tangled the nylon round its body and one wing, flapping frantically and frothing the water in the attempt, drawing visitors attention to its plight. Though now unable to fly, effecting a capture took the combined efforts of several people in the river! Fear of digging the hook in further prevented anyone grabbing the remaining length of line. A small crowd gathered on the bridge, torn between concern for the drake and glee at the increasingly wet state of its pursuers, a cheer marking the bird's final capture! It was quickly untangled and all but a foot of the line cut off as a precaution, so it wouldn't get caught up if it managed to escape again. The hook itself unfortunately, was not so easily disposed of, being too far down and securely dug in. Initial efforts to remove it from the struggling drake were unsuccessful, and further attempts seemed likely to cause major damage.

Leaving Sharon in charge, with Jan driving and Gordon holding the drake, they slipped off to the Vets by car. Evening surgery had almost ended and the receptionist had departed; they met the vet showing his last patient out. Asking them into the treatment room, he put the duck on his surgery table and while Gordon held it, endeavoured to remove the hook. The attempt was unsuccessful. Freeing the deeply embedded barbs was causing the duck too much distress and its muscles were too tense.

"Sorry Donald, I'll have to give you gas."

Jan blinked in surprise. Could a duck be put under? Did everyone talk to birds? Perhaps for someone dealing constantly with people's pets, this technique consulted the owner with less chance of disagreement – sort of, if Donald doesn't object, why should you? Certainly in this case it worked, for neither raised any comment.

The vet slipped a big cone-shaped rubber nozzle over its beak and put his hand all round the ducks head to reduce escaping gas, chatting as he worked.

"They don't make these ends to fit ducks beaks, they're for bigger animals. Turn your heads away. It's an extra charge if I put you out as well!"

They realised this apparent levity was to ease their own nervousness, for he worked with gentle care, obviously concerned not to inflict pain. The duck fell unconscious and everyone else did stay on their feet. Once resistance ceased, a little patient effort extracted the hook without great damage but the duck would not come round; still deep under the anaesthetic.

"I'll have to give oxygen," the vet looked pensive.

Five minutes later they had left the surgery and were climbing back into the car with a conscious and *very costly* drake! And they didn't need more drakes anyway – already had too many. Even if more had been needed, at least four could have been bought for the price of saving this one. Ridiculous! But they couldn't see the bird suffer.

The car refused to start at first, then Jan stalled it pulling away from the kerb.

"I'll watch the drake, you concentrate on trying to drive!"

"Trying too? It's not my driving; I've told you before, we need a new car."

"No way. I'm already holding one expensive bird and can do without another! This car is only three years old. You think money grows on trees."

"If it did, you'd have a fit each autumn!"

But they were smiling, happy that the drake had recovered. It was well worth the trouble and expense to take the bird home cured, and doubly worthwhile when displaying its recovery to the little boy who had caught it.

He was shown the hook that had been removed, and saw the much-travelled mallard lowered back onto the river. A carefully watch would be kept over the next week to check it suffered no ill effects.

At a very late tea the children demanded full details, which Jan related, particularly the giving of gas while Dad held the duck, and that warning by the Vet. Seeing them peer curiously at their father, she spoke again quickly.

"Oh, you needn't worry about him! He wouldn't fall over even if he *was* unconscious if it meant paying more money. You should have seen his expression when the vet said 'five pounds!'"

Site activity was increasing fast in early July; the weather hot with a pleasantly light breeze. One guest attempting to entice more air to circulate the kiosk while making a telephone call, propped the door open with her bag. The bag fell over letting the door slam shut. Glass flew in every direction, the whole pane disintegrating to fragments.

It was early afternoon. Jan leant against the office desk talking to Jim when the doorbell rang. The lady, fortunately unhurt, stood by the step apologetically relating her tale of woe.

"I'm so sorry. You must let me clear up the glass... a shattering experience!"

An apt and accurate description!

"Think nothing of it, we needed more air in that kiosk anyway." Jan found a dustpan and passed it over, hoping the little act of clearing up would make the woman feel better.

Jim agreed to stay on while Gordon, returning to the office after pitching a caravan, measured the size then rushed out in the car for a replacement window. Before most people came back from the beach that afternoon the repair had been made – with rigid plastic this time – it looked like glass but was stronger.

"Now it can blow shut whenever it wants to," he stood back to view the completed job, then checked himself. "Tempting providence. If it blows open often, the hinges will probably fall off!" Extracting one screw with difficulty and taking it down to the workroom, he hunted for some a good bit longer. A size thicker would have been good too, but the existing ones were already the maximum the hinge countersinking would allow. Not totally satisfied, he drove a stake into the ground to stop the door swinging right back. That should fix it! The job complete, he returned to the office.

The children had arrived home an hour earlier but were gone again now; Jan sent them out for some exercise or to find friends, saying tea would be late. Jim insisted on staying until the job was complete and having now been duly thanked, eased himself down the office steps, limping over to inspect the work then climbed on his tricycle and headed for home. He was happy. A line of willows on the left sheltered him from the wind and his tricycle ran smoothly over the tarmac surface. It was good to still feel useful. He had taken several phone calls in the office while Jan saw new arrivals to a pitch, then stood in the doorway for a spell, the few steps easing his bad leg. Three old customers wandered over for a natter; they had all gone inside and sat talking. Asking Stephen to blow up his tyres had been a good idea too, it made such a difference! He had hardly noticed over the weeks as they gradually deflated; now a couple of pedals sent him coasting along. Two people were fishing on the riverbank beyond the trees. Jim rang the bell on his handlebars, they looked up and he lifted a hand to wave as he did with everyone. Slightly ahead and on the left lay the opening to the recreation field, used for cricket and football to remove these more dangerous games from the smaller children and the caravans. Chris was working to one side, trying to make a small vegetable garden. Jim called and steered towards him, heading for some rough stony ground several inches lower than the tarmac. Turning at an angle, a back wheel dropped over the road edge while the other still ran on the smooth black surface. The handlebar twisted violently throwing one hand free. Wildly he grabbed, wrenching it round again, but too late! The tricycle was falling, overturning! He tried to stop it with his leg. A mistake! There was no agility in that painful limb. Crunch! One shoulder hit the ground hard, driving breath from his body, the tricycle on top, a wheel still spinning – but it was the leg that caused concern. Even without the loud crack that sounded at the moment of impact he knew something was badly wrong. The stab of pain was excruciating.

Within moments Chris was at his side, calling to the men on the riverbank. They came running, fishing tackle abandoned. Chris warned him not to move but Jim, still tangled with the machine, was struggling to rise.

"Help me up. Keep me on the saddle and lift, one on each side, then push me home." There was no arguing; he would have hauled himself up otherwise. Carefully they lifted and Chris pushed him back to the bungalow. Shortly after, he was driven off by ambulance to Truro hospital.

At visiting time next day, he looked white and poorly but Audrey was relieved to find him more comfortable. Recovery however, would not be fast the nurse warned. "Old bones mend slowly, he must stay in hospital for some time"

It left Audrey alone in the bungalow. As a temporary measure, Sharon moved in with her for company. There would be no further help from Jim that season!

"It means you boys helping more when school breaks up shortly," Jan warned at tea. "And somehow I have to make time to run Audrey over to the hospital most days. I don't know how we'll manage with the shop to run as well, particularly in the mornings and it's getting busy in the late afternoon as well, when people come home from the beach."

"Sharon can come down and help," Chris suggested. "She only needs to sleep at the bungalow, not be there all the time. She says Audrey already has some lifts. People taking ice blocks down ask after Jim and when they hear he's in hospital, some have offered to drive her."

Chapter 10

Wicked

"What is the matter?" Jan looked across at Gordon, seeing the grimace of pain. They were alone in the office; he had been quiet since breakfast and had come back quickly from pitching the various caravans, not stopping to talk as was more usual.

"Nothing. Indigestion most likely. What would you expect at the speed we eat meals?"

Jan nodded, not pressing and turned away, hiding her concern. Breakfast was hours past and there had not been time to eat anything since; indigestion seemed unlikely. Perhaps it was lack of food; she pushed the worries away, running back to the mobile shop as another customer approached.

At lunch Gordon excused himself, professing not to be hungry, returning to the lounge and a comfortable chair.

"What's up with Dad?" Chris asked.

"Not sure, he's been off colour all day. Better this week than next!"

"Four more days at school," Chris smiled, "Some of my friends are already here, wonder how many more from last year will come back?"

Although school holidays in most places across the country had not yet started, the many caravans and tents now colonising the valley already sported a sprinkling of children. Some were from Staffordshire, where according to one lad the schools closed earlier – the pottery holidays

171

he called it.

"Boys, you mean?" Jan asked.

"Well yes, perhaps some..." Chris hesitated again, and was saved by a noise from the hall.

"Shop," a voice called as Stephen, who had been left on duty outside, suddenly appeared in the doorway. Jan hurried off to serve the customer, returning shortly to finish the meal.

Stephen, who had eaten earlier, was now free to go and ran off to join his small group, racing round, climbing the steep side of the remaining unfinished terrace, kicking balls that deliberately ended in the river, ever on the lookout for some prank. At least they were careful to do nothing damaging. That might be luck and could change at any time, but Stephen, while never averse to mischief, had a certain ability and inventiveness. He saw little fun in merely being destructive. Today for instance, his group found a lizard lazily basking in the sunshine and pounced on the unsuspecting creature before it could make good its escape. A whispered conference found them rushing to the Ladies toilets, placing it hurriedly in a wash basin and retiring to nearby bushes. A woman entered the building but the door, propelled by its spring loaded closer had hardly swung shut before it flew suddenly wide again and she rushed off in the direction of the office. Stephen nudged one of the girls, who ran from hiding to carefully collect and carry the little creature back to its original home. When the woman re-appeared with Jan following, the young group were again crouched, hidden and listening with glee as she tried to explain that there definitely had been a reptile in the basin, and no, she couldn't possible have imagined it! Later that same afternoon in the mobile shop the full story was heard from a woman whose young daughter had boastfully provided the details.

Returning to the office and finding Gordon no longer in the armchair, Jan hurried upstairs to find him resting on the bed, saying it was more comfortable, and no, he didn't want a coffee.

Downstairs again, she and Chris were chatting in the office when a camper entered to book extra nights for her family. Somehow the subject of young sons arose and Jan retold the lizard story, finishing with a wish.

"Wish I could remember the name of the lady who came rushing in here – probably still thinks she was seeing things. I told Stephen last time not to do it again."

"He didn't, not exactly." Chris grinned, defending his younger brother. "You said not to put frogs in the ladies toilets – he used a lizard in a basin instead."

"Frogs, lizards, same sort of thing. Little devil!" Jan smiled back.

"No, He's right," the visitor shook her head, supporting Chris. "They really are different. Lizards have scales and dry skin, they're reptiles. A frog is an amphibian, wet skin and no visible scales; I teach biology."

When Stephen appeared, walking towards the office, they laughed quietly together and the visitor quickly left, but Jan said nothing to her youngest son.

Chris had been amused by the incident but was now above such things. He made no comment either, but left to join friends and was seen later sitting along the riverbank amid a mixed group of teenagers, all talking quietly together with the occasional hail of laughter. Chris and a girl were sitting very close, whether by accident or design was not clear.

With Jan busy and the boys at their own pursuits, no one noticed Gordon's more frequent spasms of pain when he returned downstairs to the armchair again. After a short while, thinking that lying down had been easier after all, he retired early, omitting for the first time in many weeks to walk round after dark checking all was quiet. But sleep would not come and the stomach attacks increased in frequency. Somewhere around midnight, Jan whisked him off to Penzance Hospital in severe pain. Appendix was diagnosed and she returned home alone in those small hours of Tuesday 15th July, four days before the first really busy weekend of the season!

"Wake up!"

"Eh?" Chris rolled over, rubbing his eyes and looking up at his mother. Struggling to a sitting position, he tried to smother a yawn, "Did I oversleep?"

"No, it's still early but we have a problem. Get up, go down to Audrey's bungalow and wake Sharon. I need you all together for breakfast – and hurry, there's lots to do. Tell Stephen to tend the ducks."

Before Chris could ask more, his mother had gone. Once outside she unlocked the service passage, grabbed the cleaning bucket and headed for the Gent's side of the first toilet building, not even pausing to enter cautiously. Turning off the gas light, the debris of dead flies attracted to the flame overnight was swept away. Basins, showers and toilets were cleaned, the seats washed with disinfectant and dried off with a special cloth; taps and mirrors polished, ashtray emptied and the waste bin checked. Scrubbing the urinal with more disinfectant followed by a quick sweep of the floor finished the job. A final look round made her wonder; had it been skimped a bit? The midday clean would be more thorough, or rather she hoped it would; but nothing was certain any more! A glance at her watch revealed this cleaning had taken over ten minutes and there were still three more to tackle. In spite of the morning's freshness she already felt sticky with perspiration but knew they must be done faster and hurried, almost running to the other Gents, entering to find it empty and started immediately. "How will we manage? What do I tell the children?" the thoughts crowded in, halted as one greasy basin demanded extra attention. "Damn! It's taking longer. With both of us working together, each compartment takes seven minutes normally... why am I thinking about normally – nothing will be normal for the next two weeks!" A smear across a mirror caught her attention, she rubbed

174

at it quickly then paused at her own reflection, face unsmiling, hair unkempt, "I look like a char-lady!" Dismissing the thought she hurried on, finally returning indoors a few minutes before seven to find Sharon cooking breakfast.

"Beans on toast Mum, it's nearly ready. Okay?"

"Oh yes," Jan sighed, relieved. "Call me, I'll be in the office. Where are the boys?"

"Upstairs. Sorting school stuff they said. Lying on their beds more likely."

Better take advantage while they can, Jan thought, walking through to the office, picking up a clip of booking forms. Eight to arrive but the regulars seldom booked, confident they would be found a space, which was true. There would be casuals too, there always were; people who took a chance, calling at any site they liked the look of. Just as well, their custom was certainly needed! She wrote the day's date in the visitor's book, then scanned the daybook for those leaving. Four to go; two from Holland were booking by the day and might stay.

"It's ready!"

Hearing the call Jan left the books, pausing to shout up the staircase, "Breakfast!" then walked through into the kitchen as Sharon added two plates to those already on the table. "Just finishing Dad's toast," she said as the boys came jostling through the doorway.

"Don't bother, it won't be needed. Turn the gas off and come, eat your own." Jan pulled out her chair, sitting down, cutting off a piece and popping it in her mouth. The children were watching her, she knew that, but found herself reluctant to start. Lying awake last night trying to decide what was best had produced no workable plan.

"Where is Dad?" Sharon's words forced a response.

"In hospital. Appendix they say, and..." she raised a hand at the alarmed expressions. "No, it's not serious, a small routine operation." she paused again, praying that it would be, that nothing would go wrong; pretending an unconcern that was certainly not felt. "It gives us a problem

175

though. They may keep him several weeks and we have to manage somehow." Jan studied the faces of her family. "Trouble is I don't really know how?"

"We can help," Sharon looked towards the boys who nodded strongly.

"Thank you. I'm afraid you'll have to; you won't get nearly so much time with your friends but two of you should be free each evening after the shop has closed; that will be our main problem, the shop. Don't stop eating, this is not the end of the world, we'll manage somehow – we have to."

For a few minutes they ate in silence, not that they normally bothered about eating and talking simultaneously, but the children were waiting on their mother and she was delaying, still searching for answers.

"Right." Jan pushed the plate aside. "The real difficulties will be next weekend, when the rush starts. Someone must be in the office all the time; that will have to be me. People will want prices and other information, will want to pay, have a receipt; with the numbers likely to arrive it's too complicated for you." She paused, probing the faces for agreement. "Chris, you must to do Dad's job, seeing them to a pitch; make sure people with dogs only go on areas six, sixteen, or twenty three; tell them to walk their animals downstream along the riverbank. You know the spacing must be twenty-feet clear? Find how many steps that is, so you can indicate quickly where each one should be."

"Seven and a half of my paces, or it was last summer, but I can check, Dad showed me. The side of our toilet buildings are exactly twenty feet; I can pace alongside counting the steps." Chris explained.

"Good. If you get any difficult customers, send them back to me. Another thing, will you change any empty gas bottles each morning and check the pilot lights are burning so the showers don't go cold. Okay? Now you Stephen; dustbins – you know what to do? Make sure those you take away are really full, right up to the top; tip others into them if necessary. We'll probably be short of bins anyway. Do them early each morning while I'm cleaning the toilets, then again midday. Just check in the evening and if they're full, change some more. You can manage that?"

"Yes."

Jan smiled at him; the little face lit up with pleasure, then turned downward and away as if shy.

"There's more you boys can do. Check round the site each morning for odd bits of rubbish, inspect the emptying points and use secateurs to snip off any branches or brambles that stick out. Chris, you must drive the mower, catch the patches where visitors leave. Do it early afternoon when people are out, okay?"

"Don't forget the waterwheel," Sharon prompted. "Staying up at the bungalow I've got used to watching each evening, a colour set too." She looked across at the boys, gloating, then realising this was not the time, asked her mother, "Shall I see to it?"

"No. I'm coming to you in a minute, but that is a point. Chris, will you clean the grid each morning so we don't lose power. Do you know how to clip people's batteries on when they need charging?"

"I do." It was Stephen's voice. Jan turned at the sound, waiting, and he continued. "Red clips go on the plus."

"Yes. Well let the caravanners carry their own batteries round, just indicate where to put them, I don't want any strained backs this week thank you! Right. Now Sharon, you do the shop, that's the longest job of all. Can you do breakfast each morning too, and cook midday if I'm busy – something we can eat in relays? It means moving back here, leaving Audrey on her own. Nip off now and tell her, then put your things in the mobile shop, I've never driven it before but I'll have to in about fifteen minutes."

"What about school?" Chris asked. "We've a test today. Last one I think."

"Hm... school it is then. I'd like you all to go but only

177

if Audrey will come and help, otherwise someone will have to stay; that will be you Sharon. Off you go to Jim's; come back with me afterwards, there'll be half an hour before bus time."

The little meeting broke up, Stephen hurrying out to start the dustbins, Chris following to handle his chores and Sharon running off, anxious to impart the news. Jan cleared the table leaving the washing up for Sharon, then made the double bed leaving the children to make their own. Other housework must wait – indefinitely! A few more minutes preparing the office and the clock read 7.50am. One visitor, standing where the shop would park, watched as she locked the outer door and walked briskly across the bridge, breaking into a jog up the road.

Meanwhile Sharon had already reached the bungalow, imparted her story, hurriedly ascertained that Audrey would help and was now collecting together books, clothes, and her favourite pillow. Within a few minutes these items were placed inside the mobile shop; the electric connection to the vehicles on-board fridges being removed as Jan appeared at the gate. A rapid exchange of words brought a promise from Audrey to walk down in half an hour. They climbed aboard. One press on the button started the engine – the vehicle was on its way!

"How does Dad turn this thing?" Jan eased it through the gateway, struggling to lug the wheel round, catching a few feet of grass on the riverbank. Once travelling faster however the steering handled better and in short order it crossed the bridge, coming to a halt in the yard. Already a queue was waiting.

At mid-morning six miles away, a few deft flicks of the knife removed the offending appendix but Gordon would not become aware of this until some time later. A painful and unpleasant twenty-four hours would follow, pushing other concerns aside, but of that too he was for the moment, happily ignorant.

Back on the site the day was moderately busy with

178

several caravans arriving. Leaving Audrey in the shop, Jan showed each to a pitch, giving less choice than usual and having ensured each caravan rested in it's proper position, hurried off again. The visitors seem happy enough, but one couple with two dogs opened the caravan door and let them run. That was the type of thing Jan hated – the need to deal with something unpleasant.

"They must be on a lead."

"Oh they'll be all right." The man reached inside as he spoke, his hand reappearing with the winder for the caravan steadies.

Jan screwed up all her determination. "No, I'm afraid they won't be all right. Call them and put them on a lead please."

"Goodness, we've only just arrived. I can't keep them on a lead all the time!"

Jan's discomfort was giving way to anger, she could feel her cheeks burning. "If you want to stay here you will. Put them on a lead *now*... or hitch up and collect your money on the way out!"

He called the dogs, clipped on the leads and passed them to the woman who stood nearby. Neither looked happy! Ah well... more pressing matters called and Jan strode self-consciously off. By eleven, trade in the shop had reduced to a trickle but another problem arose. People wanted to collect and deliver ice blocks but that was no longer possible. There was no way to freeze anything on site; nothing but mains electricity could handle that task, and with Jim still in hospital, the bungalow at the site entrance was empty. Although Audrey explained the circumstances and promised to be available in the evening, it still caused inconvenience among the visitors, detracting from the normally good service offered. Some new method must be worked out.

Knowing Gordon's operation was due sometime after ten, Jan waited until the mobile shop had gone. With warmer weather and opening the fridge lid so much more often, a midday boost on the mains had become necessary to recharge it's freezer system. She was on her own now, having driven the vehicle and Audrey to the bungalow, then run back down the road, anxious about the unattended phone and office.

"Leave the shop here until the children come home," Audrey had suggested. "Send people who want something down to me, that way I can serve freezer packs as well. Not many will come back until after four o'clock anyway."

Jan had been pleased enough to accept the idea, though it was hardly ideal for it meant more cars parked in the entrance, which made the roadway look narrow. Under those circumstances, passing caravans often drove straight on, preferring somewhere more accessible. Now however, the system offered at least a breathing space, a chance to make that all-important call – the news she needed but feared.

"Yes," the nurse replied. "He is back from theatre. I'll pass you to sister."

A wave of panic swept over Jan as she gripped the phone. What couldn't the nurse tell her?

"Hello, Sister speaking. Your husband is sleeping. The operation appeared successful but naturally he'll be uncomfortable for a while. Normal visiting starts at six o'clock, I don't think there is much point in coming here earlier."

"Thank you." Jan put the phone down. Visiting? How could she? Would the children cope entirely alone? Another caravan arriving cut the thoughts until later.

Without the shop, that afternoon passed easily enough, though at least two phone calls had been missed. Twice the outside bell high on the gable wall had rung out while she ushered caravans to a pitch. With no hope of reaching the office in time, there was nothing to be done; but this possible loss of bookings resolved the question that had troubled her all afternoon – Chris would stay home tomorrow! Something else worried her too; one of those dogs had been running free again. She glared across in that direction but continued on, leading a tent to a pitch farther downstream. On returning, the dog was tied to the caravan, lying down apparently asleep. Annoyed but relieved, she marched by and back to the office.

When the children arrived home and they sat down together for tea the phone rang yet again as it had on and off all day. Jan rose, swallowing the food in her mouth and strode through to the office, lifting the receiver, "River Valley."

"I'd like to book a place in your bed."

"*Gordon*?!"

"Part of me. Someone's pinched a bit I'm told."

"I've missed you... do you love me?" Jan paused, listening, surprised when no immediate answer was offered. "Aren't you going to tell me so?"

"Well... I... I'll tell you when I get home."

"Oh, you're not alone? Someone might overhear, yes? Never mind, I'll let you off. How are you feeling? Is everything all right?"

"Something's painful, but there's this little nurse that comes to hold my hand..."

"Nothing wrong with you! I was coming in to see you tonight, now I'm not so sure."

"Don't! Don't leave the site. Is it running okay?" He sounded anxious.

"Yes. Oh, a little trouble with two dogs." Jan went on to explain in some detail, "but don't worry I'll handle it somehow. About visiting, it was always going to be difficult, are you sure..."

"Quite sure, honestly. The fellow in the next bed had the same op. Says he'll teach me chess later. I'll be fine, but can you really manage?"

"Of course! Everything is in hand. Audrey and I can cope. Think women are incapable do you?"

"Well..." he could hear laughter in her voice; that was good. "Women are okay I suppose, as long as there's no thinking. By the way, are the takings holding up?"

"Sure. I've told everyone it's all free until you recover..." she was cut off by a strangled gasp.

"What?"

"Relax. Don't give yourself a hernia too. Naturally the takings are all right, why wouldn't they be? Probably up a bit. Two and two do make five, don't they?"

"Can't stand intelligent women! I have to go, nurse is coming."

"Leave her alone."

"No, she wants the phone for someone else, it's on a trolley. Ring you again tomorrow."

Returning to the dining room with a great feeling of relief, Jan repeated the gist of the call before discussing arrangements for the coming days. Chris confirmed his last exam had taken place and there were no more that term, so a system was agreed; he and Sharon would take alternate days off, leaving Stephen to attend regularly.

Put to the test next day the arrangement worked tolerably well, Jan dashing between office and mobile shop, Chris pitching the caravans. Returning to the office on one occasion, he reported two dogs roaming free.

"Were they black and white small collie types?" Jan asked, almost sure that they would be. Receiving a nod she knew something had to be done, and decided the caravan concerned would have to leave. For a moment she sat, hands tapping nervously on the desktop, gathering her courage – suddenly looking up to find Chris watching her.

"Is something wrong, Mum?"

"No." She gave a sigh. "Yes, there is. Those dogs will have to go." She rose, striding to the door and grasping the handle but along the track another caravan was rolling towards them, a big heavy looking job. The dogs would have to wait. Good! But the reprieve could only be temporary. The towing car was a Range Rover type vehicle, an expensive outfit. Units of that size were the devil to push, she hoped he could reverse, and half expected a suit to appear, but the man who emerged and walked to the office was casually dressed.

"You take alsatians?" The voice was coarse, a touch uneducated perhaps, surprisingly different from what had been anticipated. Damn, more dogs! It was not something she normally felt, rather a reaction to the recent trouble.

"Yes, but they must be quiet and kept on a lead."

"They'll be on a lead. Never bark. Good as gold unless anyone tries to break in."

"Really?" Jan peered through the window at the car; two large canine faces waited behind the glass. Intimidating. "Hm. How long would you like?"

The man booked seven nights. Chris stepped forward to lead the way but Jan said no, she would take the gentleman personally. "Watch the office for me please Chris, I have just the place for this one."

Gordon rang again that evening.

"Hey. Guess who showed up here this morning – walked right in, must have travelled the 300 miles straight down..."

"I already know," Jan cut in. "Frank and Ivy, your Dad and Mum. Great to see them but I couldn't spend much time; had a great list of jobs waiting. There're down at the bungalow now, visiting Audrey. How are you feeling; any better yet?"

"Not too bad. If you need to contact me anytime, I'm in women's medical. Is everything going Okay?"

"Women's medical? You sure you're all right – not delirious?"

"Moved here an hour ago. My chess friend thinks we could make maternity if there's more emergency admissions. We're in a side ward, just the two of us, nurses swarming all over – must be the novelty value. I'm sore, but back on proper food tomorrow. Have to stay in at least until the stitches come out, sister says." He paused, then asked anxiously again. "Are those dogs still giving trouble?"

"Not any more. I put a pair enormous alsatians on the

next pitch."

"Is everything else okay?"

"Sure – so far. Not looking forward much to Saturday."

The alarm sounded at 5.45am. Jan came groggily awake, stretching out a hand to feel the empty bed beside her, then, awareness dawning, reached in the other direction, pressing a button on the clock and cutting the bell. Peeping through the curtains revealed six caravans already in the yard, one of them obstructing the bridge. She dressed quickly, waking Chris.

"We're in trouble. The yard is blocked... need to start pitching early. Put two caravans on the hardstanding on Area 10 as a temporary measure, take the one from the bridge and whichever other is easiest to move. Tell the drivers to come to the office in ten minutes. Wake Stephen."

With that she was off down the stairs, entering the smaller bedroom and shaking Sharon. "Never mind about breakfast, help me with the toilets. Use Dad's cleaning bucket; you do the Ladies."

Sharon was about to speak, but her mother had gone.

Finishing the first Gents in under five minutes, having skipped the mirrors and taps, Jan was crossing to the second when a couple of things caught her eye; another caravan coming down the road, and Stephen working on the dustbins.

"Here," She thrust the bucket of cleaning materials into the boy's hand and pointed. "Clean the other Gents, leave the bins for afterwards. Sharon's doing the Ladies, ask her what to do if you're not sure." Jan hurried off again, catching the caravan as it drew up. "Come straight into the office." Stepping quickly to another car where the occupants were asleep in their seats, she knocked on the window and as sleepy eyes opened, called, "We're ready now, come into the office," then hurried inside, catching a glimpse of Chris cleaning the waterwheel grid.

While booking in a woman from the most recently

arrived caravan and taking her money, the two families temporarily placed on hardstanding entered the office, closely followed by the man who had been asleep. Jan paused, three ten-pound notes still in her hand, speaking to all those crowded into the room.

"We don't usually start before eight o'clock because people are asleep but this is different, we must start early to avoid getting jammed in. You've probably guessed from the traffic it's the year's busiest day. Now it's only just gone six, so please be very quiet when you pitch. My son will guide you." Jan held out the change, pointing to Chris who had returned and stood ready by the door.

Clearing the queue, including a further motorcaravan and a tent that arrived, took three quarters of an hour. By this time Stephen had finished the dustbins and Sharon was already cooking; breakfast must be eaten before Jan went for the shop, there would be no time afterwards. It proved to be the last sit down meal until evening; even at midday when the mobile was driven off for an hour, a queue of arriving caravans prevented more than a quickly eaten sandwich. Shortly before seven o'clock the shop finally rested with Audrey at her bungalow for its overnight recharge. Returning on foot, Jan, who had not seen the site all day, took a quick walk round, scanning the various areas, leaving the boys controlling the office while Sharon cooked in the kitchen.

Even then the meal did not go without interruptions, but that was normal enough to be of little consequence. Afterwards they sat around talking.

"How did it go, Sharon?"

"Not too bad Mum. Gas was the main problem. In the end I took the money and let Stephen deal with the bottles. Even with the midday recharge, the ice cream was getting soft towards the end; I'd opened the fridge so many times. I sold that stale loaf!" Sharon looked pleased with herself.

"How much did you charge, half price?"

"Certainly not, Mum. Full price." Sharon lifted her

head in pride. "The woman picked up a fresh one and said she was buying it for the ducks. I told her they liked stale better – it didn't stick to their beaks so much."

Smiles broke out around the table, normal rivalry between the children suspended as they worked together in the crisis. Jan turned to Chris. "I see you filled all the spaces up by bluebell wood; the ones that catch shade in the evening. I should have thought those would be taken last."

Hearing the curiosity in his mother's voice, Chris tried to explain. "Dad said something to me once, something his father, Frank, taught him when he was young. Frank sold meat; now what was it he said...? *'Any fool can get rid of the best cuts, it's selling the rough that makes a butcher'*. I think that's true here too. None of our pitches are rough, but people do choose some more than others. Grass is always first choice in good weather for instance. I know we don't let the heavier motorcaravans go on grass, but it's easier just to say the hardstanding is more level and not so soft; they choose it then without being told. Those pitches you noticed up by the wood... most of the day they're in full sun. I tell them of the evening shadow, but I also say it's very sheltered if the wind blows, which is true." Chris stopped, spreading his hands with a shrug.

Even Sharon nodded, smiling approval. Jan, happy to see the whole team pulling together, smiled at her youngest.

"Well Stephen, you've had the easiest job, but the dustbins would have overflowed today without you. Will there be enough to last the week?"

"Yus. I made more room."

"How can you do that?"

"Plastic bottles, big ones." He held out two hands indicating the size. "Unscrew the lid, jump on the bottle, screw the lid back quick before more air gets in."

The days ticked by, none quite reaching the intensity of that Saturday, and then Gordon was home again. He only sat in the office answering the phone and taking money, but that extra pair of hands completely relieved the pressure. Strolling gently round in a slack period, discussing pitches with Chris, he pointed.

"You've done very well, but take that one. Its big front window is pointing directly towards another caravan; avoid that where you can, most people don't like to be so overlooked. Next week will be more difficult."

"Why?"

"Some of these will be leaving, and more arriving. You don't want to put another one back precisely where the first caravan stood because it ruins the grass, but if you've exactly twenty feet each side, its difficult not to. Try to leave such a space open for a few days. Sometimes it pays to leave more than the twenty feet in places, so you can change pitch positions. Extra space in the middle of a group is better than at one end, gives you more flexibility. Have a scout round mid-afternoon when everyone is out and give it some thought. I'm pleased though, with what you all managed to do."

"Sharon did well in the shop," Chris paused, surprised at himself, "She added all the money up on paper. Stephen did the dustbins. He's started squashing the aluminium cans, puts them under the pedestal drill with a block of wood on top of the can, then winds the empty chuck down. Got a gang of young boys helping."

"Trust Stephen. Any problems, any difficult customers?"

"One I sent back to Mum. Wasn't any trouble at all when he returned; couldn't find out what she said." Chris stopped, thinking back. "There was one that was my fault; a motorcaravan went out without leaving anything to mark his place, that wide pitch at the rear of Area Ten. I needed somewhere for a heavy oversize 'van and forgot the other one was coming back."

"Was he annoyed?"

"Yes. I offered him a spot on the other side, but he insisted on having the old pitch back. Said he'd paid for it and the other 'van must move."

"Did it?"

"No. I told him I'd put it there for safety because it had twin back wheels. Said some child had dropped a milk bottle and I wasn't sure all the pieces had been cleared up. He decided the other pitch was rather nice after all and perhaps he'd keep it."

"Good. You been listening to your mother?"

"Why?"

"Oh, nothing."

They made their way back to the office. Later at tea Jan asked, "How did you get them to let you out so soon? Sister said it might be another week."

"A little subterfuge." Gordon made to lean forward, chin on one hand, elbow on the table, but found it uncomfortable and eased back in the chair. "It happened like this. A nurse came dashing to our little side ward like they did every morning. *'He's coming; get into bed!'* she said, warning of the Consultant's approach; 'doing his rounds' as sister called it. We crossed towards our beds but when she hurried off to warn other patients I returned to the far side of the room, picked up a book and appeared to be reading. My chess friend warned I'd be in trouble and shortly afterwards the surgeon bustled through the door, two young white-coated men and sister in train. He glared at me in surprise, then momentarily shot an annoyed glance at sister. This was it then! I dashed across the room and jumped on the bed. It was painful, but in a good cause! The surgeon lifted a hand, pointing towards me, *'Look at him go, nothing wrong with him, discharge him right away.'* That's how I managed to escape!"

***

Later in the evening as they lay together that first night in bed, Jan challenged him again, "What did make them let you out early?"

"It was like I said... really, no kidding. I can still feel that pull as I jumped. Mind you, with minor fantasies over smart white uniforms and their contents, I almost decided to stay. It was only thoughts of you that made me go through with it! That reminds me, now we're alone I can say it... I do love you." He paused, leaning towards her, but feeling a twinge, reached out and with gentle pressure guided her closer until their lips touched. After a while he let go and continued. "While I think of it, those nurses... I've got their names all safely written down, Christian names too..."

"A little black book to go with those fantasies?" Jan interrupted, laughing lightly.

"You know better. I'd like to get them something, show appreciation; I thought medical scissors, a pair each with their names engraved on the handles. Can you fix it for me next time you're in Penzance?"

"Sure. Doesn't every wife buy presents for her husband's girl friends?" Leaning forward she kissed him again, aware there was no danger tonight – a shame really, it had been a long week sleeping alone. "I suppose you'll keep me waiting for ages; the lengths some men will go to for an excuse."

"Keep *you* waiting! Hm. Remember when we were courting, how long I had to wait?" Gordon asked gently. "Years! When did we first meet? You were fifteen. And when we did get serious, you still refused, even after we were engaged. I was in the RAF then, they sent me off to Hereford one winter. Some weekends I got a 48 hour pass and hitch-hiked all the way back, two hundred miles at least, starting Saturday morning and thumbing a lift in some big lorry; they were the easiest, the drivers wanted company. One man took me a hundred miles. *'I've been driving fifteen hours,'* he warned, *'Keep talking, you're only here to stop me falling asleep at the wheel. Remember, we're carrying sheet steel, if I hit anything it will come through this cab like a guillotine, slice us both in half – so keep talking.'* It was cold, there was ice and snow along the road edges, he could easily have slid into a tree. I should have got out then but knew you were waiting. That journey seemed to take forever. What time did

I get home; late wasn't it, after midnight? You remember, we were staying at Gran's at the time."

"How could I forget?" Jan snuggled closer. "Gran and Jack had gone to bed; I pretended to, but I couldn't sleep. Thought something must have happened. You'll never know the relief when you knocked at the door. No one *ever* came downstairs faster! I had that door undone and you slipped inside, all cold through my nightdress when you hugged me. You were wicked that night, you must have known how worried I'd been, and you took unfair advantage."

"Never."

"You did! *'Just 'til I get warmed up'*, you said. And I fell for it, had felt how cold you were and wanted to help... let you slip into bed with me – and you took advantage! We lay together for a long time before your hands began to move, they were warm again by then, too warm. I tried to resist, told myself it was wrong, that you *must* go... my mind wanted you to go but my body refused, wouldn't let me. I lay there in your arms, terrified, but I couldn't push you away. Something had happened inside, certain places became so sensitive. I'd never ever felt like that before. And your fingers, when they touched me... I burned! Something in my head screamed at me to stop, but your hand brushed a nipple through the thin material and I exploded... my whole body leapt! You must have felt it, must have known. Your fingers began moving downwards – it was agony, ecstasy! I had to push that hand away. I *had* too! I did reach for it, laid my hand across your knuckles, but couldn't resist... actually felt myself pushing the hand lower, breath coming in gasps, wanting you, dreading what might happen but frightened even more you might stop. Then the nightdress, my last protection was being drawn up; up until it drew tight under my bottom. I could have held it there, could have stopped you then, but you blew soft and warm against my cheek; it distracted me, made my lips turn. As we kissed I eased upward, letting the material slide past until it lay bunched at the

190

shoulder, my whole body exposed and vulnerable. You let the material go then but I couldn't make myself pull it back, just laid there holding my breath, waiting. Your hand brushed against me, playing, making little circles, now slow and firm, then softer, more delicate, everywhere so sensitive, working gradually downwards again. When you touched the top of my bare thigh I clench my legs together tightly... your fingers caressed the skin, so light, not forcing; here, there, always moving – a feather touch. I called 'stop' but no sound came out and I didn't want you to stop... longed for you to press harder. My legs loosened, couldn't prevent them, one moved sideways, I swear it did it by itself. I could feel you; your... your shape... hot against my skin, warning me, but I was powerless – and all the while your fingers touched me. When you found the spot, my back arched; I think I cried out then, could have been in my head again. I throbbed, heart raced, and I wanted you – how I wanted you!

After a while I couldn't resist, you could do anything, my hands pulled you towards me, you came; the weight was heavenly. I was panting; it hurt a little when you broke through, but I didn't care... could feel you inside. My hands, fingers, raked your back, must have left nail marks; I was arching to meet you, something inside mounting, wanting – and then you called my name, a soft urgent whisper, our cheeks together. Suddenly a new warmth filled me, a delicious lovely warmth like nothing ever felt before, and you went limp. I didn't want that weight ever to go." Jan sighed, easing her grip on his hand, and for a while they lay together remembering.

The passing years had changed that first love. It was no less deep, but not so urgent. Sex now was for pleasure, not the pressing necessity it had been that first night.

"Do you remember how quietly we crept to the bathroom afterwards?" Gordon spoke in a whisper, still holding her hand. "I'm sure Gran knew. She always pretended not to, but she must have. You were my first too, you know. Nearly three years we'd been courting, you've got to respect a girl who resists that long. Good job I was in the forces and knew about protection. The other men were always boasting of their conquests and the precautions they took not to get lumbered... their words not mine!" He held up a hand defensively, Jan's arm raised to thump him clearly visible in the full moon's light shining through the window; but it was only a game. They understood each other so well, she would pretend to hit, he would feign fear.

Reaching forward she kissed him gently, "So that's how you happened to have that packet of Durex in your pocket that day. As a girl educated in a convent I should have objected, but as a mother, planning the time has been far better for the children. Anyway, good job you were prepared, I could never have stopped you, protection or not – but I've never regretted it. Hope you didn't boast about it to your boys back at camp, though in a way I'd have been proud to be thought your conquest. Boys do always exaggerated when they talk about women don't they; bigger..." she reached out drawing his hand closer until it rested lightly on her chest, "what do you call them in the forces?"

"Knockers – and other things; but no, I didn't breathe a word, even though I took a lot of stick for not having 'scored' of a weekend. I almost told Gran that first time."

"You didn't! I could never have shown my face again if she mentioned it. Whatever made you think of doing that."

"Not in words, I left the empty Durex packet under the bed, forgot it in the heat of the moment. Well you would, wouldn't you! It's not every day an innocent young chap like I was, gets seduced."

"I never...! Mind you, only because I didn't need to; might have done that night – if you had stopped!"

"Good job I didn't then. Not that I could have. The excitement, it was..." unable to find the words, he squeezed her hand again. "I only remembered that empty packet just before starting back for camp after Sunday lunch. Eighteen hours together, that's all we had on those weekends. Do you remember seeing me off, how we clung together as if parting was forever."

"Seemed like that to me." Jan sighed. "I fancied you again then, when you were leaving, could feel myself becoming moist, something inside, churning, wanting. You couldn't get a pass the following week; the time seemed to drag that fortnight. When you next came home, I could hardly wait. You were earlier, found a better lift, but Gran insisted on cooking you a meal. Sitting there watching you eat, waiting – that was torment. I'm sure she knew, was smiling to herself. When we got upstairs, I couldn't get my clothes off quickly enough. We had about twenty hours before you must return; there's never been a night like that. Five times! Five times we managed, the last one when you were about to leave and popped back upstairs on the pretext that your tie was crooked. You didn't even undress. That uniform was so coarse against my skin, made me feel really wicked – I loved it! I remember you bending over afterwards, picking up that empty packet, slipping it into your top pocket – don't tell me you never boasted about *that* night to the boys!"

"I never did." Gordon went quiet for a while, looking into space. Jan watched him, a shadow of a face in the soft light, not speaking until a far away smile forming on his lips piqued her curiosity, "What are you thinking?"

"I've never told you this. The lad's teased me quite a bit at camp. Because I never talked of our little indiscretions they assumed you never..." he paused, smiling up at her, "*'came across'* is the way they put it. Many boosted of a conquest, one or two of scoring more than once over the weekend. They'd discovered I had a girlfriend. I left my locker undone one day and they found your photo..."

"I know where you keep it." Aware he still found it painful to stretch, Jan leaned over again to kiss him softly,

193

"I found it one day years ago. You didn't think I knew? It's still there... stuck in the front of your air force bible. I look at it sometimes, is that where it was then?"

"Yes." He went quiet again for a while, embarrassed perhaps. "Yes, they read your name and made jokes about iceberg girl and not having what it takes – remarks that recurred regularly after each weekend away when I still didn't boast of having 'made it!' In a way they were right. Before that first night I probably was the only chap there who hadn't... who was still... pure?" Hearing a quiet ripple of laughter and feeling her head rest on his shoulder, he continued. "One evening after we'd been lovers for several months, a group of us were playing a card session, others standing behind the chairs in groups, chatting with each other and watching the game. There's a lot of camaraderie in the forces and usually someone regularly comes in for ridicule in a more or less friendly manner. It's hard to combat; the only way usually is to laugh with the others at the jokes at your own expense. If you take umbrage, that only makes them laugh louder. We were sitting round a big table on that Sunday evening, everyone back from their weekend leave, all still in number-one uniforms. A few had discarded their tunics but the billet was cold, the stove only just relit after the 48-hour break. As always, many conquests were being paraded and boasted about; tales of film-star like blondes, or redheads with insatiable appetites, told in a casual macho manner as if it were par for the course, a regular accomplishment. Many were probably true – the uniforms will do it! One claimed a vicar's daughter, his manner challenging the others to cap that for achievement. As the tales unrolled, the tellers, having displayed their own prowess, sought for less fortunate victims to be the butt of some jibe. You and I of course, came in for the usual banter. You know the sort of thing. One chap enquired, *'Think you'll make it by next Christmas?'*. Another asked more crudely in a Welsh accent, *'Checked lately, still got one have you man?*

194

Someone to the right enquired, *'This girl of yours, not under age is she, not still waiting for her sixteenth?'* " Gordon paused, the events of that evening so clear in memory.

"I was actually eighteen then," Jan whispered. "A really innocent eighteen. Did you just sit there and let them carry on?"

"I might have. It was good-natured enough, no nastiness in the taunts; young men you know – tough, fit, back from the hunt and full of high spirits, the talk non-stop. Some shouted their comments, others chatted more quietly to someone nearby – all so sure of themselves, in their prime, everyone around that table so vital, so very full of life. Those teasing remarks were directed more at you than me, nothing bad, nothing really offensive, just the suggestion that you were hardly worth the effort. They were so wrong... it couldn't go unchallenged. I reached into my top tunic pocket and grasped all those empty Durex packets we'd been so careful not to leave under the bed. Even then I was doubtful, it was our secret. I sat there gripping those little squares tighter... and on an impulse my hand came away lifting them clear. I was committed then, reaching forward to spread them in an arc with a single sweep of the hand – must have been thirty or forty. The silence was shattering. Conversation stopped like someone turning off a light! Perhaps twenty chaps around that table, stared, not a movement between them. These were hard young men, muscular and fit, most with a string of conquests of their own, but not one of them spoke.

I said nothing, just looked round the circle, meeting their eyes. Usually one outbid the other as the stories were told, but no one could top this. One or two reached forward to finger the packets, inspecting them, but they were real. Every person in that billet was familiar with the label; those little squares were a greater symbol of achievement than stripes on your arm! The Commanding Officer couldn't have created a greater impression. I doubt there was one man present who didn't wish you were his girl at that moment. If I'd had a big picture of you it would have taken over from Jane Russell beside the door for everyone to pat your bottom as they left the billet."

Gordon stopped, a shadowy gesture of his hands saying that was all. Jan reached across, smacking him gently but her eyes were shining in the moonlight.

CHAPTER 11

Brandy

Several days passed, family life gradually returning to normal, the children gaining more free time to take advantage of many friends, old and new, now staying on the site. The two troublesome dogs had stopped running loose and at mid-week they left without saying goodbye. The big alsatians that had deliberately been pitched next to them, behaved impeccably, causing no trouble to anyone. When the man came in to book three extra nights, Jan apologised saying she hoped the other dogs had not caused trouble.

"You mean that sour couple who left this morning? They didn't bother me. One of their dogs pushed its way into our awning and my pair went for it; they couldn't quite reach, their tethers were too short but it shot off with a yelp. A man came round then to complain. My dogs just sat there, didn't move but showed their teeth and growled a bit – made him nervous. My wife asked how he'd like it if our dogs ran free and visited his awning. We never heard another word... never saw his mutts free again either."

Jan couldn't resist a smile as the man left. She had hoped for something like that – so great when a plan came together. It was early afternoon, the easiest time of day with most arrivals already pitched and many people still at the beach; they were taking advantage of this brief respite to relax in comfortable chairs. Returning to join Gordon in the lounge she glanced upstream through the window. "That's unusual. Look, there's Melville walking down the road with Randy. Let's meet him on the bridge."

Melville Lawrey, owner of Gurlyn, the neighbouring farm, more often dropped by in his Land Rover. They hurried out and walked to the bridge, calling a greeting.

"Hello there stranger, long time since you've walked down. Lost a horse or something?" Gordon bent stroking Randy who had run ahead. The dog paused, wagging a tail, then headed off into the bushes.

"Exercise!" Melville strode up, halting at midstream, one foot on the parapet. He seemed slightly breathless. "This road is longer on foot, I'm taking the short way back, across the fields."

Jan asked after his wife Ethel and her son Tommy but the outside phone bell high on the gable wall sounded. Excusing herself she ran off leaving the men discussing harvest prospects. The call was from a regular visitor wanting to know if they could come tomorrow.

"Yes, do. We've plenty of space, have a good journey. Yes, early afternoon will be fine." Putting the phone down and making notes on a pad, she went to the window, wondering whether to rejoin the men now chatting by the waterwheel. Deciding they would call if her company was wanted, she took some bread to feed the ducks. Outside a dog broke from the bushes and bounded towards two elderly well-dressed ladies throwing crumbs on the water from the bridge.

A great shout rang out. "Randy!" Melville had a remarkably strong penetrating voice! The dog veered away towards its master as Jan reached the bridge.

"What did he say?" one woman demanded, standing stiffly upright, her voice a mixture of condemnation and outrage.

"Calling his dog... Brandy, I believe. You know; after the little barrels carried by those big mountain-rescue dogs. Er, St Bernard's!" Jan lied a little. "What did you think he said?"

The lady offered a cold unfriendly stare, turning to her

companion. "Come." They strode off without a parting word, noses in the air as if something unmentionable might lurk nearby. Jan watched for a moment then hurried towards the men. Melville, having seen the exchange and guessed the cause, was laughing.

"Get a little skittish, did she? Highly bred mares will sometimes. I like your wheel but what you really need is a windmill. I've got one down at Varfell Farm."

Gordon and Jan looked at each other. Did they really need a windmill? What for?

"It's cheap!" Melville encouraged, smiling.

"Cheap? I was hoping you'd offer it free." Gordon smiled back.

"I bet you do! Go and look at it." And with that he left, heading back for the bridge still chuckling, raising a hand in acknowledgement as a few final words were called back and forth, drowned eventually by the engine noise of an arriving caravan.

***

"Do you have a mantle for my gas light?" a woman asked.

Sharon was scribbling numbers on a slip of paper, moving each item across the counter and speaking the price aloud; she reached for a box on the shelf behind. "How many, just one?" Receiving a nod, a small cardboard cube with a picture of a mantle on the side was extracted, passed over and its price added to the list. This customer was the last, a queue that had stretched half across the yard finally dispersed. The woman paid and as she left, stepping down onto the tarmac, the shop rocked gently on its wheels. Sharon watched her go then bent to peer through a window towards the house. Her mother had several people in the office and two caravans stood waiting in the yard; no point in dashing over to make coffee yet.

Saturday had come again with another wave of arrivals. Chris was showing caravans to a pitch; Dad was pitching too, but he was slower and as yet unable to push if

199

someone failed to reverse properly. They appeared round the toilet building, father and son talking together and walking towards the parked caravans. One family were still in the office but three people stood waiting by the other outfit.

Thinking the man's face familiar, Gordon asked, "How good are you at reversing?"

"Terrible. We were up the hill last year, can we go there again?" A hand pointed.

"Sure. I'm not allowed to push. Appendix; had it out two weeks ago. Chris will take you, he's pretty strong now." Gordon turned, "Okay?"

Chris, not yet fully grown at fifteen, could push as hard as many men. He nodded confirmation, waited while everyone climbed in the car, then walked off signalling the driver to follow. A pause at the foot of the hill gave the visitors time to ask which pitches were still free and choose the spot they wanted – better to know beforehand, stopping halfway up was dodgy. Having made a selection, the man pointed and climbed back in. Chris ran ahead up the steep stone track, swinging into the first terrace, a broad grassy step in the hillside; three caravans were already backed up against a dry-stone wall, a wall that supported the terrace above. Running backwards he beckoned the driver on until at a signal, the car drew to a halt. The outfit now rested in a straight line along the outer edge, a few feet from a ten-foot drop to the level below. The caravan must be unhitched, swung through ninety degrees and pushed back to take its position in line with the others. This arrangement gave everyone clear views across the valley.

Most pitches were entirely flat but those carved into the hillside had been given a slight forward slope to insure any rain ran quickly away and no water was trapped. The gradient, slight enough not to be immediately noticeable, soon became obvious when they swung the caravan round then tried to force it backwards. The man was rather old

200

and not very strong. The women, a wife and sister also well beyond retirement age, made no attempt to push. That was expected; it was one of the reasons so many retired people came to the site – they could always expect help when pitching.

"Put the brake on hard," Chris advised as he held the weight, and seeing this done, straightened up, searching for something suitable. To one side of the grassy area, the stone wall swung forward in an arc and tapered down to a heap of loose rocks. Walking across he lifted one and carried it back, dropping the granite close to the caravan then bent down to manoeuvre it under one wheel.

"To stop us rolling over the edge?" one of the women asked with amusement.

"Makes it lighter to push." Chris moved to the other side, taking up position, and speaking to the man. "If we move this wheel up the slope first, the caravan will slew sideways but we'll only be moving half the weight. Can you pull from the back or would you prefer to push sideways on the hitch? Let the brake off first, I've got the weight."

Releasing the lever, the man hurried to the rear, trying at first to pull straight but soon understanding the movement must swing to one side. At Chris's request the wife stepped forward to pull the brake on again. Transferring the stone to the other wheel, the procedure was repeated, slewing in the other direction. Quite quickly the caravan sat in its intended position.

By the time Chris returned, the yard was empty except for the mobile shop with Sharon and a customer inside. As he entered to office calling his return, Jan came through from the kitchen

"Dad's taken the other caravan off downstream; it had a dog. That reminds me, someone near Bluebell Wood called in, I meant to tell you earlier. Says there's a large dropping near his caravan – see if you can remove it. There's a note of his car number somewhere on the desk.

Don't be long, I'm making coffee while we have the chance; tell Sharon on the way back. Oh, if you get time later, check the riverbank for droppings too. Dad still finds it painful to stoop."

Somehow the coffee never materialised. Two tents arrived together, followed by a stream of other visitors and a complaint about the showers that seemed miraculously to fix itself without any adjustment. Someone else wanted to change pitches because of a neighbour. More customers calling in for various bits and pieces, or information and advice took them through until the shop was driven off to Jim's bungalow for its midday refreezing session on the mains. Only at lunch with a sign on the door designed to deter the impatient, did the family get chance to sit again and chat. Never mind, it *was* Saturday; they were lucky to find time for a meal at all.

The day passed happily enough but late the following morning, trouble with the showers recurred. A customer rang the office bell, someone who had spent a holiday on site the previous year, a young lady well remembered for her attractive attire and somewhat cheeky outlook. Her dress this year was less scanty but something mischievous still lurked in the expression as she asked, "What has happened to your showers?"

"Is something wrong. Are they cold? Nobody told us." Gordon reached for the matches, it was months since a pilot jet had blown out.

"No, not exactly. You always said come round if anything was not quite right. Well I started to shower, it was lovely as always but much less power than usual, not so much water, not that it really mattered although I do like the force your showers give. There was someone in the next compartment too, but when they finished their shower, mine suddenly went cold. I stood to one side, reaching to turn the hot tap up full and the cold right down, but it made no difference. I've never rinsed soap away so fast! I turned off and got dressed, there seemed

202

nothing else to do – well I couldn't very well walk round here naked, could I? – might embarrass someone." She paused, "I really wanted to wash my hair. Can you fix it?"

"Probably. We're quite busy, could you be my chaperone so Jan can stay in the office?"

"Chaperone?"

"I don't generally barge into the Ladies unless someone checks first and gives me the all-clear. You might like to see the cause of the trouble? If it's what I expect, then I can show you; we had something similar a few years ago." Gordon put the matches in his pocket, adding a screwdriver, a small wrench and an adjustable spanner. Calling through to the kitchen asking Jan to take over, he followed the lady out, starting across the yard but not directly towards the entrance doors. "Hang on a minute, I'll check the pilot light." He ran to the service passage, entered and looked quickly at the second gas burner, the one controlling water to the showers. The pilot jet was alight but the roar of the main burners absent. Good, it was working but no one was taking a shower at the moment – or if they were, it was a cold one! Hurrying back, he explained to the waiting young woman and they walked together round the building to the entrance door, a little black silhouette figure in a skirt painted on the white surface indicating Ladies. The woman smiled at him. "Do you want everyone out?"

"No, just warn them, see that they're decent and er... stop me being attacked."

A sharply indrawn breath and her expression indicated surprise before the smile burst through. "Nervous?"

"Always!" Gordon watched her disappear, the door automatically swinging shut but there were voices inside, little ripples of laughter. Ah! He had hoped it would be empty so near to midday. Still at this time of year it was only to be expected; most grassy pitches were already full and not everyone went to the beach; a few stayed in the valley, laying back on loungers to relax and unwind. The door opened again and a hand beckoned. He slipped inside

203

and stopped. Two other women were waiting, not doing anything, not using the facilities, not even washing their hands, but waiting and watching him. They were young, early twenties probably, his chaperone the oldest at perhaps twenty-five. There was something disconcerting in those expressions; amusement certainly, but was there more? He wondered for a moment about coming back later but pushed the thought aside, unable to bring himself to allow any site facility to remain faulty.

"Hm... I'll uh... I'll test it first." He stepped sideways, still facing the women, moving carefully in a circular arc around them and keeping as much space between himself and the audience as the layout of the building would allow then asked, "Which cubicle did you use?"

The hand that had beckoned him in pointed again, this time to the nearer shower. Turning the water on while fully dressed would inevitably mean a wet arm, especially as this would not be one quick twist – for a proper test the hot tap must be opened fully; half a dozen turns at least. It would be sensible to undo the cuff and roll the sleeve up first, but he hesitated to do anything that would expose more bare flesh under the present circumstances. Leaving the button fastened, the arm reached in, the wrist rotated and water cascaded down. By no means was it falling with the usual force; an ordinary feeble shower not the satisfying deluge this system normally gave. Seeing the women move closer to watch, he hurriedly explained. "Usually it will run hot within five seconds, the heater is only just behind the wall, it hasn't far to come, but let's give it a minute to make sure. I'm not taking up your time, am I. You must have other things to do?"

Three heads shook. One woman asked, "When will we ever get another chance to watch a man in a lady's shower? Your shirt is all wet, it's clinging to your arm and..."

"I think that's a good enough test," Gordon swung back towards the shower, nervously thrusting the dry arm in by mistake. He wished she hadn't said that, they'd be selling tickets next. Realising the error the arm was quickly withdrawn, the other hand reaching in to stop the flow.

"Right. Now for the repair." He stepped in, reaching upward... "Ouch!" That appendix op still made itself felt when stretching. Something to stand on, just a few extra inches. Where...? Stepping back outside the cubicle he looked past the three women and there on the floor beneath the basins stood the very thing. He glanced up at the faces and down at the floor again – there was no way he was pushing past, then bending to pick it up, exposing his posterior as a temptation to nimble feminine fingers! Naughtiness was written clear in those watching eyes!

"Could I er... could I have one of those footstools?" A tentative hand pointed to the small wooden stools about six inches high, placed for children to stand on when using the basins. The youngest woman reached for one, going down gracefully with straight back rather than bending over; about nineteen or twenty he guessed, revising his estimate, noticing how the half-length skirt draped over a thigh as her knees bent.

Reaching out at arm's length to take the stool when it was offered, he slid quickly back into the cubicle. It gave that extra height needed to reach the shower rose, a few twists releasing the chromium head with all its little perforations. Taking it to a basin, he unscrewed the face plate and laid it to one side, then banged the main part hard against his open palm, holding it out for all to see. A liberal covering of coarse sandy grains coated the skin. "That's your culprit. The Water Board have done a repair somewhere and gravel has crept in. Because we're in the valley, the flow of water carries it more easily downhill and it ends up here. These little specs block the showers. Look." he lifted the small disk, holding it up to the light. A good percentage of the holes were blocked. Washing under the tap and banging it against one palm removed most; a pin brought along for the purpose, stuck in the end of his shirt collar would do the rest. While clearing the holes he continued to explain. "The water is heated by instantaneous gas burners, that way it never runs out. The gas lights up automatically when the water runs – but if it runs too slowly the water would get scalding hot. Under those circumstances a safety device cuts the gas; that's what has happened here. These little specks..." he cleared another hole and blew on the surface, inspecting it closely for more, "these blocked holes reduce the water flow until the gas cuts off. If two showers are in use, then enough water is flowing and it keeps working; that's what gave me the clue and..."

The door flew suddenly open and a child, six or seven years old, burst in.

"Mummy, Daddy's waiting! He sent me to fetch you."

"Tell him I won't be long."

"What are you doing?" the young girl looked with round eyes towards Gordon and at the other women. "Shall I tell him you're in here with a man?"

"Yes, you go and tell him that. Tell him we've not quite finished yet."

The child ran off and the door swished closed again leaving the women laughing together as Gordon hurriedly re-entered the cubicle, intent on restoring the shower head and making good his escape! He had intended cleaning the other shower too but it suddenly seemed prudent to leave that one for later; much later – midnight maybe!

As he fumbled with the screwdriver refixing the perforated plate, whispers and giggling behind intensified; it was a surprise that fully grown women indulged in such things. Now to refix the rose; even with the footstool it was high and awkward. Stretching up to screw it on, he concentrated totally on the difficult task, standing on tip-toe, striving not to turn it cross-thread, not seeing a naughty female arm slide forward. Suddenly, the hand touched, running rapidly up the inside of his leg... "Oh!!" A jerk ran through his body, the rose dropping with a clatter as he twisted urgently away before those soft and delicate fingers reached... "Ah!" The stool overbalanced, a flying hand grabbed the tap and clung there as a gale of laughter swept through the building. Heart pounding he hung, suspended by one arm, feet scrabbling for grip, his eyes on three jubilant faces in the doorway. Catching his breath and finding a foothold he pulled himself upright, pointing with the free arm over their heads to the far ceiling, "Look!"

As they turned, he threw himself forward, slamming the door and sliding the bolt! What now? Trapped in his own toilet by a few slips of girls – more than girls, he admitted; one was a mother. Yes! And her husband would know by now that she was in the Ladies with a man! Would he dare to enter? An ally perhaps, a means of escape... or would the wife point a finger and say *"he's in there!"*

He sought to push the thought aside, automatically stooping to recover the shower rose then reaching up to refit it, lecturing himself silently, "Don't be silly, it was only high spirits, a holiday laugh; they would surely explain to the husband?"

The outer door opening brought a stiffening of his muscles; crunch time, the husband had arrived! But it was female voices that sounded, several of them, a further group of women had obviously entered – reinforcements! He put an ear to the polished wooden door, listening.

"...believe it. There's a man hiding in the shower!"

Nervously he looked up, half expecting to see a head poke over the surrounding walls which were perhaps seven feet in height.

"*Is* there?" A new, older, sterner voice demanded. "Lend me your bowl, Hilda."

The sound of running water galvanised him into action! Quickly wrenching the shower head tight, he brushed nervous fingers tentatively over the wet shirt, gave a small nod of determination, then screwdriver in one hand, spanner in the other, opened the door and stepped out.

"There. That should be fine now ladies. Let the office know if you have any more trouble." With that Gordon nodded, forced a smile, reached for the outer handle and quickly left. The door didn't swing shut behind him as expected and he sensed they were holding it open, still watching. Without hesitation he pushed on the next door stepping into the Gents. Sanctuary! Was this how persecuted men of the past felt on reaching a church? Surely this place was sacrosanct from females!

He decided against returning to the office immediately, putting a hand to one cheek and feeling the warmth. If that Ladies shower was blocked, then every shower head on the site was probably affected. Collecting a footstool he entered the first compartment.

Back in the office, Jan wondered what was taking so long; she had started to prepare the meal and wanted to get on. After twice checking through the window, she hurried across to the mobile shop, which at the moment had no customers. The figure leaning against the counter, head inclined downwards, was obviously reading a book.

"Sharon, have you seen Dad?"

"No." The head shot up.

"He went to fix a shower. Watch the office while I check." Jan walked briskly across the yard and round the corner. A minute or so earlier would have found Gordon still in the Ladies, but instead she encountered only a group of women talking animatedly, but silence fell as she entered, silence and some half-concealed smiles as many pairs of eyes followed her progress to the showers, then back towards the door.

"Lost anything?" A laughing voice enquired.

Sensing that something had happened and not wanting to appear to concerned, Jan stopped with a hand on the door, "Only a husband, nothing important."

No response was forthcoming but wicked merriment

hung in the air. She pulled on the handle and stepped outside, catching sight of a small boy sitting on the big excavator in the rear of the dustbin area, but said nothing and strode back to the office.

"Stephen, your little friend is round in the dustbin yard playing on Max. Go and stop him please."

Twenty minutes later Gordon entered the office, his complexion long since returned to normal. "I've fixed that shower, it was grit in the head. The four Gents showers are done too. Three in the Ladies still need attention, can we set the alarm for 5.30 tomorrow."

"No. Six o'clock is early enough. Sharon can get up and help."

"Sharon will want to clean the Ladies and you'll go off to the Gents. That's not what I had in mind. I'd rather you were with me in the morning." He listened for a moment to Jan's suspicious reply, before protesting, "No, it's just that I like your company. Better with only the two of us, I can fix those shower heads and we can talk at the same time."

"What did happen out there?"

"Happen... Ah, almost forgot. Time to drive the shop down to Jim's." He took the key and made for the door.

August was busy, not so much with extra customers for numbers were similar to the previous year, but the shop added work and was a mixed blessing. People were pleased that milk and bread was now available most of the day, and a certain number of groceries too, but the range was limited and customers wanted more. Fruit and fresh veg were asked for, and postcards, books and many varieties of breakfast cereal. The range of stock had gradually increased but entailed extra journeys to cash-and-carry; yet another chore to fit somehow into busy days.

Jan was on such a trip early one afternoon while the shop was still up at Jim's bungalow for its midday re-freeze.

209

Sharon, alone in the office, booked in an arriving tent asking it to wait, since Dad was already pitching a caravan and would be back shortly. They were talking about the bird carvings on the tree behind the desk when a couple already on site stopped in to extend their stay.

"Another two nights please, that takes us up to include next Saturday."

Sharon consulted to book and found the name. "No. Two nights will only include Friday."

"We've paid for five already, two more will make seven. We didn't arrive until Saturday, so seven days must take us to Saturday again. Yes?"

Sharon checked back through the book. "No, there's only one Saturday night in a week. If you want to leave Sunday morning, it's three days."

"She is right you know." The waiting tent standing on one side, spoke up, causing the couple to turn. "Not just a pretty face eh?"

When Gordon returned, the three visitors were chatting together round the desk, happily including Sharon in the conversation, pleased to take advantage of her knowledge of the area. They left together and stood talking outside until the tent was led away to his pitch, the couple driving off up the road. Sharon watched them go, smiling with satisfaction. Chris had gone out earlier with a boy and two girls; Stephen too was away today, they took turns at being on duty now that Dad was almost recovered. Her brothers might or might not return for tea, but at sometime during the evening a chance to relate the incident was bound to occur.

Busy days moved on, good weather, happy faces. At tea one Thursday towards the end of August, Chris spoke as he severed a sardine and cut off a section of toast.

"Dad, I think there's a rat in the service passage. It lives among those spare roof tiles stored under the work bench; plays on the bench surface too, you can see the droppings."

"Get the Council's pest control man in," Jan suggested

Dad shook his head. "Have a van with 'Rodent Control' painted all over it standing in the yard? Not likely. We'll do it ourselves. Rescue one of those four-inch pipes from behind the dustbin yard for me please Chris, and carry it to the passage. If we put rat-poison in a plastic tub then slide it halfway along the pipe, nobody's pet cat will reach it. I'll leave a small dish of water in there too."

"It's cruel." Sharon murmured. "Why water?"

"Cruel maybe, but they carry disease and I don't think there is a kinder way. That's what the rodent man would do and he might not be so careful. Why water you ask? Well it's necessary to rats, they have to drink. Mice are different; live largely on moisture from the things they eat; anyway mice are no problem. Remember our mouse?" Dad turned towards Chris who had brought the creature home, "I wonder what happened to it. Your friend leaves tomorrow, doesn't she?"

Chris nodded. Many were leaving, numbers beginning to fall. All the children had lost friends recently but were themselves free most of the time now, no longer required to stay on call. It was only fair; they had worked hard through the earlier emergency and still helped occasionally with the mobile shop. This facility was proving more time consuming than anticipated. Though a queue still formed in the mornings, most of the day saw few customers but the service could not now be withdrawn – visitors liked it, found it convenient. As always, expectations were rising, comments had shown that other sites were also getting their own shops; not having one would soon be considered substandard. Buying the mobile had been the right decision but certainly the drawbacks had been underestimated! Apart from the regular re-freezing trips, there were other disadvantages. If a customer came while Gordon was pitching, it dragged Jan away leaving the office unattended. It worked in reverse too; she had lost count of the times that ringing phone had made her dash back to the office, leaving a customer alone in the shop. Sometimes she failed to make it and the caller rang off as she reached for the receiver; that was really annoying but one person could not be in two places at once! The family were discussing these problems again, wondering if an extension phone could somehow be fitted in the vehicle, but it seemed impractical and Jan changed the subject.

"What is tall, old and useless?" she smiled at the young faces then swung deliberately towards Gordon. The children followed her gaze, grinning broadly, four pairs of eyes regarding Dad intently.

"Not me! Mum's talking about the windmill, the one we discussed several weeks ago. Will the three of you take charge tomorrow morning for an hour while Mum and I pop off together to see what it's like?"

Mill was really the wrong word. When watching the sails of a wind machine, the word windmill came naturally to mind, but only those used in milling, working the large corn grinding stones, were actually windmills. This one pumped water and was therefore a wind-pump to name it correctly, but like everyone else, the family called it a windmill.

Since the day when Melville from the neighbouring farm had walked down the valley with his dog and offered it to them, the family had discussed the prospect often. 'What you want is a windmill,' he had said. But did they? If so, certainly no one had ever realised it before – didn't know where to put it anyway. "Go and see it," Melville had said as he left.

"Yes. Thanks, we'll pop in and look... sometime next month when things quieten down a bit," Gordon had called at the retreating back, playing for time to consider. A chance to inspect it was fine, carrying no obligation – offering a space to think, to find perhaps an excuse to say "No," without seeming ungrateful, for Jan and Gordon both liked him. Having themselves grown used to being tactful with customers, Melville's blunt way of saying exactly what he thought regardless, had its own appeal. Did it come from close contact with farm animals? They, at least, were seldom in a position to argue.

The wind-pump was five miles away by road; finding the route took some twenty minutes at mid-morning the next day. Viewing the tall metal tower, Jan was doubtful. It stood dilapidated, derelict and gaunt.

"I don't like it much." She turned towards him, shaking her head.

He said nothing for a while, gazing up at the old structure, trying to visualise how it had once looked, then stretched out an arm, pointing, "You see that big sail, we could paint River Valley on it. After renovation and in the right setting... say behind the house, it could be exactly right; a little piece of history like the valley itself."

Jan watched his face, seeing the enthusiasm grow, heard it in the voice; he could seldom resist a challenge that involved building. She looked back up at the bleak tower, suppressed a little shudder, and nodded.

"You may be right. It could grow on me after a while."

She watched him smile, and smiled back. If he liked it, she would give way, as he so often gave way to her. Love was more than just physical attraction.

Guessing her thoughts, he made a promise. "If you really dislike it when it's finished, I'll take it down again! But don't expect anything fast; this old wreck will take time to get back to working order."

Jan raised her eyebrows questioningly, scanning him up and down.

"The windmill, not me! I'm fully recovered... well almost," he rubbed his side where the stitches had been, then pulled her closer, kissing gently below the right ear and whispering, "You knew exactly what I meant, so you can forget that innocent expression. Anyway, I have to see Melville first and agree a price; it might be too expensive. If we do get it, remember what I said, it will take a long

213

time. This is only a hobby, it comes second to all our other work."

On arriving home, the children had so many questions, they were bundled into the car and whisked back to Varfell Farm where the relic stood. Jan, hiding her doubts, stayed behind preparing the midday meal. Later, as they ate, Chris was enthusiastic, keen on the idea and volunteering help with the dismantling, asking how it would be done.

During the discussions Jan said little, a nod here and there but remaining unusually quiet, face puckered in a slight frown of concern for her son's safety. He was almost a young man now, she could not reasonably object, did not want to be seen treating him as a child – but almost wished not to have seen the height of that tower. She was worried for Gordon too, knowing he didn't like heights, aware that having once decided he would force himself to climb. The job would be pretty well impossible to manage single handed and she certainly had not the slightest intention of climbing up herself! She would have to let Chris help. Best say nothing, restrain the urge to caution them to take care; the height itself would do that. By the time they reached the top of that narrow rusty iron ladder fixed to the outside of the tower, their fingers would be clinging to the metalwork tighter than barnacles to a rock. In spite of this resolve, thoughts were already forming in her mind of the best way to raise the question of safety when she got Gordon alone – in bed tonight might be the best time. Suddenly she became aware that he was speaking again.

"...don't think so. You'd better ask your mother."

"Ask me? Ask me what?"

"Stephen wants to help. I think he's too small to climb on the tower – certainly the first time, until we get to know what the problems are."

"I could stand on the ground," Stephen offered quietly, not to anyone in particular, a thought muttered aloud.

"I don't think so," Jan shook her head. Letting Chris go was bad enough, certainly her youngest was not getting

214

involved; she had witnessed too often his casual attitude to risk! "Things could drop from the top, a piece of metal, anything... it wouldn't be safe. Like Dad says, certainly not until they check just how difficult dismantling it will be. You stay here with Sharon and me; see if they come back in one piece." Those last words were unintended, Jan had meant to say nothing about safety but her concerns had somehow slipped out, disguised though they were as a joke. Seeking now to divert attention, she asked Sharon, "You don't want to help too, do you?"

"No thank you! I've seen it. I think they're stupid."

A phone call after lunch, arranged the meeting.

"Four o'clock over at Varfell suit you?" Melville asked, pausing for the reply then his strong voice coming again. "Yes, of course today. Get it done, don't hang about!"

Gordon hurried through the afternoon chores and was five minutes early for the meeting, waiting near the field entrance when a Landrover drew up. Melville climbed slowly out, telling the dog to stay, and they stood in the field gateway together gazing across at the tower on the far side.

"Like it do you? Told you it's what you need."

"Hm... maybe." Gordon tried to keep any enthusiasm hidden. "Cheap you said?"

"Ah! Well... £50, that's less than scrap value. Enough to buy Ethel a new dress."

The temptation to offer £40 was almost irresistible, ingrained, passed on from father to son. But £50 was generous, an offer from a friend, a favour – to quibble would devalue it. Gordon couldn't however, resist a little sigh and a sad shake of the head. "Okay, £50." He reached into a pocket for the notes, passing them over. "And thanks!"

As the money changed hands both men looked at each other and grinned.

CHAPTER 12

The Tower.

"We could start on the tower this morning." Dad suggested at breakfast. The weather outside was clear, another week had passed and numbers fallen. The school holidays were almost over, only twenty nine caravans and seven tents remained; it could easily be run by one parent now if Sharon would serve in the shop.

Chris nodded, holding his smile in check, not letting the enthusiasm show; it was not cool to be eager. He looked towards Sharon with a touch of superiority that drew a "Hm!" of derision, then noted with pleasure the envy in Stephen's expression.

"No you can't." Jan cut short Chris's muted triumph. "It's Saturday, we could still be busy early on and I'm off shopping once the first rush is over. Yes I am, no good shaking your head, and Stephen's coming with me." The statement left no room for argument; how could it, the lad would start senior school in a few days and needed kitting out. A quiet smile replaced resentment on the face of the family's youngest member. Jan smiled back at him, then spoke again to Chris. "I'm still not sure why your father wants it; we've enough work to do already."

"You shouldn't let them Mum, it's useless."

Hearing Sharon's comment and sensing a rising discord across the table, Jan regretted having spoken; it had not been intended. From the start she disliked the idea and the danger it posed, but had hidden her feelings to avoid family

216

dissension. Instinctively she sought some way to brighten the conversation. "Oh never mind. If the men of this house want a new toy to play with then I suppose..." her hands spread in a '*who can understand them*' gesture, looking at Gordon, challenging him to deny it as good humour returned to the room.

He smiled back. She was clever, pleasing Sharon with the jibe about males, pleasing Chris by refering to him as a man, and he had seen the wink at Stephen, as if the little lad were part of the joke – and it was done with a easy grace, leaving Dad to find an answer. Okay!

"Useless you say?" Gordon paused, thinking. "I'll come to that in a minute. You're right about one thing, we do have other work, more important work, but taking the tower down will take at most a few half days, it will make a break and I can't start using the excavator yet; we do promise our guests quietness, remember? And it's not necessarily useless either. It could help to boost visitor numbers. We've already had a few people come especially to see the waterwheel, this is something else to make a talking point; how many sites have both a waterwheel and a windmill? Did you think of that? And another thing, what would happen if the mains water supply failed? We have our own electric, a shop, plenty of spare gas bottles, but no alternative source of water."

"We have the river," Sharon offered.

"And will you carry buckets of water all day so visitors can flush the loos. How much easier with a wind pump. I could make it fill the cisterns that flush the toilets. It might be worth doing that anyway, to cut the water charges. Could even save enough to buy a new dress or..."

A ring on the office bell stopped conversation as the morning's work commenced. It became quite busy for a while, partly with people calling at the office as they left, some offering thanks, others wanting booking forms for next year. By the time Jan could get away there was hardly time before lunch, so she left in the early afternoon, returning several hours later. As they settled round the table for tea, Stephen entered the room to stand proudly erect by the doorway, his dark blue jumper and long, sharply pressed grey trousers obviously new.

The pending return to school, monopolised conversation during the meal, for as well as being Stephen's first day it would start Chris's final year.

After a while, Gordon asked, "Well, will you keep your mind off chasing girls this year and pass those final exams?"

Chris glanced at his father, "I don't need to chase them." The words were said with a touch of offhand arrogance, unintended probably but with just the suggestion that '*if I snap my fingers they come running*'. It ruffled Sharon's feathers.

"All right then, if you're so clever, what is a mole?"

"A nasty little creature that digs holes in our grass pitches?" Jan offered. Everyone agreed.

"No," Sharon shook her head. "A mole is the amount of a substance in chemistry, like you might get a spoonful of some ingredient in cook..." she stopped herself, "in domestic science."

As the older pair faced each other across the table, searching their minds for further ammunition, a voice spoke into the lull. Stephen, apprehensive perhaps about the change, had said little; now he murmured the question quietly. "How can you tell if a drake is right handed?"

"Ducks don't have hands." Sharon's reply was automatic but she continued to look in his direction, awaiting the reply.

Stephen glanced at Chris then at each parent, keeping them waiting; whether by choice or by accident was not clear. When he did reply it was directly to Sharon. "I said drakes, you can't tell with ducks."

Sharon waited, but no more words came and she asked with annoyance, "All right then, drakes! How *can* you tell if they're right handed?"

218

"They swim clockwise afterwards." Stephen looked down at the cloth, not explaining further. Chris grinned, but Sharon failed to understand.

The parents smiled at each other across the table.

"Do you think it's true? We must take more notice." Jan waved a hand to where her daughter sat with a puzzled expression, "I think Dad better explain."

"Tell her about the bird's and the bees you mean, like you once threatened to make me?" Seeing a startled expression then amusement on Sharon's face across the table Gordon paused, selecting his words. "The drakes, after they mate with a duck, swim round her in a big circle, a sort of lap of honour, proclaiming their achievement. The question is, does each drake always swim in the same direction. Perhaps Stephen can tell us?"

Finding himself again the centre of attention, Stephen shrugged, "Boy at school says so. His uncle breeds ducks."

Sunday proved busier than expected and it was not until mid-afternoon that they stood at the foot of the windmill; Chris with a coil of rope in one hand, Gordon beside him remembering Sharon's words, *'I think they're stupid'*. Was she right?

No rain had fallen and as they had hoped the tower was dry – dry but daunting! Apart from its height which was worrying enough, the structure was flimsy, old, and partly corroded. Four narrow legs of that steel commonly referred to as 'angle iron', ran the full height, each leaning inwards until they came together forming a point way above. At intervals, horizontal braces, again in narrow steel angle, stretched across joining the legs together. At some stage it would be necessary to stand on these slender pieces of metal to undo the various nuts, balancing in space with nothing beneath; but that was for later. A series of thin rods ran diagonally, criss-crossing the structure to give rigidity, and almost at the top hung a small wooden platform. That must be the starting point! The fan, a

219

collective term for all the little sails that caught the wind, normally spun right at the very peak but it had broken and fallen the short distance onto this high platform, forty feet above ground level. What damage that collapse had caused was not visible from where they stood. At one time the main metalwork must have been galvanised but this protective coating had largely worn away leaving the whole tower liberally splashed with rust.

Reluctantly, Gordon moved forward, placed a hand on the narrow vertical ladder and stared upwards. They had only viewed from a distance before; it seemed different close to. "Um." Heights had always been a problem; he pulled his eyes away, and seeking a distraction, turned to Chris, "Looks much taller from here. We need to reach that platform."

"I'm lighter, should I go first?" It was hardly an offer, the reluctance clear in Chris's voice.

"Better not, Mum would murder me if she knew."

"She wouldn't find out – at least, not if you double my pocket money!"

"Bandit! I'd rather risk the height." Gordon turned away, kicking the bottom rung hard; some rust flakes dropped but it remained straight and unbent. Reaching higher, he glanced aloft again.

Waiting quietly to one side Chris murmured, "How did I guess?" but looked relieved rather than disappointed, watching his father put one foot on the ladder, hesitate, then heave upward, climbing with an awkward one-handed grip, an arm trailing behind carrying the loose end of rope and the tools in a bag. Every few steps the body pulled tight against the steelwork, balancing as the leading hand slid upwards to take a higher grip.

Chris's eyes rose again, following the narrow ladder to the high platform. He swallowed; it would be his turn soon. What would it be like up there? A loud crack pulled him back to the present! The climbing figure, still clinging to rope and tools, wrapped both arms round the ladder and hung on.

Gingerly, Gordon sought the cause, he had felt the metalwork give and instinctively clung to the only thing within reach. Some movement had to be expected; this old ladder may not have been climbed for more than thirty years. One of the nuts had probably stripped a few threads. He kicked the next rung, testing it before moving upwards again. Passing the first cross brace and reaching the second, he paused, standing on one leg and hooking the other over the horizontal steel member, gripping it behind the knee so both hands were free, then threaded the rope around, pulling until it tightened.

"Okay!"

Chris heard and commenced climbing, moving faster with both hands free. At each upward movement of his body the rope round his waist loosened, then pulled taunt as his father took up the slack. It was easy enough here; he looked upward again, rose three more steps and taking a firm grip on the ladder called "Right!"

The feet above his head moved on, the rope no longer tight. They continued in this fashion, Gordon calling back over one shoulder each time, instructing the lad to take a firm grip then waiting confirmation before easing the rope and moving ahead again. He climbed with care, testing each rung and each connection point. Some sections of ladder were loose. Okay, loose was expected, but were they unsafe? He had to be sure. Only the main cross members that joined the legs offered more solid support and even those were flimsy enough. They rose higher, Chris's climb rate slowing, becoming more cautious; not by intent – the height forcing an instinctive wariness. This was something he had never done before.

The little platform near the top, just below the fan, had a hole where the ladder ended. This small opening might once have housed a trap door, it could only be entered by stretching one arm up to grasp metalwork above the platform, then releasing the grip on the ladder and pushing that arm too, upward above the head before squeezing the shoulders past.

Waiting on the ladder, Chris wondered about the hold-up. Something was happening; ripping, tearing sounds grated harshly down from somewhere beyond his vision. After a while the noise stopped, the feet above disappearing.

Wriggling through onto the rotting boards, Gordon rose carefully, one hand clenched on the section of tower that projected above the platform, calling down, "Okay, come on up."

For a while they stood together.

"Is it safe?" Chris asked.

"Probably not. Best to assume that anyway. See where I've scored the timber surface," a finger pointed to the floor. "That's where steel members run below the boarding. Be sure always to tread exactly on those marks. Anywhere else and you might go through."

Moving outward, nervous feet trod gingerly on the scratched lines. Holding the shaky handrail, broken in several places, Chris gazed around. The tops of a group of trees waved some distance below; how soft a landing would those uppermost branches make? Crossing cautiously to the opposite side, the ground seemed a long way off. In one direction sat a farmhouse, elsewhere mainly fields. The beach lay less than a mile away but rising ground and some woods deprived them of a sea view.

Gordon climbed higher; up the mast above the platform, a mast now less than a foot wide. Re-tying Chris's rope to the top, he looked downwards again at the far off ground... "Pass me that shorter rope from the tool bag." With unsteady hands he tied it round his own waist and again to the tower before climbing down, stepping with care; it was only too easy to forget always to place feet exactly on those scratched marks indicating the unseen metal angles below. How serious stepping elsewhere would be was unknown but neither was anxious to find out the hard way just how far the rot had progressed.

Attention switched from the scenery to the job in hand. The collapsed fan was in the way, it restricted movement – they shuffled carefully round to start the dismantling. Removing those eighteen blades would allow more working space. The nuts proved difficult to shift, hardly unexpected, but with perseverance the blades came away and as one followed another, began to form a close fitting stack on the floor of that high perch. The last three blades were more difficult but yielded eventually, bent and distorted by the fall. It would make them harder to carry down. One thing was certain – no one was fool enough to try straightening them on the platform, swaying as it did slightly in the wind. The thought of banging anything with a hammer conjured pictures of the whole tower collapsing in a pile of dust. Gordon, treading with all the care of a mouse in a cattery, moved the damaged blades to one side and considered the next piece to be dismantled. Chris too, he noticed was moving with precise and ultra careful steps.

The approach of evening saw numerous bits and pieces safely lowered on that first night, all carefully stowed in the car, together with every nut and bolt, not one dropping from careful if perhaps slightly shaking fingers.

At home Jan asked, "And was it difficult or dangerous? Any problems."

Chris, in spite of his new cool image was still apt to exaggerate on occasion. Aware of this tendency and seeing his eldest son about to reply, Gordon nipped in smartly to forestall any such words.

"No. Easy really. No problem at all."

Chris's eyes widened, then understanding he casually nodded agreement, asking, "Anything happen here while we were away? Anyone my age arrive?"

"No, but we had a funny tent. It wanted to camp on the top terrace, the unfinished one. A young couple from Holland, I told them there was no grass but nothing would dissuade them. In the end, I agreed. They came to the office

223

again later and booked two extra nights."

By morning rain had set in. As they ate breakfast the little battery radio, still the same one used years ago in the first caravan, gave a poor forecast for the next twenty-four hours. There were hazards enough on the tower without walking on wet slippery steelwork; further efforts in that direction now postponed. In those two days before dry weather re-established itself the children returned to school, so it looked likely dismantling would not recommence until the weekend; that tower was hardly a place to work alone. The delay was of no consequence, there were things to be done on the park and visitors to attend. The main season may have passed but a few dozen caravans, mostly elderly couples, still remained and this off-peak trade was important. Attracting visitor at this time of year when vacant pitches existed on every site was an achievement; a truer compliment than being full at midseason – and they did need the money!

The two younger children, lacking now the many friends of a few weeks earlier, regretted the delay. They had inspected those parts already brought back from the windmill; the fan blades, various odd shaped pieces of ironwork and a cardboard box of nuts and bolts. Stephen had helped unload them from the car boot, fingering the pieces with envy but saying nothing. Sharon, standing well clear, had watched with pretended disinterest, making the occasional derogatory comment but unable to stay indoors, forced by curiosity to see what had so far been recovered. At tea a few evenings later she was having an argument with Chris on how something should be done in the mobile shop and finding herself losing, sought some way to recover the situation.

"Hm! I shouldn't worry about my work, what about yours? What about that tower? There's plenty of light in the evenings but you still don't go. Frightened are you, got a few small pieces off and scared to try the bigger ones?"

She threw her head to one side, hair swinging, nose in the air.

"We'll go next weekend?" Chris looked to Dad for confirmation and seeing a nod, swung back to his sister, "Anyway, I've homework to do."

"Tough! Some of us are bright enough so the teachers don't think we need any."

Aware that his mother was watching, and sensing the faint smile on her lips was at his expense, Chris hunted for a response.

"Well..." he hesitated. Sharon and Mum were smiling openly now, challenging him. There had to be an answer. "Well if you're so clever and have no homework, why don't *you* help Dad? Go on, see how you feel right at the top when it sways in the wind!" The improvisation had come out in a flurry, without thought; Chris flicked a dubious glance to his father, half expecting disapproval, but his parents were looking at each other across the table, a smile now on both faces.

"Okay, why not?" Gordon turned to his daughter. "How soon can you be ready?"

Sharon's expression froze with alarm. "I..." she swallowed, eyes wide, "I can't."

Chris and Dad looked at each other, Dad holding out one hand palm upwards in a 'what did you expect' gesture, repeating the words, "She can't." Chris rolled his eyes to the ceiling trying to mask the expression of delight, and they shook their heads sagely at each other before turning back to the female section of the table. Stephen, who had taken no part in the exchanges, banged his fist on the teak surface. Somehow, the little argument that had started between the two older children had divided the family; boys against girls.

"She can't because I won't let her." Jan joined the battle.

"Of course. Quite right," Dad offered. "Females are not really capable; probably stop to comb her hair halfway

225

up and fall off."

"Dad! I would not! It's just that... well I..."

"Yes?" Dad leant forward over the table, chin on hand as if listening, waiting attentively, agog for the explanation. Chris, then Stephen quickly copied the stance.

"I..." Sharon struggled, "I haven't any trousers!"

Jan raised a hand to her face smothering a laugh, gathering herself together. "There you are, I told you I wouldn't allow it. You needn't think I'm prepared to let my daughter show her knickers to half of Marazion!"

Chris came home on Thursday evening without homework; this and fine weather offered an opportunity to work the tower. They climbed more quickly this time, knowing the ladder to be safe, but those first few minutes at the top were still daunting and the wind stronger. The heavy iron gearbox would be the night's big task but first the vane must be tackled. This long lopsided metal rectangle streamed out like the tail of a cat in flight. Presenting a broad face to the wind, its purpose was to automatically rotate the mast top, swinging the fan directly into prevailing air currents.

With those first signs of failing light, the vane swung clear, attention focusing now on the large gearbox. Everything that could be separated had already been removed but the ungainly iron casting and the gears it contained was still heavy.

"Chris. Feeling strong are you? Let's try it for weight. No, not from the platform; we'll need to stand on those small cross braces above, one of us each side of the tower." They moved into position, grabbing the tower legs and climbing up.

"What about the pipe?" Chris pointed to a steel tube approximately two feet long projecting downwards from the gearbox. It passed through a hole in the metal capping piece that held the top of the four tower legs together.

"That's why we're perched up here. We must hoist the

226

whole thing upwards until that tube clears the tower. For a start, let's lift a few inches then drop it back – that should show if it's possible."

The attempt succeeded but it *was* weighty. They rested the casting back.

"Plenty heavy enough! About a hundredweight I guess – er, forty-five kilos. Think you can do it Chris?"

"Not sure. Not sure if I can lift high enough."

"You did fine that time. Maybe I can take more weight. You realise the next problem?"

"Getting it down?"

"Not right down, we'll worry about that later. Better not be too much later though," Gordon cast a glance at the darkening sky. "Once we have the tail clear, I don't think you can step down onto the platform holding that weight. We'll tip it sideways to balance on top of the tower. I'll hold it there while you climb down. Okay?"

Chris nodded, reaching for the metal then waiting on his father for instructions when to lift.

"Take three deep breaths with me, like weightlifters do, then lift and keep lifting until I say."

They stood facing each other across the tower top, breathing in and out in unison.

"Now!"

It rose quickly until the tail was almost free, but Chris was a touch short. Legs braced against the metalwork they held on as the weight wavered, then with a final heave the end cleared, twisted quickly sideways and fell back as muscles gave. No need to lower it onto the tower, the damn thing came of its own accord, banging down despite all efforts to cushion the fall. There it rested.

"Whee!" Chris blew a sigh of relief, waving a fist aloft in triumph as they stood on the high perch, waists level with tower top, catching their breath, the countryside laid out in an unrestricted view below them.

A few minutes later the heavy casting lay safely on the platform.

"Well done Chris! The next bit won't be easy either."

They leaned against the tower looking again over a darkening landscape, feeling it sway in a sudden gust, not yet sure how to lower the unwieldy burden to the ground, forty feet below. There was only one rope of sufficient length, attaching it and lifting together failed to move the casting, the method of lifting rather than the weight beating them this time. The rope, less than half an inch wide, was amply strong but gave insufficient grip and they dare not wind it around their hands with a forty-foot drop below.

"What will we do?" Chris pulled ineffectually on the rope again. "Perhaps one of the caravanners...?"

"I doubt it. Look, if I can get the casting between my chest and the ladder, and you stay here taking what weight you can on the rope, I might lower it one step at a time."

"You'll be underneath?"

"Fear will boost my muscle power, give me extra strength."

Chris looked doubtful but helped manoeuvre the weight towards the opening. Lowering it through the small hole and getting a firm grip below took every ounce of combined strength, and the long task was underway! Chris braced himself on the rope, pulling with the total power of which he was capable; he had again wanted to wind the rope round his hands but had been forbidden. Below, his father descended slowly, the weighty casting, held between body and ladder. One foot extended, probing, feeling for another rung; difficult, awkward. On the next downward step the ladder moved! The unexpected jerk threw him momentarily, the weight slipping.

"Pull!" The call flew urgently upwards as he fought to retain a hold, pushing with chest and one palm, the other hand gripping the ladder. Although the ladder itself had moved, nothing else was within reach. He must hold on! Would it break away? It mustn't! The casting threatened not only to fall and shatter itself, but to take him with it.

As Chris had pointed out, he was underneath.

A stab of pain hit! Something tore into a finger holding the ladder, slicing through flesh and removing part of the nail but there was no time to look. A touch of panic lent strength that forced the sliding casting against the next rung, temporarily jamming it as he clung on, glancing again to the ground far below then back to the bleeding wound seeking a cause. Inches away, a bracket that had refused all attempts at removal stuck sharply out, its metal eroded away to a keen edge – the rusty projection now streaked with a darker red.

There was nothing to be done but ignore the injury and continue! He stepped down, chest and one palm pressed hard against the gearbox, clamping it to the rungs. The other hand still clung to the ladder with three fingers, one damaged digit sticking straight out, blood oozing from the end and dripping steadily into the void below, carried by the stiff breeze to who knows where. Thirty feet still to go! Ease the weight lower on the chest before taking the next step. Blood was running down one arm, the injured hand now higher – an unconscious precaution keeping it clear of further damage. No way to hurry; forget the pain and concentrate.

Chris struggled above, taking what weight as he could. No need for him to lower, the weight pulled the rope through his hands as his father took each downward step. At intervals a call sounded from below.

"Okay. Take a rest. I have it lodged against a rung!"

Chris relaxed his grip temporarily, flexing aching shoulders and rubbing first one sore palm against his jumper then the other, never letting go of the rope completely, always ready to take the strain again should the casting slip.

His respite was short. Below him, Gordon was in trouble, struggling with the weight, in pain and unsure of the blood being lost. He could hardly afford the pause but knew Chris would never hold his share of weight without respite.

"Okay. Ready again?"

"Yes!"

The voice floating down sounded fainter at each stop. Hopefully that was the increasing distance not weakness coming on. Above all, he could not afford to faint!

When one foot encountered a flat surface the change of angle and a moments inattention bought on by relief almost caused another slip; the casting came down in a hurry, the other foot sidestepping to swing clear and 'thump', it lay on the ground. Great!

"Okay, it's down!" He had intended to climb up again, tie the rope round Chris's waist and hold it while the lad descended but circumstances had changed. Chris threw the rope clear, followed it through the hole and clambered carefully but quickly down the ladder, his first descent without a safety line.

Waiting at the bottom, Gordon wrapped a handkerchief round the injured finger as Chris joined him. Together they carried the casting slowly across the field, resting at intervals then hoisted it into the car boot, before hurrying off to Penzance Hospital. The nurse administered an injection, cut away a fleshy chunk of nail and dressed the wound.

As they finally arrived home driving across the yard, Jan was on the doorstep, relieved but not pleased at the late arrival. Quickly she grew suspicious, noting Chris's apprehensive glances, seeing an air of expectation as her son's eyes switched from her own face to a hand Dad was concealing behind his back

"Show!" She pointed towards the hidden limb. "Don't pretend not to understand! That innocent 'What do you mean' expression will get you nowhere. Show!"

Reluctantly he revealed the bandaged finger.

"You told me it wasn't dangerous! Where did you get that dressed?" She paused regarding Chris critically, assessing his condition, convincing herself that he too was not injured. Turning back she accused, "You've been to the Hospital! That's why you're late!"

"This? Oh, it's nothing, just a little cut. We only popped in to update my Tetanus."

Over the weekend they worked on, taking off piece after piece. In a perverse way Chris was afraid but enjoying himself; they were more equal now with his father handicapped by the bad finger. Chris looked down, his feet resting on narrow cross braces, scanty strips of metal only two inches wide with an unbroken view of the ground far below. A fist clenching tightly to the nearest tower leg supported him as he worked one handed, fear his best friend; amazing how much power that void below added to the grip – and yet he felt exhilarated! By evening the remaining sections were dismantled; nuts, bolts and sundry shorter pieces weighing down the car boot, the rest left in a pile awaiting later removal.

CHAPTER 13

Small Onion

"Come on, put it on the table!" Jan waved a small pair of scissors in Gordon's direction. "You can't walk around like that." She had wanted the dressing changed on the previous day but he argued the work was unfinished; it would only get dirty again. That excuse was hardly valid now but worth a try.

"We've still the long steel sections to collect."

"When?"

"Not until next weekend," Chris supplied the answer before his father could speak.

Reluctantly the damaged hand slid across the table. Snipping the outer layer, Jan addressed Chris as she worked.

"Next weekend? How? They won't go in the car."

"Dad says we hang them underneath, roped to the front and back bumpers; tie white cloths where they stick out, fore and aft."

"Why wait until the weekend?" Jan snipped again then laid the scissors aside, lifted the wrist in her other hand and started to unwind. "Well, don't I get an answer!" A warning tug on the arm forced his attention.

"Er, be less people about, not so many going to work. We could start early."

"How early?"

"About five... Ouch!"

"Sorry, the last bit stuck. Five in the morning! Dodgy is it; illegal perhaps?" She bent to inspect more closely.

"Bit gory! Could have been dangerous if you'd been lifting anything at the time."

"I suppose it could." He caught Chris's eye and looked quickly back towards the hand, masked a smile and smartly changed tack. "Pity the sewage works is not ready yet. They say next spring at the earliest."

"That long?" Jan was silent for a while, winding on a new dressing. Having secured it, she pushed the hand aside. "Try to keep it clean. As you say, shame about the sewage, I had hoped we could connect this coming winter once the last visitors have left. By spring more will have arrived. Won't try fixing it with people on site, will you? How much mine waste is there still to shift?"

Gordon picked up a half finished bird he was carving but the damaged finger made holding it difficult, the new bandage less flexible. He put it down again. "Our sewer must be dry for those final connections. We'll do it next autumn. The mine waste... take about four weeks I'd guess, then some trimming; the trees and hedges have grown forward quite a bit," he turned to the children. "Did your friends make any comments about their holidays this season; things they didn't like or would have preferred... well, different?"

"Hair dryers; the girls still want them," Sharon offered. "And there's nowhere easy to empty waste water from motorcaravans but those lid-lifters do help. People like the showers."

"I know one thing; that mobile shop is a pain!" Jan's comment brought nods of agreement from the children. "Not bad early in the mornings when there's a queue, it's interesting then, but later when they come in odd ones and twos at intervals, you sit alone just waiting. It takes up so much time, gets hot in there too and looks unsightly parked down a Jim's. Audrey says a caravan swung round in the entrance yesterday and went away – could have been caused by the mobile. Can't we get rid of it?"

"How? The customers like it?"

"You don't spend hours standing out there like the rest of us," Sharon offered support to her mother. "Anyway the ice cream gets soft and the milk is off some evenings."

"The chocolate goes white," Stephen muttered.

Dad turned to Chris "Are you against it too? No useful suggestions I suppose?"

"My friend has a gas fridge, not small like ours, a big one as tall as I am. It runs off mains gas but wouldn't Calor gas work? That would stop the milk going sour."

Sharon, about to raise an objection, remembered that for once they were arguing on the same side, and merely asked, "Where could we put it?"

"In the garage. The pit right at the back that takes coal, we could fill a small section to stand the fridge on. Taking a few cold bottles to the shop at intervals throughout the day would keep the milk fresh."

"Supposing," Gordon hesitated, thinking. "Supposing we had such a fridge and we stopped selling ice cream? The shop could stay here all the time then; we need never run it up to Jim's."

"We'd still have to stand out there, except..." Jan paused, "Tell me, if it never moves, could you fix an extension to avoid running for the office phone?"

"I might do better than that." He leaned back in the chair with a broad smile, eyeing the family, letting the idea run through his mind.

"Dad?" Sharon prompted, wanting an answer. When he rose, making for the door instead of replying, she jumped up in pursuit followed by the others, along the corridor, past the fireproof door and down two steps into the garage.

"That's where you mean Chris?" he pointed to the far side of a wide pit stretching right across the rear wall, space enough for a ton of coal but now containing only a few hundredweight. The pit could be covered by boards and above sat a substantial window, originally to shed light on a small workbench that had long since been moved to the basement. Receiving confirmation, he gazed for a while at the space.

"As you say, if there's not many people around, having to sit out in the mobile is a bind. Leaving a bell on the counter has helped to some extent but we don't always hear when people ring. If the mobile was parked permanently outside, never moving, I probably could fix up a phone, but someone must still sit out there, at least part of the time. We have planning permission for a proper shop but that would be even worse; farther away and unnecessarily big. What we really need is one attached to the house. Why not bring it in here? I don't mean drive the mobile in – let's convert this garage into a proper shop."

Jan looked from end to end; the roof sloped down to head height on one side and the walls were rough block-work, but it had possibilities. "The door faces the right way for visitors; our car can easily stand outside. We needn't bother about rust problems, I don't intend to keep it long enough."

"You'll be lucky!" Stephen murmured with emphasis, seeing alarm in his father's face.

"Don't worry," Jan smiled at the lad, "I won't want a new one for a few years; remember how the mini-van lasted. Hm? If we do get a big gas fridge like Chris said, we could stock butter and other dairy produce. There's more space here too; room for greater variety, caravan spares, water carriers, clothes-airers, the things people ask for." She turned to the children. "What d'you think?"

"We'd get more free time then?" Sharon asked eagerly. "Less hours sitting waiting for customers?"

"Yes, I think you would. This year was exceptional anyway, you know that. Dad better not be ill next peak season or I'll... I'll put him in that coal pit and cover him over quick! Come on, back to the lounge and work out the details."

"How much will our help be needed with the building?" Sharon asked as they sat down.

"You personally? Not at all, nor the boys much. We need planning permission first but there is one thing. The coal needs shovelling through the hole into the basement. Stephen, will you do that please?" The young lad glared at his older brother in annoyance, Chris smiling broadly back.

"There's another job," Gordon pointed a finger at Chris, taking away the smile and bringing a grin to Stephen's face. "Bottles. I want to knock a hole down in the pit first, a hole to connect it with the outside air. When that's done then we need enough bottles and jars to fill the entire space; there's plenty still in the dustbins but they need rescuing before Thursday. Stack them in empty bins and bring them in here. Sharon can help."

"Delve around in other people's rubbish? I wouldn't know how!" Sharon looked aghast, moving towards her mother for support.

"Ask Stephen, he's handled the bins all season," Jan advised, then turning to Gordon. "No good enquiring I suppose, why you can't fill it with soil like any normal person?"

"By normal, you mean someone who doesn't know any better. For an engineer there's a good reason to use bottles; they weigh very little, won't put much extra load on the foundations. I'll cover them with a layer of plastic then five inches..." Gordon paused, "no, eight inches of concrete – reinforced of course. Does that answer your question?"

"You sure eight inches will be enough? What about this hole you want to knock?"

"Ah. That's secret. Something I plan for the future. You'll like it."

"Not a lot." Jan muttered quietly, but asked no more.

"Not a lot is right!" Sharon wiped a hand unconsciously against her dress with a little shudder. "I don't like it even a little! It's unhygienic, feeling down into other people's rubbish with your fingers."

236

"No." Stephen shook his head. "Never reach inside, just tip the bin into an empty one. When you see a bottle, stop and drop it into another empty bin. Plenty of empties this time of year."

"There, the voice of an expert." Jan smiled at Stephen, surprised by the long speech.

"I still think it's wrong. Girls don't do things like that." Sharon frowned sulkily.

"Tell you what," Dad bent nearer, whispering loudly. "As you're a very special girl, I'll..." he paused seeing Sharon's smile broaden, "I'll ask Chris not to tell too many of your friends and school."

The smile froze, changing to alarm then anger, much to the boys' jubilation. The wordy melee that ensued did little to advance the discussion. Time would be required for the necessary planning permission so no immediate work was possible, nor could moving the final few thousand tons of mine waste be undertaken while customers remained. Trimming hedges however, a quiet but essential winter task, would save time later.

There were still the long windmill sections to collect, but Tommy from Gurlyn Farm next door had volunteered to transport them with his tractor. Gordon drove to the farm at the prearranged time to find the tractor ready but the attached trailer still piled high with sacks of potatoes. He jumped up to help as Tommy and another man loaded them onto a lorry parked alongside. A competition developed as the paper sacks were hustled onto the waiting vehicle. Good fun! Sweat soon ran freely; few loads of spuds ever moved quicker!

Unloading the tower sections from the trailer later, they suddenly realised the pump was missing. The old base had been so overgrown with brambles that no one thought to check. Telling Jan of their intention, father and son sped off again, arriving once more at the field. Cutting and pushing aside a mesh of thorny runners revealed a cast iron pump bolted to the foundation. Removing four nuts and some prising and chipping of concrete released the compact cylinder, which was whisked away to reside with the rest beside the house. And that, for the time being, was that. Other tasks were waiting!

The season drew towards its close. Sycamores were turning brown, the leaves falling now, missing those more vivid yellows of beech and maple. At Jan's instigation, photos were taken facing northwards down the valley, showing an almost continuous backdrop of colourful oaks, now mellowing to the rich russet of autumn in the still sunny days. In the foreground, in the very centre of the road, a pair of Mallard slept peacefully. One eye in the drake's brilliant green head opened momentarily as the tripod was set not ten feet away, an eye that closed again, content no danger threatened.

Jan watched from one side, wondering at the ducks choice of bed. "They've lived here long enough to know it's where the cars go; long enough I suppose, to realise that drivers will stop. Does it give them a feeling of power? Perhaps the black tarmac surface holds the heat; their equivalent of a warm bed?" She moved behind the camera, taking in all it would see. This was the best time of year for those oaks, better even than spring; the valley was beautiful now; but then, even in the bleakness of winter few places could compare. Thinking back to their first arrival, she remembered how primitive life had been and how remote. Whatever made her agree? She shrugged, who knows? The nights were drawing in, the season ending. Life was no longer so primitive but would be just as remote and isolated again in a few more weeks. No parties or high life here, but who needs it, she sighed, swinging slowly round again towards the eastern valley side; more ducks were approaching, hoping for food as they always did. I miss the goats she thought suddenly for no reason, smiling to herself, remembering that trip taking Judy to the billy goat. How much lonelier would it be when the children grew up and went away?

Later as dusk fell, they sat together round the small television. Jan, affected by thoughts from earlier in the day, quietly watched her family, wondering again about the future. A knock at the door pushed those thoughts aside. Dusk had fallen outside but a motorcaravan stood dimly visible in the yard beyond, one of the last this season. Gordon opened the door to a young man, inviting him and his lady companion inside to book them in for the night. The couple apologised for the lateness, explaining they were actors from a touring company now playing in Penzance. That was normal enough, many such shows were put on throughout the area in the summer season, though most had now finished for the year. The rest of the family continued to watch the film, but with the sound switched off. As the couple stood chatting, the tree filled with carvings drew the young man's attention and he turned to the girl.

"Oh *Darling*. Model birds." The words were spoken in a highly affected, terribly posh voice, drawing out the *darling* in that way actors sometimes do.

A flurry of activity ruffled previous stillness in the other part of the room. Through the archway that divided office from lounge, Chris choked into his handkerchief, Sharon buried her head in a pillow and Stephen rushed from the room. Jan sat unmoving, a rigid expression on her face, jaws clamped tightly together.

Gordon pushed the signing in book towards the arrivals, not daring to speak, knowing he could never make it with a straight face. As the young man wrote, the rest of the family fled, leaving the room to join Stephen. Several doors were heard to close. The certainty that wicked glee was even now erupting, bursting forth from happy faces in the kitchen, made Gordon's task no easier. He took the money and showed the actors rather hurriedly to a pitch; struggling to resist the laughter within. The short walk back to the house gave a chance to smile in the gathering dusk, rejoining the family in time to hear Stephen's fair impersonation,

"Oh Darling. Model birds."

They were not usually inclined to laugh at visitors' mannerisms, though often at themselves. Jan could remember no other occasions when this had occurred in connection with the bird carvings, although customer's comments on the colourful display were common enough. The near uncontrollable merriment came totally from the manner of delivery! Being actors, had it been deliberate; was playing for effect in the blood and irresistible? Would he have been offended or pleased had he known his audience's true reaction? Who can tell? A hangover perhaps from some recently performed aristocratic part? He probably played a terrific role.

As autumn mellowed, the mystery of the windmill's missing parts had been solved. Many exposed pieces, mainly moving parts of the mechanism, had never been galvanised and in consequence had rotted away with rust. Stephen remembered seeing a similar tower earlier in the year in a little nursery opposite Wendron Forge, or Poldark Mine as it had recently been renamed. This model was smaller, but obtaining permission from the owner, sketches were made and measurements taken; they could be adapted later.

Having sorted the shapes and sizes, what now? A forge was certainly needed, a lathe too if possible. Evening classes in metalwork at Chris's school provided the answer. This was not so much a class in the recognised sense, more a hobby shop. One chap worked on wrought iron gates, another welded an exhaust pipe, and yet another toiled at some unknown device, the lecturer giving words of advice only when asked. Chris had a project of his own, a metal weather vane in the form of a cockerel, complete with mounting and bearings; Jim had mentioned he would like one for the bungalow. That left Gordon working through a list of items in his notebook.

Bending of shapes, cutting screw threads and a little

240

welding, both gas and electric, together with some milling and other work were to extend over many weeks, but as Jan had once said, what else could he do on a dark winter evening? There was no particular hurry, the tower was unlikely to be started for another year, perhaps two. It first needed re-galvanising and any money currently available was unavoidably destined for other uses. One aspect of this delay to the tower's erection did cause regret; Melville would never see it finished, for sadly he died in October.

The month drew on, November was only a week away; the site would close then and Max's engine could start earlier, at first light. A planning application to convert the garage into a shop had been submitted, but would permission be given? Only time would tell.

Chris was unhappy, resentful, struggling unwillingly with more homework in this his O-level year. Even a fine weekend like today, was no longer free. Pushing the books aside he strode off, wanting to be alone, thinking of the future. Aimless steps took him down the valley, pausing near the chestnut tree and remembering the old tunnel found long ago. Pushing a way through, sliding down into the gully and leaning on an overhanging branch, he looked at the big pipe. "I'm taller now; if I crawl inside will it still be possible to squeeze round in the cavern beyond?" Deciding not to try, he walked away intending to look for the old brick path that crossed the river underwater, to see if it was still visible among the shingle, but the excavator engine farther downstream deterred him from choosing that direction. Arguments had arisen recently. Dad, intolerant sometimes, urged him to study harder, still treating him as a boy – that was unfair. Some friends, hardly older than himself but with birthdays before September had already left school and were working, now independent and earning good money! He moved away, staying concealed by the trees until well clear, then crossed to follow the river upstream.

Sharon saw him from the kitchen window, watched him kick a loose stone into the river, then stroll on towards the house. Her homework too, was increasing now. She glanced at his books still on the table and could sympathise but felt a touch of pride that her own study was going well. School was a place of many friends, an enjoyable place; aware of her brother's desire to leave she could not share that wish. On impulse, she took some bread and went outside, timing her exit to meet him near the bridge, tearing the slice apart and offering half. A man from one of the last caravans stopped to ask about the waterwheel. They stood talking, exchanging a brief greeting as Stephen wandered over, joining them to listen but not contributing to the conversation.

"I know it charges batteries because it charged mine," the man said, "but what else does it do?"

"Everything. Our lights, television, batteries for the shaver points in the toilets, the electric drill..."

"And Mum's food mixer and the vacuum." Sharon added to Chris's list.

The man shifted his stance, looking thoughtfully toward Stephen for any further suggestions. The lad stooped picked up a small pebble, perhaps the size of a currant and flicked it at the water. A trout rose to investigate.

"I thought they only did that for bread." The man watched the fish disappear. "Will they chase anything?"

Stephen paused, then struck by an idea suddenly ran off, collecting a milk bottle from a crate left in the yard for that purpose. Filling it quickly at the tap he raced back to the bridge and kneeling on the low parapet, tipped carefully letting a few drops fall on the river below. Three trout darted out, circled and disappeared again. Further efforts failed to attract them.

"The fish aren't that stupid then?" The man suggested.

As they watched the clear river, colourful patches of weed streaming out in the current, Stephen tipped the bottle letting a continuous trickle fall to the surface below.

242

The man watched; his eyes somehow drawn to the falling water, then suddenly hurried off towards the toilet building.

As he went Jan appeared in the doorway and strode over to join them. "I saw you from the kitchen talking to the caravanner; he left pretty quickly." Nothing wrong is there?

"Gone for a small onion," Stephen spoke quietly with a grin, picking up a tiny pebble and tossing it to the surface below, watching another fish rise to investigate.

Jan looked at the older two, surprised to see them grinning. "Why would he want an onion?"

"A leek." Chris supplied the answer, "A little leak – the loo. Stephen emptied water from a bottle slowly over the bridge to dribble on the river below and he rushed off."

"We say, gone to play the violin," Sharon offered. "Just a saying; it started in our music class."

"The violin," Jan shook her head, but saw immediately that Chris and Stephen understood.

"Had a fiddle, Mum, that's rhyming slang. It's only what they say at school," Sharon added quickly, seeing her mother's expression of disapproval, then seeking a diversion asked, "Any chance of Dad raising my pocket-money?"

"None at all! And don't think you can fool me by changing the subject. It may be a school expression but it's not very ladylike. Anyway, if you really need more pocket-money, go ahead and ask; you do deserve it but choose your moment, catch him in a good mood." Jan headed for the house, the three youngsters talking in a huddle until they too dispersed to their various pursuits.

The sound of Max's engine marked Dad's return in the falling gloom; the children were already inside. Knowing the power supply would still only last for one film and not a long one at that, forced a choice every night. Sharon usually read for a while lying on the bed in her room until viewing time arrived, but tonight she sat in the lounge, apparently playing cards with the boys. Jan smiled, shook her head secretly again at their chances of success and pretended not to notice as whispered comments passed between the three.

The door opened and Dad came in, visited the bathroom, changed from his working clothes then sank into an armchair and asked what time the film was.

"About an hour, want a coffee?" Jan rose, knowing what the answer would be, and made for the kitchen. The sound of a kettle being filled drifted back in.

"Dad," Sharon rolled over on the carpet to sit upright, the playing cards still in her hand. "Does your appendix still hurt?"

Having lit the gas, Jan returned to resume her seat while the question was still being asked. Gordon looked up, surprised and pleased at the concern in his daughter's voice.

"Sometimes, if I move wrongly. Why do you ask?"

"Oh... nothing really. It was awful that morning when we woke up and you were gone. Mum told us all at breakfast."

"Thank you." He glanced at Jan, eyebrows raised in surprise; pleasure and pride on his face.

"It's true," Chris agreed, smiling at his sister then facing back to Dad, "It was difficult without you."

Stephen nodded solemnly in agreement.

With a big sigh of contentment, Gordon looked back at them, seated on the floor, cards strewn all around. They didn't often play together like this these days with Chris almost a man and Sharon growing fast; it was like old times in the caravan. He smiled, "You managed fine, all of you – did really well helping Mum cope with everything. We could never have managed without your help; I'm sorry it lost part of the holiday for you. Was it really bad?"

"No... er," Sharon hesitated. She knew exactly what she wanted to say, but felt somehow guilty. They had been concerned, that was true enough; they had even been keen to help, pleased to know they could do it, could handle adult visitors, persuade them to do things, make them laugh sometimes; it gave a feeling of maturity. But that was not her purpose now and she felt somehow uneasy. "It did keep us from our friends but we enjoyed it, well most of it, but... do you think we deserve more pocket-money?" She was struggling, it was in her face now; even Dad, not always the most sensitive creature in the world where the children were concerned, could see it. He leaned forward stretching out an arm. There was quietness in the room. Sharon took her father's extended hand, squeezing tightly as if asking understanding.

Jan watched from the other chair, seeing the brightness in Gordon's eyes as the two hands clasped; saw him nod slowly, knowing he had understood the situation – not only what had been intended, but understood too the reason for Sharon faltering. As father and daughter looked at each other, Jan tried to read an answer in his face; she had expected opposition, had been prepared to add her own weight, to say how much they deserved it, but no way could she do that now.

"How much did you have in mind?" He spoke quietly, directing the question not at Sharon, but at Jan.

She looked evasively towards the window, then back to see a smile hovering faintly on his face. That too, was a surprise. She realised he knew Sharon's purpose but had not expected him to guess that she herself had encouraged it. How had he penetrated her feelings so easily. Her eyes flicked down to the carpet, then back again, a little shrug and a wave of the hand saying it was up to him.

"Suppose I offer twenty percent? Only those who work out the exact amount can have it. You might think it worthwhile to check each others figures before claiming the increase?"

Planning Permission to change the garage to a shop came through the following Tuesday. An advert in a trade magazine offered second-hand shelving (from some supermarket that was being refitted the small print claimed) but it was in London. Gordon drove off early and alone, returning from the long drive at around midnight, tired but pleased. The shelving, in first class condition and remarkably cheap, would be delivered sometime over the following month, whenever convenient transport became available. Another step in making customers happy!

Jan dressed quietly in the morning and for the first time that year, provided breakfast in bed. The children were already at school when she placed a tray of steaming coffee and toast on the bedside chest and perched lightly on the edge of the mattress, asking about the trip, the shelving and when it would be delivered. Gordon sat up, yawned, stretched a bit and in doing so, reached to pull her down but she evaded him, slipping to the door with a "See you downstairs."

As single garages went, this one was large; twenty-three feet long. At the time of building Jan had asked, "Why so big; when are we buying the Rolls?"

Those words had stopped Gordon in his tracks, inducing a lecture on profligate spending. The size however had been justified, for at one time it housed not only the car, but two mowers, the coal and a workbench. Fortunately the entire garage had been built with a cavity wall – to make it stronger of course, but it removed any danger of damp penetration that might otherwise have affected the stock.

The single window must be removed. Two screws on each side of the frame were normal but this particularly window was much more liberally endowed with such fixings. It yielded eventually to a prolonged assault, a new wall quickly sealing the opening. The floor however, was another matter; it sloped approximately a foot downhill towards the entrance, constructed that way to follow the lie of the ground and so any rain water carried in on the car wheels would drain back outside. A decision must be made.

"Do you think people will mind? There's a lot of work to change it. We'd need two steps at the entrance."

"Um?" Jan surveyed again the downward sweep of

the floor. "It will have to be flat. When did you ever enter a shop where you walk uphill? Mothers will find their pushchairs run away. If it's wet, people may slip. I can help mix the concrete and Chris has offered a hand."

"Thanks. Another excuse to avoid studying? No, I didn't mean that, and it's not so much the concrete anyway. See that beam over the doors. Eleven inches wide, fifteen inches deep and over nine feet long, that's..." he reached for a scrap of paper and doodled with some figures, "about 1800 pounds, er, three-quarters of a ton! It will have to go and I can't let it drop, the foundations might crack. Any suggestion how we remove it?"

"Can't it stay?"

"If we leave it there and raise the floor twelve inches, only dwarfs can enter."

"I wonder," Jan asked quietly, as if to herself, "How many single garages have a three-quarter-ton beam over the door? You put it up there, now let's see you get it down. Can I help?"

"You could take a few roof tiles as I pass them down, just the ones at the edge. Might as well start now. Let's remove the old doors, then I'll get a ladder."

The tiles came away with a little persuasion, the block-work following and as teatime approached the debris was already being cleared. Work stopped when the children raced across the bridge, impressed by the beam's size now that it lay fully exposed. Taking off rubber gloves, Jan stepped across to stand behind them, her hands resting on Sharon and Stephen's shoulders, directing a question to Dad.

"What next?"

"Two great piles of concrete blocks, one under each end, and wide enough to slide the beam forward, clear of the existing walls."

"How will that help," Sharon sounded doubtful.

"We move the beam outwards, then lift one end, take away a layer of blocks and lower it again. Just keep doing

247

that at alternate ends. Simple?"

"Sure," Jan turned to Stephen. "Ask him who will lift it."

Stephen frowned at the beam, a question on his face but he said nothing; no words were necessary, everyone knew Dad had heard.

"We use our small hydraulic jack; we'll need more blocks to put it on and..."

"Who will carry these blocks?!" Sharon interrupted, suddenly suspicious, a doubt confirmed by the smile that spread across her father's face.

Half an hour later, with tea postponed, great stacks of concrete building blocks stood where the doors had been only hours before. The children, having done their part, gathered round to watch Dad at work but soon lost interest and wandered off.

Halfway down, no problems had occurred apart from a liberal covering of sweat. "From exertion or fear?" Jan asked, reaching up and wiping a finger across his forehead, then holding it downwards and watching a single drop of liquid drip off to splash on the floor below. "Come on, give it a rest, the meal is ready and the children want to eat."

Some time later, rested and refreshed, battle recommenced, Jan watching with some concern from a safe distance. The beam now rested eleven blocks high; nearly four feet to go. Another five layers came satisfactorily away but it was swinging outwards, the right hand stack becoming shaky and unbalanced. As the next was being removed, the jack tilted, the whole pile beginning to crumble on the outer side. Throwing his weight against the beam proved hopeless and Gordon jumped clear, watching the slow motion slide until it stopped, the far end still perched precariously against of the other pile. A swift kick and shove from the inside sent it down with a thud! All that remained was to tidy the mess and shift the beam with crow bars. It ended up ten yards away in a ditch, probably to lie there forever.

"Why do we need a sink with two bowls?" Sharon asked a month later. She was standing in the new shop, the front face had already been rebuilt with a normal size door and the walls were now plastered.

"Public Heath requirement," Jan shrugged. "One bowl for washing hands, the other for utensils. I know we have no utensils because everything's prepacked, but that's the regulation, two bowls and hot and cold water. In the mobile we didn't need water at all, hot or cold, or two sinks, in fact not even one sink. To do exactly the same thing here we must have the works! No wonder prices go up all the time. Some politician did promise red tape would be reduced; promised to remove unnecessary rules before breakfast, before lunch and before... Who was he kidding!"

"Will we have a proper till to add up customers bills?"

"No. Stick to your slips of paper. Tills are electric, they need mains current. Dad's fixing a radiator tomorrow; says it's especially for you. Over there," Jan pointed at the rear wall and seeing Sharon's smile of pleasure, shook her head, wondering when her daughter would learn a little more suspicion. "Do you really think you'll need one in summer; might not his real reason be keeping the stock in good condition in winter?"

Three weeks later the walls were painted and the shelves had arrived.

"What size screws are you using?" Jan asked, watching as he started knocking the hundreds of holes for screwing them to the walls.

"Inch and a half number tens. Stainless steel of course."

"Oh, of course. Bit big aren't they?"

"There'll be a lot of weight on these shelves." He went on to give a whole list of weighty items.

"Really? Are you absolutely sure these will be strong enough?"

"Oh yes. Well," he paused, thinking. "You know, I've some two inch number twelve's in the basement, I think

I'll use those." He laid down the hammer and rawlplug tool and disappeared.

Another week saw the shop complete; one of the year's prime objectives achieved. There were no windows now; light entered only through the glass door. Strong Cornish sunshine could not send the chocolate white here! For use in the evenings, three lights from the waterwheel had been mounted on the ceiling, though it was hoped they would seldom be needed.

"How soon will we sell the mobile shop?" Sharon asked at tea.

"Next week possibly, I phoned the advert in yesterday. That reminds me," Jan turned to Gordon, "There's a bit in the paper about a new Race relations act. Will it affect us?"

"The chance would be a fine thing, we've never had anyone black yet. I'm more concerned about the last water bill. Did you know they've put the rate up by twenty-three percent this year?"

CHAPTER 14

Cheaper

Jan felt edgy, had tried several times to settle, first scanning a magazine then sewing, only to rise again and head for the kitchen, returning shortly with two cups of coffee. Determined to cast the restless mood aside, she picked up a novel and sat reading in the armchair for a while, absentmindedly sipping the hot liquid then rested the empty cup down. It was dark outside, a rough night. The wind gusted to a howl drawing her attention. When it ebbed again to a softer note, the swish of the waterwheel, normally so constant that it went unnoticed, seemed louder. Focusing again on the page she remembered nothing of the words read only seconds before and laid the book down, to rise, walking round the room adjusting curtains.

Gordon watched guardedly without appearing to do so, saying nothing. He could sense her tension, her restlessness, noticed the involuntary clenching of a hand, the indecision as she started in one direction, suddenly to change tack and headed off in another. He too, had felt like that once or twice, but there was always work to immerse himself in and by evening the physical exertion had normally pushed such feelings aside. Jan crossed back to the chair, standing beside it. He looked up, "What's wrong?"

"Nothing's wrong!" the retort snapped back, immediately defensive. "Why should anything be wrong?" swivelling on one heel she strode away to the kitchen, filling the kettle with no purpose in mind, a reflex action for idle hands.

Gordon dragged himself from the chair, laid down Roger Phillip's book *Grasses, Ferns, Mosses and Lichens*, collected the empty cups and walked through to join her.

"Can I help." He put the cups on the draining board. Automatically she picked one up.

"No you can't. Go away!"

The cup in her hands slipped and fell to the floor, shattering in a dozen pieces.

"Damn! Now look what you made me do."

"No I didn't," he spoke quietly, walking towards her and holding her shoulders gently, "You're just a difficult age."

She gave a wild shriek, lunging forward, hammering his chest with the sides of tightly clenched fists. Dropping his arms down her back he pulled closer, restricting the movements. The blows gradually lost their force and as her shoulders sagged, he bent forward to kiss her. Up came the head, eyes blazing, like a snake ready to strike!

"Don't you dare!" she wrenched herself away.

"Go and sit down, I'll clear the broken cup. If you really want more coffee, I'll bring one for us both." He guided her gently out through the doorway.

Five minutes later, sitting together in the lounge she was quieter, more under control but an underlying tension remained; the uneasy mood out of character with her normally happy disposition. Gordon held her hand, not forcing conversation, waiting as they continued to sit in silence.

After a while she started to speak, hesitated, then tried to explain. She had no idea what caused the mood, had just felt like screaming, throwing something through a window, pulling her hair out, or better still someone else's hair out.

"Perhaps I'm lonely with the children at school all day. I miss them now; sad they stay at Audrey's to watch the longer films, like tonight. Couldn't we get a bigger battery and watch together as a family right here?" She paused, but before he could answer, spoke again. "I rang Mum at teatime to make sure they were all okay. Sad we get no visitors in winter. Shame you've finished the shop shelves; it doesn't help to have you working so far down the valley. With the wind in this direction I don't even hear Max's engine."

"That means you miss me?" he asked, pleased.

"Miss you! Hmm. Bighead!" She wouldn't admit to it but just the chance to deny any such thing seemed to cheer her up. They smiled at each other, her mood improving. She remained thoughtful for a while, working out something in her mind. "We both know you could take time off now; it wouldn't be catastrophic. That's one of the unsettling things, we could have a break but you don't want to! Most of the site is already laid out... well quite a lot anyway, certainly enough for last summer's trade. We must have as much grass as we need for the moment. Why do you still work all hours? Don't tell me; because you like it I suppose; or is it habit? What about me?"

He made to reply, but she stopped him. "No. I didn't mean it to sound like I don't enjoy the valley any more. I do, but I get this feeling occasionally. Couldn't we get away; some longer trips, not necessarily this year but maybe next?"

There was some truth in what she said. Those longish hours could be partly from habit; but not entirely. Some things must still be finished this winter. He paused for a minute, thinking, then nodded agreement.

"Okay. If you like. A few trips around the world won't hurt at all." Seeing the broad smile that these words brought to her lips, he glanced towards the window and the drawn curtains that kept them snug as the wind howled again. The valley beyond, a scene so busy last summer, was devoid of people now, even the rabbits would hide on a night like this. He turned back to Jan. "When we do eventually go, it will have to be before the site gets busy. We should need someone to run it while we're away. A few years yet perhaps – would you mind?"

"No. Not really. It's something to look forward to; to dream about when I start feeling sorry for myself. You won't mind spending the money? Is it a promise?"

"Well yes, I promise. We can visit caravan parks abroad; see what people from those countries expected on holiday."

A small fist thumped his ribs. He stepped back quickly, arms covering up in self-defence, surprised to see loving exasperation had replaced her smile.

Shaking her head she sighed, "I should have known. Single minded, that's what you are!"

"Single minded? Me? Never!"

"Oh no? Why else would anyone spend a holiday inspecting other people's toilets?"

"Not just toilets; the roads, the grass, how big are the pitches, how far apart do they expect to park, is there hot food, or a shop, do they mix caravans and tents together, do..."

"All right! If it makes you happy, we'll inspect some other sites. For peace and quiet, okay? What would you do if I refused?"

"Ah, but you can't!"

"Oh?" Jan took a step forward, fist bunching again. "Why not?"

"You promised to obey... when I bought you, remember? And don't forget the honour bit too!" He took another step backwards but found himself trapped against the wall fending off her make-believe blows... and then they were together arms round each other, lips meeting. After a while they leaned back, he checked the clock on the opposite wall; the children would be home soon.

"You needn't think this means you've won," Jan smiled, not attempting to break away. "I had my fingers crossed in that bit of the ceremony. We'll inspect a few sites if it's important, but how much will you learn, what

254

advantage will it really be?"

"I'm interested. We think this park is the best, but is it? We learn all the while, even from the children. You think back. Stephen thought of those handles on the toilet buildings for tying dogs to; Chris heard about that hose for filling motorcaravanner's fresh water tanks. It cost very little but they all use it now. We'll be making that special drain-out point for their waste water tanks as soon as the sewer is connected. That's the sort of thing a trip might show, but there's more, something very important. On a trip to inspect caravan parks, you become cheaper!"

"Cheaper? Not very flattering to a girl. Anyway, how could I?"

"You become tax-deductible!"

They stood still locked together, Gordon holding her arms tightly to restrict any blows, but the phone rang.

"Lucky you! Saved by the bell," Jan reach for the receiver, listened then replied. "No, tell them to stay there, Gordon will come down in the car." Another pause as something was said at the other end then, "Yes, he will won't he, soaked probably. Serves him right!" and she put the phone down, pleased with herself, smiling and telling him to fetch the children, knowing he could hardly refuse.

When the car returned, they rushed into the house, full of life and excitement, talking non-stop about the film, often all at once, only Chris showing some reserve befitting his growing years. With the plot discussed and dissected, Sharon mentioned the heroine's clothes, asking hopefully, "Did we make a lot of money this year?"

"Yes. We did rather well," Jan turned to Gordon. "Tell them."

"Mum's wrong. Actually, we are down on last year, I worked it out this morning." He reached for a scrap of paper. "Here, 6805 caravan days rather than 7374, a seven percent drop."

"I'm not wrong! Go on, answer Sharon's question. Tell her about the money."

Gordon rose, crossed to the desk, reached in a drawer and extracted a file. "Um, we made a profit of £2774, not very..."

"Better than last year!" Jan cut in. "Don't think you can fool me, I checked the figures too. That's £157 more; we could both buy new dresses with that."

Sharon's face lit up in a huge smile at her mother, but the smile faded as Dad waved a warning finger.

"There's no way you're spending that much on dresses! And you *are* wrong. In real terms we really have gone down; inflation was nearly seventeen percent."

Jan shrugged, "No dresses then?"

Gordon smiled with relief, realising now she had teased. "Perhaps a skirt, a blouse or jumper too if you wait for the January sales," he leaned towards Steven and Chris, "See the problems you'll have with expensive women when you grow up and get married. Do you know, I already give your mother twenty-five pounds every week!"

"Expensive!" Jan exploded, and was about to say more but Sharon and Chris were already arguing loudly. Hearing them, she leaned back waiting, then noticed that Gordon was gazing studiously at the wall. No smile showed but she could tell from that innocently vacant, *I don't understand* expression, that he was laughing. In that moment, their eyes met and she mouthed the words silently, '*wait 'til I get you alone*'.

When quietness was restored, Jan winked at Sharon, "If inflation has gone up so much, don't you think the housekeeping money should rise?" Switching attention to Gordon, she spoke more seriously, "Okay, you may be right, perhaps we haven't done so well, but buying food each week gets increasingly difficult. What will you do with the money anyway?"

For a while he rubbed his chin, trying to decide how best to explain. "You *should* have a rise, I know that, but can it start from next Easter when visitors are coming again?" Receiving a nod, he continued. "Quite a bit has already been spent on the shop but some should come back when we sell the mobile. I'm hoping there's enough for more tarmac; the stretch of road below the terraces and maybe the one in the front field. Those sections are very dusty in the dry weather, a proper finish would be much nicer for caravanners. Can you think of anything more important?" He watched the circle of faces, waiting for suggestions.

"My friends," Sharon offered, "the ones that have dogs and pitch along the riverbank or those with a tent at the far downstream end; they say it's too far to walk for a shower. Couldn't you build the third toilets instead?"

"I could and as you say, it is more important. It's only December; I could probably have it built before we open but the sewer is not ready yet. The officials say the works should start receiving effluent in about five months. That's well after Easter. Our pipework is ready but I still have to dig down in several places to make the new connections. That can't be done in the season; extra manholes are involved and the pipework must be dry. It will have to wait for next winter. Okay?"

Sharon frowned and was about to say more but Chris spoke first.

"Dad means that if we build the other toilets now, they must stand empty and locked all season. That would annoy people more than if the building was not there at all." Chris turned to his father, "That pipework; even in the winter the house water runs down. How will you keep it dry?"

"I'll put in a drain plug to hold up the flow, and no baths for a week unless Sharon wants to use the river again?"

"Next winter will be costly then," Jan raised an eyebrow. "What about this year?"

"The tarmac – expensive but quick. A day is all it will take. We might get lucky with some topsoil to grass a few more pitches. The site is already looking better don't you

257

think?"

"Tell you tomorrow; we'll walk round together. You won't forget that little job I want done in the house?"

When the children left for school next morning, Jan climbed the valley side, guided by noise from the digger to where the trailer was being loaded.

The engine died, Gordon climbed off and limped towards her.

"Affecting your leg again, I see." Jan pointed to the sizeable remaining mound of mine waste. "How long?"

"Hm, bit stiff, wear off in a minute. About a month before it's all gone."

"You said that last time. Come on, the walk will do you good." She took his hand and they strode off, the limp soon disappearing.

Standing on the bridge a few minutes later, the bare hedgerows could be ignored; only the very earliest visitors would see them without leaves. The front of the house however would not change with the seasons. It looked uninspiring; they had discussed it before but found no solution.

"Couldn't you try something; alter those concrete steps, they're too small, or some plant tubs or a Cornish wall in front... maybe a patio?" Jan tilted her head to one side trying to imagine the various possibilities.

"I could draw some plans. Easier to move things about on paper than to build a wall in the wrong place and knock it down again later."

They walked on past neatly cut grass areas, the valley looking good, the bareness of naked branches broken here and there by an evergreen shrub. Nothing really needed here, a few extra trees perhaps. Passing a niche where the third toilet building was planned, Jan stopped.

"Where will the cars park? Don't expect them all to walk! I've seen visitors drive less than fifty yards, park outside the toilets then drive back to their caravan. It's quite a way to the farthest downstream pitches; in bad weather most will come by car, you can't expect otherwise."

"I suppose they will." He crossed the road. "This rubbishy area under the oaks; I can level a hard surface for... let's see; about six cars? It should be enough. I can do it now, over the coming few weeks; save time next winter."

They walked past more grassy areas until the road petered out, the surrounding land still undeveloped. Some of these lower sections were not far from level in their natural state, but the ground was poor, so poor that few trees grew except along the western fringe. Even the gorse was sparse, a few widely spaced spindly stems, patches of brambles here and there restricting easy access. These areas required little filling, just cut the undergrowth and level off. A coating of topsoil would help; no decent grass would grow on the present sandy gravelly mixture. Still, the porous subsoil might offer good drainage and become less soft in any wet spells.

Returning they took the upper road to higher ground, passing Bluebell Wood. A few trees needed removing, one decayed with age, others overwhelmed by the sheer weight of ivy strangling them; several were elms.

"This is the section of road I want to tarmac," Gordon swept an arm forward and back indicating a curving 300-metre stretch.

"Make life easier without potholes to repair." Jan nodded and they moved on, veering right, up the hill again to where Max was parked, then wandering to the very edge of the top terrace. From this high perch, the major part of the valley floor was visible; grassy pitches with several birds hunting the turf for a meal, a solitary rabbit that scampered into some bushes but not a single person in any direction; the contrast with August was marked.

"Be nice to get rid of that before the season." Jan pointed to the mobile shop; it looked much smaller from here. The vehicle had been advertised but no interest yet shown. "When will you order the tarmac?"

259

"I'll ring Mr Crowle this afternoon, get an estimate, tell him he can do it when he likes as long as it's before March; cheaper that way."

"Will you finish your work by then?"

"A fraction over two months until we open; should be enough. The hedges are mostly trimmed, a bit still to do if we get the time."

January passed and now at last all the mine waste was gone. So it should be after nearly seven years work! With this task finished, the big five-ton trailer was sold. Never a thing of great beauty, it could serve no further useful purpose. The road to the bottom of the site was now complete, its stony surface leaving something to be desired. Elsewhere, the extra tarmac had already been laid but money was tight; a third at least of the roads remained just stone. The tarmac gang with their special machine had laid a super-smooth surface on the selected section, completing it as predicted in one day, much to the children's admiration.

Seeing the finished road after school that evening, Sharon asked again, "Mum, why can't Dad work that fast?"

However, in spite of appearances he had not been idle and the winter had shown good progress. The recreation field part way along the entrance road had received attention, being flattened and levelled for easier mowing and a better playing surface. That should please boys in the eight to fourteen age group who wanted cricket and football; older teenagers found other pursuits, seldom playing with the youngsters. All the terraces were complete now except for a lack of topsoil, though some were planned to remain as hardstandings.

"What happens if we ever do get a very wet summer?" Gordon asked. "Heavy vehicles could destroy the place, cut up all the turf and make life miserable for those coming later – miserable for me too; I'd have to put it all right! The hardstandings stay!"

Opening day approached; trimming hedges, bushes and trees resumed. No garden-like neatness was intended; rather the removal of foliage and branches was deliberately irregular to maintain a natural appearance. Standing on the ground it was possible to reach some eight feet in the air, but taller overhanging boughs were beginning seriously to encroach on many pitches. The grass too had started to grow and needed a cut.

"I'll cope with the mowing," Jan promised sweetly as they sat for a mid-morning break. It was no hardship, she normally tended this chore out of season.

"Thanks?" Gordon smiled, waiting for the rest, for the *'but'*. He guessed why the offer had been made. Jan wanted the lounge wallpapered. He had promised to find time, but tasks he once thought would be completed soon after Christmas had somehow dragged on, taking longer than expected. Partly this was over-optimism, partly an increasing stiffness of the left leg caused by driving Max. Nevertheless, the weather being mainly fine, the wallpapering had been put off in spite of numerous small reminders. Now the subject was about to be raised again; of that he felt sure!

From the chair, he peered carefully up under shielded eyes, knowing by some instinct that she was watching. Catching the intense stare, he continued to straighten, as if looking out across the river had always been the intention. "Not much sign of leaves growing yet." The remark seemed casual but he was having great difficulty keeping a straight face.

Jan continued to wait, silently watching, seeing the ghost of a smile that no one else would ever have detected. He had agreed to redecorate and he would, she knew that, but it had been put off all winter and she wanted it started; wanted it done before people arrived! Still sitting, he turned, apparently to gaze through the other window, leaving her watching the back of his neck. A slight tremor

261

of the lips as the head swung away made her aware of his difficulty containing a laugh. She should be angry, but somewhere inside a laughter of her own was forming. Rising, she moved close to stand above him. Lunch break was over, he must rise and return to work any moment; a little patience, that was all it required.

Minutes passed, the battle joined; they waited, neither speaking. A restiveness within him, a need to get back to work, to get on, could not be concealed – at any rate not from her. With a sigh he rose and they faced each other.

"Why the hurry? What are you working on?"

"The hedges, they're growing too tall. Must get on." He made to leave.

"I was about to suggest, if you stand in the excavator's big front bucket, I'll drive you slowly along the hedgerows so you can reach – like a tall handsome man would?"

The idea stopped him, it might be the answer. Jan's round, unquestionably; he gave a nod of acquiescence and they were together, hugging.

Shortly after, Max's engine roared into life. Equipped with bow-saw and branch-loppers, he climbed aboard to be lifted in the air. The big machine moved off, Jan taking her direction from the outstretched arm in the bucket above.

The system had advantages, it saved time, brought those taller parts within reach without using the stepladder which in any case had been unsafe, the legs penetrating the soil unevenly and tending to tip over. They had ignored the hedge tops for several years, not realising the branches were growing so high. Some that now overhung grassy areas would continue to drip water onto caravan roofs long after any spell of rain; others more upright, hid the sun that most people wished to enjoy. Perching high in the bucket had its own hazards, stretching for branches at the limit of reach then shouting down instructions above the engine noise, but it was certainly quicker.

During a break for coffee, Jan suggested, "This must be saving quite a bit of time; leave you more for little jobs around the house."

"Um, possibly."

She frowned at the non-committal reply but said nothing more. When he climbed in the bucket again she pulled the lever hard, sending it abruptly upwards, stopping high above with a jerk. Catching his balance then leaning over with the intention of protesting, he was stopped as a gear grated and Max jumped forward. There had been no argument but the great good spirit of earlier in the day had somehow lost itself in the difference of opinion, each feeling niggly with the other. The machine went over a bump faster than it should; high in the bucket he gripped the side more tightly to avoid being thrown out, recovering to shout down something uncomplimentary about women drivers.

An angry voice floated back up, "You want woman drivers, I'll give you woman drivers!" The engine revved, picking up speed and simultaneously the bucket lowered to a mere four feet above the ground.

Gordon clung on with both hands; they were heading straight for a big clump of gorse at a speed that would take them straight through and out the other side. Automatically he let go with one hand, holding it to protect his face. Without warning the bucket tipped as if dumping its load and Max braked, skidding to a halt. He shot forward, crashing through the spiky tips, the gorse stems below bending to break his fall. As he came to rest the engine note grew again, reversing rapidly, swinging round to drive smartly off.

Maybe he'd better do some wallpapering!

***

"Did you know the chromium plating is peeling off the soap dishes in the toilets?" Chris asked as they ate.

An inspection when the meal finished, showed it to be true. They were not only peeling but the metal beneath, whatever it was, seemed to be rotting away to a white powdery substance. Jan sighed. Even the best-laid plans could go awry. The lounge walls had been washed and rolls of wallpaper lay ready in a pile in one corner, chosen and paid for the previous day – a white background of course, with a tracery of gold pattern, something suitably reflective to help their small lights. This new discovery would mean a further postponement; she realised that. The site was open in a few days and anything affecting customers took precedence. A search of various builders' merchants catalogues offered several types of replacement dish, but every one with inadequate screws.

"Look at the fixings." Dad pushed a catalogue towards the boys. "Only two small concealed woodscrews and a grubscrew so tiny you can hardly see it. That will never be strong enough."

"Why does everything have to be strong?" Jan shook her head. "They only have to take a cake of soap!"

"No." Stephen shook his head. The single word intervention was unexpected, drawing attention, forcing him to say more. "Young boys hang on them because the taps are high."

"That's right," Chris nodded, "makes it easier to reach. Some older ones will too, trying to climb up and look over the partitions when a friend is in the next shower."

"You see," Dad addressed Jan and Sharon, still obviously doubtful, "they do need to be strong. We can make our own. Brass tarnishes badly and stainless steel is difficult to bend; aluminium will be best."

"Will they be shiny again like the last ones?" Sharon asked.

"Chrome plated you mean? No, I don't think so, that would have to be on brass. I read it up last winter; fancied using our spare waterwheel current for electroplating but the chemicals involved are dangerous. In the future maybe but not this year, there's no time. I want that last area at the bottom of the site levelled and... er," he glanced across at Jan, "I believe Mum wants a little job done in the house."

264

A firm at Deveron supplied aluminium off-cuts. These bits, too small for normal use and therefore really cheap, would be fine for soap dishes. Working on the basement bench the metal was cut to shape, drilled, the edges bent up to stop the soap slipping off, and everything carefully rounded and smoothed. By the following morning they were being fixed to the wall near the taps in each shower.

Alone in the house, Jan moved the lighter furniture from the lounge, covered the floor in dustsheets, then mixed the wallpaper paste. A cheap folding table lived somewhere in the basement, she descended the stairs, finding it in one corner of the workroom, noticing in passing that there were still five new soap dishes on the bench. He had forgotten them... no he hadn't! Four must be for the third toilet building, the one not yet built, and the fifth? She shook her head, switching the light off and lifting the table, finding difficulty manoeuvring it up the stairs and into position with armchairs partially blocking both hall and office.

Approaching ten o'clock, Gordon appeared, stopping inside the door and shaking his head. "I want to finish the levelling downstream. Why..."

"Don't worry, this will keep. No need to do it now, I just thought getting ready would save time when you start. Sorry about the mess, we're open the day after tomorrow but customers won't notice, will they?"

Shortly after a late lunch, the wallpapering was finished, the dustsheets gone and the furniture back in place. Jan was aware the indoor work had not been planned for that day, his hand forced by the state of the office as she knew it would be. Blackmail perhaps, but it had worked! She watched him reach for the excavator key and hurry off – now he would try to catch up.

CHAPTER 15

Pegs

"Sewage works. It's started." Stephen spoke quietly, then resumed eating, as those around the table looked up sharply. It was still early March, only the third day since the site opened. The sewer should not be live until May or so they had been told.

"How do *you* know?" Sharon beat Dad to the question.

"Boy at school."

"What about this boy at school?" Gordon asked, a touch of urgency in his voice.

"His father's friend works there." Stephen cut into his poached egg and toast, taking another mouthful, not attempting to give the circumstances behind his discovery, not tempted to elaborate as Sharon might have done.

"Won't try to connect until winter, will you?" Jan hoped not. She knew that now they were open it would mean working all hours to get the job done quickly and the system functioning again. "No real point is there? The third toilets aren't built and everything else works fine the way it is. Anyway, there are two caravans already here."

"True, but if they leave we could close for a few days to get the final bits of pipework done. I know it would make no difference to visitors this year, but it *would* mean we were officially joined to the sewer. I'll ring the works tomorrow, get permission to connect. It's important!"

"Why..." Jan saw Gordon's head shake slightly, and his eyes flick towards the children. It stopped her. With a

266

wave of the hand she passed it off, "Okay. If you want."

Not very interested in the sewage works, Chris changed the subject, "I need a door key."

"No." Dad's reply was rapid and definite. "You lost the last one, I had to change the lock. We'll wait up."

"I may be very late." Resentment showed in Chris's face.

"That was back in last summer," Jan jumped to his defence. "Even if he lost it again, there's nothing to steal at this time of year."

"And suppose someone picks it up? What's to stop them keeping it until peak season when the house is full of money? Tell me that."

"It's all cheques, no use to anyone. Any cash we take you pay to the tradesmen."

"*I* know that, and *you* know that, but would a burglar know?" Gordon turned back to Chris, "How late?"

"Depends how I do. If things go really well I may stay overnight with... a friend." Chris looked down at the table with a silly grin.

"Oh?" Dad hesitated. "I see. If you're not back by the time we go to bed, I'll leave a key outside."

"Really?" Jan's spoke with extreme sarcasm. "Someone may come and find it, break in and pinch... what?" she raised an arm to encompass the whole room. "What would you steal if you broke in? Hm!"

It was true enough, there was very little worth stealing, certainly no money, and houses that ran on waterwheels were not notable sources of electrical goods.

"Not where I shall hide it, they won't. And it doesn't even go out there until we go to bed."

"Where will you put it?" Sharon asked.

"Never you mind. That's between Chris and me, and don't think we'll put it in the same place every time."

Sharon looked at her mother with a frown. Receiving only a shrug, she turned her resentment to Chris. "I bet he's arranged to see that film with somebody, the one we can't watch because it's over two hours long."

Chris's smile confirmed that her charge had hit its target. Irritation and resentment masked both the younger faces, Jan saw it grow and sought for words of comfort.

"We can turn on for the last hour if you like, but be fair, it's not Chris's fault. You watch sometimes with your friends from guides and come back late."

"I know," Sharon smiled half-heartedly to her brother. "Dad did say once he would buy a bigger battery."

Chris left shortly after, having first taken a shower in the toilet building rather than having a bath in the house, and spent some time in his room dressing. Watching from the office door as he cycled off up the road, Sharon leaned close to whisper something in Stephen's ear.

Jan stood in the background during the departure, wondering whether to wish her eldest son success or failure; she saw Sharon's whisper and watched a grin spread on Stephen's face, his clenched fist flexing inward at the wrist, the arm bending up from the elbow. Ah yes, her youngest was growing up too. They would both probably go out for the evening, pity about the television.

"Well, what was so secret at tea?" Jan spoke as they watched the two children walking off down the road, guessing they would end up at Jim's for the big film. "You wouldn't really close the site just to join the sewer, would you?"

"Yes I would, and now we're alone I'll tell you why. It's the tents. We've hardly spoken of it all winter, but the problem is still there. You know the situation as well as I do; until we join the sewer, we remain on the temporary permission that allows tents. Fine. But once we connect, then we're back on the original planning, which refers only to caravans. We need two more years before the Council notice the discrepancy. We're not safe until two years *after* we connect to the sewer!"

"You really think it's worth all the hassle of closing, turning people away, just to save six months?"

"I do..." He had intended to say more, to mention that it would also allow a special emptying point for motor-caravans to be made for this season instead of next, but realising the significance of those two small words just uttered, he stopped short. As Jan waited, a questioning expression on her face, he eased himself away, glancing towards the window trying to make the backward step look casual. "It's just that I promised myself never to use those words again."

"No wonder you moved out of range." They stood looking at each other, then Jan reached out a hand and when he took it, guided him into the lounge where they sat, looking out over the river and the valley.

"Okay." Gordon looked across at the other chair. "So you want something. Just what is it you intend persuading me to do? Don't put on that innocent look. I offer a little insult and you smile instead of hitting me, then pull me across to a chair and sit quietly down. That sort of thing can raise a chap's blood pressure." He looked at the open door leading to the rest of the house, "Is it wallpapering another room?"

"Wallpaper? That would be nice but I hadn't thought about it. How much other work is there still to do? Have you finished using Max?"

"I think so, I should paint the old machine really. All the intended pitches are levelled now. Some parts I've left rough deliberately, for the wild life; our type of customers expect the country not Kew gardens. They like the wild flowers, the butterflies..." he broke off with a movement of the hand, fingers opening to say 'you know.'

She nodded, they had discussed it often enough. "The new batteries Sharon spoke of; how long could we watch TV with those?"

"Indefinitely. Our existing lead-acid ones take twenty amp-hours in their present condition; a set of nickel-alkaline batteries the size we need would hold up to ten times that amount, but they're expensive, several hundred pounds.

269

That's more than we have left. Next year perhaps."

"Next year Chris may be gone. Sharon hopes to make university in a few years too." Jan paused, then hurried on. "Your leg gets better every summer with the excavator put away; rather than paint it again and have trouble keeping children off all season, why don't you sell Max?"

There was no reply. He stared blankly into space giving no acknowledgement of having heard, his body present in the room but mind elsewhere, running back over the years. It was true Max could do little now, even trimming the hedge tops was complete and would need no attention for several years. What about the third toilet building? Only the foundations would need a digger; half a day was all it would take, cheap enough to hire one. Little worries about the machine's future had bothered him from time to time as the groundwork drew to a close, but in those lonely hours he had pushed such things immediately aside, refusing to consider them, half believing that Max might sense his thoughts. Now he must decide, weigh up the merits, consider the family. What Jan said was right, his leg did get better; recovered completely in summer, and it *would* be difficult again this year to stop children climbing and playing on the old machine; it always was. Not that Max would mind, he liked childr... Stop it! He forced the thought away. Max was a machine; a machine that needed maintenance, greasing, servicing; time that far exceeded the hours of useful work now ever likely to be needed. And it was a dangerous toy when children climbed aboard, they could easily slip and get hurt. A sale seemed the only sensible solution. Max might even be happier somewhere else with more to do. Was he bored standing idle all summer? But would another driver treat him right, ease his bucket upwards as he loaded rather than ram straight in scrabbling the tyres and making them sore? No, Jan was right, he... it – must be sold. The logic was inescapable but a certain nostalgic attachment prevented any immediate decision; there must be other jobs that

270

would need doing?

Jan had not moved. She sat silently watching; had opened her mouth once to add some persuasive touch but decided against. Selling had only been a suggestion, it must be his decision.

A phone call the following morning revealed the sewage works would not be officially commissioned for at least a couple more months, scotching any ideas of an early connection; perhaps it was just as well. Leaving the office, Gordon walked slowly round to where Max was parked and stood looking at the machine. After a while he returned indoors for a bucket of soapy water and a soft cloth.

Early the following month the sale finally took place. Even before the decision was made, Max had been given a fresh coat of paint. The old machine had served the family well, had earned proper care and attention, but it was time to part. In any case, the site had a garden tractor with a mower mounted beneath; toy sized by comparison but lightweight and with wide tyres to avoid damaging the turf. There was a trailer too, a miniature version for transporting soil or branches; of course loading and unloading would be by hand but no great quantity of soil moving was expected and having loaded the trailer, grassy pitches could be crossed without leaving deep ruts. Crossing such areas had always been difficult with the heavier machine, particularly in winter months when most work was done. Max fetched £825, more than twice the amount paid some seven years earlier but the balance had certainly been lavished on care and maintenance since. So all those years of use had been practically free and it would leave in vastly better condition than on arrival! Quite satisfactory, at least it had seemed so when the bargain was struck. However, when the collection lorry arrived one morning and the faithful machine was driven onto the low platform behind the cab, things seemed less clear. Doubts, feelings of having in some way done wrong, assailed him. As a series of broad straps were looped round Max's wheels then wrenched up tight for the journey, Gordon winced, wishing the men would be more gentle, wanting to tell them but knowing they would only laugh. Instead he turned away, recalling the day Chris had watched his goat loaded on a trailer to be taken off to a new home. It was silly but as the lorry drove away he sensed Max reproaching him, like an old friend discarded, sent off to an unknown home after serving so well. His eyes followed the departing lorry feeling slightly wretched, wanting to snatch the excavator back. What a cad to be so ungrateful.

The children, on arriving home, noticed the machine's absence from its normal place. They had already been briefed on the sale, opinion splitting as expected, Sharon in favour, the two boys reluctant to see it go. Stephen in particular regretted the departure though he said little. It was one of his earliest memories.

The new battery arrived the following week and at Jan's suggestion was installed in the basement and the charging sequence started without a word to the children. The following day a thick cable was run under the basement ceiling to a point just below the corner where the television rested. Moving aside the furniture and turning back the carpet, a small hole was made that allowed the cable to pass up through the concrete floor and connect directly into the set. All was ready and back to normal long before the children arrived home, a rush job but with reason; a particularly good film was showing that evening!

"Okay, I fixed everything just the way you asked but they won't want to watch it," Gordon warned. "They know it's too long; over two hours. You won't fool them, they always look up the times."

"I've arranged something with Audrey. They start watching here and we tell them that when the power goes, you'll run them down to Jim's bungalow to watch the end. They'll keep expecting those dark margins to appear round the screen as the power fades, but it won't happen. You

272

are sure? It really will last?"

"I'm sure, but why bring Audrey into it; why not just pretend you've made the arrangements?"

"Two things; Sharon will probably ring up and check, particularly if *you* make the suggestion. She's become very cynical recently about boys telling the truth."

"And the other reason?"

"Me. I'm cynical too, about male honesty. I still think it may not work!"

In the event Sharon had no need to ring Audrey. She had checked the programs before breakfast and when calling in at Jim's bungalow that evening as they usually did on the way home, had asked if she might come back later for the long program. Audrey, being briefed beforehand, suggested the exact arrangement that Jan had proposed.

Before the program started, Dad was forced by weight of numbers to turn the car round so it faced in the right direction and place the keys on the desk ready to grab. When an hour had passed and still the picture remained strong, disappointment and a certain impatience showed in the young faces. By the time the film had ended however, good humour all round was restored and Jan led down the basement stairs, along the corridors and into the workroom. In one corner stood the expensive battery set, the top shielded from dust by a large plastic cover, an old discarded rooflight from a caravan. Gordon stood in the background waiting for the reaction, expecting the family to turn to him which a great show of appreciation but their enthusiasm was muted, the faint praise leaving him deflated.

As evening wore on and the parents sat alone, Jan said quietly, "You know why, don't you?"

"Why what?"

"Why they were less pleased than you expected. They were hoping the supply would run out; wanted it to so they could watch the rest up at Jim's." She stopped and smiled at the surprise on his face. "Jim's set is in colour!"

273

Easter approached, another quick trip to cash-and-carry laid in extra stocks but the shop shelves were still half empty – there were so many, so much space compared to the mobile. Some things, biscuits for example, were short dated. A case might hold twenty-four packets, so buying in April was out of the question; the sell-by date would expire before the main season. The new fridge had proved a success – low and somewhat erratic numbers made it difficult to guess how much to order but not a pint of milk had so far been wasted. That looked about to change! Two families travelling together had left unexpectedly on bad news from home; they had been big milk drinkers with a tribe of young children between them. The departure left six bottles standing unused on Thursday evening. Friday saw five of them sold, leaving one that now, on Saturday morning, was three days old. It could not be offered to a customer. Jan fetched the bottle through to the kitchen, expecting to tip it away but tried some first in a teaspoon. It was fine.

"Mum," Sharon called, "Do we have any tent pegs?" She was serving in the shop.

Jan came through from the kitchen, "No, sorry." She reached the communicating door and saw a teenage boy, perhaps fourteen or fifteen, standing at the counter, "Are you short of some?"

"My parents forgot them; packed the tent and left the pegs behind. I hoped you'd have some to stop the argument. They're blaming each other; I think we might end up going home. Where could we get some?"

"Scorrier," Jan offered. "I'll tell you how to..."

"Not me. I'm not going anywhere with them right now. I'll send Dad in; tell him the route!" The lad hurried off.

Sharon's eyes followed; there was no one else her own age on holiday at the moment. Aware suddenly that her mother was watching, she looked away, then muttered,

274

"Pity he's a boy."

Jan nodded, "Good-looking isn't he. Let me take over; the father might be angry."

"Angry with us?"

"He might think a camp shop ought to stock tent pegs; we should really. Make yourself scarce, he'll be here soon, I've finished in the kitchen anyway."

Sharon left, walking through into the house, turning as if to her bedroom, but once hidden from view leant against the corridor wall waiting. Shortly after, hearing voices in the shop, she eased open the basement door, slipping silently down the stairs and into the workroom. Dad occasionally found tent pegs the hard way; with the mower. Sometimes they flew away like missiles, one dented a caravan once, but often they clattered round inside the blade housing to drop flat on the grass and be left behind. Whoever was mowing always stopped to search and pick them up; left lying they could damage the blades again at the next mowing. These pegs were put in the dustbin if Mum was mowing but Dad seldom threw things away; any relatively straight ones might still be on the bench.

A search revealed only two. Disappointing. One was badly bent. Putting an end in the vice, she pulled steadily, unclamped and moved the angle slightly then pulled again. Dad would have finished off with a hammer to get a more perfect line, but it was good enough; besides, such noise would bring unwelcome questions. This was just an idea, a flight of fancy never before attempted that might work out – or it might be abandoned with no one ever knowing. The pegs sat snugly in one hand but could not be carried openly, some hiding place essential to avoid embarrassing explanations. She was wearing slacks with no pockets and an old blue jumper that had become a little tight. Pushing the thin metal up inside a sleeve concealed them, but she wanted something else! Taking the secateurs from a shelf and easing them under the other sleeve was fine but the shape showed clearly through the already tight material.

Looking around for inspiration, her eye fell on a box of broad elastic bands; there were others upstairs in the desk drawer, a couple more added each day, coming with the mail, used by the postman to hold the letters together. As always Dad stored them away. Undoing the buckle and slipping off the broad heeled brown shoe, a fashion she had recently persuaded her mother to buy, Sharon slipped three bands over her foot and up round the ankle. Replacing the shoe and resting it against the wall, she pulled up the trouser leg, reached again for the secateurs, then worked the circles of elastic upwards to hold the tool tight to the outside of her left calf. That would be the side farthest from Mum when she passed the shop door. Pulling the trouser leg down, two experimental paces and a spin on one heel assured that nothing showed. She felt good, just like that girl in a movie they had watched recently, with a gun strapped inside her thigh. Adopting a supposedly seductive pose, then switching through a series of others just as the girl on screen had done, Sharon imagined herself in the part, gave a small giggle and headed for the stair, returning briefly to pull the light switch cord.

As she appeared in the hallway, Jan called from the shop, "They've gone; gone to Penzance for a meal and if they can't buy tent pegs in the town they're travelling home overnight. They can't cook unless the tent is up."

"Did they ask for their money back?" Sharon really wanted to ask a different question, but held back at the last moment thinking it too obvious.

"No. They only paid for one night to see if the location suited before booking more. They want a shower before travelling and said the night's fee would cover it. Generous, but I didn't argue. Just the parents went, not the boy, he must still be on site somewhere."

Sharon let her breath out slowly; that was the question she had wanted to ask. "I'm going out for a time, while it's quiet. Okay?" She saw her mother nod and hurried to the office door, then made for the service passage. Four more tent pegs lay on the bench; two were bent but there was no vice here. The bench top was made of old railway sleepers, at one point they fitted badly. Pushing the first peg down between the timbers, she leaned against the outer sleeper and pulled towards herself. The peg straightened; the other quickly followed.

Locating the tent was merely a process of elimination; only in one very restricted area did tents and caravans mix, a place reserved for families travelling together; elsewhere tents were on their own separate areas. Hurriedly she looked at each and in a niche between trees towards the downstream boundary saw bright orange canvas lying on the ground. Some distance away a lad stood on the river-bank. She had never approached an unknown boy like this before; nervous self-consciousness almost turned her back but he was watching and had seen her, that was obvious; she could not turn away now without feeling stupid.

The young visitor had indeed noticed, had seen the approach from some distance but knowing she worked on the site he was unsure, thinking she might be looking for another, afraid to signal in case she ignored him.

Sharon walked on along the road, not yet turning to cross the grassy strip. Why didn't he wave or make some acknowledgement? For some reason the tool still strapped to her leg heightened the tension, recalling again the film. Would he reach any moment for his gun and would she dive forward drawing her own? Her eye fell on a bush that would provide cover but she passed it by. Coming level with where he stood on the riverbank, she turned and crossed directly towards him.

"I found six," she held out the four pegs, then remembering the other two, pulled them out from under her jumper sleeve.

"They've gone to get some. They're still shouting at each other so I stayed here, but thanks anyway."

"Six is enough for the main guy ropes," Sharon glanced towards the tent, trying to keep her voice even.

"We could have it half up by the time they came back?"

"We?" He was uncertain. "You'd help?"

"My job." It was said defensively. Sharon started towards the tent, walking quickly to keep ahead so he couldn't see her face.

Reaching it together, the boy produced a mallet, tossed it on the ground, then picked up one of the poles. As he tried to lift the canvas one handed, Sharon took the pole from him, squeezed inside and wriggled it into position, heaving upwards until it stood erect – holding on while he secured the first guy rope. Within a few minutes the poles were in position and the main guys stretched. Now the shape was there but the bottom hung loose, moving at every small puff of wind.

"Pity we only have six," the lad seemed uneasy, unsure what more to say. After a pause he spoke again. "My name is Ken..." As if regretting the words, he rushed on, "Do you work here often?"

"I live here. I'm Sharon. We could make more pegs."

"How?" He looked surprised.

She smiled, pleased with the reaction, not telling him the technique came from Guides. "Come on, I'll show you." She turned, sprinting off heading toward the downstream areas where the land had been levelled but not topsoiled, seeing from the corner of one eye that he followed. There were still thick clumps of foliage here, much of it hazel.

"Look!" Her fingers ran over a branching stem. "Dad intends to trim these next winter. If we cut just below the fork, then cut one stem off long and one short, we have a tent peg."

"How do we cut it?"

"The best girls go prepared," as Sharon spoke she lifted one foot against a nearby trunk, lent back to smile at him and slowly pulled up the leg of her slacks. The boy took a step backwards, almost tripped, and grabbed a nearby branch to steady himself.

Sharon felt good! She gave the slacks another pull and

278

leaned forward, slipping the first two rubber bands down, letting them rest round her ankles. Pulling the secateurs free and letting the third band stay where it was, she waved them in the air as the woman in the film had waved the gun. Reaching for the selected stem and placing the blades carefully, a hard squeeze forced it through. Another two cuts and the improvised tent peg fell to the ground. Stepping back, she let Ken pick it up then passed him the secateurs. The pressure required had hurt her hand but she had no intention of letting it show. "How many do you need?"

"Twenty at least, is this one a bit long?" Ken held the peg against another junction; using it as a template to copy, several could be made from the same branch.

"Long? Yes it is a bit, but if there's room, cut them all like that until we see how soft the ground is. How come you're on holiday at this time of year."

"Dad's factory is moving, he has to take it now." Ken reached out to make another cut but Sharon stopped him, confidence growing by the minute. "Remember they're upside-down. Make the top cut sloping to give a point; that end goes in the ground. The bottom cut must be flat, that will be where the mallet hits; it leaves a flat cut on the tree too, not a point someone could fall on."

Half an hour passed before the pegs were all in and the left over branches tidied away; Ken had been for leaving them where they fell but Sharon insisted. Inside, the tent consisted of a main area and two sleeping compartments, one large, one small. Extending in front was an open awning and it was here that they unfolded and erected the aluminium frame and windshields forming the cooking arrangements.

"Did they leave you any food?"

"No. They were angry. Said I had two choices; go with them or stay hungry."

"What do you like? We can get some at the shop." All shyness had gone, Sharon sensed herself in control now,

279

leading, dictating events; a position she loved.

The boy reached in his pocket, "I've very little money."

"Don't worry. Your father can pay tomorrow; what are Dads for?"

"Well I... he might not like it. He's not very generous?"

"What's new! All Dads are mean, mine calls it being careful."

"Suppose they argue so much that they leave anyway, even though we've got the tent up?"

"They've paid already. That will cover what we want. I'll pay for my own."

"You're sure it's okay?"

"Yes. If they do leave then I can tell my Dad I gave you the food free – his hair will probably fall out."

The fingers touched as they laughed together; Sharon's hand suddenly snatched away, comfortable with the boy's company but not quite ready for closer contact. Embarrassed by her own reaction she looked down at the floor, then determined not to let anything spoil the new friendship, pointed towards the office, "Come on!"

She had a three pace lead as they raced up the road but he caught her easily and ran alongside until they slowed, recovering their breath over the last hundred yards. There was no one behind the shop counter. Sharon hurried to the communicating door, "I've got it Mum."

Wondering where Sharon had been for so long, Jan came to the door anyway and seeing the boy, stopped. "Oh?"

"We're just getting some food. The tent is up."

"I didn't see the car come back."

"It hasn't. That's why Ken and I need some food. I'll see to it." Sharon's tone and the body language said, 'Go away Mum!'

On the point of asking more questions, Jan decided not to, and returned to the kitchen. Sharon looked at the shelves, extracted two eggs from a square stack of cardboard containers and put them in a paper bag. "Okay, that's one egg you owe, I'll write it down, say four pence. We need potatoes in the house so let's split this five-pound bag and," she hunted round inside, "take the two biggest. Now cheese..."

In the end they carried away eggs and potatoes from the shop, and from inside the house Sharon rescued a single chipolata sausage, a chunk of cheese, one apple, a tomato, two long carrots and a few lettuce leaves. A small plastic bag contained a mixture of frozen peas and sweet corn liberated from two packets in the tiny freezing compartment of the small house fridge. Two rashers of bacon, an almost empty bottle of cooking oil, a spoonful of coffee in another bag and some milk completed the haul.

"How much does my Dad owe?" Ken asked as the last items were laid on the counter. No one else had entered the shop, few did at this time of day. Sharon consulted her list, "Half of everything, not counting bits like the lettuce that might have gone to waste anyway, near as I can figure, twenty pence."

Ken fished in a pocket, pushing three coins across the counter, one ten and two fives. "There. We'll be independent." As he collected the various bags, Sharon dashed into the house, reappearing quickly with pepper and salt pots in another small plastic bag, a box of matches hidden in the other hand. Jan stood at the lounge window, watching the retreating backs, pleased, but with a tinge of concern.

Back at the tent, they inspected the cooking equipment; two gas burners, one large frying pan and two average saucepans. "We don't cook much, can you manage with these?"

Sharon looked at him and grinned. Not only was she in her element but the situation was novel and intriguing. Chris and Stephen would never congratulate her on a meal however good, but Ken might. "I think I'll manage."

"I guess so. A girl who walks round with secateurs strapped to her leg is scarcely likely to be worried about

281

saucepans." His eyes were shining as he glanced down at her slacks then round at the tent. "What do we do first?"

Sharon had seen the glow in his eyes and the direction; it made her feel special, warm in a way she found pleasant but disconcerting. She had seen his appreciation as he looked at the tent, erected where his parents had failed, and noticed his gaze rest momentarily on the secateurs still lying in one corner. She had forgotten them, remembering now that the elastic bands were still round her leg. "First we fill a saucepan with water and parboil the potatoes."

"The water carrier is still in the car, I'll fill the saucepan. Where is the tap?"

"Use the river, it's nearer." Sharon paused, "Don't look so worried, we're boiling it anyway and it's only for cooking."

"I'll run to the tap." He bent down and rummaged in a box, "I'll fill the kettle too."

He returned shortly, leaning close to place the saucepan on an already lit ring, not noticing the secateurs had again disappeared.

Sharon slipped the potatoes in, adjusting the gas to burn more fiercely, tipping oil into the frying pan ready for later, then sliced a carrot, laying the disks in a pattern on two plates, adding pieces of lettuce and segments of tomato. All were arranged round the rim, stretching two thirds of the circumference and leaving the middle empty. The potatoes were still cooking ten minutes later when the remaining carrot joined them in the same boiling water. Lighting the other gas to put the frying pan on, she added a fraction more oil, the single sausage and the bacon, then while keeping an eye on it, cut the cheese into slender sticks and arranged them round part of the remaining plate rim. Ken found a cooking bowl and on instruction, broke the two eggs into it, sprinkled in some pepper and salt, then beat them gently. Another five minutes had passed when Sharon rescued the potatoes and carrot, slicing both and French frying them in the pan, cutting the sausage in half, pushing it to one side then adding the now unfrozen peas and sweet corn – a deeper pan would have been helpful. Moving the still boiling water aside and placing one of the plates on top to warm, she put the other saucepan on that ring, added a dash of oil for safety and carefully emptied in the stir-fry mixture to keep hot, leaving the frying pan free.

"Should we have bought bread?"

"No, we're using omelette as a base." Sharon emptied half the beaten egg, watching it sizzle in the pan, drawing in the edges before flipping it over then onto the plate still sitting above the hot water.

"That should keep mine warm. Cut the apple in segments and add it to that remaining space on the rims, will you."

Pouring the remaining egg into the pan, she finished the omelette quickly and flipped it onto the plate, then emptied half the stir-fry contents of the saucepan on top. Adding the rest to the second plate, turning out the gas to one ring and putting the kettle on the other, completed the preparations. Carrying their meal outside, they sat together on cushions. Ken had put his a bit close Sharon thought, and was about to comment and ease her seat sideways to give more room when their arms touched. It was not unpleasant – things the older girls at school had hinted at came to mind. Suddenly less sure of herself, her eyes turned downward to the plate in her hands. The meal looked terrific, her confidence returning! They had scarcely started to eat when a car appeared, rolled to a halt and Ken's parents stepped out.

Much later, back at the house when the family gathered for tea, Sharon waited with suppressed eagerness, expecting Mum to ask how the meal in the tent had gone. She sat with impatience as Chris somewhat unwillingly, answered questions on preparation for his final exams. As this conversation fell away, Sharon looked several times to her mother, longing to tell but sensing the impact would be lost if she raised the subject herself. Jan was aware of these glances, understanding the reason but not absolutely

283

sure she wanted to hear, particularly with young Stephen present. The silence lengthened and eventually it was Dad who spoke.

"Two people came in earlier to book an extra week, apparently their son insisted they stay until next Sunday evening. Strange couple, something to do with Wonder Woman, they said, and to ask my daughter?"

As the family's attention swung towards her, Sharon positively glowed, unable to suppress a smile. Straightening up, she tossed her head throwing back the hair which was growing again and had fallen in front of one shoulder, a hand automatically rising to brush away the remaining few strands before speaking.

"Ken's parents came back just after I finished cooking us a meal in his tent. We were sitting outside eating when their car drew up. They were impressed!"

In the ensuing conversation Sharon went into minute detail about the meal, embellishing it in a way that would have done credit to Chris.

"They told me they couldn't cook because they had no pegs to put the tent up?" Jan raised an eyebrow.

"That's right. We put it up first, before we came for the food."

"How could you without pegs," Chris challenged "Did you find some in the basement?"

Jan shook her head. "She carried nothing when she left here. There's no pockets in that outfit."

"We made them; cut them from those bushes Dad said he's trimming back next year. But Mum's wrong, I was carrying something when I left... and I still am!" Sharon rose taking three quick paces to the middle of the kitchen where all could see. Pausing to check everyone's attention was on her, a neat pirouette with hands held aloft displayed nothing was hidden. Leaning backward and balancing on one leg, she kicked the other high in the air, pulling back the slacks to reveal the secateurs, simultaneously punching the other fist upward.

Chapter 16

Billy and Bessie

Easter saw many old customers return, a nice sprinkling of fresh faces too. Several asked after the mobile but were pleased when shown over the new shop. It now contained a variety of caravan and camping accessories, including tent pegs of three different lengths purchased from a firm called Joy and King. The boost to finances that this early influx of holiday-makers gave, came as a relief. The shop conversion and stocking, together with last winter's tarmac and the bigger house battery had stretched resources again, leaving them low. Half expecting it, Gordon had continually urged caution; his own fault, he realised, for trying to push the road surfacing forward too quickly. Certain planned purchases of clothes had been delayed and Jan was buying cheaper food as continuing high inflation ate into her weekly allowance. The children of course, from whom the financial circumstances were partly hidden, put all economies down to Dad's natural reluctance to spend, or as Stephen muttered at lunch, "He's just stingy."

"No he's not," Jan contradicted, then leaning closer whispered loudly, "He's giving me a rise! Remember, he promised back in January I'd have an extra £5 a week once the season started." She turned to Gordon with a sweet smile, "that is right, isn't it dear?"

"Well, I... Hm, trade always dies down after Easter and..." he stopped, suddenly aware that the family were nodding to each other; Chris and Stephen grinning broadly,

285

Sharon looking annoyed, Mum's face crinkled with amusement. Straightening up, he looked fiercely back. The ruse might have succeeded but one glance at the stern expression and Jan burst into laughter.

"Oh, all right then," he waved a hand in the air, "Easy come easy go. Start next week."

"Not this week? Pity."

Something in her expression warned him. "Ah, I see. You already took it, yes?"

"Spent it too." She nodded confirmation.

Billy and Bessie arrived by arrangement with the R.S.P.C.A; they were old, a pair of mute swans bullied by younger birds and needing a place to recuperate. When released on the riverbank, they waddled with ungainly steps down to the water. However, their grace when swimming more than compensated; long curved necks complementing wings that arched angel-like above the back. Their imperial progress through the water showed no apparent means of propulsion, no movement in the upper body balancing strokes of the webbed feet below. How different from a moorhen that walked the banks surveying these recent arrivals, its neck bobbing forward at every motion, one of the few regular swimmers not to have webbed feet.

There were other ducks enjoying the water, muscovys, mallard, a few aylesburys and some recent additions, four young but fully feathered shelduck from Mousehole Bird Hospital.

With this, River Valley's first pair of swans, came the possibility of mating and nesting; unlikely perhaps in view of their age – the possibility a mixed blessing for the male bird, the cob, can be quite nasty at such times. Would the joy of seeing young swans also drive off the mallard? All the ducks were free to leave if they so chose. In some bird sanctuaries where his protection is not needed for survival of the young, the cob may be clipped and taken miles away, leaving the female, the pen, to raise the family alone. They will meet up again after he has moulted and grown new feathers but by that time the cygnets are sufficiently large and his protective instincts have cooled. There were no plans for such action here. Whatever transpired Billy and Bessie were old, and age should limit their disruptive potential.

The pair were popular with visitors; apprehensions of younger children being afraid seemed unfounded as both swans liked their bread tossed on the water, waiting like true nobility for food to come to them rather than chasing after it. This reticence lost them many a meal for the other ducks, as always, ran up the bank to crowd round anyone approaching with bread in their hands, some tolerant enough to let the children stroke and play with them, but only so long as food was on offer.

Nevertheless, in spite of this shyness, the swan's grace and size drew people's attention, ensuring they received an ample share. As days passed and extra nourishment strengthened them, they grew more daring, floating to the river's edge to take bread from the hand; Chris was first to succeed in feeding them directly. Billy began to make short flights with that wonderful whistling sound swans generate when they fly, so unmistakable once heard. Bessie found her wings a week later but after a short circuit round the house, crash-landed in the middle of a large patch of brambles and was trapped; totally unable to free herself.

Stephen dashed in with the news and accompanied his father, secateurs in hand, to the rescue. Bessie, unable to run away, stretched a long neck out defensively, warning the pair off, weaving and hissing as she attempted hope-lessly to free herself. A swan may not have teeth, but it can break a person's arm with a wing. Gordon approached slowly, carefully snipping away at the outer brambles as Bessie continued to struggle. Coming within range, he shot out a hand, grabbing the waving neck, cutting her off in mid hiss. Leaning into the thorny thicket, his right arm slid over wings and body, hoisting her clear. Stephen moved forward, picking secateurs from the ground then stroking the breast feathers and lower neck, the effect somehow calming; both swans had become thoroughly used to children.

Carried carefully back to the river's edge and lowered gently into the water, the swan showed no gratitude. For days afterwards she would accept bread from everyone else but when Gordon came near, just put her head in the air, for all the world like turning up her nose, and sailed to the other side of the river, refusing to have anything to do with him. Quite beneath her dignity.

One more failed flight brought a call from a lady in the village, a distance of half a mile. She was getting stronger.

"There's a swan on my doorstep!" the lady sounded distraught. "I can't get in my door; every time I go near it stands up tall and hisses at me. Can you help?"

"I'll send Gordon," Jan put down the receiver, opened the office door and called, "One of our swans is stopping Mrs Barber getting in her house. I don't know where she phoned from. Can you go?"

A quick trip by car and he parked close by, jumping out and slamming the door, waving to Jim and Audrey in the bungalow. Crossing the road and stepping into the driveway revealed a stand-off, the lady waiting to enter, Bessie on the porch with wings half extended, head held high and hissing, not prepared to let anyone approach.

"Not frightening our swan are you?"

"Me frighten that! You must be joking." The woman smiled, more relaxed now. "I only took the front door key with me. He won't let me in."

"It's a she, Bessie. Wait a minute," He walked straight up, grabbed the neck, stepping in quickly to pin the wings under an arm before any damage could be done.

"Brave! Thank you. How will you take her back."

"Could you come and open my car door? I need both hands until she's settled."

They walked out onto the road but in spite of the hand on her neck, Bessie hissed as the woman leaned closer, making her jump back then stretch gingerly for the handle.

Seating the swan on his lap, right hand holding the neck and right elbow preventing the wings lifting, Gordon asked, "Shut the door for me please," and drove one handed, slowly back up the site entrance road to the house.

Seeing the big bird placed on the river, Jan waved a cup from the window, calling, "Is she all right? No problems?"

"Females are always a problem!"

Eventually Billy flew off not to return; it was a surprise, everyone expected them to leave together. A few days later Bessie was missing; no one saw her go, perhaps he came back for her. Neither returned; the river too small, too shallow and fast running to be ideal for such big birds. They had almost certainly found a more suitable stretch of water. A few people missed their presence and enquired at the office but the other ducks were probably pleased.

As May arrived life was easier than in previous years, partly because numbers were again down, but this was not too depressing, being counterbalanced by other factors. Firstly, in spite of a wish to keep site prices unchanged, the continuing high rate of inflation had forced a modest rise so actual takings had hardly fallen. Second and more importantly, advance bookings for the peak season were higher than ever before, far outweighing any temporary fall in numbers. Adding to the leisurely feeling and lack of stress was the fact that everything on site was now in top condition, with no further development work planned until the season closed at the end of October. Even if the odd load of topsoil arrived unexpectedly it would merely be tipped in convenient out of the way heaps to be used later. The time of year was passed when seed could be set.

It was perhaps this change in the tempo of life that lay behind a decision that a year ago would have been unthinkable. Everyone, well nearly everyone, has moments of madness. A vacancy had occurred on the Parish Council and after talking to one or two members, the task seemed not too time consuming, so Gordon offered to join. Why should he do that? Difficult to say; a chance to become involved in the parish maybe, or someone other than Robin to talk to when the long winter months returned? Who knows?

Why the local Council should accept him was an equal mystery – perhaps no one else applied? That would not have been surprising for this was hardly a body that made earth shattering decisions! Very few members of the public ever attended, though there had been that great burst of interest some years back when the District Council tried to introduce street lighting. In general, footpaths were the main topic, with a variety of other small matters cropping up. For instance, on one evening an hour passed discussing a plastic bag of rubbish someone had dumped beside a road; enthralling stuff! Who would sit at home watching TV when they could listen to this – well, 99% of the population actually.

However, public support or not, this being Jubilee year, it fell to the Parish Council to find something to commemorate the great occasion. A fete was chosen. Some years had passed since a big event was held in the Parish; most Councillors and many other local people were helping. Marquees, ice cream, various competitions and displays were arranged. The chairman suggested more stalls were needed, and asked for ideas in that direction.

At the site, trade was still very quiet; the opportunity had been taken to cut a large overhanging branch from a lopsided oak, there were one or two such branches in various places that needed attention. Its size triggered the idea of skittles. Having no lathe, the timber was shaped with a spoke shave, a two-handed plane originally used by wheelwrights and coopers; the ten skittles took many hours to produce, mainly in the evenings. It would have been preferable to season the wood for a lengthy period, for unseasoned timber was almost bound to crack eventually. Never mind, the event would be over before that happened. Activities for folk to let off steam were needed now, not in a few years time! The skittles proved quite heavy to knock down, so substantial wooden balls were made from a weathered ash branch snapped off in the wind some years before and still lying in Bluebell Wood.

Seeing the finished skittles and testing them on the grass, the family became interested, wanting to be involved, Chris suggesting a slippery pole would create fun and drain energy from the younger children. It sounded good, and here Sharon proved particularly helpful; a support was needed at each end of the pole and she had just learned the knots for making tripods at guides. These would hold the pole in a horizontal position at a suitable distance above the ground; not too far for the younger children to fall, but high enough to prevent older ones from steadying them-selves with one foot on the ground. It allowed for a good thickness of straw, to be provided by John, a local farmer. The pole itself was an old dead tree trunk that age and a dry spring had made very hard and smooth. Trial and error soon found the best height.

Sharon decided that if Dad managed the bowling and Chris ran the slippery pole, she must have a stall too. The first effort was a device for testing steady hands, a bent wire gadget, where a bell rang if touched by another wire with circular hole.

"I'll need a table or bench to put it on. My friend is helping, we could manage something else too." Sharon suggested. "Could we use one of those large jars of sweets?"

"What would you do with them?"

"One of the girls last summer, one of the visitors... I went in their car and we visited a show-ground. One of the stalls had a big jar filled with beans. People had to guess how many."

"Yes, Okay. It's in a good cause, perhaps afterwards we could give the sweets away, maybe throw them in the air for the children to catch. Better choose wrapped sweets, not the loose boiled ones; then it won't matter if they drop on the ground. Maybe I could make a ballista."

"A what?" Sharon frowned, glancing at the palm of her hand where the rope had rubbed while making the tripods.

"No," her father shook his head. "Not a blister, a ballista; it's an ancient war machine. How can I explain it? In a textbook I once read, it was described as, let me think... a device designed to propel fortification shattering projectiles at besieged battlements, to harass and demoralise the defenders. What they mean is, it lobs great chunks of rock at castles. Don't worry, our ballista will be a tiny one, a toy – but it should still work."

It did. On the great day, when loaded with sweets and with a great sea of children all waiting eagerly in front, it was a thing of gaiety not terror. Some of those children were from caravans and tents staying on the site. The ballista arm was released, flying up in a short arc to whack with a resounding bang against the top cross member! A shower of sweets glittering in variously coloured wrappers, shot forward, spreading out over a wide area as the crowd jumped, arms outstretched then dived in a seething mass on the ground. At a suggestion from one of the helpers, when the bottle was nearly empty the last few were saved for tiny tots who had not managed to catch one.

Gordon Floyd, the parish chairman, was in charge. Almost every Councillor ran a stall or judged or organised in some way, with a brass band, the first for a long time at a parish function, and a variety of activities run by other local people. The whole affair proved a great success and it didn't do the two nearby caravan parks any harm either! Visitors like joining in events and meeting the local population. Caravanners and campers from River Valley put over one hundred prizes in a tub full of shavings for a lucky dip, and Mr & Mrs Carlow and several other visitors helped at the event. The local Caravan Club site contributed too, Mr Sherwood from their head office in East Grinstead helping greatly, and in the end St Hilary raised more for the Jubilee Fund per head of population than any other parish in the district. Parish Councils come in for considerable criticism one way or another, mostly to the effect that they seldom do anything but talk. That, it must be admitted is largely true, so it was nice just for once, for the whole Council to receive a few pats on the back.

***

"Hey, look at this. We've got one at last!"

Another caravan had drawn up in the yard, a tall dark man stepped from the towing car, strode to the office and signed in. The first black customer had arrived, a Mr Andrews, his wife white and much shorter, an unlikely contrast of size and colour. He was a cockney, like Jan, but with a real cockney accent that she had never acquired. Gordon had always thought of Robin as a cocky cockney, this visitor was more so! Probably in his early twenties and outgoingly extrovert with it – you couldn't really help liking his cheek. A day with him could give any normal person an inferiority complex. He had good clothes and a real flash car, modern, powerful; hand painted 'go faster' stripes down the side; the lot! The couple were shown a few pitches and it was so easy. No sense of reserve, no problem with decisions, he spoke without hesitation, "We'll have that one." A long black finger pointed.

Gordon returned to the office. "Our first. What do you think?"

"Handsome," Jan smiled. "Bit overpowering sometimes I imagine. Are you prejudiced?"

"Probably. Depends what you mean by prejudiced. At Imperial College, back in my London University days, most of my friends were black, from India and various parts of Africa. My best white friend was Polish. I've never been very nationality conscious, it didn't seemed to matter; we were all faced with a greater enemy, the mathematics of Structural Design! Lately I'm not so sure. This new race relations act... it may be counter productive; emphasises differences that once seemed unimportant. How can I explain? Look, sometimes we turn people away – not often, one in a thousand perhaps, if their dog keeps

293

continually barking or if they persist in playing loud music at night and upset other people. Strikes me we may not be able to do that now if they're black. That doesn't seem fair, makes me feel a bit anti when I never was before."

"I suppose it might." Jan considered. "Keep a list of the coloured families that stay and are happy in case we ever need to prove we're not biased?"

"Good idea. One thing's sure; our Mr Andrews isn't prejudiced, nor is his wife. Should be a prize for mixed marriages. Ah well, back to work. I'm off to cash-and-carry, have you got that list?" Taking the offered slip of paper, he left the office and drove off. The shop stock had been limited so far and it was time to start buying more. Gradually the range on sale must be expanded.

Ten minutes later the office door flew open. "It's stuck!" Stephen stood, out of breath, facing his mother.

"What is stuck?" Jan had been watching two caravans approach down the road and wishing Gordon were still here. She could do without further problems just now!

"Big motorcaravan with stuff on the roof." Stephen held a hand in the air indicating height.

"That monster with the air conditioning equipment, the one parked on hardstanding behind the toilet building. What about it?" Jan glanced toward the arriving caravans now pulling into the tarmac area in front of the office.

"Turned the wrong way. Got Stuck. Caught under a tree." Stephen looked over his shoulder as people emerged from the two cars.

"Go see if you can help. No, tell it to wait until Dad gets back. He'll be..." she looked at the clock, "Perhaps another hour."

Sensing his mother's attention was no longer with him, Stephen turned away, stepping aside to make room for the new visitors. An hour? Did it matter? The road was blocked but the downstream pitches were almost empty; two tents only and both of those were out. Slipping into the service passage he grabbed a long coil of rope, not sure how it might be used but having a vague idea it could help. Hanging it over one shoulder he headed off at a run.

The driver was waiting. Seeing only the eleven-year-old lad, he stood back with a sigh, looking upward again. Somehow, the slopping front of the gear on the roof had forced a branch upward until it slid along falling back into a gap between two parts of the cooling system. He had been travelling slowly, heard the bang and stopped abruptly, backing up a few feet to relieve any sideways pressure but was now at a loss how to proceed.

Stephen ran up with the message, offering the rope but the man signalled it away with a dismissive wave of the hand, turning to open the vehicle's door and talk to someone inside. Voices were raised and shortly a woman emerged, the couple striding off in the direction of the office. Watching them go, Stephen felt little sympathy; they had practically ignored him. Their discomfort would have been pleasing if not for the obstruction this motorcaravan would cause when people in the tents came back later. Slipping his head through the coil of rope so it rested diagonally across the body rather than hanging from one shoulder, he looked up again before starting to climb the tree. A low bough on the far side of the trunk, the side remote from the road, supplied the first foothold; a slender limb but he was light enough. Reaching a higher level, it was easy to walk out along the offending branch, arms held horizontally, balancing his way a mere five paces to the vehicles roof; he had crossed much more dangerous places. That roof worried him though – would it bear his weight? Thinking it better, he remained on the branch, steadying himself with fingertips on the gear alongside until he reached the far edge, then bending, still balancing, leaned out as far as he dare to tie on the rope with a series of knots. Satisfied he stood, swivelling on one foot to face back towards the tree. The branch was heavy, thicker than his arm even at this distance, branchlets spreading to both sides. This one would not move easily! Kneeling he reached for a leaf, plucked it and rose again, feeling the texture, looking at the shape; there was no real need, he knew already it was sycamore. A flick of the wrist sent it sailing away. Still avoiding the actual roof, small feet followed the timber and reaching the main trunk, climbed higher, selecting another stout branch well above to pass the rope over, its free end falling towards the ground. So much for preparation! He lay back casually against the tree, standing on the branch, arms hanging free and peering outwards, the foliage was too thick to see much. Taking up the rope and bracing himself, a strong pull heaved the branch upward, but not enough. Climbing again to pass the rope over a higher branch improved the angle, making the pull more vertical. Dad had said, always get at right angles to what you want to pull for the maximum force. He tried again. Yes! The branch rose just clear enough – but how to keep it there? He wasn't strong enough to hold on one handed while tying the end round a branch?

Letting go, the young lad straightened. There was still no sign of the man returning. What to do? Looking where the rope draped over the branch, he pulled it up and tied a loop; a stirrup for his foot. Below this loop he pulled up the trailing rope, passing it under a lower branch and back up over the higher one again. Good. Stepping into the loop took up the slack and he reached forward with both hands, heaving upward. The branch rose until it was clear. A quick pull with one hand on the other loose end tightened the whole thing, the bodyweight on his foot in the loop helping now to keep it taut while a knot was tied.

At tea that evening the matter came under discussion.

"When the driver and his wife came to the office, what did they say?" Sharon asked.

"They were hardly polite," Jan waved a hand, uneasy with the memory. "I told them a vehicle their size should not have driven round the site, and I sent them back to wait. What else could I do, the two new arrivals were still in the office? I wished you were here then Chris. Anyway, after satisfactorily pitching the caravans and with Dad still not returned, I left Sharon in charge and walked down to help but it had gone. I could see the branch still tied up; I suppose the driver must have managed somehow though I hardly thought him capable. Wonder why he left the rope behind?"

"Another job for me?" Gordon shrugged. "I'll go down sometime and untie it, then cut that branch off and drag it to the bonfire place; burn it next winter when I start trimming again."

Stephen passed no comment. When the driver came back he had still been in the tree, too high in the foliage to be seen but had heard the shout of surprise. Shortly after, a door below had banged shut, the vehicle reversed up the road, turned and drove away. Attempts to undo the rope had not succeeded; the knot pulled tight by the branch's weight. Stephen remembered giving up and had been about to climb down to fetch a knife when Mum arrived; he had just seen her through the leaves and had frozen. Now, as he sat silently listening, a little grin hovered round his face.

Early June was not a busy time, particularly midweek; there just were not that many people about yet. It was still possible to do odd jobs in the middle of the day, though being away from the office was not such a good idea, little rushes that required them both occurring from time to time. The roped up branch did however demand attention, since no one knew how secure it was. Probably the flush of spring growth, the weight of spreading leaves, had pushed it lower, though a vehicle of such extreme height had never been expected in that particular place. Maybe other branches should be inspected? A shame though to cut too many; overhanging foliage in moderation added to the sense of countryside.

Unwilling to fetch a ladder Gordon stood below the tree looking upward. He lifted a foot to the slender low branch that Stephen had used when climbing, but it seemed unlikely to bear his weight. Reaching to hang the bow-saw on a high snag, he stepped to one side, knees flexing to leap arms outstretched, grabbing a thicker member above, then swung upwards, hooking a leg round and pulling himself aloft before climbing higher to find where the rope was tied. It came away with difficulty and looked like their own, the one kept in the service passage. He began to wonder, but pushed it from his mind and climbed down to where the bow-saw rested. With sycamore it was best to sit on the branch and cut at least a metre out from the trunk. This type of wood usually split before the branch was cut right through unless the weight could be supported; that would be difficult to do while sitting in the tree! "Okay, here goes." On the nineteenth stroke, the branch dropped away, splitting as expected. Never mind, the weight was gone. Finding a foothold on a slightly higher branch and leaning down, another cut close to the trunk left a neat finish; twice the work but twice as good.

Dropping to the ground, he stretched and stepped back clear of the tree's shadow to look at the mess. That June sunshine was hot, there were occasions when one regretted living in a valley so sheltered from any breeze. The longest day; was it next week? "Should have eaten a smaller lunch, I feel like sitting on this branches not hauling it off to the bonfire." Prompted by the thought, he moved back into the shade, leant against the trunk and looked idly at the long bough. Should it be cut into three pieces, or maybe five? Where was Robin? Sleeping off his morning feed cadged from the visitors no doubt. Blackbird was there already, looking under the leaves; the sight of the bird recalled to mind something else black – Mr Andrews. "He could probably talk this branch into place, don't you think?" Automatically, Gordon had spoken aloud, chatting with the bird as he often did at other more lonely times of year. Quickly he glanced round; no caravanner had crept up unseen, no one had overheard. He spoke again, "Did you know we have a black person staying?

That should please you."

"I've seen him. Splendid looking specimen for a human. Lovely colour!"

"Suppose I prefer white to black. I don't necessarily, but just suppose?"

"I spoke to a pigeon yesterday, it flew in from London, been to Wimbledon for the tennis, got chased off the court. An expression used by one of the players seems very apt, 'You cannot be serious, man'. Black is the colour par excellence, a little French expression heard from a martin last spring, for your benefit it means, without equal. And I can prove it!"

"Go on."

"Bird's bones are hollow, very thin and easily damaged. That's natural. In order to fly, everything must be lightweight. When attacked by an enemy a bird's natural reaction is flight. It's the nervous bird who survives, not the brave one, so evolution has bred the instinct to flee when danger approaches. You follow so far?"

Gordon nodded.

"A bird is most at danger when it cannot fly – at night! Knocking even a small branch in the dark could break those fragile bones, a wing for instance, and again evolution has bred an answer. The instinct after dark is not to flee but to freeze and hope the enemy will not detect you. And here is the point – What colour is most difficult to detect in the dark? Black! I rest my case."

"Good argument," Gordon adjusted his position against the tree. "I still think white is better sometimes."

"Why should you, your ancestors were black."

"You can prove that too?"

"Oh sure. Birds have been around longer than humans. Much longer! In the early days you most resembled apes, no weapons, no clothes and living in equatorial regions – must have. Where else could you survive without clothes? Even with a thick pelt of hair you don't have the body for a cold climate – ears too big, body too long and thin, a

cold climate origin would have given a more compact heat conserving shape. Starting life near the equator, the sun would dictate skin colour. No doubt about it, your ancestors were Black!"

"Um... yes, convincing enough, but my turn now!" The bird's head cocked up farther, appearing to listen as Gordon spoke aloud. "So, long ago all humans were black but learning to wear clothes allowed a move into colder lands. Evolution ensures any change that helps survival is maintained. Since indigenous people from all cold lands have changed from their black origins to white, there has to be an advantage in that. Right? Well then, what is it? I've three ideas. First, vitamin D is created by the skin from sunlight. There's less sunlight in cold countries, so maybe white allows more to penetrate and be absorbed. Secondly, a reason from our schooldays. Two hollow cubes, one black, one white, are filled with hot water. The black cube radiates more heat and gets colder quicker, so a white skin may keep you warmer. Thirdly, camouflage. Many Arctic animals can turn white when snow lies on the ground. Is this man's attempt to match his surroundings? What do you think Blackbird?"

"A passable argument. Take it further. Is the process reversible? If you go to Africa, not just to visit like the Swifts but to settle there, how many hundreds of generations will it take before you are a nice handsome black again. Would you like the rain forest, with flies landing on your face..."

Suddenly wide awake, Gordon could feel them – reaching up a hand to brush the offending insects away. What was it? Ah, hanging on a little thread from his raised hand was a small spider, a shaft of sunlight through the leaves reflecting off its back. He walked over to a bush and set it carefully down before picking up the bow-saw and setting to work on the waiting branch.

CHAPTER 17

Buzzard.

A shout drifted in through the open fanlight. Chris tried to ignore the distraction, but a chorus of voices made him look up. A group of visitors, including several children all younger than his own sixteen years, were clustered on the bridge leaning over the low parapet, some pointing down at the water below. One boy held a small rod, its line thin enough to be invisible from inside the house.

Chris glanced down at the drawing-board perched across the arms of the chair where he sat by the lounge window. Several sheets of paper scattered the board, a partly written essay in preparation for the final exams at the end of term, but the topic had no real interest; he leaned back in the chair. This position commanded an excellent view of the river, a feature that was no accident. When building the house four years before, care had been taken to arrange most main windows facing at least partly towards the river and bridge, the only way a vehicle could enter or leave. From here he could look under the arch or over the top to the water beyond.

The boy outside should not really be fishing. That short stretch upstream of the waterwheel was restricted, fishing not allowed; a conservation measure. After all, having created a camp site and attracted so many young fishermen, some part must be protected or trout stocks would eventually be exhausted. It served another purpose too; adults and young people alike threw bread from the bridge and the trout

301

grew very tame, a delight especially to small children who under normal circumstances would have great difficulty seeing a fish in the water. For many, this was their first such sighting and it fascinated them.

While safe from human anglers (except the more sneaky ones who occasionally hid behind the bridge with a hand line), the trout still ran certain risks. They were by no means safe from other predators. At six in the morning when the family rose, it was not unusual to see a heron walking along the riverbed or standing statue-like waiting to spear its unsuspecting prey. Few holiday visitors rose early enough to witness this feathered poacher.

Chris turned back to his work; essays were the worst, writing not a favoured subject or one at which he shone, something more practical and active suited better. Pen poised he re-read the last sentence but a derisive cheer from outside pulled his head up; "Ha! They missed it again!"

He knew what was afoot. From time to time eels found their way upstream, particularly it seemed, in years when the weed was thick; a fishery officer once claimed these eels fed on young immature trout and were best removed. That was why fishing the forbidden stretch had been allowed this evening – a big eel had been sighted.

"Well, if *they* couldn't catch it, perhaps someone else should try?" Chris lifted the board aside, rose and ran nimbly up the stairs for his tackle, then to the kitchen to cut small cheddar dices, half the width of a sugar cube, from a hunk of cheese. Coming through from the shop for a dry teacloth, Jan looked curiously in his direction. He held up a cube, pushing it carefully onto a number eight hook, then added two weights very close to the bait. She nodded and left again.

Chris moved to the window, checking on the crowd, weighing up the possibilities; the approach was important in making an impression. Quietly he gathered the gear and left, slipping the catch on the office door since his father was absent and his mother still in the adjoining shop.

Reaching the bridge he moved to one side, not too close to the other young fisherman, and hiding the hook with one hand dropped it quickly over the side into the water. It was done with a casualness so that few noticed his approach. The bait lay ready and waiting on the riverbed before most visitors saw a second fisherman had joined them, but word quickly spread. The cheese had landed in a clear space between tufts of red-topped grassy weed, every strand of which showed clearly in the crystal water but the eel was not in sight. Sinking the cheese rapidly was important, the two weights had dragged it down; trout showed little interest in anything lying on the bottom; that was the eel's hunting ground. Seconds passed and a murmur ran through the watchers; a blunt snout poked carefully from a downstream reed clump. The target had smelt the bait from several metres away.

Odd shouts of encouragement mixed with pieces of facetious advice that had previously flowed forth from the watching visitors died away, replaced by anticipation as interest intensified, a host of eyes following the scene below. Slowly the dark form emerged, not swimming straight like a fish, but sliding forward in a series of arcs as it headed into the current. Above on the bridge no one spoke, all watching as it made unerringly for the bait, seemed to hesitate momentarily, then snap! – breaths were drawn in as the jaws struck. A second later, line, bait, hook and writhing eel rose in the air, the onlookers stepping hurriedly backwards as Chris swung the creature round at arms length for all to see.

Normally, fish caught in the river were returned unharmed, but in view of the fishery officer's warning, this eel had no such luck. As the caravanners dispersed, Chris packed his gear away before returning to the essay but concentration was hard. There were still two months before he would be free and the exams over, his schooldays past. He had started helping at the Mechanical Music Museum two miles away in Goldsithney on some weekends, but had

303

no real idea yet of his future career. He helped on site too but had fallen out with Dad several times recently, disagreeing on the way work was done, baulking at restrictions, arguing over late homecomings and disliking the constant encouragement to study. Working at home was a possibility, but he fancied more independence.

Jan appeared from the shop and asked through the doorway, "Where are Sharon and Stephen."

Chris looked up, "Sharon is off with that new girl, the one with red hair. Stephen went downstream looking for the mallard and her ducklings."

"Did either of them say what time..."

"Are you open?" a voice floated through. Jan turned, stepping quickly along the corridor and into the shop; a woman was standing at the other doorway looking in. It was evening, trade had picked up, a decent number of caravans and a few tents were now spread across the valley, almost all occupied by couples.

"Yes, come on in; what can I get you?" At this time of day custom was only sporadic but the shop had been well received; it was busier than the mobile last year, even one or two from the village came occasionally to buy things. The new arrangement made life easier, too. Freedom from a need to dash off each morning and collect the vehicle from Jim's bungalow was a boon, and with the big gas fridge, milk kept fresh and was served cold; people liked that. A hand bell once used in the mobile had been placed on the shop counter so Jan could sit or work in the house rather than stand in the shop. It operated well, clearly heard now, not like the previous year. However, this particular part of the arrangements had not proved an entire success; that very afternoon a customer had been found standing waiting, not realising the bell's purpose; it had happened once or twice before. Even carefully printing a folded cardboard sign failed to work with some children and foreign visitors.

Having finished serving the customer, Jan re-entered

the lounge, saw Chris writing busily and changed her mind, intending to head for the kitchen, but he looked up and spoke.

"Neither said anything about time but Stephen shouldn't be long unless he's driving the ducks upstream. When will Dad be back?" Something in the voice made Jan wonder.

"Anytime now I should think. Trouble again?"

"No. Well, just a disagreement... about study. He thinks I don't work hard enough."

"Do you?" Seeing Chris shrug and turn away, Jan let it go, asking if the cheese had worked.

Later at coffee the conversation lagged, not flowing as it generally did, a certain reserve creeping in between father and son, especially when Sharon raised the topic of school work by speaking of a project her friend was doing while on holiday.

Seeking a less divisive topic, Jan asked, "We had another customer standing waiting at the counter earlier this afternoon; can't you fix a bell on the door so it rings in the house when someone enters? It wouldn't use much current would it?"

Current was not such a concern now with the bigger battery, but the waterwheel would produce less as the river fell to summer levels. Caravanner's batteries carried in for re-charging would increase too, as the season blossomed.

"Bells use hardly anything." Gordon walked to door, looking to where it might be fixed on the corridor ceiling. "It would run for weeks on a normal 6-volt lantern battery; a bell or a buzzer, whichever you prefer. Nip to Penzance and buy one."

By early afternoon the following day it was working, connected with long wires attached to two bent pieces of copper pipe fixed to door and frame in such a way that they touched and the bell rang every time the door opened. At busy times, a small piece of Sellotape over one of the contacts would prevent it ringing – simple but effective, a temporary measure that worked so well it seemed likely

305

to become permanent. When things were slack, no one need sit in the shop; customers could not now enter unannounced. A brilliant move, Jan said, explaining it to the children that evening when the bell suddenly interrupted tea.

The old mobile shop had gone, sold at a considerable loss but its absence enhanced the entrance. Improvements to the house's frontal appearance discussed earlier in the year must wait until autumn – River Valley could not afford a Spanish type reputation by letting building work continue at holiday time. A single load of topsoil arrived but was tipped in an area not yet in use and left untouched; it was too far from the office with visitors regularly arriving. And those visitors were happy, pleased with the better shop and the winter's work on grassy areas. The finished terraces had greatly improved; the riverbank too was healing over with new growth. Some heathers had been reset but years would pass before it fully recaptured the old glory. Still, it was more acceptable now, less sign of the sewer's passage remaining.

This happiness on the part of both caravanners and campers gave a certain relaxing satisfaction that one might, without stretching the imagination too far, call idleness. There were as always, certain chores; the cleaning, satisfying customers needs both in the shop and elsewhere, and of course seeing arrivals to a comfortable pitch, but between these essentials there was time to spare. One felt able in the middle of the day to sit and do little, and this year, because the site had progressed so well, it could be done without any feeling of guilt. Early afternoons were often the slackest, most people out sightseeing or lying on some beach; a time of day when it was possible to read a novel or look forward to watching Wimbledon from a comfortable armchair – civilised living; a great stride forward!

One afternoon they sat together in the lounge, reading. Jan's book subsided gradually onto her lap as she fell into a light sleep. Seeing the eyes close Gordon continued reading quietly until a caravan appeared way up the track coming slowly towards them. He rose crossed to the other chair, dropped on one knee and gently kissed the sleeping lips. As the eyes opened, the contact lingered until he drew back slightly to say, "You don't really deserve it."

"I was thinking along different lines. 'Help! What have I done to suffer this!' Anyway I do deserve it, I'm a good girl, I am." Jan was born a cockney, and though she had no such accent normally, she used it for those last words.

"Hm." Gordon rose, looking fondly down. "Nobody kisses a good girl! How about serving some customers? There's a caravan coming."

A little later, with the visitors comfortably pitched and few people returning yet, they sat together again.

"You look too comfortable. Laziness is catching, you once said; that must be true." Jan waited, wanting to say more but not sure. After a while, choosing the words carefully, she spoke again. "If you can sit idly there with a clear conscience, perhaps it's time to stop telling Chris to work harder?" It was not a rebuke, just an apparently light-hearted half-joking remark, followed by a long silence. They both understood.

"Sorry. I try not to but..." Gordon stopped, not sure what to say. A spirit of competition had always existed between the children, often pitting themselves against each other in ways that were sometimes unfriendly. A similar spirit had recently sprung up between father and son as Chris grew, testing the bounds of his independence. Gordon knew he had not always reacted well, the same thing had happened with his own father a generation before; he should have learned from that, but found it difficult and was now at a loss to explain. The silence lengthened again.

"How long before another batch of ducklings hatch?" Jan asked, breaking the mood. She had attained her purpose, registered her concern – labouring the point would achieve nothing.

Chris, when he returned home in the evening, was equally uneasy. He had reached a point where his life, his whole attitude was changing. At school he was very much a senior; no one tried to tell him what to do, not even the teachers unless he stepped too far out of line. His freedom to decide, to choose this way or that, had never been so great. When he passed with his friends, younger children stepped back giving them passage, not necessarily from fear but from respect, from a wish to be as big or important as most seniors were seen to be. It gave a feeling of power, a boost to the ego and to confidence; made him feel a man, as he nearly was.

At home it was different. He was treated... not exactly like a child but as having less maturity, prevented sometimes from doing things the way he wanted. Mum was more understanding, but Dad – not always. Sometimes his father would discuss a point, give reasons, occasionally even give way, but often he still took the line 'I pay the bills so I call the shots', and would insist that some point or job be done his way with no argument. That was frustrating; once or twice Chris had deliberately disobeyed and caused a crisis. It made for uncertainty, Gordon trying to hold the line, resenting the change in their relationship, but something inside Chris driving him on. He was feeling his way, pushing where he dare but other things were unsettling too; the end of term lay only six weeks away. Previously the route forward had been clear, another term had always lain ahead; but not this time! What would he do? He wandered outside to sit on a low branch behind the house, a place to be alone, and watched a bird soar over trees across the river. There had always been buzzards flying in the valley; the one above circled effortlessly on a thermal, the sunlight catching white patterns on the underwing as it banked to glide off downstream.

It was Wednesday evening. Even though still early in June, Chris had hoped some friends from previous summers

308

might arrive but none had appeared. Crossing the bridge, he wandered off into wooded ground on valley's north-easterly side, catching sight of the big bird occasionally. One had caught a young rabbit the previous day and flown past with it hanging from talons below; the nest must lie somewhere to the north. It was a passing idea without any intention to deliberately hunt but his footsteps now wandered in that direction, mind elsewhere, thoughts still a disconcerting jumble. The terrain was not difficult; plenty of tracks, made by cows probably, criss-crossed beneath the spreading foliage, mainly willow and hazel with the occasional taller oak or ash. Ahead sunshine marked where the wood ended; he headed toward it and saw a buzzard skim low overhead, watching the big bird as it swept on to land in a distant tree. Curiosity made him follow, not directly but a more circuitous route keeping under the leafy cover, approaching carefully. The nest was easy to see; in a tall oak at the top of the main trunk where limbs branched in three directions, a place with no small twiggy branches to hinder access of the adult birds' large wings. Chris knelt, watching. He had heard before that buzzards seldom bothered to hide their nesting place, the higher and more exposed the better, easy access and a good view more important to survival. The nest itself, an untidy jumble of sticks, had the appearance of falling apart, certainly not the work of accomplished builders. There was movement; the top of a fluffy young head perhaps, low on the nest and indistinct. Watching was somehow restful, lifting other concerns, his mind more at ease now than it had been since arriving home.

After a while, Chris crept away but returned later with binoculars. Resuming his original position he focusing on the tree, the ground below strewn with discarded prey, the wing of a magpie, part of something black that could once have been a crow, and pieces of greyish rabbit fur. Drawn to these tasty morsels, were hoards of flying insects, scores of them, their tiny bodies brought closer by the powerful

309

lenses, clearly visible as they caught in shafts of sunlight. Crouching half-hidden by leaves, he wondered why there was no smell; too far away probably, or the dryness of summer? Perhaps he was downwind but no breeze was detectable. Even from this comfortably safe distance, he now saw that two young had hatched, one much larger than the other. That was normal with birds of prey; the female started incubating the first egg immediately it was laid, causing one fledgling to hatch first and thereafter being stronger, to take the major share of any food. The second chick was mainly insurance, a reserve if anything happened to the first. Usually it was pushed to one side getting weaker as its older sibling grew. Only in really bountiful years would both survive.

Chris watched for a while, then wandered back, telling his mother but asking her to say nothing; feeling an odd sort of kinship with the birds, envying their wild free spirits. For some reason it was important they should survive, should remain undisturbed. He hoped now, his friends from previous years would not arrive that week. If they did, he would tell them nothing; the nest's location would remain his secret. Unable to keep away, he returned the following night to find the second chick weaker, and on Friday it no longer stood in the nest, but clung to a branch below. What to do? Studied through the binoculars, it hardly moved, making no attempt to climb back. At least it lay beyond reach of the bigger chick; perhaps the parents would feed it now. He decided it was right to do nothing. In any case, reaching the fledgling would not be easy; the tree had no lower limbs to climb and buzzards could be dangerous! They had been known to attack anyone approaching their nest. Perhaps it was time to get help? He thought about asking Dad but decided against, and that night looked for an opportunity to get Mum alone, but either the two younger children or Dad were always present, so he said nothing.

Chris rose early on the Saturday and ignoring heavy

overcast skies, hurried off – but the weaker fledgling was gone.

Jan, serving breakfast when Chris reappeared, put another plate on the table and saw him sit, morosely toying with the food. She wanted to ask what ailed him but guessed it concerned the buzzards and remembered his insistence that no one else should know. The slightest hint would find Sharon asking questions, Dad too probably. Things were better between father and son the last few days, Chris seeming preoccupied, less keen to be difficult. Gordon too had gone out of his way to be helpful, raising no objections to things that might previously have caused an argument. Was it a result of their talk a while earlier?

As Jan cleared the plates she noticed one was only half empty. Hm, unusual. She could tell Chris had gone to the basement, could hear sounds of someone at the bench. Before long he reappeared, spread school books on the table and started work but his head kept rising to gaze through the window. After a while, unable to settle, he put down the pen swept the papers into a heap and picked up a book but was not really reading. Eventually he rose, donned an anorak and left.

A heavy drizzle fell; Jan watched him stride off in the direction of the nest and wanted to call him back, but he was a young man now, soon to leave school. She must let him make his own decisions; he would anyway whether she liked it or not. Nevertheless, during the next hour she stared often at the gap in the trees where he had disappeared, knowing he must be saturated and wishing he would return.

Approaching the nest, Chris slowed. Without binoculars, the usual position was useless, he needed to move closer. The buzzards noticed his arrival. They had been aware of his presence since that first day, that much had been obvious but he had stayed at a distance, never near enough to seem threatening.

How would they react now? Crouching beside a bush

he wondered, then rose, moving a few steps forward into full view. These were not half-sized, half-tame like the young buzzard he had handled seven years ago, but fully grown wild birds – and with young to defend! Would they attack? If the chick was still alive it must be near the tree; would they let him approach, let him search? He moved forward slowly. There appeared to be only one parent bird on the nest; the head turned, looking down at him over a fan of tail feathers. Those talons that gripped the nest were big, he could see one from this distance. Defence! What about defence? The rain still fell but he knelt again, reaching round to ease off the wet anorak. Held out in front it would protect his face and eyes, giving chance to back away. No good to turn and run, those talons might drive in the back of his neck. For a long time he waited, crouched to the ground, eyes scanning ahead, feeling the wetness now seeping through jumper and shirt. There was no sign of the chick but the undergrowth was tall and varied. Gingerly he rose, took a couple of forward steps, then glanced upwards again. The buzzard above had not moved. Pity; it should be hunting. Where was the other one; would that too be so tolerant? He moved forward again.

Back at the house Jan waited. Between phone calls, serving in the shop and welcoming arrivals, she continued to gaze from the window, but in an apparently casual way, remembering her promise to tell no one of the nest. Both Sharon and Stephen had left the house when an hour later, Chris reappeared coat in hand, wrapped in a ball and held out in front as if the contents were fragile or perhaps explosive. She watched as he entered the house, laid the garment on a kitchen worktop, then carefully drew back the corners to reveal a wretched, bedraggled object with wet dishevelled feathers and drooping eyelids.

"It was a long way from the nest," Chris said quietly, one hand reaching to touch, but there was no reaction. "Must have spread its wings as it fell. Instinct I suppose?"

Plainly the bird was almost finished. The nearest suitable food was a tin of steak and kidney pie filling. With the aid of tweezers, several small pieces were tucked down its throat, the bird offering neither resistance nor encouragement but remaining passive. Chris put a cardboard box lined with newspapers on a chair next to the dining room radiator, turned on the heating and lowered the buzzard inside.

"Now get yourself changed," Jan urged as they stood back regarding the fledgling sadly. "You're soaked."

Lunchtime came and the younger pair arrived home; they had been at Jim's bungalow, Dad fetched them in the car to avoid the continuing rain.

"Will it live?" Sharon asked

"Probably not," Jan said quietly as Chris turned away.

At intervals throughout the afternoon, everyone visited the kitchen to look again at the young bird. Once, Chris carefully poked extra food in the unresisting beak and was tempted to give more but resisted the urge since nothing came out at the other end. No sign of improvement showed as family retired for the night. The feathers had dried but were untended, the poor dishevelled creature looking even more wretched. They could only expect the worst.

Dawn had come when Chris, still in pyjamas crept again down the stairs, his parents not yet risen to clean the toilets; five-twenty the clock hands said. It was warm with the heating left on all night, crazy in June but like all birds, the buzzard's natural body temperature was higher than humans and it needed the radiator. Quietly Chris opened the door, hesitating a moment before stepping inside, knowing that in all probability he would find a limp body lying in the box. The room was dim but not dark, light filtering through the thin orange curtains. Another pace, one hand reaching out – and he stopped! A little face looked over the cardboard side, eyes bright, head up, and the feathers had been preened! A great surge of elation lit

313

his face but he controlled it quickly, looking round as if someone might see; his delight now covered by a defensive 'what's so special' look that adolescent teenagers often adopt. The 'play it cool man' reaction had been automatic, habitual; but aware he was alone and satisfied no one could arrive unheard, the mask slipped away. Reaching in, he lifted the fledgling and held it close, being careful to aim the talons away. On an impulse, one cheek was laid softly against the bird's back, eyes facing downward out of reach of the beak; it might need time to know they were friends.

After a while Chris placed the little bundle back in the box, looked quietly in the cupboard and found an ovenglass pudding dish. Filling it with warm water in the bathroom and adding a splash of Dettol as his father had explained, he fetched the buzzard, dipped its feet in and left them submerged for perhaps thirty seconds before lifting clear and setting the wet talons down on the bathmat. Two eyes followed him but made no attempt to move away as he emptied the bowl, thoroughly washed it out, took it to the kitchen and returned. This time when the bird was lifted, its talons were allowed to rest on his pyjama sleeve. They did not dig in as the feet shuffled slightly, lifting and adjusting without much sideways movement, settling to a comfortable stance as it might one day in a tree. The feathered head turned upward, then swung to stare this way and that, rotating a full 180 degrees to look over the tail feathers without the slightest movement of the body. No human could do that. When Chris took the first forward step, the talons tightened and he stopped abruptly! They had only pricked the skin and were probably safe from infection now, but he moved forward with more caution, careful not to unbalance his charge and was sitting quietly at the table when a face poked round the door.

"Thought I heard someone running the tap." Jan was in her nightdress, a pile of clothes in her arms. "It's recovered?" She saw the nod and turned to leave, "Dad's just getting up; we'll be back in twenty minutes."

Standing the bird on yesterday's newspaper on the table, Chris opened the beak one handed and pushed in a slither of meat; it proved more difficult than the night before, strangely enough a good feature in a bird not used to humans. Somewhere inside a great feeling of joy spread through the young man. It would live! He wanted that as if his own life depended on it. Any fool could kill something, how many could bring life back from the brink? He felt good, doubts about his own future fading, seeming less important. After a few more pieces the young buzzard was returned to its box, carried there with all the care a mother might lavish on a new baby. Washing in the bathroom, he rushed upstairs to dress in record time and was back with the bird on his arm long before either parent returned from cleaning the toilet facilities.

Sharon and Stephen were also up and dressed when the office door opened and Jan returned alone. "The fox has been at the dustbins again, Dad is collecting the bits in a plastic rubbish bag, says he'll check the whole site and to delay breakfast." She looked towards the bird on Chris's arm. "Have you fed it yet?"

"Yes. It was more difficult."

Stephen moved closer and held up an arm; reluctantly Chris eased the new lodger on. After a while Sharon too stepped forward, but more dubiously, stopping first to drape a towel over her arm.

"He won't hurt you. Just don't move suddenly," Chris took the bird back and moved close to his sister, easing it forward again with his free hand. "You don't really need a towel! He has been disinfected."

"Oh yes I do! Not for the claws; to protect my dress. What will we call her?"

"Her?" Stephen uttered the single word, turning towards his mother.

"I've no idea. Dad could check but he says it's not fair

315

on the bird. Do we really need to know? Choose and in-between name. Where shall we keep it?"

"In my bedroom." Chris moved protectively towards the bird on Sharon's arm.

"Fine while it stays in the box, but after that... we'll see what Dad says."

Chris frowned, turning away. It was none of Dad's business where he kept his own bird. Jan saw the lips tighten and automatically sought to forestall any trouble.

"It's not just Dad. *I* won't want it flying free up there either, making droppings on the carpet and the beds. It needs to live in the house now, needs the radiator, the warmth; but when it recovers, well, we'll have to see. Think about where it would be happy, talk to Dad later, he'll be back soon." She reached out, stroking the feathers. Although looking far better than the night before, it was weak and underweight and might still deteriorate.

Jan was serving the meal when the office door opened again and Gordon strode through to the kitchen. He looked at the bird now back on Chris's arm, smiled and reached to ruffle the chest feathers with a finger.

"Eat while it's hot." Jan whisked a plate to Dad's position at the far end of the dining annex. "Chris was wondering where we'll keep it when it gets stronger."

"Oh? Where did you have in mind?"

Chris eased the buzzard back into its box and sat down. "In here for a day or two, this radiator is better than the bedroom ones, then up in my room in a bigger box but Mum thinks it should go outside when it starts to fly. There are chicks in the duck shed; could we make somewhere in the service passage?"

"We could," Gordon cut another segment of toast, added some egg and popped it in his mouth, chewing thoughtfully. "Probably fly up into some corner of the roof and be difficult to reach. Wouldn't you rather keep him indoors?"

"Yes! But Mum thought..." Chris, not wanting to

316

mention negative things like droppings, wished he could take back the words, "Great! Our bedroom?"

Gordon looked towards Jan, waiting for comments, but she was not about to object to a suggestion that looked like improving the harmony between father and son. He turned back to Chris.

"There is a better place, provided you can persuade your mother. Why not the bathroom, there's no carpet; any droppings will wipe up easily enough."

Buzz, as the bird became universally known, was moved the same day. The bathroom was better, a hot water cylinder in the airing cupboard maintaining warmth even when the radiators were turned off. One side was torn from the overnight box allowing freedom to come and go; placed in a corner near the end of the bath it was no longer a prison but still formed a favourite retreat.

Growing bolder as days passed, Buzz was tended and played with by anyone with a spare moment but this attention, while frequent, was intermittent. Chris's final exams approached and visitor numbers were increasing; other things too demanded time. Early summer showers had kept the grass growing longer than usual. It was greener too; a spreading of nitrogen rich fertiliser in April proving to be somewhat heavy handed, adding unexpected vigour. Fortunately, hot sunshine had slowed the growth now. Dandelions and plantains dotted the turf, a stiff rosette of leaves marking the extent of each plants territory, forcing the grass aside. Occasionally one member or other of the family took a knife and cut through the lower roots to remove a few dozen of these airborne invaders but the task was endless for no weedkillers were used, the ground kept safe for babies. Grass care without such chemical aids was an art. Weeds thrive on lime, so sulphate of iron and sulphate of ammonia, both harmless, helped keep the soil acid, lessening the problem without curing it. In winter the grass was allowed to grow longer, further suppressing weeds like daises that preferred it short. But the valley's turf would always be interesting rather than perfect; among it germinated all manner of other gate-crashing seeds, few of them noticed by visitors. An attachment had been bought that towed behind the mower, a series of wheels with large spikes for aerating the ground; spring rakes too, were sometimes used to remove the thatch. It was strange that caravanners in general, many of them keen gardeners at home, should give so little thought to the difficulty of keeping grass in good condition when it was regularly compressed and compacted by car wheels.

Jan had noticed something else. Where the first tarmac was laid over two years ago, the turf had needed raising at the edges to meet the new black surface. The good soil used for that purpose had given the grass extra vigour; it was extending itself out over the road. Hearing of this discovery, Gordon promised to cut the turf back and started early next morning, working quietly, sliding the blade with great care across the tarmac surface so as not the wake nearby customers. The time was shortly after six with most of the site still soundly asleep. One man however did wake, but that was only discovered later in the day.

Sometime after eleven, a voice called, "Gentleman here with a complaint."

Gordon rose from the desk and hurried through into the shop, relieved to find both Jan and the man smiling.

"I was just telling your wife, I was woken a bit early this morning by a noise, quite faint, gradually approaching our caravan. For some minutes I lay, hardly aware, then it gradually impinged on my consciousness. This faint scraping seemed to come from outside but not far away and as more minutes passed it seemed to get nearer. My wife was asleep. I dare not get up and look through the window for fear of rousing her and I certainly didn't want the children awake for another hour at least. I lay there and the sound stopped for perhaps a minute, then resumed again almost outside the caravan. In the end I couldn't stand it; the curiosity beat me. What the hell *was* that?

318

"As I slipped from the bed, my wife woke, calling me back. I slid in, whispering in her ear so not to wake the children. She couldn't detect the noise at first, then she heard it. We lay together for a few more minutes, listening.

"I must look! I said, and made to slip out again, but she clung to me – that bit was good; like ten years before! If it hadn't been for that damn noise we might have... but I could see myself failing, wondering what it was again just at the vital moment and failing. Grrr! I slipped from the bed, hearing a whisper to be careful, and moved across to the window. That was when I saw you, working along the road edge near our caravan. If thoughts had power you would never have survived. In that instant I wanted to throw something; to rush out and wring your neck. What idiot, what dumb stupid idiot worked at 6.30 in the morning? And I'd seen you walking round after ten the night before! Suddenly I wanted to laugh, relief perhaps or just the absurdity! I lowered the curtain, you didn't even look up. Back in bed I told my wife, whispered to her under the clothes. The conversation went like this. 'It's that chap who showed us the pitch. He's out there with a shovel clearing grass from the road edge.'

'What time is it?'

'Just gone 6.30'

'Don't be ridiculous. How long has he been out there?'

'No idea. Ten minutes for sure, but could be all night for all I know.'

"We laughed a lot, but ever so quietly under those blankets. It turned out to be quite a morning in the end. In view of how things developed, you're not such a bad chap after all; a total fruit cake working at hours I didn't really believe existed, but not so bad. When we did eventually get up, you were gone and the road edge had been neatly trimmed round the corner and out of sight. Anyway, we'll always remember it." He picked up his purchases from the counter and left.

The young buzzard continued to gather strength, and

now liked to perch on the bath rim, reaching it with a leap from the floor and a flap of the outstretched wings. When anyone wanted a bath, the bird was first moved to the window-sill providing the curtains were open, which was invariably so since no one bathed after dark in early July. Chris did most of the feeding, carefully adding a little hair or fur for roughage; buzzards need it for their digestion. Hair was at a premium, the female half of the family were certainly not prepared to part with theirs, and Chris, Stephen and even Dad could spare little more without taking on a crew cut look.

One long haired lad who drove up in an old car with a tent tied to the roof-rack, looked as if he could lose a hank or two without noticing. He rang the bell to ask if there was space and what price for camping?

"Yes, we have room," Gordon offered. "You can stay in exchange for a chunk of that hair; just a minute, I'll look up the..." But the visitor was off, not waiting for the price, sprinting across the yard, into his car and away up the road.

As Buzz grew stronger he learned to fly for short distances, a sort of half fly, half jump; usually from window-sill back to bath rim while it was in use, then stood there, head on one side, observing. Chris was delighted at the acquired prowess and pleased to have it near, but Stephen expressed himself not too keen at the direction of the bird's gaze!

Sharon too was dubious. "It's lovely, but not very nice when you use the loo. From the window sill the beak leans over and pulls at your hair trying to get attention. I move it to the bath edge, then it just stands watching your every move.

One day a shriek sounded from the bathroom. "Help!"

Gordon rushed in to find Jan covered in soap, sitting very still in the water with her neck stiffly erect, Buzz balanced happily on her head looking pleased with himself.

She spoke without turning. "Sorry. It startled me; dug

in a bit when he landed but it's not too bad now."

"Shall I take it off?" he moved to sit on the bath edge, looking her up and down.

"No. I'll be fine now. I can reach up if necessary." She lifted both arms, stretching up to the feathers above to demonstrate, and seeing where his eyes rested, dropped them again. "No, I'll keep him – take yourself off instead."

A few minutes later she called again, bringing him back. "Can you lift Buzz clear after all, please? As long as I make no sudden movement it's comfortable enough, nice even, but if I turn sharply his talons dig in, I suppose like he would on a branch in the wind. He did it again just now when I tried to lift him off."

Offering an arm under the bird's chest, Gordon moved it upwards slowly and Buzz stepped on. After that it became a regular event for him to land on Jan's head, but on no one else for some reason. "The talons were much gentler after the first time," she said. "I carry on washing, every move done in slow motion."

When Gordon poked his head in to watch one evening, Jan suggested with a superior smile, "Buzz obviously prefers my head because my hair looks softer and nicer."

"I think he just a yearns to be back where he came from. Remember how untidy buzzard's nests are!"

She would have thrown the wet sponge but dare not move suddenly to unbalance the bird, and instead put her tongue out, then from the side of her mouth spoke to the bird above. "Kill Buzz!"

"So unladylike." He slid quickly out through the door as the office bell rang.

321

CHAPTER 18

Dishonest?

A man rang the office bell and stood waiting, a large motorcaravan parked in the yard behind.

"How much to fill up with fresh water and empty my waste tank," he asked when the door opened.

"Hm. Another one," Gordon thought silently, glancing away momentarily at a sound from behind as Stephen and Chris entered the adjoining room, then turned back to give the standard reply. "It comes free with the night's stay."

"I'm not staying. Just need water and a place to empty the waste. We like to park by the roadside close to the sea."

"Okay. The charge is seventy-five pence, that's half what a night's fee would cost. Have you been in the area long?"

"No, we arrived a few hours ago, been looking round since. Seventy-five is a bit steep."

"Your first night? I guessed it was – and the best of luck to you! It is a bit dear I'm afraid but water is our most expensive item; on a meter you see. Sorry."

"I suppose it would be. What did you mean, best of luck, is anything... er, wrong?"

"Oh no, most likely not. You'll probably be fine. Don't worry, nine times out of ten it doesn't happen."

"What? What might happen?"

"Oh nothing. The water is from that hose in front of the toilets." Gordon walked off, turning on the tap and aiming the hose in the air, then leaning over to catch a

322

mouthful, showing it was good.

The man nodded but instead of driving over, he leant on the cab door and stood for a moment chatting to someone through the window before calling across, "My wife suggests we stay the night. Just 'til we get used to the area you understand."

"Of course, get your bearings, sensible idea. Your wife will love our hot showers, they're free, no meters. Let's go in the office."

Helping the motorcaravan top up its tank then offering a sheltered hardstanding pitch, Gordon also showed the waste water manhole lid and the special lifting handles before returning to the office to find the whole family waiting.

"What did you make that poor man think might happen to him," Jan demanded, pointing a finger. They were all grinning.

"We heard everything," Chris accused. "It would have been quite safe."

"What d'you mean? I did tell him not to worry."

"And I suppose," Mum smiled again at the children, nodding her head, "it was only after you said that, that he really became concerned and decided it was safer to stay."

"Well it is. The police sometimes wake up roadside caravanners and move them on."

"I suppose he thought it worthwhile if he had to pay half a night's fee just to fill his tank. What's this about water being our most expensive item?"

"Well it's almost true. I could hardly be totally honest and say the most expensive thing on site was not water, but my wife, now could I?"

"You tricked him into paying. That's..." Sharon paused searching for a word, "dishonest!"

"Not really. Let's see if I can convince you. Remember that three inch water main we laid from the village?" He waited for the nod. "Good, and remember the work we did building the septic tank and laying pipes everywhere, yes?

Well that all comes into the cost, and our water bill *is* pretty high, too high really, I've been concerned about the way it's rising." Gordon paused, pleased to see Chris nod agreement. Sharon was still shaking her head. He tried again. "Before you reach a final decision, let me put it to you this way. The man paid £1.50. With five of us, that's thirty pence to spend on each; thirty pence say towards a new dress. Now, on reflection, don't you think that was fair after all."

"Well, er... yes Dad, perhaps..." Sharon spoke hesitantly, torn between virtue and practicality. The latter won, a huge smile spreading on her face, accompanied by a simultaneous nod of the head and downward movement of one arm, like banging a small clenched fist on a table, except there was no table where she stood. A rush of words followed. "Yes! He might have got stuck on soft ground or run over a bottle, or anything!"

"I was always in favour," Chris agreed.

The family turned to Stephen who had said nothing from beginning to end. He stood looking up under unruly hair, lips pursed thoughtfully together, aware they were waiting, some comment expected. Slowly a small hand lifted and a quiet voice asked, "Can I have my thirty pence now?"

The two parents looked at each other. At a slight nod from Dad, Jan reached into the desk draw, withdrew two coins and held them out.

Little Stephen took them, eyes shining with pride, a challenge on his face saying, 'Beat that!'

Chris raised an open hand, Sharon following instantly. Both parents looked to each other again, shaking their heads. This had been a special prize, not a general handout. "Don't you think he deserved it for being clever?" Jan asked of Sharon.

"No Mum. We know more than he does."

The quiet voice came again. "Dad says the water bills are high. I know why – do you?"

Attention swung back to Stephen then to Sharon, awaiting her reply, but she had nothing to offer and in the end could not resist asking, "All right then, why are they?"

But it was not to his sister that Stephen directed the answer; he turned instead to Dad. "Our taps are too high and children often fill water carriers. Can't hold them up once they start to fill – too heavy! They put them on the ground, then half the water misses and runs down the drain."

Quite a speech for Stephen, but no one could disagree. He had earned his bonus.

Jan smiled at him, glancing at Chris and Sharon and receiving their confirmation, turned to Gordon. "Will you lower them? Remember they're push taps."

The water company had insisted on taps that only ran while the tops were pressed down; to save water they said. They were mounted so a person of average height could press them without stooping. Small push-on flexible ends had already been tried, added to the taps many years before but continually worked loose and in the end had been abandoned. At that time the matter had not been important; the agreement with the supply company included a minimum quantity clause that in those early years actually covered more water than was used, so any waste had not affected the bills. Water was dearer now, and as the years passed two things had happened; site numbers had grown and facilities inside caravans were improving, both leading to greater usage. The method of collection was changing too. In the past, many people preferred one gallon water carriers that stood by the sink. Such small containers were easier to tip into kettles and when being refilled at the standpipes, were light enough to hold close to the tap. Now that most caravans had foot operated pumps taking water direct to the sink, bigger outside carriers were normally used. Some, the aquarolls, were never lifted but rolled along on wheels of their own that were constantly in contact with the ground. They made light work of fetching

325

water but were not so easy to position exactly under a tap. Stephen was right!

"As Mum says, lowering the taps would be a mistake; make them awkward to hold down by adults," Gordon paused, looking at Chris, "or tall young men. That motor-caravan I just pitched; he won't waste much because the hose takes it straight to his tank. I'll fix a hose to each tap, not too long, just enough to reach a normal water carrier. Okay?"

***

Chris, having taken all but one of his final exams, no longer attended school regularly, going in only on selected days when a class on the remaining subject was due. Today, early afternoon, he sat in the kitchen, Buzz standing on the shoulder of his dark green shirt. Mum sat opposite, sewing. She put the needle aside and tossed a small leather strap across the table. It was sewn into a circle, the circumference less than that of an eggcup.

"Now all we have to do is get it on his leg!"

Chris looked at the band, pulling it for strength; there was no give, neither stitches nor leather stretching. Good, but the hole was small, much smaller than those extended talons. He reached up offering the band. Buzz's hooked beak snatched at it. Chris held on, resisting briefly, but feeling the claws clamp through his shirt as the pull strengthened, he let go before they penetrated the skin.

Jan watched the leather tossed around. This buzzard was not like the last one they had helped; that had been an older bird, more developed, only needing feeding for a while then sending on its way. This one had been but a few days old; it had learned nothing from its parents. They had written to Dr Hurrell, the Devon naturalist, asking advice on rearing the bird and getting it back to the wild. The reply with instructions had arrived that morning. Firstly, it must become familiar with the area, and above all it must not escape too soon, not until able to fend for itself.

Having nibbled and played with the soft band for a

326

while, Buzz judged it inedible and let the leather drop. Chris put it to one side and raised an arm to his opposite shoulder, easing upwards under the feathered chest, extending the yellow legs until they stepped aboard, then lowered the arm again to rest on the table. The feathers were growing in fast, little sign now remained of the downy fluff they had first seen. The arm tipped forward until Buzz stepped off to stand on the cloth.

For a while Chris played with the bird, stroking it; gently scratching itchy places, then carefully lifted one foot. Buzz objected, pulling away but Jan moved in close on the other side, laying a hand on one wing as Chris reached again for the foot. Though the actions were strange, the people were familiar; those hands had always brought food and safety, never caused harm or discomfort. This time he allowed the talon to be lifted, baulking a little as the claws were eased together and the band slipped over, but it was quickly done. That however was not the end. Jan must now sow the leather together in the middle forming a figure eight shape, one small circle tight to the leg, the other sticking out alongside and providing a place to tie a cord. This would give freedom to ride on someone's arm or shoulder when outside the house without allowing a premature escape. Jan reached for her needle. Small holes had already been pierced to make sewing easier but Buzz seem to think some game was in progress. However, five minutes later all was secure. Tying on a long length of cord, Chris took the bird on his arm and strode out through the office door to follow the river downstream.

Rapidly Buzz adapted to these fresh air walks, becoming familiar with the valley's layout, an essential part of the training. He enjoyed the time spent outside, riding on the arm or shoulder of Chris when he was home, or of anyone with a few free minutes to spare. Thinking of Buzz as a 'He' had become convention, though out of respect no one attempted a confirmation. In the evenings he sat often with one or other member of the family as

327

they watched television, an old towel draped over them and a wet cloth nearby to deal with the inevitable droppings. At other times he still lived in the bathroom and as his abilities increased, the door remained firmly closed when nobody was with him. That was especially true when the family gathered for a meal. Food contaminated with buzzard droppings, now quite substantial, was definitely to be avoided.

One morning, though apparently closed, the bathroom door was not properly clicked on the latch and it sprang open a tiny crack when Jan swung a kitchen window wide to clear some steam. Buzz saw the opportunity; he had become very agile and quite intelligent about houses; with talons extended he eased the door backwards then pushed it wide, a talent he was to display frequently in the future. At that time Jan, alone in the kitchen preparing the midday meal, knew nothing of this new achievement. The family would return shortly to eat; various items of food were coming together in the oven, on gas rings and on surrounding work benches, a cloth already on the table. Five dinner plates were balanced on a large saucepan, warming partly in steam from the food boiling within and partly from gas heat that always rose round the edge; not a very effective method for the bottom plate tended to get very hot while the top one was scarcely warmed. However, with the gas oven having no warming draw, this dubious method was the best that could be done for the shelves inside were both in use. As she reached lifting the stack, a soft flutter of wings caught her attention and Buzz landed on the table, flexing his neck to look directly at her, proud of himself.

"Oh!" Jan stopped in surprise, then addressed the bird, "A buzzard to lunch? What will you have Sir?" Suddenly, heat penetrated the thin teacloth with which the plates had been lifted and she straightened up, dropping them smartly on the worktop and shaking her fingers. A camera lay on the sideboard nearby; a quick snap captured this landmark in achievement for the latest member of the household.

Site numbers were increasing quickly, so when one man in a suit drew up in a car, his arrival was viewed with little enthusiasm. Reps could be done without at this time of year. Chris, having finished that final exam, was now helping on a regular basis at the Music museum in Goldsithney, and Stephen and Sharon were still at school. That left the parents on their own, Gordon sitting at the desk catching up on notes in the daybook, Jan by the window watching the newcomer.

"Tell him we don't want any and to go away," she suggested as two pin-striped legs appeared. The man emerged, straightened himself, buttoned his jacket then leaned back in. Jan expected a case with samples or at the very least a folder of photos, but it was neither.

"Gordon! He's got a clipboard."

In a moment he was at her side, glancing quickly towards the now busy tent area then back to the car. Another Council inspection? They waited, any thought of dismissing this man with a curt "No thank you," was now out of the question. Those tents; had someone found out? Even the children had not been told; the subject studiously avoided. On those rare occasions when it was discussed, they made sure they were alone and spoke only in the vaguest of terms – in case walls really did have ears. Who had made the discovery? Gordon swung the door wide with a smile as the man approached. The smile might not be genuine, but he would go a long way to keep this man happy – to divert his attention.

"Good afternoon." A hand came forward holding out a card, slipping it almost immediately back in a pocket. "Water Board inspection department."

"Ah!" Casting a look at Jan and disguising a sigh of relief, Gordon stepped back. "Come in. You're here about our sewer connection?"

"Sorry, not our department. We monitor the water

bye-laws. Your park is listed as not being checked recently. We like to turn up, er, unannounced... make spot inspections of the facilities and everything."

"We had one already, several years back. All underground pipes are eighteen inches below ground and the toilets are fed from separate tanks in the roof, right?"

"Good, but I need to check." As the man spoke, another caravan followed by a separate car drew up in the yard and someone was walking towards the shop.

"Help yourself. I can't come with you at this time of year. If you need me, can you come back after the children get home from school?"

"Not necessary, we prefer to work alone. People get upset sometimes." And he walked off.

The caravan booked in, the car behind was a tent, the daughter's boyfriend. They wanted to be together. Fine. A couple of areas were used for mixed parties now. Reaching a suitable pitch, the caravan was set forward and the tent behind with its entry facing the rear zip up door of the caravan awning. In many places the arrangement would have looked incongruous, but beside the large tree in the chosen corner, the tent hardly showed at all. That was obviously what the younger couple wanted; a way to come and go at any time without other prying eyes watching.

Jogging back to the office, Gordon caught up with the water inspector and fell in alongside. "Did you find anything?"

"Not much. Very good as standards go. Better than we usually expect but there is one thing." He walked at an angle across the road to one of the standpipes, grasping the attached hose near the top and waggling it so the end flipped up and down. "These have got to go."

"Why? I only put them on last week to save water."

A small lecture followed on why such hoses were absolutely against the bye-laws. It could for instance, be used to fill a bucket containing weedkiller. If it was and the poisonous mixture reached the pipe – which it easily

330

could – the man wagged a finger, then that poison would remain on the end of the hose and be carried into some unsuspecting kettle! After a few further examples of the possible dangers, he stopped, run out of ammunition possibly, and asked, "What was that about wasting water?"

Gordon reached for the tap, wrenching and twisting the attached length of hose until it came free. "Now, pretend you're an ordinary caravanner, and you bring a five gallon water carrier along to replenish your fresh water supplies. How do you go about it."

"I hold it to the tap, naturally."

"Five gallons of it? Pretty heavy! Many of my customers are retired people, they put it on the ground, press the tap and wait until it fills. Look!" Gordon pointed to a man way across the site filling a cloudy white plastic container. "You can see from here that there's only a small opening at the top. Try for yourself; press this tap and see how the water spreads now the hose is removed. What about a shorter one, not long enough to get contaminated, but something to aim the water with?"

The inspector tried the tap, stepping back as water splashed around. "Yes, I could accept that; have to be really short, less than nine inches." The length was agreed and he left. Gordon made for the basement, collected secateurs, screwdriver and tape measure, then hurried away to make the adjustments. He was out of sight before a caravan appeared in the distance.

Stephen came to the office door with Buzz, he wore no protection, just a thin denim coloured open neck shirt with short sleeves, the buzzard perching on one bare arm, its talons spread, careful not to puncture the flesh. Stephen hesitated by the step, wondering whether to call his mother but not wanting to startle the big bird. Any surprise move was apt to make the claws tighten, a shout would certainly cause it; even the office bell might. He walked away into the yard, watching the caravan roll to a halt, a big one from Germany, he could tell by the car number; HH was for Hamburg. A man alighted from the far side, walked round the car then stopped, swinging back to speak to someone inside. A woman joined him and they strode together toward Stephen and the bird.

"It is tame?" The woman reached out a hand but Buzz spread his big wings, not exactly taking flight but hopping to land on Stephen's shoulder, pivoting to face forward with wings fully extended and pointing to heaven. The bird's unbalanced body now rested against the boy's head, hair and flecked brown feathers almost indistinguishable. Still moving it swung again, Stephen leaning back with the movement, his young face smiling out at the visitors as Buzz settled, head facing to the rear.

"Ha! He hurts you, no?" The woman looked on in surprise, seeing clenched talons gripping the shirt, the black steel-like claws already disappeared in the fabric.

"No. Buzz uses the material. You want to hold him?"

The woman put up a hand defensively, shaking her head, then reached out tentatively to touch the feathers. "He lives in the house always?"

"Until he's stronger, then we set him free. Like that one," Stephen pointed high in the sky.

They stood for a while, the woman now stroking the feathers, saying something to her husband in a foreign language. Shortly, with a few friendly parting words, they headed for the office and Stephen went on his way.

Hearing the bell, Jan wiped her hands and made for the door. She was about to say 'Good afternoon', and invite them in but the man spoke first.

"You have please, the electricity points?"

"Yes, for shavers; inside the toilet buildings." Seeing a puzzled look she made a shaving motion, stretching the skin on her cheek with one hand, pulling the other down as if with a razor, then regretted the action in case they thought it was she who shaved.

"No." The man shook his head. "The electricity for the caravan," he made his own little mime of pushing a plug in.

"For the caravan? No, we don't. Sorry."

"Ah." He looked disappointed. "We can stay one night?"

"Yes you can," Jan agreed and took the money, asking them to wait by the caravan while she put on some shoes. As the couple left, a group of ducks barred the way; there were no ducklings now, they had all grown to full size, and in growing had become very tame and fearless. The woman stopped, reaching out but expected the duck to dart away, looking up with an exclamation to the man when it allowed her to stroke the black and white feathers.

The day, as always in the school holidays, would continue to be busy, this August proving particularly good for business. Undoubtedly the shop was helping, used in the evenings as well as for breakfast trade.

"Trips to cash-and-carry are more difficult to manage now," Jan thought as she pulled on the shoes and hurried to lead the caravan off. Approaching a corner two boys on bicycles whizzed into view; she moved a hand up and down signalling the pair to slow but they tore past, the one disadvantage of smooth tarmac. No chance of catching them now, a word with their parents later might help but first the caravan must be made comfortable. She walked on.

Stephen, having been delayed by a group of visitors, made his way down the centre of the site, then back up the riverbank, stopping at the bird's favourite place. Buzz had now mastered the art of tearing up food and was being fed regularly at a small table, a fifteen inch square of plywood mounted shoulder high on a post driven in the ground just downstream of the house. This raised unobstructed platform suited a buzzard's natural preferences. Any of the family, whoever happened to be free, would take Buzz for his evening meal at this special feeding place. Often enough some other member of the household would follow with a camera. Many caravanners too, gathered to watch. Stephen stroked a wing, catching the end primary feathers and opening it wide to see the colours on the underside but Buzz pulled away. Stephen shrugged, knowing his brother

333

could have done it, for Chris was still the bird's favoured person, the one he was most tolerant of. Those, after all, were the hands that had rescued him, providing the first comfort and affection Buzz had ever known, for there had been no such tenderness in the nest; a place of starvation and bullying by the larger fledgling.

Later that evening Sharon took him to the feeding table. Food was offered at a regular time; this would continue after the release in case the bird failed to find food. A group of people were waiting by the waterwheel. As she crossed the grass, sudden excitement arose; a dog tried to escape from one of the watching visitors. Buzz, on her bare arm as usual, overbalance in alarm then clung frantically on, talons tightening and wings spreading. Fortunately the dog was whisked away by its owner and calm re-established with nothing more than a few red marks on the skin. But for the thin lead, the incident could have had tragic consequences. If the bird had been free to fly away prematurely, it would almost certainly have died. Those wings were tested quite often now, and not just when danger lurked; it was natural enough, all young birds need to practice.

Jan took Buzz out one evening and was standing in front of the waterwheel when the wings opened and he half flew half hopped to a shoulder then to that favourite place, on her head. There it stood proudly looking round as it would one day in the wild, choosing a high stump with unrestricted vision was normal. For a young buzzard, a person's head was a natural choice but the campers she was talking to quickly moved back a few paces.

Another week passed and the long business of training for the wild was drawing to a close; a release date fixed. On the day, Chris ate lunch in silence, responding to questions in monosyllables and having finished, walked off alone with Buzz on his arm, not reappearing until shortly before the appointed time. Reluctantly he placed a piece of rabbit on the feeding table, quickly returning to the buzzard he had left inside, not seeing a reporter from the local newspaper arrive, camera in hand. For a long while Chris stayed in the bathroom gently stroking the feathers. Stephen and Sharon waiting in the hallway, became impatient and urged Jan to make him hurry but she sent them outside, going with them herself and explaining to the waiting reporter and the R.S.P.C.A man who had been so helpful, that there would be a short delay. Back in the bathroom, Chris continued stroking the feathers, his fingers probing those itchy places that Buzz liked. Bringing the bird near, he rubbed a cheek against the coarse wing feathers, knowing this was the last time – it would never return, never again allow a human near enough for physical contact; and that was as it should be. He wanted a successful release, to see the bird flying high, soaring on the air currents, but... With a sad face he rested his forehead against the softer chest feathers and breathed deeply the odour of buzzard, feeling the hooked beak comb gently through his hair, searching for insects. They would be waiting outside. He moved the bird back to arm's length, looking at it, eyes bright, standing for a moment longer – then reached for a thin pair of scissors, slipping them into a pocket, and opened the door.

A ripple ran through the little crowd standing outside; not too many people for it was mid-afternoon and most were at the beach. Chris strode over, showing the bird to one person then another, delaying the inevitable. He posed for the cameraman, noticing that Dad too stood in the background with his own camera. Shortly, having no further reason for delay, he took the bird towards the table; it flew the last twenty feet with Chris running after so the lead remained slack. As Buzz settled to his meal, Chris took the scissors from his pocket, gently felt for the band on the leg, fed the steel point carefully in, snipping the stitches a few at a time. Lifting the yellow leg, he eased the band of leather down over the talons. Buzz was aware of this activity, but that pair of hands had always been welcome; he trusted them. Chris stepped back and the bird was free;

free but not aware. It continued feeding as the young man backed slowly away, not towards the watching crowd but round the corner of the house, taking a few more paces until he stood out of their sight. In this position he was alone but still near the buzzard and watching it feed, half wondering if it would fly back to him. Time passed, five minutes, ten, fifteen... he continued standing long after the others had gone, knowing he could still walk up, hold out an arm and take it indoors again but resisting the temptation. It was almost half an hour before the buzzard flew off. He watched, saw freedom in its flight, gathering speed, veering slightly as if uncertain or perhaps spoiled for choice, then disappearing into a neighbouring wood across the valley. His emotions were confused; a mixture of sorrow, pride and something more elusive, a certain kinship, a touch of envy – off into the great wide world for the first time! How often recently had he wished for that? One fist clenched tightly at the thought. Feeling something, he opened the fingers, glancing down at the soft leather band still in his palm.

A picture appeared in the following week's issue of 'The Cornishman', showing the buzzard on Chris's arm, its beak close to his nose – an affectionate farewell?

Most people will know that to let a raptor anywhere near their face can be unwise; you need to be very sure of your bird and there are few it would be safe to allow too close. An eye could be lost quicker than it's possible to blink, they can be very fast. Even after living with a bird for so long, there is always the possibility of a mistake, a miscalculation, a sudden movement creating an unexpected reaction, a moment's inattention causing the most undesirable of consequences. During the early stages of any new avian visitors, the family either held the bird well away from their face, or sometimes wore goggles to allow more freedom and confidence in handling without undue risk. It was a measure of Chris's rapport with the bird that complete trust had existed between them.

CHAPTER 19

Generous

"Don't keep it to yourself! What is it?" They were dealing with the morning mail, one booking, several junk items, then a plain brown envelope which Gordon had just opened. He frowned, leant back and gazed at the ceiling, leaving Jan waiting in the other chair.

"Er, what?" Caught unprepared, he looked up. "Oh, one of the trade magazines. They want next year's prices."

The season was past its peak, numbers beginning to fall but so far had declined only slightly. "Already? Tell them to wait."

"Can't. This is a directory, a free entry; too valuable to lose. I'll have to tell them something. Do we increase, or stay as we are?"

"Sharon would say increase, so she can have another new outfit," Jan mused aloud, not sure of her own opinion. "Perhaps we should... a little? How much will you spend on the site this winter?"

"That doesn't really count; it's this year's money we'll be spending... bound to leave us short again. The sewage works at St Erth is active now; first job will be altering the pipework and getting connected; you know what depends on that!"

"The tents," Jan nodded. "And that special emptying point for motorcaravans. What about tarmac? Those remaining stone roads are quite dusty."

"Not this year, not enough cash. The third toilet building;

I promised people who like to stay downstream that I'd build it this winter. They don't like walking so far, you know that from the children, from what their friends say. Besides, with inflation over fifteen percent again, materials can only go up; the sooner we buy the better." Elbow on the table, Gordon rested his chin on a thumb, blowing through his fingers. "Things will be tight, might have to wait until next season gets underway to buy all the fittings. I think we should go up; inflation was bad again, that's over thirty percent in the two years. We're falling behind, getting too cheap – it's dangerous. Have a good rise this time then try not to alter again for at least three seasons."

"True." Jan agreed. "All the very cheap sites we ever stayed on turned out to be noisy dumps. It's the people they attract. But why is one larger rise better? Surely three tiny ones would be less noticeable."

"I'm not so sure. The real advantage is in advertising; not for next season, but if we stay level for say three years after that, then the adverts we take in the trade magazines can boast, '*No change of price this season!*' That sort of thing catches the eye."

"And this coming year? What will you say in those adverts?"

"Don't know," He sat, drumming fingers lightly on the surface. "How about, '*Come for a day, you'll probably stay a week!*' How does that grab you?"

The office bell went again and Gordon hurried off to find a man on the doorstep, a car battery at his feet.

"Bring it this way," He led the customer round the house to where several other batteries formed a group on the grass, all connected by a series of jump leads. Changing a few connections, he returned inside to Jan.

"We're getting more batteries to charge this year."

"Oh, that reminds me," Jan clicked her fingers, trying to recall the details. "I meant to tell you at the time but so many other things were happening. We had a continental couple arrive, er, from Germany; they wanted some sort of electric supply for the caravan! The man showed it to me when I took them to a pitch; a socket on the caravan side with a long lead and a plug. Inside, fixed to the ceiling were electric lights, not gas lamps. They booked one night, said their batteries would only last that long. Does this mean trouble for us in future?"

"Well... No, I wouldn't think so. It will never catch on."

***

Like the multitude of flowers that bloomed everywhere, wild animals were part of the valley's attraction, to be encouraged and preserved. The tourists loved them, happily ignorant of the drawbacks. Badgers were highly favoured though seldom seen except by the most determined visitors, and even those who did catch a glimpse were unaware of the damage the big claws could cause to the grass in frosty weather. Rabbits, particularly young ones, were endearing enough to watch, but adjoining farmers objected when numbers rose too strongly. Ah well, you can't please everyone! Animal problems seldom work out as predicted.

Way back in April the first young stoats of the year had appeared, a family of five, though there may have been more for they ran in and out of the undergrowth so quickly it was difficult to count. With small ducklings already about, trouble might reasonable have been expected, but it was not to be. Young rabbits, their normal diet, were particularly numerous that spring and so, instead of being a nuisance to the ducks, they actually helped to hold the balance of nature and lessened the rabbit problem for local farms.

Just after reading the water meter one morning, Gordon heard a rustling in the hedge and stood perfectly still on the road. A stoat dashed across from one side to the other, appearing and disappearing at speed without the slightest hesitation as it entered the tangled growth. Two more followed in quick succession, one running back, then a chase round the road by two of the kittens, one almost running over his foot. The tails lay horizontal, flying straight out behind as if in a wind, occasionally to shoot up in the air, the darker tip bent over like a shepherds crook. One of the parents re-emerged to sit bolt upright on hind legs, nose twitching, the white bib and tummy giving an aristocratic touch. Gordon didn't move a muscle, he was standing close to a willow and must have appeared to be part of the bush for the game resumed, more joining until five were visible. The frolics continued for two or three minutes, then movements of the grassy tops receded, the rustlings fading and they were gone. This family had become very bold as the season wore on, to the delight of many caravanners who would sit quietly watching, and luckily those little predators never did develop an interest in ducklings.

Squirrels too, frequented the site; there had never been very many, just the odd one or two, but cheeky with it! One was seen sitting on a dustbin, nonchalantly eating a hole through the lid, disregarding folk walking along the road not ten yards away. It was not the first such hole to appear; a small annoyance but not too serious. The other problem they caused was stripping odd pieces of bark from Sycamores. Since these trees grow quickly, dozens of saplings establishing themselves every year, the loss of a branch here and there had no great importance. Strange though, how on balance these vegetarian squirrels were more destructive than the purely carnivorous stoats had been, but visitors liked them and they too were left in peace.

The first intimation of more serious trouble came in the form of a gentleman who marched to the office door, gas bottle in hand, entered quickly, annoyance clear on his face. About to speak he realised only Sharon was in the room and hesitated, reining himself in, the accusation in his voice muted but still obvious.

"This gas bottle you sold me yesterday – it's empty!"

"Not me, I was at school." Sharon, seated at the desk, rose, reaching for the internal door. "Dad is pitching a caravan, I'll fetch my mother."

Jan entered from the kitchen, listened, then took the gas bottle feeling its weight. It was quite empty. "Oh yes, I served you, about 10.30 yesterday morning. We'd run out in the shop, I remember fetching one from the shed. It was certainly full then; harder to carry."

He stood saying nothing, not contradicting, but obviously not believing a full bottle could run out so soon. There was no way to prove otherwise so Jan replaced it free, sure he had mixed his bottles up; most caravanners carried two.

"Will you tell Dad about the free one?" Sharon asked when the man had departed.

"What are you grinning at? You think he'll mind? It's better than losing a customer but we'll keep our eye on that one."

"He might stop it from your housekeeping?" Sharon's grin was broader.

"Just let him try! Anyway, he doesn't pay me, I take what I want. We agree a figure between us and I stick to it... well, more or less. And not because I have to; it's the way marriage works."

"You mean Dad is not really stingy?"

"No," Jan smiled back, "Careful perhaps, that's the way we got this house and the site. Several times our money has nearly run out, he worries about that. I'll tell him about the gas bottle."

"Can you do it when I'm back at school?" They laughed together.

A few minutes later the man was back again, ringing the doorbell.

"There's a great hole in my gas pipe." While not actually accusing, his words made it clear that someone on the park must have caused the damage! Turning on the new bottle, the smell had been so overpowering that he turned it off again and had spent several minutes inspecting each junction, only to find it was not a joint at all but a hole in the rubber hose connecting the bottle to the caravan. Gordon returned during the discussion; Jan drew him aside for a quick word before he accompanied the man to his caravan. The characteristic teeth marks of a squirrel were easy to see. Hearing the explanation, the man peered closely, not fully convinced and not happy even if it really was a squirrel.

"I paid my fees. I'm entitled to a safe pitch! A site owner shouldn't let his animals damage customer's caravans."

"My squirrels? What do you think – that I train them to bite through gas pipe to increase sales? It *is* a wild one you know, I don't tell it what it can and can't do."

They stood for a moment, sizing each other up before Gordon pointed to the damaged tube. "Measure the length of your pipe then come to the shop, we sell it."

"Sell it? Don't I..."

"No, certainly not! Think yourself lucky the extra gas bottle was free!" The refusal was outright, no question of compromise. The cost would be small enough but somehow, paying for everything seemed to admit liability. Helping a customer was one thing, putting right his every woe for free did not figure in the service. In the countryside, one had to expect country things. Gordon continued to stand, feet solidly planted, waiting.

The visitor gave a little shrug, "I'll come round now. Can you lend me a tape measure?"

Gordon bent to reach the pipe, going hand over hand along it. "Four and a bit hands, that's eighteen inches you need. Cost you twenty pence."

The man smiled at the trivial amount, happy for the first time.

Later, as the family sat at table eating tea, the office bell rang again. Stephen went, and came back quickly. "There's a man in the office, something about a squirrel. He's not very happy."

Gordon rose, disappearing into the corridor and shortly, voices raised loud in argument were heard. After a while the office door banged loudly and Gordon returned, sitting

342

hard faced at the table.

The children looked at him, then back to Mum.

"Well," Jan asked, "Don't keep us in suspense. What happened?"

Instead of replying, Gordon rose, striding out to the corridor, stopped to pick up a key then opened the outer door and hurried off. The family who had also rushed through to the office, watched the departing back.

Jan bent over close to Stephen, "Think you can follow without being seen?"

The young face lit up; not saying a word he pulled the door open and slid through. Minutes later he was back. "Dad's looking in dustbins. What about tea?"

"It can wait." Jan ruffled his hair, "I want to know what goes on."

Scarcely had she spoken than Gordon reappeared, heading towards the first toilet building carrying a one gallon plastic container. They watched him enter the service passage, the one where the diesel tank was stored, and in a little while re-emerge, locking up and striding back. Quickly everyone disappeared, off to the dining room end of the kitchen and were only just settled when Dad came in, the container still in his hand, just the suggestion of some pink liquid washing about in the bottom. Crossing to the sink, he held the bottle under a tap adding a dash of water, then leaving it on the draining board, opened a cupboard and rummaged inside. Pepper was first added, shaken in through the open top, other ingredients followed, then the top was screwed on that the mixture vigorously shaken. Taking it with him, Gordon left, crossing to the bathroom, from where the sound of running liquid went on for some time. Jan thought it sounded... she was not sure... but not quite like a tap.

When the bathroom door opened, the container looked much fuller. He put it down on the floor, not on the draining board this time, then went back to the bathroom to wash his hands. Jan wondered if that was significant.

343

Sitting back at the table, he looked much happier, the stony expression gone, even a ghost of a smile replacing it.

"Well?" She waited.

"Oh, it's nothing really. The squirrel came back. He chased it off but the new pipe is already fitted and he's worried. Says he can't stay in the van all day watching and that I should control my own animals."

"Cheek!" Chris spoke first, nipping in while Sharon still gathered her words. "Control them? Doesn't know much about squirrels, does he."

"I hope not." Gordon looked toward Jan, took a slice of bread and began to butter it.

She saw the roguish grin and wondered apprehensively what was intended. "Okay, is it secret, or can we all know?"

"Well, to get rid of him, I suggested he hurry back in case it came again, but that I knew of some special stuff; expensive but very effective. I'd see if I could get some and bring it round to him. Chris, get me one of those sticky labels, the big ones for reusing envelopes."

Chris hurried away, hearing a voice shout after him. "And two pens, one of them red!"

Searching the desk, Chris picked up a black Parker pen, then found labels in a drawer, but no red biros. Another drawer contained a cluster of perhaps two dozen pens held together with an elastic band. Dad never threw anything away. No less than five were red, but did any work? He tried the first on some paper; no good. The rest proved equally useless. Discarding the fifth, he picked up the labels and black pen to return to the kitchen, then on a thought took all five red biros too. Laying them all on the dining table, he took a red at random, crossed to the sink and held it under a tap until the water ran hot, then tried it again. A thick red line marked the scrap of paper.

"Shall I throw the others away?" Sharon asked.

"No!" Dad looked up sharply.

"Why? What use will they ever be?" Jan joined the argument.

344

"Some may work, like this one does," He took the pen from Chris. "Anyway, they can still be useful even after they run out. I think I read somewhere, that a Doctor once used one on a bus to do a Trac...a Trach... an operation on the throat. Someone couldn't breathe and he made a little slit then poked the empty biro casing down into the windpipe and saved him. You see, never throw anything away!"

"And I suppose that's why you keep them; in case a customer suddenly chokes on his bubble gum in the office? Hm! Men!" Jan looked at Sharon, receiving a nod of agreement.

Gordon, pointedly ignoring the remark, placed the sticky label on a big table mat and using the red pen carefully wrote, 'FELIS LEO' in big block letters and underlined it. Changing pens, he scribed in a looser hand 'Urgent. By courier to:-' and below that, the name and address of the park. Leaving the table he fetched a wet pad from the office, moistened the label crossed the room and knelt, sticking it to the plastic container then returned to continue the meal. No one else was eating, they knelt together in the kitchen, reading.

"What is Felix Leo?" Sharon demanded.

"Felis, not felix. A lion, in Latin." Jan supplied the answer, and when Dad looked up in surprise, she stuck her tongue out, quickly withdrawing it so the children wouldn't see. "Thought I wouldn't know, eh? Forget did you, that I went to school in a convent?"

When Gordon carried on eating, she tried again. "Well, if this is supposed to deter squirrels, shouldn't you take it round to him?"

"No. Too soon. The courier hasn't arrived yet."

"Hasn't arrived? It's standing over there in the corner."

"Ah. You know that, but he doesn't. Got to get the timing right, make it seem realistic."

"Don't be stupid. He'll never believe that! Go and

345

give it to him." Jan waved an arm towards the door.

"Give!" Gordon looked scandalised.

"You're never going to charge him?"

"Certainly. If it's free he'll think it worthless. Actually I'm feeling generous."

"What do you mean generous, and what is it made of?" Chris butted in before Jan could ask.

"Come with me when we've finish eating," Gordon invited, and turning to the others, "No more questions until later."

After the meal, Dad signalled Chris aside. "Listen, he hasn't seen you has he? No, I thought not. You've dealt with enough customers, you can pull this off. Just carry the container, make it look precious, appear to handle it with great care. Oh, and call him *Sir* when you pass it over, then leave. Put your cycle clips on first."

They walked off together still chatting, the rest of the family watching. Chris looked back twice, smiling broadly. As they approached the caravan, the man was waiting.

"It came back again!"

"Don't worry, the stuff has arrived. It's a bit expensive I'm afraid, £3, but I'm only charging you half price, £1.50. I don't suppose there'll be any left, but if there is, let me have it back, don't throw it away." Gordon waved a hand towards Chris who held up the bottle so the man could read the label.

"What is it?"

Gordon looked around as if to make sure no one was listening, then leaned closer. "The formulae is secret, but the main ingredient is Lion urine. It's a fear bred into squirrels, a fear passed down through countless generations from those times thirty-thousand years ago when this country was joined to the Continent and lions roamed freely. Just dribble a little over anything you want protected. If there's enough you can make a circle right round the caravan." He flicked another glance over his shoulder, holding out a hand, palm upwards, rubbing thumb against

346

index finger and at the same time whispered even more quietly "Don't tell anyone the price I let you have it for."

The man also looked round, somehow catching the spirit of the occasion, then reached into a pocket, bringing out a note and fifty pence, reaching to place it in the outstretched hand. As Gordon pocketed the money, Chris stepped forwards, offering the container. "Be careful Sir, it shouldn't be shaken."

The man, stopped momentarily by the warning, reached back into his pocket for a twenty pence piece and passed it to the lad, carefully taking the container in return.

"Thank you Sir," With a slight inclination of the head, Chris turned smartly round, strode off a few paces then broke into a jubilant run.

"In a hurry isn't he?" The man watched the receding figure.

"Got to get back to the depot I suppose," Gordon shook his head and sighed. "I better start back too. Oh, don't get it on your hands, they tell me the liquid is quite strong." With that solemn caution, he left.

Arriving at the house everyone was waiting and obviously Chris had already told his story, his eyes were shining as he tossed the coin in the air.

"Lion urine?" Jan demanded. "Is that why you were so long in the bathroom?!"

"Got to give it the proper tang. There's a touch of diesel too; what you might call the active ingredient – most animals don't like it."

"Clever. Chris says you charged £1.50 and called it half price. That, I suppose, is what you meant by feeling generous?"

"Fair don't you think? Almost the price of a bottle of gas. My father, Frank, would have been proud of me."

"*He would!* I'm not sure I am. And stop leading Chris astray." But Jan was pleased to see such rapport between father and son. Turning with a smile to the boy who already reached her own height, she asked, "I hope you don't approve of your father's behaviour?"

"No. Definitely not! He should get the details right!" Chris, also smiling shook his head. "Dad told the man that squirrels' fear of lions was hereditary, from thousands of years ago when Briton and Europe were one big continent." He waited looking round the faces for comment and receiving none, continued with a shrug. "Grey squirrels came from America not Europe, and they only arrived in the last century."

"Dad, What will you do if it doesn't work?" Sharon asked.

"It will," Chris answered with assurance.

"How do you know! Rain may come in the night and wash it all away."

Chris turned to his father, "Perhaps we should put it off and sell him another lot tomorrow first?"

Gordon nodded thoughtfully and was just about to answer, when Jan demanded, "Put what off? What are you two up to? Come on, give!"

Glancing at his father and seeing a little movement of the hand indicating he should go ahead, Chris turned to Mum, "We're catching it. The cage we tried to trap mink with, the one that closes when something treads on the bottom; we're setting that at first light tomorrow, up by the trees where the squirrel lives. Peanuts will be the bait."

"First light is early. Why not set it tonight?" Sharon asked, and turning to her father, "You won't hurt it?"

"No, I'll take it five miles towards Camborne and let it go in a wood. Tonight would be no good, we'd have to wait until dark so no one saw us, and badgers are nocturnal; you know how they love peanuts."

"Why must you catch it?" Jan asked. "No confidence in this Lion brew?"

"Every confidence, but if it does work our nibbling squirrel may just choose another caravan for its attention. We have to get rid of it somehow and I'd prefer to do it alive."

348

"Why all the secrecy then; what does it matter who knows? I suppose you're worried this chap might want his money back?"

"Yes, he might, but there's more to it than that! If we can remove it quietly without anyone knowing, what is he going to believe?" Gordon smiled, turning to Stephen for a reply.

"He'll think it works." Stephen grinned back.

"Exactly. And not only that! Probably he'll talk to everyone around that area, tell them how effective our special formula is. Will you look through the dustbins tomorrow and rescue some more plastic containers."

Chapter 20

Connection.

Site numbers were falling quite fast. Jan stood in the shop, looking round at the shelves. A big mistake keeping every line in stock after peak season passed; no way to sell all this before closing. They would be eating leftover tins and packets forever – well, most of the winter anyway.

Her eye fell on another shelf. The practice of ironing had intensified that summer. She satisfied those first requests in the usual way, by loaning a large old fashioned flat iron for heating on the gas stove, the one used in the house and before that, in the caravan. People had been amused but the solution seemed to everyone's satisfaction; a touch of nostalgia perhaps. One iron had proved insufficient as the season developed – visitors rising expectations again. She had located more, buying two extras so several could be lent out at once. The three irons stood together now on a shelf near the counter.

Glancing through the glass door onto the front field, only a few caravans still remained. That was one of the children's areas. Most visitors at the moment were pitched behind the house, places reserved for units with no children; the majority were retired people. That almost empty front field was discouraging to new arrivals, she must try to persuade more caravans to pitch there. It showed something else too; the grass was growing strongly again and needed cutting, that always happened in late September. This year was different; Chris no longer helped with the mowing. Still gazing outside, she thought of her elder son. He had worked part time on site for a while in the summer months to earn extra money; it had not been entirely successful, father and son often disagreeing – the lad sought something different, more independence. He had not returned to school for further studies but taken a job at the Mechanical Music Museum two miles away in Goldsithney, details of the work emerged sometimes in conversations at tea. Mainly it entailed the repair of old musical instruments; one early task the re-pinning of ancient barrel organs. Now that he was earning and no longer totally dependent on financial support, his desire for independence had grown. She wondered where it would lead, hoping the family would stay together but knowing it unlikely; most young men left home eventually. Life was easier now, more comfortable, not like those first days in a caravan when the children were small. Remembering the way they had lived and how the family had drawn together gave a feeling of warmth – warmth and a touch of sorrow that such times could never be recaptured. Eight years had passed; good years but... with a sigh, she left the shop, wandering back into the house, not expecting more customers this morning. The younger two were already back at school, their seasonal friends long gone. Sharon, now fifteen and a senior, was hoping to transfer to the Girl's grammar school next autumn.

"To get away from boys, that's why!" she had retorted tersely in reply to Chris's taunt one evening. "You should have stayed on too, and taken A levels instead of making barrel organs for monkeys to sit on."

"Repairing antique instruments and bringing up the old wood is an art. You use a find grade sandpaper, always in the direction of the grain, then damp the wood down to raise any loose fibres and sandpaper again, sometimes as many as six times. Anyway, I was in charge today." Chris lifted his chin and looked round the table. "The boss had a business meeting somewhere and left me to do the tour;

show visitors round the mechanical pianos, violins, organs and other instruments, tell them the history of each machine. That's the first I've done; we only sold six tickets but it's always slow at this time of year. He told me the practice would be good and I might do it next summer."

Throughout the conversation, Stephen had remained quiet, but in a lull he asked, "When will the sewer people pay up?"

Compensation for damage done during sewerage work was still being argued over by solicitors. Apart from supplying facts and figures the family had not become involved but it was more than two years now that they had waited.

"I've no idea." Indeed, that was true, but Dad knew why the question had been asked, could see it in the faces round the table. Most likely one of the others had put Stephen up to it again. They wanted many things but top of the list was a colour television, one with a bigger screen too. It was a possibility now, as autumn brought increasing electrical power from rising river levels. The new house battery was big enough to store this extra current overnight and through the day. With that help the waterwheel could cope; it could run a colour television. Naturally, when the stream fell next summer and demands for recharging caravanner's batteries rose, current would almost certainly be in short supply again. If they did eventually buy a colour TV, the existing black and white set must always be kept in reserve. However, that decision remained in the future. Money from the sewer settlement had not arrived.

Dad looked at the faces. "I hoped it would be settled this year, but it seems unlikely. I chased them again only last week and they promised to... er, what did the man say... Oh yes, 'expedite it!'"

"How well have we done this season," Sharon asked.

"Pretty good, actually. Wait a minute," Gordon rose, leaving the room, reappearing with a slip of paper that had been hidden away. "We reached just over 7500 caravan-nights, I count everything as caravans, including tents.

That's up on last year." He looked up to see smiles from the children but Jan waved a threatening finger.

"When did you work that out! You never discussed it with me. Give it here." She held out a demanding hand. "Where did you hide this?"

"In the bottom of a drawer; you don't want everyone seeing our business."

She looked at the slip for a while then held it out pointing to a figure, "Is that the 7500?" Seeing a nod, she asked, "Why has it got a decimal point after the seven?"

"To confuse anyone if it falls into the wrong hands, of course."

"And this heading scribbled at the top, 'Spacing of pitches in metres', that's just another little precautions so no one will know what the figure represent... just a minute! This other column, the one that ends four point nought five five, that wouldn't be cash would it – £4055? Don't look over your shoulder as if someone might overhear!"

"Well, yes." He spoke very quietly, putting a finger to his lips to indicate that nobody should repeat the figure. "That's profit for the year... now don't go thinking we can lash out on luxuries. I know it's nearly doubled but remember the new toilet building. I don't know if we'll have enough money to complete it before spring but I hope so. We certainly can't afford to employ a builder so I plan on hiring a machine for a few hours next week to dig the foundations."

"The base for our windmill tower too?" Chris prompted.

"Never mind the windmill, what about connecting to the sewer?" Jan turned to Gordon, "I thought you wanted that done first."

"There's still a few caravans on site; I'll start as soon as they've gone. I had hoped to tarmac more roads but with the sewer settlement not forthcoming we can't afford that either. The tower must wait too."

A week before closing, a caravan arrived and asked

for eight days.

"Sorry. You can have seven, we must close on the last day of the month."

"Oh? We're collecting our grandson from near Helston on the first of November. Can't collect him before because of a birthday party."

It raised a problem, the licence stipulated that the site be closed at the end of September. This meant a caravan could stay that evening, provided it left by midnight! Theoretically, staying until the following morning would breach the licence conditions. How seriously would the Council view such an infringement?

Gordon explained the problem. "I'll charge you seven-and-a-half nights, that's up to midnight on the thirtieth. Of course I shall be asleep by then, so if your car won't start or your lights fail and you can't leave until daylight – just don't wake me up!"

By the time this caravan left, the new building's foundations complete with underground pipework were finished, checked and approved by the Council's inspector. With the site now closed, attention turned to the new sewer connections. The necessary holes had already been dug and everything was ready for the changeover, but water from their own bathroom and kitchen still ran down the old pipework and that must stop! In a manhole some distance from the house, Gordon forced a four-inch drain plug into the pipe end. Tightening a screw compressed a thick rubber ring, forcing it outward to grip the pipe and form a seal. This would stop any house water damaging the fresh cement. That done, he worked fast to make the new connections; the cement used was stronger than usual to make it set faster, but even so at least three days must pass before the plug could be removed.

That evening Sharon wanted to wash her hair but on being invited to use the river, decided perhaps it could wait another day. By limiting water use to the very minimum it was hoped the pipework above the plug would hold sufficient to allow essential functions such as the toilet to remain in use – a miscalculation! Late on the second day, murky effluent began seeping up round a manhole lid close to the house. The drain was full! There were plenty of alternative toilets, twenty of them to be exact, but all ran straight to the main drain. Definitely no good! The cement around the changed pipework must have at least another day, preferably two, to fully set. An extra drain plug solved the problem, temporarily blocking off another pipe run and allowing one of the toilet buildings to be used, but Sharon complained again about her hair.

On the fourth day in the evening when the system was judged ready, the family gathered as Dad lay on the ground by a manhole. Reaching in, he attached a length of cord to the first drain plug to prevent it washing down the outlet pipe and causing a blockage. Tying it tightly, he straightened up. "Who wants to unscrew the plug?"

Stephen stepped forward but Chris, standing next to him said quietly, "I wouldn't if I were you," and backed away a few paces.

"Get on with it," Jan urged, knowing a pile of dirty crockery stood by the sink. She had washed up in a bucket for the past three days, tossing the water away over the grass, but since breakfast had let the dirty plates accumulate, anticipating a return to normality.

Lying down again, Gordon reached for the drain plug; this was the one on the shorter run of pipe – the easier of the two. The arrangement was like a large wing nut. He made the first turn, waited a moment, then turned it again. Nothing happened. Glancing up, he saw the family had gathered round listening to Chris, the lad's arms swinging suddenly apart, flying outwards as if demonstrating an explosion. Gordon smiled grimly; that was about right! Squinting down over the extended arm, no sign showed of any water trickling free. This stage was tricky – under considerable pressure from the weight of trapped effluent above. The aim was to ease that screw so it just held, then stand clear, yank on the cord and hope to dislodge the plug; but it didn't always work like that! He took another turn of the thread, saw a trickle of water and instantly rolled aside, rising to a kneeling position at a safe distance then jerked on the line. The plug came away, a spurt of spray flying up as the water below surged clear. Following Chris's lead, Stephen and Sharon ran to the edge of the chamber watching the thick soupy liquid topped with pieces of floating debris gush along the pipework. Dad stood with them untying the line, waiting until the foul mixture drained away before stooping to retie it to the second plug. This one was under more pressure; a longer pipe run containing a greater volume of effluent. The chamber was messy now, soggy brown lumps clinging to the walls; he tried to avoid them, working with fingertips, turning his head upwards at intervals to inhale a lung full of fresher air, noticing the family had again retired to a safe distance. With the knot secure, one hand gripped the wing nut, starting to release the pressure. The first three twists produced no result, he leaning backward and waited, then gingerly started another... Wham! The plug flew free, hitting the chamber wall, the air around suddenly alive with putrid spray. Although already at a safe distance, Jan sprang backwards in alarm as a gusher shot upwards.

Gordon tried to roll clear but too late, his head already drenched where he had not moved fast enough, undesirable pieces of detritus clinging to his hair and around the old working jumper.

"Hey! He's in the... er, fertiliser!" Chris adjusted his words just in time, whooping at the sight

Sharon, her mouth hanging open, recovered quickly, an expression of delight spreading on her face. Stephen wore his elfin grin – no hope of sympathy from this crew!

Gordon ran for the river, took a dive to the edge, leaned over and stuck his head underwater; the stuff had run down his face and no way was he licking his lips! The river could wash it away. Rising to shake like a dog, he jettisoned the jumper, dunking it twice and leaving it at the river's edge, then headed for the toilet building. Only a shower would do! Thank goodness he had the foresight to light the gas burners before starting.

Now the system was live, it needed inspection and approval, which it quickly received. The children were absent when the inspector left, Gordon and Jan watching his departure with satisfaction.

"Our tent permission clock is ticking now?" she suggested. They smiled together.

Winter brought more than dark evenings to the valley. An uneasy truce lay between father and son, a truce balanced precariously by Jan's efforts. Work on the third toilets was going badly, the high inflation of recent years taking its toll. Progress was both much more expensive than expected, and slower. With Chris no longer helping and Jan busy re-painting inside the existing toilets, Gordon found himself not only laying the concrete building blocks, but fetching them from an untidy pile where the lorry had tipped, and also mixing his own cement. It all took longer, the walls not growing at the expected speed, adding to the gloom and making him less tolerant. It had been hoped that when the time came, someone could be found to apply a coat of cement render to the building, both inside and out. Although that work was still some months away, it already looked doubtful if money would be available – in all probability he must do that himself too!

It was then, unfortunate when Chris wanted a new shed built! His employer at the Music Museum kept Toggenberg goats but had decided to turn their grazing area into an extra car park. These goats had not been put to the Billy for sometime and were therefore not in milk, a factor making them difficult to dispose of. One remained, and without consultation Chris had agreed to keep it until a better home could be found.

"Keep it here?" Dad looked doubtful. "Just where do

you propose to house it?"

"We could build a shed – use it for the ducks when the goat has gone," Chris proposed hopefully.

"We? I've more than enough to do. You build it. Draw it out on paper first and show me – I want it strong, not something that will need attention for evermore. What use is a non-milking goat, and who'll look after it?"

"I will. It's my goat! I don't care about milking." Chris put two hands on the table, staring back at his father with more than resentment, the two squaring up for a row. Jan stepped in quickly.

"I'll tend it in the daytime. Be nice to have an animal around again even if it is only temporary. You design the shed Chris, Dad will look at in the evenings and offer any helpful comments." She turned to Gordon. "Won't you!"

"Hm... Yes, okay." He nodded agreement unwillingly.

"Good." Jan's smile was not reflected in either face but she hurried on. "We wanted a duck shed nearer the river so they leave less droppings across the yard. This is the answer."

The shed was built and the goat duly arrived, its coat a soft brown, but relations continued to be strained. Out of the blue one evening the following week with all the family present, Chris addressed his father.

"If you want help erecting the windmill, better do it soon. I'm thinking of getting a flat!"

"Ouch!" Jan pricked herself with the needle she was using on a seam that had come undone in a pair of Stephen's trousers. She looked up sharply, bringing the finger to her lips... it gave chance to think before speaking. Gordon's head had risen too, she saw him hesitate then look down again. Sharon and Stephen showed no surprise; the subject had obviously been discussed before.

"Where?" Jan asked, forcing an understanding smile. She had hoped such a move could be avoided, had been caught unprepared by the sudden announcement, and yet... it was not so unexpected.

358

"Goldsithney probably."

Little more was said and Chris slipped away to his room; darkness had fallen an hour before or he would probably have walked off to be with the goat. On the pretext of lighting the kettle, Jan stepped into the corridor pulling the door closed as she went, then slipped silently up the stairs, entered his room and perched herself on the other bed. For a while they sat, Chris's face uneasy but welcoming.

"I've been expecting something like this," Jan spoke softly, so no one downstairs would be drawn to the voice. "Is it Dad?"

"No. Well, in a way. These last few weeks he's been... he seems more dogmatic, harder to get on with."

"The third toilet building is not going well. We're running out of money, not enough for all the materials... he's worried, not so much about the work but by not being able to finish this year like he promised people. Pity that settlement doesn't come. I think he misses your help too. Makes it slower."

"Dad is not the only reason. Some of my friends have flats, are their own boss, do what they like. And in a way it's you too."

"Me?" Jan's eyes opened in surprise. "I only try to keep the peace."

"But in a pinch, you'd always support Dad." Chris paused and seeing his mother about to protest, hurried on. "No, I don't mind. Wish I had someone who would... but it's not that. If I bring a girl here, you make her welcome but keep flicking a glance at us to see... you know. If we walk off down the site I half expect you to send someone to follow us. What would you do if we both went up to the bedroom?"

"I'd..." Jan stopped, not sure how to reply.

"When you were young, didn't you... never mind." Chris looked at the floor, colouring, realising what he had been about to ask his mother.

359

"When will you go?"

"Next week if I can arrange it – would you mind?"

Jan sat not answering. Of course she would mind but what good would that do? However genial family relations might become he would leave anyway, soon. Perhaps better if he went now, on amicable terms; then he might come back some day? She pushed the thoughts aside. "Mind? No, not really. I'll miss you. You can always come for a meal, bring a friend if you like – I'll promise not to pry! We'll look after the goat until you find it a home." Jan rose, leaving before her face gave her away.

"Look what I've found." Sharon placed half a dozen grubby, moisture stained papers on the table; scraps torn from notebooks or similar and folded to pocket diary size to push through a small opening. "Stephen hid my homework list and I thought it might be in the suggestion box in the telephone kiosk. I unscrewed it and found these – left over from last season."

"Why would he take your homework?" Jan picked up one of the papers.

Sharon shrugged. "We had an argument over a book, one Chris left behind when he moved out. Stephen said it was his room now and I couldn't come in. I kind of borrowed it anyway."

"By force I suppose, and he pinched your notes to get even. I wonder if Chris will come back?" Jan gazed vacantly at the wall, then remembering Sharon's presence, looked down again at the paper in her hand. "This note; it's obviously from a youngster. Wants a BMX track. Bicycles are a pain; dangerous the way some ride them."

"There's room in the recreation area; maybe Dad could make one?"

"Don't suggest it, he's enough to do."

That was true. Christmas had long passed and he still worked on the third toilet building. One thing had improved, the ducks had taken over Chris's shed – a good home at last found for the goat. Jan was pleased; the task of moving its tethering during the day had fallen to her; like all goats this one could not run free, a point it had once well proved by escaping and gnawing the bark from half a dozen young saplings. She looked down again at the note. A BMX track? How many more cycles would that attract? Written by a child almost certainly, the letters scrawny and uncertain as many such messages were, expressing with varying degrees of illiteracy a desire for more active pastimes, games rooms and the like. At one time a survey had been taken over several months, the overwhelming result of which was a desire to avoid any such facility!

Even without these noisier pursuits things went wrong sometimes – arguments occurred between neighbours that someone had to sort out. Following such incidents other messages occasional appeared in the suggestion box, notes with less helpful suggestions; an invitation for instance to take a long walk on a short pier – though they were seldom couched in such moderate terms. All were read and analysed in the hope of doing better in future. In general, notes that caused laughter were given more consideration. Fortunately, a high percentage of praise and congratulations appeared, counteracting the cruder, less frequent but depressing messages. Jan unfolded another note and read its contents. The number of people asking for hair dryers had increased and recently the lack of a laundrette had been mentioned, but almost no criticism was levelled at the toilet buildings. Indeed, so practical and trouble-free had the original design proved that in building the third toilets, few changes had been made. However, unlike the previous buildings, this one stood against a hedge at the rear, the absence of external taps on that side allowed the service passage to be shorter, the space used to enlarge one shower in both Ladies and Gents. It was also found possible to include one extra WC in the Ladies, seven instead of six. Now in mid-January, the walls were almost complete, but although a stack of tiles and the roof timbers lay nearby, none of the toilet pans or wash basins or other fittings had been ordered – money had run too low.

Jan looked down again, picking up the final note. It was bigger, folded several times, written in a small hand from a mother refering to the antics of Stephen and her own three children; amusing – a nice note to end on.

Chris's absence continued for many months, but he often came home for lunch on Sunday. Any animosity between father and son seemed to have disappeared, talk flowing freely, Sharon and Stephen in particular seeking information. Jan was delighted, though careful not to appear prying, but on one occasion could not avoid showing concern when Chris arrived pale and unwell.

"Food poisoning," he admitted. "I had this liver in the fridge, it had been there almost a week but it smelt okay... tasted a bit funny but there was no other food so I ate it. I was off work Thursday and Friday – stayed in bed yesterday."

It emerged too, that Chris's job was not going well. The lack of prospects caused concern rather than the work itself. The whole family and particularly his grandfather Jim, offered encouragement when he spoke of applying for the police. Having ten months to wait until his eighteenth birthday, it was only possible to join the cadets and he had learned that on making such an application, his home might be inspected. It gave the excuse that everyone wanted; he would come back to his old room.

When he left after the meal to make the necessary arrangements, the whole family accompanied him to the door. On the threshold Jan reached for his hand, gripping it tightly, standing until he broke eye contact and swung away. With an arm round the other children, she watched the diminishing figure as he cycled away up the road.

By March and opening day for the new season, the family was whole again – but for how long? When Chris made his application, would it be accepted? Work on the

362

third toilets had ceased, apart from some cement rendering still being done intermittently on the inner walls. For appearances sake the outside had been properly finished including the main doors but the windows remained unglazed. Hopefully that would be done when an influx of people at Easter provided the cash. For the same reason, the new emptying point for motorcaravans was also postponed, as were the extra standpipes planned for some downstream areas. If only that settlement for the sewer damage would arrive!

It was evening, Easter had come and passed. The new toilet building windows were now glazed and Spring Bank Holiday approached.

"A successful day wouldn't you say," Jan whispered with a grin as she started to undress. "One or two more like that and your hair may turn grey. Was she convinced in the end, that you are really quite a normal fellow?"

"I think so. Embarrassing though. What did she say to you?" Gordon whispered back, trying not to wake the boys in the next room.

"Told me a funny man was using the far Ladies toilets, and that he'd locked the door afterwards. Wanted me to come and unlock it again so she needn't walk so far – asked if it was safe or would that chap be back. She didn't know they were unfinished; I thought you were apologising and telling everyone?"

"I am, at least I mention it to the ones who go down-stream, but she's up by Bluebell Wood, nearly as close to the centre toilet building. Anyway, I didn't show her to a pitch; at least I don't think so. Must have come while I was at cash-and-carry; that's why she didn't recognise me." Sliding into bed, he surreptitiously reached under the pillow, pulling her nightdress down under the covers and hiding it, then watching the final clothes drop to the floor.

"She'll remember you in future, that's for sure! I told her I'd send my husband to see her. How did you lull her suspicions?" Jan tossed something lacy aside and stepped towards the bed.

He watched, seeing the shape of her upper body change as she leant forward, one arm reaching under the pillow and feeling nothing, leaned farther and tried again.

Understanding what had happened, her eyes swung up meeting his own, accusation in her face. Seeing his grin, she drew herself upright, turning slightly sideways to offer a better profile, tummy pulled in, one foot sliding smoothly to the rear. Daintily, both hands floated to rest softly on buttocks behind, drawing the shoulders back and emphasising the breasts. "Well, have you seen enough?"

Suddenly she drove off that backward foot, springing totally naked onto the bed, raining down blows then trying to break from his grip as he grabbed her wrists and pulled her closer, warning, "Shush... the children."

The struggle subsided and they lay together, one inside, one outside the bedclothes, her wrists now free as his hands moved over her shoulders and spine.

"Why do you like your back rubbed so much? Come inside, you'll get cold."

"What about my nightdress?"

"There's a price. Are you willing to pay?"

It *was* chilly above – slipping inside and squeezing close for warmth she asked, "Well, are you going to tell me? What did you say to that girl?"

"I went to her caravan but she saw me coming and wouldn't open the door. I heard the catch slip as she locked it, then moved to open the window a fraction. Even when I explained who I was she was dubious." He paused, his hand continuing to wander over her body, leaning forward to whisper even more quietly.

Jan let out a small peal of laughter "She didn't!"

"Yes she did. When I invited her to come see for herself, she moved back from the window as if I was dangerous. Stop laughing. Don't you think I could look sinister? Sh! The boys will wake. She told me not to come

364

any nearer, then slipped out of a door I couldn't see on the far side; must have run into the next caravan. I was about to give up when she appeared again with another woman, a friend probably, perhaps travelling together."

"Weren't they terrified of my big, bold, naughty man any more?" Jan asked, pretending surprise and burying her face in his chest to stop the giggles.

Her laughter was infectious. He felt himself slipping, caught up in it – this was not at all what was meant to happen just now. Suddenly a hand touched him below.

Sensing a changed Jan had reached out, checking. "You'll never make it now. Better give up and pass me that nightdress" They both collapsed into howls of quiet laughter, and he had to admit she was right. For a while they lay together, Jan breaking into renewed bouts of giggling but eventually asking after the final outcome.

"Hm. Not very flattering." He spoke in a whisper, still hoping the boys had not woken. "The two women made me lead the way and when we stood before the door with its continental Ladies sign painted on clear and sharp, they wouldn't enter, just stood back and peeped in while I held it open. The bare appearance inside was enough, it convinced them. They came in then and made a thorough inspection, saw that nothing was ready, no basins, no pans, the floor not surfaced. It changed their attitude completely, they were most apologetic but one of them, the one that came to see you – she kept sniggering every time she looked in my direction... it was disconcerting. As we left, she rubbed her fingers over the sign, but withdrew them quickly when a group of people passing on the roadway gave us a funny look. She went quite red then; the two of them thanked me and hurried off."

"Did she still have the same short skirt?"

"Oh yes. Very good. Swayed nicely; smart top too, nicely cut and... Ouch!"

"Probably got a husband who buys her dresses!"

"I nearly bought you one once." Gordon paused,

reaching for her hand.

"You bought me several before I let myself be dragged off into the wilderness."

"Not like this one. We were working in Knightsbridge, a building called... Fraser house I think it was. It overlooked the end window of Harrods. One morning a gold dress appeared in that window, stiff looking shiny gold material, it stood all alone on a model – not another item to be seen. A high collar upright behind the neck, curled over and swept round to form big lapels, leaving an open Vee where the front plunged down to a small belted waist. You would have been incredible in it. I looked at it every day; must have stayed for a week. A whole window to itself for a week in Harrods! Can you imagine what it would cost?"

"Did you ever find out?"

"No. I could picture some flunky behind the counter saying 'If you have to ask, then you can't afford it.' He'd have been right too, but I wanted it for you."

They lay enjoying each other's closeness for some time; in one respect the evening might be classed a failure but they fell asleep happy, hands still lightly clasped.

In the morning the family were standing around the room chatting after breakfast. Stephen was missing, gone outside for some purpose known only to himself; looking for a young friend, probably. With a glance at her mother, Sharon asked an unexpected question.

"What was all the giggling last night?"

"Giggling? Surely you couldn't hear it from your bedroom?"

"No. Stephen told me. It woke both the boys. What were you doing?"

Jan looked across to where Gordon lounged against a bench, saw the grin on his face and knew that Sharon had seen it too. Should she explain? She hesitated, her daughter would be sixteen in the coming autumn; old enough surely. "Dad and I were..." she stopped, searching

366

for the right words.

"Making love?" Sharon asked, seeing her mother's eyebrows rise.

"Well actually no, we were intending to, but started laughing and couldn't..." Jan stopped, not quite comfortable with the explicit talk, making a gesture with her hand as she turned away, looking across to Gordon with a smile, remembering – and saw Chris move from the corner, heading for the door. As he passed his father he spoke.

"They don't laugh when I get them to bed, Dad!"

And with that he was gone, leaving three faces lost for words, staring at the empty doorway.

Sharon too, left shortly after. It was Saturday morning, the shop already open but few of the people on site rose early.

"Do you believe him?" Jan asked, "or was it adolescent bluster."

"Good luck to him," Gordon smiled. "You notice the 'They', as if there are lots. Maybe they don't laugh – perhaps our son has hidden talents?"

"You approve then? You must do, you said 'our son'. When you disapprove you say 'your son'. Getting on better now, the two of you I think? Will he leave again if his application to join the Cadets is not approved?"

"Maybe. Pity they're not recruiting in Cornwall though. London is a long way, we won't see him very often. Your Dad and Mum are pleased. Jim hopes Chris will go to his old station, Rochester Row."

"Shame that sewer damage settlement doesn't come through," Jan shrugged, "we could help him more. We could have finished the third toilets too, if it had. Are many people grumbling?"

"A few have but usually I satisfy them." Gordon smiled, knowing she would ask how, and hurried on when she dug him gently in the ribs. "I carry the key with me now to show them inside, let them see, tell them we ran out of money; it makes them realise campsite owners are not part of the idle rich, opens their eyes to find we have money problems too – makes them more sympathetic. After promising to get the building working by next year, I say every extra caravan we get buys a new basin or toilet pan, so will they recommend the site to everyone they meet please."

"Trust you! Someone else yesterday, wanted an electric hook-up; a foreigner again, Dutch this time."

"I had one a week ago, from France. Someone wanted a laundrette too, but only a handful of families have asked. When you consider the cost of a mains supply, it could never be economic – could it? I still want to win that Best Site award... wonder if we can in the next few years. We should build the windmill when the season ends – if Chris is gone will you climb the tower and help me?"

"No way! Don't smile at me like that, I'm not going to! Look, Chris is running back, and Sharon. You know why; the post is coming." Jan pointed to a red van driving down the road. "He's hoping to hear about the cadets sometime this month."

As the van stopped, Jan ran down the steps, Chris joining her, but only one letter was passed through the window. The initial was 'G'; disappointment showed in Chris's face but he followed the letter indoors, saying the initial might be a misprint. Sharon and Stephen came in as well.

"Typewritten address. A bill I expect." Gordon took the envelope, reaching for the slitter. A folded foolscap sheet came out, something attached to it by a paper clip. He turned it over, a smile spreading. "Hey, someone has sent us a cheque!"

"Must be a good one; mind the corners of your mouth don't split. How much?"

"Only ten thousand pounds! Anyone fancy a shopping trip?"